PRAISE FOR *QUICKSAND OF MEMORY*

'One of those rare authors who can turn what could be an interesting read into something extra special, the sort of book that dominates your every waking moment'

'I can genuinely say: fiction doesn't get any better than this'

'A tautly written revenge tragedy about secrets, lies and the past coming back to haunt you … beautifully conceived and brilliantly plotted'

'A great, absorbing thriller with plenty of twists and turns'

'If there is one thing guaranteed when reading a book by Michael J. Malone it is that the writing style, the complexity and lyrical nature of the narrative will elicit from readers a multitude of emotions'

'A superb example of a page-turning thriller at its best … it kept me turning the pages late into the night'

'A beautifully crafted story with a brilliant ending'

ABOUT THE AUTHOR

Michael Malone is a prize-winning poet and author who was born and brought up in the heart of Burns' country. He has published over 200 poems in literary magazines throughout the UK, including *New Writing Scotland, Poetry Scotland* and *Markings. Blood Tears*, his bestselling debut novel won the Pitlochry Prize from the Scottish Association of Writers. Other published work includes: *Carnegie's Call; A Taste for Malice; The Guillotine Choice; Beyond the Rage; The Bad Samaritan* and *Dog Fight*. His psychological thriller *A Suitable Lie* was a number-one bestseller, and the critically acclaimed *House of Spines* and *After He Died* soon followed suit. Since then, he's written two further thought-provoking, exquisitely written psychological thrillers, *In the Absence of Miracles* and *A Song of Isolation*, cementing his position as a key proponent of Tartan Noir and an undeniable talent. A former Regional Sales Manager (Faber & Faber) he has also worked as an IFA and a bookseller. Michael lives in Ayr.

Follow Michael on Twitter @michaelJmalone1 and on his newsletter: michaeljmalone.substack.com.

QUICKSAND OF MEMORY

MICHAEL J. MALONE

**ORENDA
BOOKS**

Orenda Books
16 Carson Road
West Dulwich
London SE21 8HU
www.orendabooks.co.uk

First published in the UK in 2022 by Orenda Books
Copyright © Michael J. Malone, 2022

A catalogue record for this book is available from the British Library.

ISBN 978-1-913193-96-6
eISBN 978-1-913193-97-3

Typeset in Garamond by typesetter.org.uk

Printed and bound by CPI Group (UK) Ltd, Croydon CR0 4YY

For sales and distribution, please contact *info@orendabooks.co.uk* or visit *www.orendabooks.co.uk*.

Prologue

Fifteen years earlier

The boy was so cold he could hear his teeth knocking together. He was sitting on the floor of his tiny bedroom because his mattress, quilt and sheets were soaked through after his new foster mother had poured a bucket of cold water over them. An action she had taken with the expression of a beleaguered saint – *See what you made me do*.

He pulled his knees up to his chest in the empty hope it might gain him some heat. Then, despite the numbness in his fingers, he bent forward to have another shot at tying his shoelaces. Because untidy shoelaces were just one of the many things that sent his foster parents searching for a way to punish him. A smart appearance was the measure of the man, they said, so make sure your laces are tied neatly and that the loops aren't any longer than the ends. Which was impossible to achieve when your hands were this cold. But he had to try, because if he didn't, they'd know. Not trying was next to Godlessness, they said. And the punishment for Godlessness was ... well, he didn't know. He'd managed to avoid that sin. So far.

Being next to it was bad enough.

They were never violent. Not physically anyway. That was beneath them. Words were the currency of their punishment. A constant drip into the mind, letting you know that you were worthless and unloved.

Cold room.

Cold-water bathing.

Bedding doused in iced water.

Tiny portions of food from the fridge. Congealed with fat and often so dry it was hard to chew.

Still, when you're not worth that much and you're a burden on everyone, you deserve what you get.

Right?

He could hear a knock at the front door. Footsteps. The creak of hinges, and then a sound swelled into the space. Children singing. Even from here in the half-dark he could detect the pattern of a song about Christmas.

It would be children from his school, rounded up by the teachers to go carolling door-to-door to raise money for charity.

'Oh, come and see this, dear,' he heard the man say.

Footsteps, and the woman replied, 'Oh, how cute,' with a sing-song tone in her voice he'd never heard before. And in his mind's eye he could see them arm in arm at the door. The image of the perfect, Christian couple.

He thought of the previous Christmas.

Before all of this.

Before *that*.

His big brother bounding into the house with a large holdall full of stuff. He couldn't be bothered with wrapping, so you just got the toy or whatever in its box. Knowing what it was straight away didn't detract from the pleasure. It was his big brother – his hero – giving him stuff.

'Five minutes, some paper and tape. That's all it takes,' his mother said. 'Keep the magic alive for the bairn, you arsehole.'

'Did you nick that?' his father demanded.

The talons of the memory ripped at his chest, seized his heart and squeezed. They reached into his gut and twisted and pulled and burned. A sense of near-crushing loss built up from his bowels. He felt his bottom lip tremble.

But he didn't cry. Wouldn't.

'Big boys don't cry,' his new 'mother' intoned in his ear.

And he was proud that he managed not to.

He was a big boy now.

Right?

Chapter 1

Luke studied his diary. Two appointments today. None tomorrow, and two the day after that.

He was hardly winning at this new therapy business, but still, it was better than last week, when he'd had a total of two.

Slowly, slowly, his network of peers all told him. It takes at least a year to build up a business in alternative medicine. Don't expect it to happen overnight. Perhaps the end of the year, leading up to the holidays, wasn't the best time to launch a new practice.

All of it meaningful and well-intentioned advice, but he guarded against accepting it as The Truth, because if he lowered his expectations too much, he felt sure his new venture would fail, which couldn't happen. He had bills he was struggling to pay and a child to feed.

Looking around his work space – essentially a posh shed in his small garden – he examined it as if he were a client. Would this suggest a successful practice?

A friend had given him an old table for a desk. He'd sanded it down and applied a light varnish that, instead of hiding the old stains, served to highlight them. But he liked that; it gave the table a worn look. *See*, it told his clients, *I've been through a lot, but I'm still standing.*

An old dining-room chair sat behind the desk, varnished in the same way. In the space in front crouched a matching pair of the most comfortable armchairs Luke had been able to find. They were second-hand, but the mechanism that allowed one of the chairs to tilt back was still in perfect working order. That and the soft grey mohair throw combined, he hoped, to make the client set aside their apprehensions about talking to a complete stranger and telling him their deepest fears.

In the other corner he'd set a small, sanded and painted coffee table with a jug and glasses, a kettle, cafetière and some mugs. So far people preferred water, but in between clients he found that at least for himself, coffee was required.

A few scattered plants and black-framed qualifications – nutrition, hypnotherapy, counselling, CBT – pinned to the walls completed the look. He'd debated whether or not he should have a picture of Nathan on his desk: thought it might be too cheesy, but then went ahead anyway. But with the image pointed at him rather than his clients.

He touched the photo briefly, over the boy's smile, and felt warmed through by this simple action. Despite not being Nathan's biological father there was a resemblance. Or so he liked to think. But there in the eyes was his mother, Lisa. Dead three years since. The breast cancer had been treated, but it came back with a vengeance. His throat tightened and he felt his eyes mist as he remembered those last days.

He had been there, at the end, along with her mother, Gemma. Both of them sobbing, unwilling to let go, unable to deal with the remorselessness of the disease. Lisa, pale as bleached bones. Graceful in her stoicism.

'Something...' Lisa gripped his hand '...that reassures me.' Her smile was a tremulous thing, laced with fear but gilded with hope. 'Nathan has you.'

'Don't,' Luke had said. 'You're going nowhere.' He bit his bottom lip. Be strong for her, he intoned in his mind over and over, like a mantra. 'You'll be there holding his hand, first day at school.'

Her eyes lit on his, and she poured strength into him. Strength and acceptance. 'He'll be skipping in the school gate,' she said, her gaze off in the distance, seeking a golden future for her little boy. 'I can see him. Excited. Swinging his wee bag, with his lunchbox and everything.'

'Don't,' Luke said, unable to hold back a sob. 'Please.'

'You're a good dad, Luke. The best. We're so lucky to have you.'

'No. Don't. You'll be there,' he replied. 'Every step of the way.'

She raised her eyebrows. 'Better believe it.' She managed a laugh. 'Listen to the wind. That'll be me whispering in your ear.' Then she adopted a mock scolding tone. 'Don't let him watch too much TV. Once a month is fine for a Big Mac. And for goodness sake don't buy him any more dinosaurs.'

They laughed through the tears.

She died sometime later. Her mother holding one hand. Luke the other.

Gratitude was the thing, she told him over and over on those last days, that will carry you through. At the time he'd refused to listen. Couldn't listen. How could he be grateful when she was dying? But now he saw the sense of it. Now he could be grateful she'd been in his life, that she'd pulled him from the fire. The only person who knew everything about him, everything he'd done, and still she loved and trusted him. He was a better man for her affection and attention, and for that he would be eternally thankful.

There was a knock at the door.

A single contact.

Getting maudlin there, Luke, he scolded. He rubbed at his eyes. Took a deep breath. Time to get to work.

There was a louder double knock,

Luke looked at his diary to remind him of the client's name. Jenna Hunter. She'd booked online and filled in the notes to say she was dealing with crippling anxiety following a relationship break-up, and the chronic and complicated ill-health of her mother.

'Just be with you,' he shouted. And he walked to the door, excited to be seeing someone new. Excited to be in a position to offer to someone else the help he'd needed to rebuild his own life.

Chapter 2

Jenna looked around herself. This wasn't necessarily an area she would have expected a therapist to live and work in. A modest street with small, one-bed bungalows on one side and what she guessed would be mainly ex-local-authority houses on the other. The house she was visiting looked like it would be one of the latter. A narrow end-of-terrace with one window, top and bottom, facing the street, the render painted white. The garden was small, but the grass was trim and planters crammed with winter flowers dotted here and there offered splashes of colour.

She'd followed the instructions on the website, walked in the gate, down the path, around the side of the house and down the garden to what looked like a prefabricated outbuilding that nestled under a giant fir hedge.

It hardly screamed 'thriving business', but the fees were relatively low, and the guy's website was full of glowing testimonials.

At the door she raised a hand to knock. Then she allowed it to fall as she turned away.

What was she doing? She wasn't the kind to see a therapist, surely?

Then the heaviness she felt every morning when she woke from a fractured sleep filled her mind. Butterflies with ice-tipped wings rose and fell in her gut, and her heart sent out a loud and fast semaphore of anxiety.

She couldn't go on living like this. On the way over she'd fantasised about speeding up on a bend and crashing into a tree. Anything to stop the ceaseless monkey chatter of self-accusation that ran on a loop through her mind.

Before she could move away she turned and knocked. Then, thinking she couldn't leave now, she knocked twice more.

The man who opened the door had a bright, friendly face. His dark hair was greying at the temples, and the few lines radiating from his eyes seemed hard-won.

'Jenna Hunter?' he said, and stepped back. 'Come in. Have a seat.'

Jenna entered, spotted a low armchair that looked like it had been designed for a winter's evening and a good book. She sat.

The man talked on:

Nice morning.

Mild for this time of year.

There's a flock of sparrows in the hedge at the end of the garden, I hope they don't chirp so loudly they disturb us.

The man seemed almost as on edge as she was. No, she thought, as she looked into his face. Not on edge. Keen. Anxious to be of help. And that keenness silenced some of her doubts.

He was behind his desk, leaning towards her. Arms on the table, sleeves rolled up enough to show forearms corded with muscle and flecked with dark hair. Not at all what she expected from a therapist. He looked more like someone who spent their working day with a shovel in his hands. Before she'd seen the photograph on his website, she'd imagined someone older, a sun-mottled pate with whispers of white hair, perhaps in a cardigan with spectacles hanging around his neck on a silver chain.

He was talking; offering her something.

'Sorry?' She felt her face heat. God, she was such an idiot.

'Or I can make you a tea or a coffee?'

'Nothing, thanks,' she said. Drinking something would only delay the inevitable. She was here to talk, and now that she was seated, in this space, she wanted to get on with it.

Crossing her arms and her legs, she sent him a smile of apology. Perhaps she should have a drink. He looked disappointed that she'd said no. But she shook her head. Jesus, stop second-guessing everything.

Jenna watched wordlessly as Luke opened a folder on his desk and picked up a pen.

'I just need to ask you some basic questions for my records,' he said. 'This is the only formal part of the process.' He smiled and brandished his pen. 'Name, address, occupation, etc. And a short medical history, if that's okay.'

She nodded her assent, and they began.

Chapter 3

'Can you remember what was going on in your life when the anxiety first started?' Luke asked after he'd completed the admin part of the session.

As he waited for her to answer he discretely looked her over, searching for clues to her life. We all wear a disguise, or in this case a hat, but often that attempt at camouflage gives away more than we intend.

Luke had been around a fair few gyms in his time and it looked like this young woman was no stranger to them either. She was all in black: leggings, T-shirt, gilet and baseball cap, her black hair in a ponytail, pulled through the hole in the back.

'My last boyfriend left me...' She coughed. 'For another man.' She laughed and shook her head. 'When it's another woman and you still want him, there's a chance you can compete. Or you kid yourself you can. Lose a few pounds, get a new haircut, you know, all those surface, shallow things? But it's never about you, not really. That stuff is just grasping at straws. We know that.' She said the word 'we' as if speaking for her female peers. Then she stopped – as if she was afraid she was rambling.

Luke motioned to her to continue.

'We can't stop ourselves from making that effort, eh? So much of what we read and see is about projecting the perfect image. How to get yourself a man, and once you've got him, how to be a good wife. All that shite.' She tossed her head as if mimicking a perfect-ten model in an ad campaign, and Luke found himself warming to her self-deprecation, to the glimmer of attitude that showed she was a fighter.

'But when your competition's a man?' Jenna continued. 'You can't suddenly grow the right body part, can you?' She paused as she gathered her thoughts. 'Is that offer of a drink still on?' she asked.

Luke got to his feet and stepped across to the drinks corner, asking her what she wanted as he did so.

'Water will do, thanks.'

He retrieved a drink for her and held it out. She took it with a small smile of thanks.

She sipped.

Luke moved back round to his chair, and as he sat it occurred to him that this might not have been the first time Jenna had been let down by love. And while she appeared to be upset about this particular situation, he couldn't help but feel there was something else going on. He'd only been working as a therapist for eighteen months, but he'd quickly learned that more often than not the problem the client initially presented with wasn't really the issue they needed help with.

But he couldn't rush it or he might lose her. He'd have to trust that by providing a non-judgemental ear she'd come to trust him and really open up.

'And there's my mum,' Jenna said after a long silence.

'Yeah?'

'We have a woman who comes in, but I'm her main carer. She *was* such a vibrant woman. Full of vim. The life of the party.' She paused, her expression lapsing into candour. 'Actually, she was a judgemental pain in my arse. All that money she spent on my education, and I end up working part-time in a bookshop. What a let-down. But she was also very kind. Very caring.' She stopped talking as a wobble appeared on her lower lip. Her head fell and her shoulders shook. 'She was there for me when I really needed her. And now it's my turn to look after her, and it's just so hard.'

Luke retrieved a box of tissues from the shelf behind him and pushed it across the table top. Wordlessly, Jenna helped herself to one and dabbed at her eyes.

'God, you must think I'm a horrible bitch. My mother's had a bleed on the brain, and all I can do is complain about how she's making my life difficult.'

'You can still be a caring person while struggling with your obligations,' Luke replied.

'Yeah, well, that's a nice thing to say, but it doesn't make me feel any less of a cow.'

'When you started talking about your mother, you talked about her in the past tense.'

'I did?' Her eyes were large with surprise.

Luke nodded.

Jenna looked away, and bit her lower lip, as if considering Luke's statement.

'There's just this old version of her and the new, post-injury version.' Jenna tugged at her left earlobe. 'She's very much alive.' She looked into Luke's eyes. 'But, God she's hard work. Used to be she'd rather die than be heard swearing. Now she swears like a navvy.'

Luke realised that allowing Jenna to remain stuck on the track of her perceived failings wasn't going to help her. So he thought back to her first answer – when she'd responded to his question about when her anxiety started. She'd paused before answering, the movement of her eyes suggesting that shadows were chasing her thoughts. Then she'd arranged her features into a non-committal expression.

There was more here. He had to decide whether to press for it now or to let it unfold over the next few weeks of her therapy.

Instinct had him bin the cautious approach and press on.

'Can you tell me the very *first* time you felt this level of anxiety?' he asked.

She looked up at him, startled, as if worried he'd read her mind.

Eventually she broke her silence.

'It happened a long time ago.' Her eyes were heavy with shame and self-recrimination. 'Someone died.'

Chapter 4

Part of him – the distant part – knew what he was doing when he tried so very hard to please them. But he still couldn't stop himself.

Look at me, am I not a good boy?

Watch while I play with other children and demonstrate that I'm a credit to you both.

Listen while the teachers praise me for my hard work and attention.

What he was doing was really not that much different from the other kids. Putting on a performance to please the grown-ups, then, when out of sight and earshot, behaving in ways that demonstrated a conscience was yet to develop.

And while the compliant part of him did what he could to win smiles from the adults, the distant part watched on, like a cat curled up in the corner, with its tail over its nose, one eye open.

Waiting for just the right moment.

And the right target.

Chapter 5

Jenna sat back, crossed her arms and her legs. She was aware that the therapist would read this as a defensive gesture. And he would be right, but she was already regretting being quite so open.

'Listen,' she said, 'I really don't want to talk about that.' She pulled her baseball cap from her head and hooked it over her knee. It fell off, and feeling her face redden she bent forward to pick it up.

Luke just sat there. Watching. His head cocked to the side.

She rushed to fill the silence.

'I mean. It was horrible, you know, but it has nothing to do with what's happening now. Really.' Without thinking about what she was doing she uncrossed her legs and then recrossed them the other way. 'And besides, we'd finished. I chucked him actually. The relationship just wasn't working anymore.'

But at the start there was something wildly exciting about him. She couldn't put her finger on it, but the minute, no, the second she saw him she was fascinated by him.

She was volunteering at a Christmas dinner for homeless people at her local church. He was picking up an old friend, she later found out, but when he saw her he pretended he was also one of the volunteers.

A dusting of beard, blond hair slicked back, his gaze bright with what she judged to be a street-wise intelligence. 'Come here often?' he asked, the glint in his eye sprinkling his opening gambit with a suitable amount of irony.

She couldn't help but laugh, and he stood beside her, picked up a serving spoon and began to dole out the roast potatoes. As they served the men and women in the queue their conversation adopted an easy rhythm, ranging from all the things they loved and hated about the time of year, favourite movies, and, strangely, the stand-up comics that irritated them.

By the time he'd finished pouring cream over the Christmas puddings she was handing out, she suspected she was in love.

He was the first mature man to pay her any attention; previous boyfriends were just little boys by comparison. And he was everything her father wasn't. Dad was an accountant, overweight, rarely seen without a perfectly knotted tie and never heard using what he called 'inappropriate language'. This guy was as lean as an elite marathon runner, wore faded jeans and T-shirt, and peppered his sentences with 'fuck'.

Years later she would mock herself for the attraction. They say the path to hell is paved with good intentions, she'd told a friend. I'm thinking those intentions are mostly from women who want to change their man.

There was nothing he did that day, or on most of their subsequent days together, that suggested he was a bad boy, but there was an edge to him, a suggestion that he didn't much care what people thought of him. It was a world away from the 'mind your Ps and Qs' drill she'd heard almost every day growing up with her parents, and she therefore found it deeply attractive.

She was brought up to be a middle-class nice girl, always ready to smile, ready to acquiesce, never to make a fuss, and she was deeply tired of it. This was her chance to rebel. He was her chance to earn a disapproving word from her parents. To show them she was her own woman, not their little girl. And she grabbed it with both hands.

Her mind drifted to the end days. He became exhausting. Loud, with enough energy for six people. Then quiet and withdrawn for days. And utterly dependant on her for his happiness, or so it felt. She remembered that last day they were together. His eyes empty in the moment before he saw her, then, when he was aware she was there, he lit up as if he'd received a charge of energy. It was suffocating. It felt like he was relying on her presence to keep him together.

'I can't be without you,' he said, slumped back into the sofa.

'But we've been together less than a year.'

'Eleven months, one week and three days,' he said with a little flare of triumph in his eyes. 'Which is a guess.' His smile was straining with hope that his little joke landed well in her mind. 'Some people get married after knowing each other for a day.' He was pulling at her hand, his eyes beseeching.

She reared back at the word 'married'.

'It's too much,' she said, every inch of her wanting to be far from him. 'You're too much.' As she spoke, her eyes flashed to the bin in the corner of the kitchen, where she'd thrown the used pregnancy test. Its little blue lines like neon in her brain.

'What the fuck does that mean?' He was back on his feet, and it looked like the clench of his fists was lengthening his arms. Not for a moment did she feel threatened by him; her worry was that he would harm himself. Slam his knuckles into a wall, or a window or something. Or worse, take it out on someone else. When they'd first got together she'd heard the talk about his capacity for violence, but when he turned out to be a sweet, vulnerable guy, she was sure those rumours must be about a different person. There was no way the guy who cuddled up to her, the guy who cried at soppy adverts, was the one these people were talking about. It was ridiculous.

'I'm not what you need. Can't you see that?' She hadn't told him about the baby yet and was dreading having to do so.

'Everyone else has fucked off. You can't leave me too,' he shouted. Who the *everyone else* were he never actually said. He rarely mentioned family, saying he missed his little brother but couldn't take the shit he'd get from his parents if he went to see the wee fella. He did once talk about a guy. His oldest friend. They'd had a massive falling out, and it was clear that whenever he was down, which was often, this still bothered him greatly. But when she pressed him on it, he clammed up, as he did about every other part of his life.

'We used to be out all the time. You were the life and soul of every party, but now we're here every night...' She looked round his living room. The vanilla-coloured woodchip on the walls, the three-bar electric fire from another era, the curtainless windows. '...While you drink vodka and smoke hash.'

'But nothing else matters. Just me and you, babe.' His eyes searched hers for agreement. 'We've been good together, yeah?'

'Yeah. But...' The 'yeah' referred to the early months of their time together. He was her first real boyfriend. He seemed so worldly and solid. And he took her places for posh meals and weekends away. The trip to London to see Beyoncé in concert was a real highlight. It was continuous excitement, and she'd felt so, so lucky. Chosen, almost. And it was a huge difference to the world she inhabited before.

'Me and you. Against all the bastards out there.'

'That's the problem though, eh?' she tried to argue. 'Your "them and us" way of thinking. You haven't even had me over to meet your family. That's just weird.'

'You know how I feel about my family.' His face darkened.

'I don't. Not really. You barely talk about them.'

The therapist shifted in his seat, pulling her from the quicksand of her memory.

'We had a massive falling out.' She cleared her throat, the re-membered guilt gnawing at her vocal chords. 'I did what I had to do. There was no real choice. He was...' She thrust out her chin and chased emotion through her mind, searching for the right word. 'Damaged. Seems horrible to write anyone off, but I always had the sense he would die young, you know?'

She sipped from her water, suddenly aware of how dry her mouth was.

'I was twenty-one when I met him. You think you know every-thing at that age, don't you? But I knew *nothing*.' Her laugh was self-mocking. 'Young and daft. Attracted to certain men for all the wrong reasons.'

Silence followed. Jenna sought a way to change the subject. She looked at the clock on the wall. There were fifteen minutes left? Heat was building in her chest and neck. She pulled at her top. God, she just wanted to leave. She shouldn't have come.

'And you're probably thinking that's why I'm so bothered about being there for Mum? That I wasn't there for my old boyfriend?'

'You think it's some sort of displacement?'

'I'm not saying I think that. I'm saying you'll think...' Aware she sounded short, she got to her feet. 'Sorry, I need to go.' Her fingers were tingling. It was too hot in here. Her lungs were scratchy, she couldn't breathe. 'I'll go onto your website and book another...'

Seconds later she was out of the door and walking back up the garden path, her past like an anchor behind her, the weight of it gouging into the earth. Her thighs trembling with the effort of pulling. It was so much a part of her she no longer registered exactly how much work it took.

Chapter 6

Luke was listening to a young woman in her late twenties, the folds of her barely contained by the spacious armchair she was sitting in. Her face was florid, and a bead of sweat was cresting her hairline, about to spill onto her forehead.

'I lost over a hundred pounds five years ago. I was on the shakes an' that,' she said. 'Minute I stop: boom. The weight goes back on.' She started crying. Luke leaned forward and held out a paper handkerchief. 'I'm just so tired of it, you know?'

'Exactly what are you tired of...?' He sought her name in his mind. Looked at the papers in front of him. 'Susan.' That was close. He'd almost called her Jenna. Ever since Jenna had left his office he hadn't been able to stop thinking about her. He'd worried he wouldn't see her as a client ever again. It was in the hang of her head and her studied steps as she walked away from him up the garden and round the side of the house.

The information she'd given him included her job as a part-time bookshop assistant. And there was only one little bookshop in the area. He'd found himself walking past the door several times over the last few weeks. But he hadn't gone in. The client-therapist line was something he wouldn't – couldn't – cross. But there was something about her. Something familiar. Something engaging. There was a vulnerability there. And a strength he suspected she didn't know she had. And when she smiled, he felt himself react, trying to find other things to say that might winkle another smile out of her.

She was a pretty girl. Very pretty. Reminded him of Lisa, if he was being honest. She had the same large eyes and full lower lip, but where Lisa's hair was auburn, Jenna had a mass of dark-brown, shoulder-length curls.

Whenever the phone rang he would take a moment before looking at the screen, not wanting to be disappointed when he saw it wasn't her. Every new ping of an email gave him a little frisson of pleasure. Just in case.

A few days earlier he'd spotted her in the supermarket, over at the fish counter. He allowed himself the imagined treat of going over and saying hello. Savoured her imagined smile in response. But of course he didn't. His personal rule when he was out and about was only to respond to clients if they said hello first. He would never initiate contact, in case they didn't want whoever they were with to later question who he was.

Luke brought his attention back to Susan, feeling bad that he'd been so easily distracted. She was talking about the stares of strangers, the looks she got whenever she ate anything out in public.

'*You* can eat a slice of cake, or a packet of crisps or whatever, outside on a bench in the park, and no one will blink an eye. People see me eat and the judgement just pours off them. It could be the only thing I've eaten that day, cos I'm on a ridiculous diet, but still they judge.' She shook her head and dabbed at her eyes with the paper hanky. 'They even shout stuff at me. Make grunting pig noises.'

Susan had booked in for a hypnotic gastric-band session. It was obviously way less invasive than an actual gastric band, she'd said, and if she could be convinced she had a tiny, tiny stomach, that would be totally fab.

'Not that I want to turn away the business,' Luke said. 'But we're not that far away from Christmas. Do you want to be going through this with all of that added temptation? Sweet treats everywhere you go?'

'I don't go anywhere,' she said, her face limp with sadness at her admission. 'Besides, no time like the present, eh?'

Luke nodded his understanding, paused, took some notes, and then prepared to give Susan first some words of support, and then a hard slice of truth.

'Your struggle with weight is not an indication of a fault in your character, so please push that belief right out of your head,' he said softly.

She looked him in the eyes. 'I know, right?' Her own eyes were hooded with a contradictory doubt.

'You're not a bad person, Susan. This is a massively complicated issue. Do other members of your family struggle with this?'

She nodded. 'Mum's side are all pretty big.'

'Right, so genetics play a part. Also, there are a number of hormones involved in the weight-gain process. If you've been eating the wrong things for you over a long period of time, your hormones may be out of whack. Then there's the emotional side of it. Do you turn to food for support?'

Susan offered a little smile.

'And you try to apply some logic to that? Give yourself a talking to?'

Another smile of recognition.

'And how's that working for you?'

'It's not.'

'These kind of patterns of behaviour are imprinted deeply in our brains. Applying logic to something that is illogical is ... illogical.'

Susan laughed.

'And, something else people don't take account of is how the processes that lots of our foods go through is designed to hijack our brains to make us eat more and more and more.'

'It is?'

'Absolutely. Our body is designed so that we stop eating when we're full, but these processed foods switch off that feeling of satiety. Ever wondered why one Hobnob is never enough?'

'God, I love Hobnobs.'

Susan's body language had changed over the last five minutes; her chin was up, her shoulders back, both feet planted, and her eyes were bright with interest.

'And there was even one piece of research where a woman's body type changed after she had a stool transplant.'

'You what?' Susan grimaced.

'Don't know why Hobnobs made me think of that,' Luke joked. 'But from that experiment it's clear that the micro-organisms in our gut also have an impact.'

'So how do I fix that?'

'Great question. And that's where the long-term solution to your problem is; but first you *have* to believe me when I say this is not a character fault. Again, you are not a bad person, Susan.'

'Okay,' she said in a small voice, as if she was preparing to accept that idea. She dabbed at her eyes again.

'I'll do the gastric-band stuff, if that's what you want. But...' her face fell at the 'but', so he rushed to reassure her '...there's something deeper here. We should try to uncover *why* you overeat – the emotional component that drives you to food – and deal with that first, or I'm doing you a disservice.'

Susan sighed.

'Trust me, Susan, the gastric band on its own will possibly only be one part of the overall solution. If you want to deal with the habit of turning to food for emotional support, there's some work ahead.' He leaned forward and touched the back of her hand. 'But I'll be here with you every step of the way. Okay?'

*

Once Susan had left he typed up her case notes and checked his diary. That was him for the day. He looked at his phone. 2pm. The wee fella would be home from school soon. Time enough for a quick visit to a certain bookshop? He did actually want to buy a book. A highly regarded work on trauma called *The Body Keeps the Score*.

Some minutes later, having finally managed to find a parking space, he walked past the shop window, feeling very self-conscious as he did so, pushed the door open and entered.

Chapter 7

They allowed the boy to live with them until his eighteenth birthday. Wasn't that kind of them? they asked. Besides, they said, no one else was rushing to look after him. Even his own sister didn't want anything to do with him, the woman added with a self-satisfied smile.

He could only nod while looking down at the small suitcase at his feet. It contained every last one of his possessions, and still had room to spare.

'I have to leave?' he asked.

'Time to stand on your own two feet,' the man said.

'The charity we told you about will make sure you're okay,' the woman said. They were holding hands, standing in front of him like a twin barrier. Matching expressions. Eyes empty of care.

He took a step towards them. Just a small one.

In unison they backed away.

The part of him that had watched and waited all these years felt the thrill of their reaction. He caused them worry. They were actually a little afraid of him.

Good.

But the part of him that had obeyed all these years shrank. He could feel his lower lip trembling. He was being discarded. They'd thrown out an old sofa the previous week with about as much emotion.

They'd taken him round to his new place a few weeks back. A large house split into what amounted to bed-sits. Space enough for a bed, a table, and a kitchen small enough to fit into a walk-in cupboard.

The windows were all barred. The doors were as heavy as if they were armour-plated.

'Well, isn't this cosy,' the woman had said, the momentarily startled look in her eyes giving the lie to her statement.

He would have his independence there, he tried to tell himself.

But still, even though the couple had treated him harshly, their attention was all he knew.

There had been good times, once. Long before the couple.

But he barely remembered them.

A mum and a dad.

They were always fighting and drinking, and calling him nasty names, but still. They were his mum and dad. Then there was a big sister and bigger brother. Watching cartoons. Plates heaped with beans and toast, and eggy bread. And chips. And the occasional glass of Coke.

Then his big brother died.

Whispers swarmed around his head. Conversations ran into the brick wall of him entering a room. His sister was no help. She pretended to be in the know, but knew as little as he did.

His mother wore the same set of clothes for months, arms permanently crossed over her black cardigan as if that might contain the grief.

Desperate for information, for any detail at all, he began to creep around the house, pausing at doorways for long moments before entering, sure that he'd catch some snippet of information.

Then his father got lost in the bottle. Many, many bottles. Killed his mother and himself, in a twisted echo of his eldest son's passing: drunk driving on the way to Danny's graveside on the anniversary of his death.

That was then.

Now was more important.

His foster parents turned to leave. No hugs. They didn't do contact. Of any kind.

No encouraging words.

But he had silent words for them.

Sleep well tonight, he thought. *But sleep with one eye open.*

Chapter 8

Jenna had been surprised at herself after her therapy appointment. She hadn't talked about that part of her past for ages. A memory of him popped up in her mind. Unshaven, wearing a T-shirt and boxers. Looking tired. He always looked tired towards the end. As if he'd given up. Yet when they first met he was always immaculately turned out: neat beard, expensive clothes, and shoes with a shine so deep you could use them as a mirror. And he was always the most vibrant person in the room. He was the sun around whom everyone else would orbit, hoping for a word, a nod, a smile.

She cursed herself for being an unfeeling bitch and not looking after him better. Could there really have been any other outcome? It was his fun and energy that drove her to him. When had he changed? She rubbed at the memory a little more and felt some of the emotion of that time leak into the present. She held a hand to her stomach, and a tear wound its way down her cheek.

He died just a few days after they'd split up, and she'd been tempted to use her old skills as a local journalist to find out exactly what happened. She'd done some digging and took some notes. Then, when her father died of a sudden heart attack soon after, she put the notebook away in a box somewhere and consigned that episode of her life to history. Besides, the system was happy, the people concerned were punished, and that should be the end of it. Right?

Within minutes of her appointment ending, Jemma's phone had rung. Hazel, of course calling to find out how her session had gone.

'Did he do any of that hypnosis malarkey with you?' she had asked, as if both thrilled and terrified at the prospect of experiencing such a thing herself. At times they spoke almost every day, she and Hazel. Then they'd have long silences. They'd been at university together, lost touch, and reconnected on-line a few years ago. But they only ever chatted to each over the phone or by messaging. Her other friends thought it strange that they never met in person, but Jenna was happy with the relationship as it was. It just sort of worked. It suited how they were with each other. Nothing was off the table, and Jenna worried that if they did meet in person they would lose some of that magic.

'It wasn't like that,' she replied. 'We just ... talked.'

'Is he hot?' Hazel asked. 'He looks hot in his website photo.'

Jenna laughed. 'What are you like?' She paused. 'To be honest, I felt uncomfortable. I wanted to trust him. Tell him everything, you know? But something held me back.'

'You'll know when you're ready,' Hazel said. 'And you know you've got me, babe. Anything you want to offload, I'm here for you.'

'Thanks, Haze,' Jenna replied. 'I appreciate it.' As she spoke she thought about the things she had always shied away from talking about. She couldn't bear the thought of anyone knowing about that; facing the judgement in their eyes. Could she go back and discuss all that with him?

No, that was a cross she'd have to bear on her own.

Jenna's thoughts were interrupted by the chime above the door telling her someone had entered the shop. Her only customer so far that morning had been one of her regulars, Mrs MacPherson.

'It's got a girl with a red coat on the cover,' Mrs MacPherson had asserted. She was a lovely old soul. Never left her house without her trolley-bag and a blue rinse. Bought loads of books, but often set her these interesting challenges. It was good training for dealing with her mother.

'Oh,' she said when she turned and saw who her next customer was.

'I'm looking for a book.'

'You're in the right place.'

Luke smiled. 'It's by Bessel Van Der Kolk.'

She couldn't help herself. A giggle bubbled up. 'That's an interesting name,' she said. Then she squirmed a little. Feeling bad that she hadn't been back to see him. 'I'm guessing he's not from Airdrie,' she added.

'I think that would be a good guess.'

He had a nice smile. It took years off him.

'Let me, eh...' she turned to the computer '...check.' She felt her face heat.

Wait a minute – was she attracted to this guy?

'It's called *The Body Knows the Score*.'

'And I'm guessing that's not a reference to the latest Rangers versus Celtic match?' She instantly regretted her attempt at humour.

He laughed. She stared at the screen. It really hadn't been that funny.

The door chimed, and a woman in a blue coat came in. This was Mrs Docherty. She'd ordered the latest Martina Cole, and it had just come in that morning.

'Do you mind if I...' she said to Luke.

'Not at all,' he said, and stepped to the side.

Mrs Docherty took a long second to give Luke the once-over before she bustled up to the counter.

'Is it in, hen?' she asked.

'Just arrived this morning,' Jenna answered, reached under the counter to the pile of arrivals and picked out Mrs Docherty's book. She put it in a bag, along with a couple of bookmarks and rang the cost up on the till.

Mrs Docherty paid, took the book and put it in her bag. Before she turned to leave she leaned forward, tilted her head towards Luke and in a stage whisper said, 'Good choice, hen.'

Then, as if she'd approved the love match of the year, she sashayed out of the shop.

'You must get a lot of characters in here,' Luke said.

'You don't know the half of it.' Jenna smiled. Before working in the shop she'd seen reading as a solitary pastime, but working here had shown her that readers were a community of the best kind of people, and now she couldn't imagine working in any other kind of place, in spite of her mother's chagrin.

In guilty moments she'd prayed that the change of personality in her mother following her head injury would result in a less judgemental side emerging. But she couldn't have been more wrong.

'What a waste,' her mother had said that morning when she called in to check on her. 'Waste of an expensive education. We put you through private school and for what? For you to work in a bookshop? What about that journalism degree, eh?' If her mother had ever held back her opinions she was now free to say exactly what she felt. All filters removed by what the doctor likened to a storm going off in her brain.

'Yes, Mum,' Jenna said while checking the cupboards to make sure there was enough food in the house. 'And for the millionth time, I didn't throw it away. I was made redundant. People don't pay for news so much nowadays, and the bookshop was the only place that would have me.' There was a hugely capable woman called Martie who came in daily to make sure her mum was clean and dressed and fed, and Jenna was happy to let Martie do her job, but she needed to salve her conscience by coming in every day to check. Which sadly also meant her running the gauntlet of her mother's insults and accusations.

'I suppose you've taken up with another druggie arsehole. Just don't be thinking he's going to get any of my money. It's all under lock and key, m'dear.'

That was one of the more recent tirades, and no matter how many times Jenna told her she was done with men, her mother kept at it.

While Jenna opened her computer and accessed the ordering system, Luke wandered off to look at the bookshelves. Jenna was always interested in what other people liked to read, so she watched as he scanned the fiction section before landing on the self-help books.

To be fair that was relevant for his job. Maybe that was all he read?

The book he'd asked about popped up on her screen. 'It's in stock at the warehouse,' she called over to him. 'Would be here in a couple of days. Are you happy for me to order it?'

'Yes, please,' he replied.

'Excellent,' she said. It meant she would get to see him again.

But there was the issue of him being her one-time therapist. She wasn't going back, so it really was a one-time deal, even though a quiet voice asserted she still needed the help.

She pressed the button to order the book, and asked for his name and address in a reverse echo of their first meeting.

'That's your book ordered, Mr Forrest,' she said.

He smiled his thanks and said, 'See you in a couple of days.'

Disappointed he hadn't lingered a little while longer, Jenna watched as he walked towards the door.

As he opened it a young man stepped inside and paused.

Not him again, she thought. He'd been hanging around for weeks. Seemed harmless at first, but now he was giving her the creeps. He'd begun by walking past the big shop-front window and stealing glances inside. Then he graduated to standing over at the crime section, casting glances her way before leaving empty-handed.

It was Mhairi, the shop owner, who first spotted him.

'I think you've got a fan,' she'd said a few days earlier.

'Nonsense,' she replied.

'Yup.' Mhairi nudged her, grinning. 'It's only on the days you're working that he does his walk past. He even went so far as coming in the other day. When he realised you were off he actually ordered a book.'

'Why would he do that?'

'So he could come back?'

Jenna shivered. 'That's creepy.'

'Ocht, he's harmless. Look at him, he's barely started shaving.'

She heard the young man apologise. Then there was a pause before Luke spoke in a tone it was difficult to analyse. Equal parts pain and pleasure.

'It can't be,' Luke said. 'God, you're his spit. Jamie? Wee Jamie? I used to run about with your big brother. Man, you're his spitting image.'

Chapter 9

Recognising that he was feeling an attraction to his one-time client, while trying to play it cool and professional, Luke felt his cheeks flush as he pulled open the door. He was so distracted he almost wiped out the young man who was trying to enter as he exited.

He looked up at the guy, saw an expensive wool coat, faint stubble on a sharp chin and a short haircut. But then he stopped as if he'd walked into a wall.

The eyes, the nose, the colouring of both his skin and hair, and it was like time had reeled him back to another era. To another young man. The resemblance was uncanny.

'Jamie? Wee Jamie Morrison? God, you're his spit.'

'Sorry?'

'I should apologise,' Luke said, hand over his heart. 'I only saw you the once, as a kid. Your brother had to bring you along with him this one time.'

'You knew my big brother?' the lad asked.

'We ... eh ... grew up together,' Luke replied.

'He died, you know,' Jamie said. 'Long time ago now.'

Just then an elderly man approached the door and made as if he was trying to get in.

'Ah've seen everything now,' the old man said with a wink that included them both. 'Bouncers on the door o' a bookshop.'

'Sorry,' Luke said, wondering if the old man had come across him doing his other job: doorman at the local pubs and clubs. He aimed a wave to the desk at the back of the shop. 'Thanks, eh ... miss. I'll come and collect my book in a couple of days.'

He stepped to the side, indicating to Jamie that he should too.

'How the hell are you? God, you were only a wee mite when I saw you last. But, man, that face. You're a Morrison and no mistake.'

'Yeah, well,' Jamie said, and crossed his arms. He looked away and then back. 'I only have a few memories and some tatty photos to compare.'

Luke examined the young man and, thinking through the years, guessed that he would be in his mid-twenties. A kaleidoscope of memories pushed through his mind. Some good, some he wouldn't want to look at unless he was sedated with whisky, or in the presence of a good therapist.

He could feel his pulse hammer in his throat and his mouth dry.

Would the guilt ever leave him?

'Listen, it's great to see you, man,' he said as he began to turn, thinking now that he had to get away.

'Hey, man,' Jamie said. 'I know next to nothing about Danny. I was so small when he died, but in some ways he was so big in my imagination.' Jamie looked into his eyes, and there was a *please* framed there. 'It would be great to talk to someone who actually knew him. You got time for a coffee? You can tell me all about the good old days.'

The good old days.

Little about those days was good, thought Luke.

'Sorry, mate. Another time, eh? I've got to go and pick up my wee man from school.'

'Ah, okay,' Jamie said as he stuffed his hands into his pockets, and Luke felt a charge of guilt. Whatever his big brother's sins were he shouldn't judge the younger man by the same measure. Besides, in spite of all the therapy he'd undergone he was still to examine those times properly. Perhaps a chat would prove helpful to them both.

'Listen...' He fished out his wallet, pulled out a business card and handed it to Jamie. 'Here's my number. Give me a call and we can arrange to meet up sometime.'

Jamie looked from the card to Luke. 'The Therapy Shed? That's you?'

'Yeah,' Luke replied, his tone a request for clarification.

Jamie waved the card in front of him. 'This is weird. I've got an appointment with you next week.'

Chapter 10

After Luke had fed Nathan, played on the Xbox with him and got him ready for bed, he pulled out his laptop to check his online diary.

'Daaaad,' Nathan shouted down from his room the moment Luke settled on the sofa. 'It's too dark.'

He'd never stop loving hear Nathan calling him 'Dad', but a wee break to get on with his work would be great.

He shrugged off his frustration with a shake of his head. Just a few years ago he would have given both his arms to be in this situation: being needed and loved.

Setting the computer on the sofa, he left the room and took the stairs two at a time, making a silly mooing sound. As he neared Nathan's door he heard the little boy giggling.

This was their private sleep joke. It had been a week or so after his mother's funeral, and Luke felt it was time for the boy to go back to his own bed. Cows were bigger than sheep, Nathan replied, when Luke told him to count sheep to help him sleep. So wouldn't they take longer to jump the gate, and watching and counting them would be so boring he'd fall asleep faster?

Luke had laughed so hard at Nathan's thinking that Nathan joined in with his infectious giggle. Seconds later they were both helpless with mirth. Luke felt a healing in that moment, a slice of light piercing the dark, laden skies of their shared grief.

From the door, by the light from the hallway, he could see Nathan was sitting up, his expression one of relief.

'Hey, buddy,' Luke said. 'You too warm?' With this question his intent was to throw the boy out of the state he'd worked himself into with a nonsensical question.

'Kinda?' Nathan replied, his expression now one of puzzlement. What did being warm have to do with anything right now?

'Will I lie on the bed beside you to heat you up?'

'Pfft,' Nathan replied, his lips pursed. 'That's silly.'

Luke helped the boy back under his covers and lay beside him.

'Want to count some cows?' he asked. 'Then I'll leave the door open when you fall asleep, and by morning the room will be full of cows.'

'But they'll wake me up. And isn't it 'posed to be sheep?'

'Pfft, anybody can count sheep. It's the smart guys that count cows.'

They faced each other. Nathan's smile was huge before he broke into a fit of giggles.

*

Half an hour later, confident the boy was asleep for the night, Luke made his way back downstairs and joined the laptop on the sofa. He made straight for his online diary.

Right enough: Jamie Morrison. 11am. Monday the ninth.

It had been an online booking, which was why he hadn't twigged.

He thought about the young man who'd appeared in front of him in the bookshop. Trim, well dressed and clear-eyed. Looked like he was taking care of himself. Which was a relief given the family he'd come from. He had a faint memory of someone saying that Danny's brother and sister had been adopted separately – or perhaps it was fostered – following the death of their parents. Must have been tough on them. He'd have thought the authorities would have done everything to keep the siblings together. Mind you, the boy was looking good on it. Whatever happened he appeared to have come out the other side thriving.

*

'Nice wee set-up you've got yourself here,' Jamie said when he took a seat in Luke's office, bang on time.

'Is this weird for you?' Luke asked. 'I can't decide if it would have been better for us to meet and catch up before your appointment, but I just didn't have any time. Nathan's gran usually steps in to babysit for me, but she was away for the weekend.' This wasn't true, but Luke was struggling with the idea of spending any time at all with the lad and wasn't sure on which side of that debate he was going to land.

'S'fine,' Jamie said as he crossed his legs. 'Whatever order it was in was going to be tricky.'

'I won't mind if you just want to sit and blether about old times, and you find someone else for therapy. That won't be a problem at—'

'Nope.' Jamie held a hand up and smiled. 'I'm here now. Besides, it took me ages to find you, and I need to do something about these night terrors. They're doing my head in.'

He did look worried, and now that he was closer, Luke could see that Jamie's face was tight with fatigue, and his eyes were edged in shadows.

'Okay,' he said. 'If you're sure.'

'I'm sure.'

'Then let's begin...'

Luke pulled a blank form up on his computer and began the process of interviewing his new client. As he asked questions, listened and typed in the answers he tried to read between the lines.

What was this young man's story, where had he been all these years and what had been the impact of all those deaths while he was at a vulnerable age? And then being taken in by another family. Luke prayed they were a good match and were kind to him.

It was a little too easy to take the facts that he knew about Jamie's past and attribute the night terrors to that. There were also the facts about his brother Danny's death, and Luke's involvement there. It would all be online, in the papers. Easy enough for Jamie to check. Should he bring the subject up? Or wait for Jamie to ask questions?

Man, what a mess. He was regretting having walked into the bookshop the other day.

'Listen,' he said as he pushed himself slowly to his feet. 'I can't do this. You need to know something first.'

'I know, Luke,' Jamie said. As he spoke there was a stillness about him that Luke couldn't read. 'I know you were driving the car the day Danny died.'

Chapter 11

Guilt was an ever-present for Luke. It wrapped itself around his heart and mind, weighed down muscle and bone, and invaded his sleep. Every waking moment arrived to him through a filter of shame.

All he could do, he determined, was to make sure he acted in the present in a way that his future self would be proud of.

It helped if he thought back to those days and reminded himself about how manipulative and dangerous Danny could be.

He realised that as a young man, he'd bought hook, line and sinker into the notion that education was not for the likes of working-class kids like him, that places of learning were for their betters. And rather than see them as unattainable, it was preferable to dismiss them in the harshest possible terms, view education as something that was at best deeply questionable and at worst a sign that you thought you were better than those around you.

That was the way your peers pulled you back. Pulled you down. Quashed any ambition to make something of your life. There could be no greater insult than: 'Who do you think you are?'

But Luke did crave to be better, to get better, to do better.

All he saw in front of him was an existence in which he was low down a chain of petty criminals, was in and out of prison, and was married to a wife who hated the sight of him and who bore him a couple of kids who had the exact same life journey ahead of them. A life of lack.

So, determined to go one better than his mates – a notion he simultaneously shrank from and embraced – aged twenty, he signed up for night classes at a local college. First he would get some higher grades, then he'd apply for university. Engineering. That was a good occupation, he thought. And it paid well. Enough to get him the fuck away from the people around him.

He told no one.

And yet...

One month into his lessons, where he'd unexpectedly found that he had a facility for French, he was walking towards the college when he saw Danny sitting on a low wall by the gates.

Luke stuck out his chin, determined to stare down his friend. As he walked the long path towards Danny he rehearsed what he was going to say – how he was going to let his friend know that whatever he was doing was none of Danny's business. But when he reached Danny, he got in first:

'I need you to deliver something.' It wasn't a request.

'I'm busy,' Luke said, and moved to walk past, but Danny jumped to his feet and was in his face, hot breath scouring his skin.

'This cosy wee life you've got planned for yourself,' Danny said, 'isnae happening. You're scum. You'll only ever be scum.'

'Piss off.' Luke pushed him away, but Danny was straight back.

'That night? You and your old pal? I'm the only one who knows, remember? And should I happen to start blabbing...'

'What?' Luke's stomach went into freefall. 'Why now? After all these years?'

'Because, buddy boy. *Because.*'

Luke processed what this meant. If Danny told everyone what he knew there would be no coming back.

'Now,' Danny said, his posture one of the victor. 'About that delivery.'

Chapter 12

Neither of them could be bothered cooking, so after driving to the nearest takeaway Jamie pulled into the wide drive of the two-bed bungalow he shared with his sister in the West End of the city. It was a handsome house, with large bay windows either side of a pillar-box red front door, set plump in the middle of a large garden, to the front, rear and sides, full of mature shrubs and trees. A suburban dream for some people, he was sure, but every time he entered the drive and heard the pop of gravel under his tyres he felt a slow burn of resentment.

Amanda had been living like this while he was suffering with the Richmonds, and not for the first time he wondered whether, if he hadn't sought her out, he would still be on his own. They argued about it often.

'Dirty old man taking advantage,' Jamie would say, feeling his face form a sneer. 'What age were you when you met him?'

'If it wasn't for him we wouldn't have any of this.' She'd look around as if taking in the totality of the spacious home and large garden. Jamie wanted her to sell up and move to the coast. A house like this, in this part of the city, would be worth a fortune. They could buy something similar in Ayrshire and have money left to support them for decades.

To be fair, he'd miss the garden if they did sell up. Often, when he was out of sorts, he'd go out back and sit on the stone bench that squatted under the branches of an ancient Scots pine. When a breeze pushed through them, it seemed like the needles were whispering to him. And depending on his mood and need, when he sat there, those whispers could be either menacing or soothing.

It was only when he'd got his own place and a part-time job stacking shelves in the local supermarket that he'd felt strong enough to look for Amanda. They'd probably still be strangers if he hadn't put in that effort. She'd made none herself, though. How was that for sisterly love?

They were together now, he reminded himself, a family of sorts, and that's all that should matter. But still, the fact that she'd met Ted and married him while he was stuck with that nasty couple burned in his mind.

Maybe he should have a proper therapy session with Luke. Talk through his feelings about his sister. She was all he had in the world, after all. He recognised the need to connect with kith and kin, that urge to belong – but he simultaneously despised it as weakness.

Other people only held you back. They promised you love and support, and then failed to deliver either. No. Self-sufficiency was the only way to sustain equilibrium in this life, because when you let someone in and they failed you, as they inevitably would, the crash and burn that resulted led only to one state of mind. A long, cold stare into the void, wondering whether or not you should jump, and whether anyone would notice either way.

He pulled his keys from the ignition, and while the engine cooled and ticked, he thought about his meeting with Luke. He was disappointed he hadn't managed to ask him if he knew the woman who worked in the bookshop. Jenna. She was hot. And she didn't realise it, but they'd met before. A long time ago. He'd been a kid, prepubescent, but just old enough to be curious about girls.

And he'd never forgotten her.

He looked at the bag of hot food on the passenger seat. He'd better get that in the house before it got cold.

Inside, Amanda was in her usual armchair in the conservatory, fingers prodding at the computer on her lap. Even from the door Jamie could see a smear of jam on the side of her mouth, a wound dissecting the puff of her cheek, as if she'd been gashed by a short, sharp knife.

I wish, he thought, and wordlessly handed her a paper bag containing two Big Macs and two portions of French fries. Like him, she had a large appetite and never seemed to put on any weight.

'You're like my feeder,' she said, her eyes bright with anticipation.

'Have you even left that chair this afternoon?'

'Pfft.' She waggled the fingers of her right hand in the air before pulling open the paper bag and peering inside. 'Moving's for losers.'

Jamie took a seat in front of the window with his own food in his lap and started to eat. Late-autumn sunshine radiated through the glass behind him and heated his neck, which was a pleasant surprise given how cold it was outside. The warmth provided a little soothing, and he felt the muscles of his shoulders loosen.

'Any new customers today?' he asked as he chewed.

'That last social-media ad we used really worked,' she smiled. 'Good idea, brother.' Jamie could tell that last comment was grudged.

'Maybe someone will find true love, then,' he replied.

'Wouldn't that be nice.' Amanda tilted her head to the side and made a little kissy shape with her mouth.

Around three years ago, after Ted died and Jamie had moved in, realising they both had a facility for computers, they'd built a dating app, and to their surprise it took off. The income was decent and remarkably steady, and allowed Jamie to give up his supermarket job.

Amanda looked up from her screen.

'Where were you this morning?'

'Nowhere,' he replied automatically.

'You went out for two hours in your car and you went nowhere?'

'Sounds about right.'

She snorted. 'You were mooning over that bitch in the bookshop again, weren't you?'

'Jesus.' He jumped to his feet. 'Every time I confide in you, you manage to make me regret it.'

'Sorry, love,' she smiled. 'I can't help it. You're so bloody serious about *everything*.' She closed the lid of her laptop, and a calculating expression formed on her face. 'Have you had your appointment with Forrest yet? He'll take one look at you and know exactly who you are.'

He thought about his 'therapy' session earlier and shook his head. Then, looking away from her, back down the length of the garden, he wondered why he didn't want to tell her.

'Why are we doing this, sis? Keeping tabs on the guy?' he asked.

'I'm just...' she tossed her head '...curious. He even changed his name. Luke Forrest,' she scoffed. 'Who does that? Someone who's got something to hide, that's who.'

'It's making me uncomfortable.' He shivered. '*You're* making me uncomfortable.'

'Me?'

'This obsession with him, just because he was in the car with Danny. It's not healthy.'

'He killed our brother, or have you forgotten that?' Amanda shot back, steel in her eyes.

'No, but—'

'Sorry, brother, but it just does my head in. Our family went to shit, and he's out there living his life. It's not fair.'

Jamie crossed his arms and stared off into the distance as if memory resided there. 'I've only a few memories of Danny, to be honest. And when I think of Mum and Dad I struggle to see their faces.'

Amanda shot him a reproving look. 'That's ... I'm shocked at you, Jamie. How could you forget them?'

'I was just a kid, Amanda.' Jamie turned away from his sister and was back in the appointment with Luke. He had worked hard to dredge up any recollections from his childhood. In particular, those moments he'd shared with Danny. But the more he pulled, the more his memory resisted.

Danny had been fifteen years older than he was and seemed to lead a life of unattainable freedom. Everything Jamie did was constrained by his parents. Be there. Do this. Don't do that. While Danny was old enough to do exactly what he wanted.

He vaguely remembered other lads Danny's age waiting by the gate. Smoking cigarettes, kicking a ball about, or leaning against their cars, arms stretched across the roof as if to confirm ownership.

'Bloody boy racers,' his father would say.

Young men and their jungle laws. Kids often shrank from Danny a little when they walked past. Even at his young age Jamie recognised the power Danny and his friends wielded. And it transferred to Jamie himself. On the way to school or to the shops, he'd been aware of other kids looking at him, whispering, 'That's Danny Morrison's wee brother.'

'Alright, wee man,' they'd shout over at him.

The implication being that he was protected.

Until the day he wasn't.

His sister was still staring at him. Challenging. As if her eyes were peering directly into his soul. He met her gaze, determined he wouldn't be the one to look away first.

She simply smiled and blew out a dismissive puff of air that said, *I could win this game if I wanted to*. Then she looked away.

Why was he withholding the truth about his meeting with Luke Forrest? When he'd first seen the man he was filled with hate for him. Blamed him for everything that had happened to him and his family. But now, having spoken to him, observed the care in his eyes, the remorse, he was unsure of his earlier judgement.

If he said as much to Amanda, though, she'd scoff. Typical of you, she'd say. Mood and mind all over the place.

'I bumped into him last week.' He spoke out loud without realising, part of his mind acceding control of events to his sister. She'd wheedle it out of him eventually anyway. 'In the bookshop.' He scanned his memory of that moment, trying to assess any interaction Luke might have had with the woman in there – Jenna.

'Oh. Really? *Her* bookshop?' Amanda sat up. Her eyes narrowed. 'Best you keep away from her, Jamie. I know stuff about that woman that would make your toes curl.'

'Really,' Jamie said flatly. He was unwilling to believe her, but he did know that she loved to gather other people's secrets, the way a magpie collects shiny things. He wouldn't have put it past her to have noseyed around the woman's affairs the minute he told her he had a crush on her. And then use it against him. 'Piss off, sis,' he said as he left the room.

An image of Jenna rose in his mind. She was smiling. At him. Warm and interested.

That smile. He would happily die to have that smile turned on him forever.

Chapter 13

Amanda walked into the sanctuary of her bedroom. Whenever Jamie annoyed her, and it was often, she'd come in here, sit in her favourite armchair and look out of the window at the bird table and the back garden. The antics of the sparrows that roosted in her conifer hedge could entertain her for hours.

But today her perch wasn't working its usual magic. Why was Jamie being so difficult? She could tell he was lying. She could always tell when he was lying; she just couldn't work out why on this occasion. To her mind his fixation on that woman in the bookshop was unhealthy.

With a sigh, she pushed herself up from her chair and moved across the room to sit at her dressing table. There, hanging on the edge of mirror was a small pair of ballet slippers. The silk was still in good condition and the ribbon only a little frayed at the edges. These were the only things she'd managed to hold on to from her old life.

She recalled a photo shoot for her old dance school. She was one of five young girls in leotards and ballet shoes, posing in the various positions. She herself was in the fifth position: both hands overhead, fingers pointing inwards, one foot in front of the other.

It took ages for the photographer to organise the shot, she remembered. All the girls had just found out they had been accepted on a scholarship for the renowned Barton School of Dance, and as a result they were fit to explode with excitement.

Amanda recalls she was the only one, despite being the youngest at ten years and eight months, who behaved professionally. As soon as the photographer detailed what she wanted, Amanda had gone into position and held it until she was told to move, while the other girls giggled and squealed, and itched with energy. She understood what it would take to make the most of this opportunity and was intent on doing whatever was necessary. She burned for the bright lights, the music, the applause, and fuelled her obsession by watching TV talent shows every night. She lulled herself to sleep every bed-time imagining the life she would lead. Photographers following her everywhere she went. Being a guest judge on *Strictly*. All the rich and famous people she'd have among the contacts on her phone.

Her parents were proud of her, she knew. Girls from her background didn't go to dance school. It just didn't happen, so she was determined to make the most of it. Most kids she knew couldn't even spell the word 'ambition'. Most of their parents were the second generation forced to live on benefits. An actual job was something that happened to other people, living in other areas of the city.

The fact that she'd learned to dance in the first place was remarkable. She recalled a young woman with an exotic-sounding name leading a class at the local community centre. It didn't last that long. Lack of funding probably. But it was long enough for Amanda to learn and practise so that she could win that scholarship.

That night, after winning the award, everyone in the house was giddy with excitement. Her dad, beer can in one hand, cigarette in the other, danced around the living room, going up onto his tip-toes and trying to spin.

Neighbours from across the landing and one door down came in to join in the party. Then it became all about the drink and the pills, and her mother demanded she put on her tutu and leotard, and show off a few of her moves.

More people arrived, and they had to clear a space in the living room for her to dance.

She felt herself shrink into the memory.

One of her dad's pissed mates, staring, commenting on her developing breasts. 'Gaunnae huv big tits like her maw,' he said.

Amanda had crossed her arms, burning with shame and shrinking from his hot eyes, and waited for her parents to defend her.

That didn't happen. Instead, they laughed, heads back, fillings on show, mindless of their daughter's deep discomfort.

She ran from the room, dived under the sanctity of her duvet, but was pulled out by her wrist. 'Don't give me your prima-donna shite and dance for wur guests,' her mother said as she pulled her back into the living room. 'And don't embarrass me like that again.'

After, when they'd got bored with her and pronounced that it was all just fancy crap, her mother let her go back to her room, saying, 'Don't worry, doll, it's only tits. You'll be glad of them one day. Fun bags for the men in your life.'

She didn't want to keep the men happy. She wanted to lose herself in the dance. To be someone. Travel the dance world. Win all the plaudits.

Then Danny died.

And her dreams turned to ash.

Mouth twisted, she put the photo away in a drawer, wondering why she tormented herself with the life she could have had. Then she remembered, pulled the image back out, wiped the silver with a sleeve and placed it carefully in full view: it was fuel. It fed her determination to watch him suffer, the man who started all of her pain. It was a reminder of all that she had lost, that all the horrible things that had happened in her life stemmed from his actions.

Jamie thought she was odd, wanting to keep tabs on him. Maybe she was, but resentment simmered under her skin. It propelled her through her day. One day his life would turn to shit, because how could someone like him, who'd committed a terrible crime, lead a good life?

It had been a close-run thing when he came out of prison and met that woman and her kid. But then she died. Tragic for her, really. So sad. No young woman should be allowed to die like that. Even Amanda couldn't take pleasure from such a situation.

But watching his grief from a distance sustained her. And when it all went wrong again, she'd be there. Watching. Gloating.

However, if it all went smoothly, maybe she could be the one to make that tide turn? No way could he live happily ever after. That just shouldn't be allowed to happen.

Chapter 14

Luke and Jamie quickly decided that therapy wasn't the best option, given their shared history, so they'd spent the rest of the hour talking about Danny. Or more accurately, talking about a version of him that Luke sanitised.

When he walked back in the house, Luke heard the drum of feet, and a small boy launched himself into his arms. 'Daddy.' Nathan grinned. 'You're home.'

'I know,' Luke replied, unable to restrain his smile. *Home.* He'd hardly been a million miles away. Holding the boy away from his body he looked into his large, blue eyes. Then, feeling the solidity of the child in his hands, the weight there, he placed him on the floor.

'Daddy.' Nathan tugged at his hand and pulled him towards the living room. 'Gran's getting quite good at Ninjago.'

'Really?' Luke asked, his tone mock stern. '*Quite* good, eh? I thought you hated these games?'

Gemma pulled her blue cardigan over her bosom and shrugged from her position on the sofa, facing the TV. 'Aye. Well. Kids should be outside, not have their faces stuck to a screen.'

Luke reached the sofa, picked up a handset and offered it to Gemma. 'Why doesn't Gran show me just how good she is?'

Gemma snorted. 'I'm not doing it while you're here.'

Nathan and Luke laughed.

'Why don't you show Gran, Dad?' Nathan challenged.

'Sorry, buddy. Don't have the time. I've got lots of work on today.' He didn't really, but he needed to get on with some marketing to try and drum up some business.

'Awww,' Nathan pouted, and Luke felt a surge of guilt. He didn't spend nearly enough time with the boy.

'Alright then. Five minutes.'

Luke sat as Nathan cheered, and they set about besting each other on the screen.

Thirty minutes later, after allowing Nathan to accumulate more points than him, Luke stood up, plucked his shed keys from this pocket and hefted them in the air to signal that the session was over. He made his apologies to a protesting child and made his way to the door.

Gemma followed him.

'You look tired, Luke,' she said, crossing her arms, as if in judgement. 'Did you get any sleep last night?

'Enough,' he answered, and felt a wave of fatigue. He'd fallen asleep quickly, but woke up around an hour later and then spent the rest of the night worrying about money, drawing out one catastrophic vision of his and Nathan's future after another.

'Liar,' Gemma said, and smiled and patted his shoulder. 'Getting any more clients?'

'Not nearly enough.'

'Last time we spoke you mentioned getting a couple of shifts at Neon.'

When he was released from prison, after serving eight years of a sixteen-year term, an old contact got him the odd night's work on the door of a local nightclub. As an ex-convict he wasn't sure that such close contact with booze, drugs and the odd flash of violence was a wise move. But at the time it was a case of needs must.

'Not sure I want to go back to that.' He didn't want to do anything that might attract the eyes of the system. He'd been punished. Served his time, and never wanted to go back.

'You've an old head on you now, son...'

'Cheeky,' Luke replied with a grin.

'You know what I mean,' Gemma said as she swatted at his arm. 'I'm sure you know enough to keep the young ones in line.'

'We'll see,' Luke said. 'If the business doesn't pick up soon I'm going to have to do something. And keeping drunks out of bother is preferable to stacking shelves in the local supermarket.'

'And I can help out if...' Gemma looked pointedly at her handbag.

Luke shook his head.

'You're looking after my grandson when his real dad can't be arsed. It's the least I could do.'

Nathan piped up. 'Did you say a rude word, Granny?'

Gemma made an apologetic face – because the boy had heard her bad-mouthing his biological father, Luke assumed. Something, in spite of her strong feelings on the subject, she'd vowed never to do.

'Try not to put so much on yourself, Luke. Lisa would hate to see you worry your way into an early grave.'

'Gemma.' He leaned forward and kissed her on the forehead. 'Stop worrying so much. I'm fine.'

'I'm fine. I'm fine,' she parroted. 'You men and your "fine".' Her face sagged with loss, before she rearranged her features into her usual expression of benign support. Luke knew what she was referring to. Gemma's husband, Ben, had died just days after his sixty-fifth birthday. He'd ignored a persistent cough. Replied to Gemma's nagging with 'Leave me alone, I'm fine' – and succumbed to a massive heart attack. Dead before he'd even hit the ground was how the doctor put it.

How could she deal with all of that loss? A dead husband and daughter in a matter of a few years. Luke ignored his instinct to give her a hug, because he knew that would set off the lecture one more time.

'I'm going to take advantage of you being here and get some shopping in. When I get back I need to try and find a way to drum up some new clients.' He pulled open the door. 'And thanks again. I don't know what I'd do...' He heard the catch of emotion in his voice and swallowed it down.

'Tsk,' Gemma said. 'How could I not?' She waved off his appreciation. 'Go on. Get off and leave me to show that boy how a Lego ninja game should be played.'

Outside his front door, he stepped on something lying on the door mat. He looked down and saw a photo. He picked it up. And almost dropped it again in shock when he saw that the image was of him with Nathan on a recent outing to the park.

He turned it over. The back was blank.

Why on earth would someone take a photograph of them and leave it there?

To send a message? But what kind of message?

It was simply a photograph of him pushing Nathan on a swing. Luke remembered the day well. On several previous trips, Nathan had watched other kids playing on the swings. He'd been unable to keep his eyes off them, but his body had been turned away. Luke had recognised Nathan's fear. Ever since his mother had died Nathan had changed from a boy with zero sense of danger to one who had an overpowering sense of his little body's vulnerability.

It took a great deal of gentle coaxing to get Nathan to even leave the house at first, but his naturally high energy levels and drive to be outside eventually won over. And after seeing other children play on the swings, Nathan allowed Luke to sit him on one and give it a little push. And that was when the photo must have been taken. In a moment when the swing was a little too high. When the child's eyes and mouth were open wide in a photographic distillation of equal parts delight and terror.

Chapter 15

When Jenna returned to her flat after another day in the shop, her feet were less a collection of skin, muscle and bone, and more like one hot throb. With a firm, mental *to hell with it,* she filled a glass full of white wine, landed on the sofa in her living room and mentally scanned the fridge.

There was a well-intentioned bag of salad, some coleslaw, tomatoes and feta cheese. She snorted with self-deprecation. Could she eat that lot? Not a chance.

One of those apps on her phone, she thought, could get her something hot, delicious and devoid of nutrition. Just what she was needing after a day on her feet.

She thought about Luke, the therapist guy. He was cute. And he had a nice smile. As she sipped from her glass she felt herself grin and acknowledged that she may just be growing a crush on the guy. And what was wrong with that? She hadn't fancied someone for ages.

A run of three terrible dates with guys she met online had cured her of that way of meeting men, and since her social life consisted of the odd visit to a wine bar, gathering with the girls in someone's house or going away for a spa weekend with them, she didn't come across many available and fanciable guys.

Jenna allowed the possibility of her and Luke actually being attracted to each other. And over the next five minutes her imagination had them fall in love after a string of romantic dates, move in together, fall out after a stupid argument and end up in a dispute about who got what from the house.

She laughed. *What are you like?* Going from strangers to disillusioned lovers in the space of a few minutes. No wonder she hadn't had a steady boyfriend for years; her expectations of relationships were so low.

There had been that one guy she began to tell Luke about.

She shivered. What a waste of a life.

In any case, she'd visited Luke for therapy. Anxiety was a regular visitor in her life. There beside her on the pillow every morning when she woke up, like a discarded but worryingly persistent lover. Sure, it eased off when she kept herself busy, but at night, with the weight in her mind and the acidic twist in her belly, she'd struggle to get to sleep.

Her phone buzzed an alert. It was a text from Hazel:

Free for a blether?

Feeling the need to talk to someone, Jenna pressed the call button.

'Didn't want to wear out my thumbs,' she laughed when Hazel answered. 'Thought we'd do this the old-fashioned way, and like, actually talk.'

Hazel laughed. 'I hear you, babe.'

'What's up?' Jenna asked as she tucked her legs under her on the sofa, settling in for a long chat.

'Just bored,' Hazel said. 'And wondering if you've arranged to see the cute therapist guy again?'

'He is cute,' she replied, 'but I don't know...'

'You don't know about his cuteness, or the need for therapy?'

'Well...' Jenna laughed. 'Both. He'll probably have some ethical thing to stop him dating clients, to be fair. And...' She wondered how much she should say. 'I don't know if I'm ready to talk about stuff. Some things are better left buried.'

'But it sounds like it isn't buried though. If it is, fair enough, let it lie, but if it's bothering you, something needs to be done.'

Jenna made a non-committal noise.

'There's a man at the heart of all this, yeah?' Hazel laughed.

'How did you guess?'

'Can't live without them,' Hazel said, 'can't live with them. I went out with this guy once. Totally the love of my life, you know? Lasted two years, and when he chucked me I thought that was it. I'd never experience love again. And my next couple of boyfriends

I compared against him.' She paused. 'He was so high on this pedestal despite *him* chucking *me* that these other guys were always going to lose out. Is it like that with you? This old boyfriend made such an impression that everyone else pales in comparison?'

'Sorta,' Jenna replied as she thought it through. 'This Luke guy is the first man I've even been remotely interested in for such a long time, and it's stirring up some uncomfortable feelings.'

'Like what?'

'Och, you don't want to know.'

There was a long moment's silence before Hazel spoke again.

'Sounds heavy. I take it there was a difficult ending?'

'I'll say,' Jenna replied. 'And it all started so well,' she added wistfully.

'Oh, you can't leave that there, Jenna. Forget the bad stuff,' she said. 'Tell me about the good stuff.'

Jenna laughed. 'What are you like?'

'A terrible gossip and a sucker for a love story. Go on. Spill.'

'The first wee while – the first six months or so, to be fair – were just lovely, you know?' She was aware that as she spoke her voice softened with the remembered affection. 'I was a trainee reporter with a local rag, and I used to get home after spending the day on my feet, chasing down stories, to find he had a tub of hot water with some magnesium flakes in it ready for me. All I needed to do was kick off my shoes and luxuriate.' She let out a small groan as if the memory had her there, feet immersed. 'And while I did that he'd put the dinner on.'

'Sounds too good to be true,' Hazel said. 'Was he a good cook?'

'Good enough,' Jenna laughed. 'Spag bol was his speciality.'

'Hey, don't knock it. You cannae beat a good spaghetti bolognese.'

The memories rushed at her, and Jenna tried to ignore their power, but before she knew it she was sobbing softly.

'Oh, babe,' Hazel said. 'I so wish I could come over there and give you a good cuddle.'

Jenna pulled her sleeve over the heel of her hand and wiped her cheeks.

'Sorry, Haze,' she said. 'No idea where that came from.'

'No need to apologise,' Hazel replied. There was a pause, and then she asked, 'He sounds lovely, pet. Where did it all go wrong?'

'Oh, hun,' Jenna sighed, feeling the weight of her regret, 'it would take too long to explain.'

'Better out than in,' Hazel replied.

'I got pregnant,' Jenna said.

'Oh? You never mentioned you had a ... Oh.'

'Yeah, I lost it.' Jenna started to cry again.

'Shit.' Then. 'Hey, these things happen. It's frighteningly common. My—'

'I shouldn't have said,' Jenna interrupted, uncomfortable about a truth coated in a lie. 'Listen. I need to go.' She felt her anxiety build, and she cut the connection.

Chapter 16

When Luke had picked up the photo, he'd run out onto the road to see if there was anyone nearby who might have left it.

'You alright, Luke?'

Luke turned to see Jamie climbing out of a large, dark-blue car, his face full of concern. Luke wondered how Jamie had come into the money for such an expensive-looking vehicle.

'I'm ...eh ... fine, thanks,' Luke said, craning his neck to look up and down the street. It was its usual stretch of quiet. 'Why are you still here...?' He turned his gaze back to Jamie and focused on his earnest young face.

Jamie waved his phone in the air. 'Trying to sort some stuff out for work. Some people seem to be able to drive and work. I don't trust me, or other drivers.' He paused, blushed, clearly realising how what he'd said applied to Luke's own driving.

During their meeting Luke had been as honest as he could be, without divulging too much. Jamie had done his research and knew the bare bones of it: that Luke and Danny had been at the exhausted end of a drink-and-drugs binge, and that Luke had been driving when their car hit a tree. Luke was charged with causing death by careless driving while under the influence of drink or drugs. He'd only served eight years of his sentence, earning time off for good behaviour.

'You didn't see anyone at my door while you were sitting there?' Luke asked.

'No. Is there something wrong?' Jamie stepped closer.

Luke worked a smile onto his face. 'Nope. Just a...' He gave himself a mental shake. He didn't want Jamie to think he was some sort of weirdo. 'It's nothing.'

'By the way,' Jamie said, hands in his pockets. 'Thank you for your honesty in there.' He looked away, then back, directly into Luke's eyes. 'It can't have been easy for you after all this time to talk to a family member.'

'And thanks for not making it harder,' Luke said. 'Can't have been easy for you either.'

'To be fair, I didn't really know him. I was too young, you know? And it was an accident. Besides, it could just as easily have been you in the passenger seat and Danny driving.'

'Yeah...'

'And you have done your time. So...'

Luke felt the stiffness in his shoulders ease a little. 'You know I wasn't really looking forward to you coming in today. Meeting you brought it all back.' He shook his head slowly. 'I was responsible for someone else's death, and that haunts me, every single day.'

'Anyway,' Jamie said, and reached forward and put a hand on Luke's forearm. Just for a moment, but the short hit of heat from his hand gave Luke a lift. 'I need to go. But let's do it again, yeah?'

'Sure thing,' Luke replied.

As he watched Jamie get back in his car and drive away, he thought what a fine young man he'd grown into. His brother, had he had the capacity to think about anyone else in sympathetic terms, would have been proud of him.

*

Luke entered the staff room, stood in front of his locker and stared. The last thing he wanted to do was clock in for a night on the door at Neon. Work as a bouncer was too close for comfort to the life he had before he went in to prison, but needs must. It was taking longer than he hoped to earn enough from his therapy work to pay his bills. So here he was in his black trousers, white shirt and black bow-tie, ready to face down the drunks.

'You look like somebody took a piss in your pint,' said Ken Connolly as Luke roused himself enough to empty his wallet, car keys and mobile phone into his locker. Ken was grinning. Ken was always grinning. If a girl scored a stiletto heel down his calf while her boyfriend tripped and doused him in lager, he'd brush it off with a smile while politely 'showing' them the door. Which of course made him perfect for the job. That and his six-foot-seven frame and 210 pounds of muscle. He never reacted, which more often than not was all that was required to defuse a situation. However, on the very odd occasion when the disarming smile wasn't enough and his patience was no longer required, Ken was more than happy to switch into default mode. Which was where the two-hundred-plus-pounds wall of muscle came in.

Luke was relieved he was sharing door duties with Ken. The big man's geniality was just what he needed. If someone gave Luke lip tonight, he couldn't swear that his reaction would be appropriate, or even legal.

He couldn't push the fact of that photo of Nathan from his mind. An ache of worry flared in his gut. If anything happened to the wee man, he didn't know what he would do.

'You alright, wee man?' Ken's deep bass interrupted his thoughts. 'You don't seem yourself.'

Luke looked over at Ken, who was buttoning up the black shirt of his uniform.

'You're far too nice for this job, Connolly,' Luke replied. 'Away and kick a cat or something. Get yourself into the right headspace to deal with the morons who come in here all the time.'

'Luke, Luke, Luke.' Ken placed a meaty hand on his shoulder. 'You attract more flies with honey than with vinegar, my friend.'

'Who wants to attract flies? They produce nothing but maggots.'

'How's the wee fella?' Ken changed the subject. 'Still kicking your arse on the video games?'

Luke couldn't hold back a proud smile and read the pleasure with which Ken observed it.

'Piss off, you big asshole.' He punched Ken on the arm. 'Stop trying to fix everybody.'

'Just call me Gandhi.' Ken crossed his arms, his biceps threatening to tear the seams of his sleeves.

'Aye. Work in a nightclub. Save the world, one drunk at a time. I can see the biopic now.'

The door opened and their boss, Anna Brady, stuck her head in. She was a good-looking woman, Luke thought, every time he saw her. And under that perfectly straightened, bleached head of hair was a brain full of street smarts.

'We've got the dream team on tonight then, eh?' she smiled. 'Good to have you back, Luke.'

'Nice to be back,' he replied.

'Liar,' she grinned. 'But there's a space here for you anytime, alright?'

'Thanks, Anna. Appreciate it.'

'How's the wee fella?'

'Grand,' Luke replied, feeling his face light up again with a huge smile.

Anna gave him a look. A sort of unsaid *good on you*. She'd once told him when uncharacteristically drunk that taking on the wee boy after his mother's death made him 'a good man, and sexy as fuck, by the way'. Luke had been too full of grief for Lisa at the time to investigate where that random statement might lead, but as time passed he wondered if he should explore it further. But, then, she and her club were a possible stream of income, so why jeopardise that?

When Anna left, Ken gave him a look.

'Anything you need to tell me?' he asked.

'What?'

'Don't come the innocent with me. You and boss lady. Looking to get all hot and sweaty with her?'

'Away and howl at the moon, ya nutcase,' Luke said, punching his friend on the arm again.

'Would it be so wrong?' Ken asked, pretending to rub at the sore spot. 'It's about time you got yourself back out there.'

'Yeah, well, maybe,' Luke replied, wondering if there was anything more to his hesitancy. Was he in a place where he could be emotionally available again?

'I'm pretty sure Lisa would want you to be happy,' Ken continued.

Luke felt his neck heat. 'Jesus, we've turned all serious here. Can we go move on to talking about the weather, tits and football?'

Ken grinned. Looked at his watch, and then made a buzzer sound. 'Too late. Show time.'

*

The evening started slowly. This time of year, before all the Christmas work parties started, always saw a lull in attendance, opined Ken. People started to trickle in after 10pm, in groups of twos and threes. Men and women, faces bright with booze and eyes large with anticipation. The trickiest moment was when a group of lads from a local football team were just a tad too excited. One in particular having overdone the drink beforehand.

Ken stepped in front of the lad, who stumbled back when he saw the fleshy bulk looming before him. 'Too drunk,' Ken said. 'One of you,' he scanned the rest of the guy's mates, 'need to take him home.'

'Ah telt yeeze,' one of them said. 'Fletch doin' his usual. Spoilin' it for everybody else.'

'You,' said Ken pointing at the man who spoke. 'Get him in a taxi home.'

The rest of the group laughed at him. 'See ye, Mosh. Enjoy your early night, mate,' one of them said.

'Piss off,' Mosh replied, looked wounded as he assessed the situation.

'Then when you come back,' Ken said to the lad, 'I'll see you get in for free, alright?'

Mosh punched the air. 'Ya dancer.'

After Mosh pulled his inebriated friend to the taxi rank and the rest of the group vanished inside, Luke turned to Ken. 'Nicely handled, big man.'

Ken shrugged. 'One less fee at the door's a small price to pay for one less twat who can't handle his...' He tailed off as something caught his attention. Luke turned to see what had distracted Ken.

A woman stood before him, her smile a hesitant hello.

'Though it was you,' she said to Luke.

It was Jenna.

Chapter 17

It was Jenna's oldest friend, Kate's birthday, and to help her celebrate, a mutual friend, Debbie, hosted a party. One pink champagne led to another, and before she knew it Jenna had been dragged along to the local nightclub.

She and the birthday girl were the last women standing. Well, Kate was. She was inside, sucking on the face of a much younger man, taking just enough time out to say to Jenna that she was perfectly safe, having a great time, and if Jenna wanted to get herself a taxi and go home that was fine.

'Thought it was you,' she heard herself say to Luke, who was standing in the doorway, looking good in his bow-tie and black bomber jacket.

'I didn't see you come in.' He looked beyond her for a possible companion. 'On your own?'

'You must have been on your break,' Jenna replied, crossing her arms. She'd known it would be a waste of time to come here, but she didn't want to let Kate down. Now she just wanted to get home and get into her pyjamas.

'My friend...' Jenna waved a hand in the direction of the door '...is fastened on to some poor guy.' She laughed self-deprecatingly. 'I'm way too old for this kind of thing. What's the female equivalent of a pipe and slippers? That's what I need in my life right now.'

'Prosecco and an episode of *Strictly*?' Luke grinned.

'Have you been peering in my window?' Jenna laughed, enjoying how in mere moments they'd sparked a connection.

'Listen,' Luke said. 'It's a quiet night, and I'm due another break. Why don't I drive you home?'

'I couldn't impose on you like—'

'It's fine, honestly,' Luke said. He looked over her shoulder, and Jenna turned to see a benign expression on a very large man.

'Aye, on you go,' the mountain said. 'I'll hold the fort.'

'C'mon,' Luke said, and turned in the direction of the street. 'My car's just over here.'

His assumption that she'd accept his offer didn't rankle, strangely. There was something solid and reassuring about him. She caught up with him and offered him a shy thank-you.

'No bother,' he said, turning to the side and smiling.

As they walked almost shoulder to shoulder, she sensed his heat and felt such a draw to it that she slowed down. What was she thinking? She wasn't in her right mind. She was breaking one of her cardinal rules: taking lifts from strangers.

'Just here,' he said, pointing at a small, dark car. A beep sounded. He opened the passenger door wide, stepped back and looked at her expectantly.

Biting the inside of her mouth, she gave him a little nod, moved past him and took a seat.

*

Just a hundred yards away, a hooded figure watched. Shadows obscured his face like they were part of his costume. His heartbeat thumped insistently in his neck, and his hands flexed in and out of fists, like lungs drawing in breath.

Chapter 18

All night long Luke's mind had run on one track.

Jenna.

The light in her eyes. The way she held her hand to her heart when surprised or pleased. Her gutsy, unfettered laughter when he'd told her a crap joke just before he dropped her off.

He ran through every word and gesture. It was clear she appreciated the lift, but was her kiss on his cheek just before she climbed out of the car a sign that she was interested? Might she *like* him, like him, or did she simply like him?

The next morning, Luke was in the bookshop, picking up the book he ordered. For good measure he requested another. Then he heard himself say one word.

'Coffee?'

It was out before he could stop it.

'Sorry?' Jenna replied, looking startled.

'I mean, it would be nice to meet up for a coffee some time,' he managed. It had been so long since he'd asked a woman out he wasn't sure where the line was. 'Or we could go for a walk? Or I could come back in two days' time and order more books?'

'Order more books,' Jenna grinned. 'The boss will love me for it.'

'Does that mean the coffee's out?'

'Oh, no, coffee would be nice. We could even walk while we drink it.'

Luke laughed, enjoying the fact that she was teasing him about his awkwardness.

*

Coffee was a success so they had a meal out together the following night. And the next night Jenna invited him in to her flat.

'You know, our relationship as client and therapist never really got off the ground,' Luke said as he put one foot on her doorstep.

Jenna's brow dipped in puzzlement. Then the realisation hit her. 'Would it matter if...?'

'Absolutely.'

'Well, then, good job I ran out of there before that first session was completed.'

'Without paying me.'

'I didn't even pay you?' Jenna's hand shot to her mouth. 'I completely ... That's awful.'

'Turns out to be a blessing in disguise,' Luke said as he stepped in close.

'Why's that?' Jenna cocked her head to the side.

'This.'

They kissed.

Chapter 19

Jamie's head felt muffled, his limbs weighed down into the mattress, and his eyes were grainy with fatigue. It felt like he'd been staring up at the ceiling, without moving, for days.

There was a knock at his bedroom door.

'Go away,' he said, managing only enough energy to whisper.

'How long are you going to sulk in there?' Amanda demanded. 'I need you to go out, Jamie,' she persisted. 'We've run out of stuff.'

Order online, he thought, like other people.

'I can't order online,' she added. 'They always get it wrong.'

'So, take a Gala apple instead of a Cox for a change. It won't kill you.'

'Please, Jamie,' she wheedled. 'I've got lots of work on today.' Pause. 'Please?'

Jamie closed his eyes. And there, burned into his memory, was the moment when he watched as they kissed.

Luke and Jenna.

How could he?

How could *she*?

He felt betrayed. Jenna and he had a bond. And Luke, of all people. Jamie was just beginning to like the man. There was something about his easy way, the gentle light in his eyes and the very real care that made him consider talking. Actually talking, rather than pretending to go through a session as he had with countless therapists over the years.

'What do you remember about Danny?' Luke had asked him.

'He scared people,' Jamie answered without hesitation. Then he studied Luke's face for a reaction, but he got none.

'Why do you think that sticks in your mind?'

'I was so small, power and the powerful fascinated me. Danny had it, and by extension so did I.'

'How so?'

'A boy tried to bully me in class this time.' Jamie was back in the past, acutely aware of his lack of strength, quailing at the thought of violence, aware of the bristle and threat from the other boy.

Then another kid piped up. 'Touch him an' you're dead. That's Danny Morrison's wee brother.'

'So what?' pig-eyed boy said as he squared his shoulders. Then he stepped back. Slow, as if he was determined to save face. 'Next time,' he said and pointed at Jamie, his finger like a blade.

'Then, when Danny died, that protection died with him?' Luke asked him.

Jamie nodded. And remembered being cold to the bone, hiding in a cupboard.

'Do you want to talk about losing that protection?' Luke asked.

Jamie ignored the suggestion. 'He was also generous. Couldn't do enough for me and Amanda. Always bringing us the latest toys and sports gear.'

'Sorry.' Luke sat up. 'I keep forgetting to ask you about your sister. How is Amanda? Do you guys keep in touch?'

'We barely talk, to be honest,' Jamie lied. Aware that he was crossing his arms as he spoke, he forced himself to relax and allowed his hands to drop onto his lap.

Luke said nothing, leaving a space for Jamie to fill. And Jamie did so willingly, despite spotting Luke's tactic. He thought it might be good for Luke to feel he'd opened up a little more. Allow him that small victory.

'I have so much resentment, you know? She was older than me. She could have looked me up, found me and taken me away from those arseholes.'

Pause.

'But?' Luke asked.

'She didn't. Once I was older, I was the one to seek her out.'

'Where had she been? What happened to her?'

'Fostered, same as me,' Jamie shrugged. 'Older couple. The

woman died when Amanda was seventeen. A year after she'd moved out.' Jamie hadn't prepared what to say next. How much of the truth did he want Luke to know? 'She'd kept in touch with the couple and moved back in after the wife died. Live-in maid, kinda thing. Only that relationship became more ... intimate. They started fucking...' Jamie wanted a reaction.

He got none. Luke was too professional for that, and, besides, he'd heard it all before.

'And then they married. The old man died.' Shrug. 'Amanda inherited his estate. Landed lucky.'

'But at what price to her, I wonder,' Luke said.

Jamie didn't much care what gaining that inheritance had cost his sister. He doubted it had had any impact on her.

'She forgot all about me. She doesn't care about anyone but herself.'

'So you feel resentment towards her?'

'Wouldn't you resent your last living relative if they did nothing to help you when they had the chance?'

'She was effectively still a child. We don't know what she was going through. Maybe she just didn't think it was possible. Maybe her difficulties made it—'

'Why are you defending her?' Jamie shot forward. 'You don't even know her.'

'Correct. I don't.' Luke held a hand up. 'And I'm not defending her. I'm suggesting there might be another way to read all of that. A different perspective can help reframe the situation. Help you not feel that resentment.'

Jamie sat back in his chair, pretending to allow Luke's considered words to mollify him. Just for a moment.

'There's a few lines I remember in a poem I got taught at school. Rabbie Burns. I think it was about Tam O'Shanter's wife, sitting at home, nursing her wrath to keep it warm.' He set his chin in defiance. 'That's me. Keeping my resentment warm, cos if I don't have that I have to start forgiving her.'

'Is that so impossible?'

Jamie crossed his arms again. Aware again of the picture he was presenting. He offered Luke the ghost of a smile. 'We can talk about that once global warming's been fixed.'

Now, Jamie heaved a sigh as Amanda knocked at his bedroom door once more. He knew she wouldn't barge in: she insisted he abide by her rules on personal space, so she never impinged on his.

That personal space, however, was limited only to time in his bedroom or bathroom. In almost every other area of his life Amanda was an unending stream of questions and a ceaseless demand for answers.

'C'mon, Jamie,' Amanda wheedled. 'We've run out of Jaffa cakes. You know I can't do without my Jaffas.'

Despite himself Jamie huffed a laugh. In one of their earliest, most furious, rows Amanda's claim about these treats had felt so ridiculous to them both that the fight ended with them doubled up with an attack of the giggles, and since then it had become shorthand for 'time's up'.

'Besides,' she added. 'There's something on your fancy woman's Facebook page you need to see.'

He reached the door and pulled it open. 'She's not my—'

Amanda was standing in front of it holding out a cup of coffee for him. She wrinkled her nose. 'You need a shower.'

He took the cup and shut the door on her.

'You don't want to see her Facebook page? Your bookshop crush?'

He opened it again.

'Leave it, will you?' It would never do to show Amanda that something was important to you; like any detective in any decent cop show he'd watched, she'd use it against you.

She held up her phone. He took it from her and read two updates.

'What's this?' he asked, knowing but dreading what was coming. 'These are screenshots, not the actual page.'

'Yeah, I recorded it for posterity. You need to get over her.'

'Fuck off,' Jamie replied.

In one, the owner of the page had shared The Therapy Shed's page with the comment: *Most highly recommended.*

In the other: *Jenna is in a new relationship.*

Amanda studied him, then, as if she'd noted his lack of surprise, she asked. 'You knew this. How?'

'What does it matter if they're together?' He fought to hide his feelings. 'This stalking thing you've got going on, it's not natural, Amanda.'

'It's not stalking. I'm just keeping tabs, and this...' she stabbed the screen with a hard little finger '...is not on.' There was a cold, hard light in her eyes. 'It's not fucking on.'

'What do you mean?' Jamie asked. There was a subtle change in his sister. A little more steel in her spine. More snap to her speech.

'I'm not having it, Jamie. After what we lived through, that guy gets to live happy ever after? We'll see about that.' Her eyes were off in the distance, as if in her mind she was already dealing out imagined havoc. 'We'll fucking see about that.'

Chapter 20

Jenna propped herself up on her elbow and looked down at the man sleeping in the bed beside her.

He was on his back, his mouth open. As were both of his eyes. Just a little.

She waved a hand in front of them to check. No reaction. He was sleeping, but the eye half-open thing was creepy.

But how wonderful to find out that Luke was anything but. He'd been a real gentleman since their very first interaction. And now here he was in her bed. Naked.

She traced a light line from the hollow at the base of his neck and down his chest to where the quilt rested halfway down his stomach. There she resisted the impulse to move any lower. Let the man sleep, she thought. He always looked so tired, as if sleep was a rare gift.

He stirred.

Jenna removed her hand.

His eyes opened. He smiled, his teeth flashing in the pale light.

'Hey you,' he said, and then yawned, and stretched.

'Hey,' she replied, feeling a flutter in her stomach. It had been a long time since a man consistently provoked that reaction.

'Sorry, I must've dozed off.' Luke pushed himself up onto his elbows. 'What time is it?'

Jenna craned her neck to look at the alarm clock on the bedside cabinet beyond him. 'Just gone midnight.'

'Shit.' He sat up. Offered a smile of apology. 'I'd better go. My babysitter will be wondering where I got to.'

'Maybe next time you'll be able to ask her to stay overnight. Would be nice to wake up in the morning and you still be here.' Jenna reached out to hold Luke's hand.

'I'd like nothing more,' Luke said. 'But softly, softly, eh? Nathan has to be my priority. I don't want to spook him by introducing a new girlfriend too soon.'

'Why, when was the last girlfriend you brought home?' Jenna worried her tone was defensive so she added a smile.

'I haven't,' Luke replied.

'You mean…?'

'There's been no one since his mum died.'

'But that was over two years ago. You must have been lonely.'

'Grief was the over-riding emotion, to be honest. Didn't leave much room for that kind of loneliness.'

Jenna shifted position on the bed, bringing her head up to rest on Luke's chest. 'Does it make me egocentric that I'm stupidly pleased that I was the one you chose to be the first since…'

Luke laughed. 'Does it make me egocentric that I'm stupidly pleased that you would be stupidly pleased?'

He moved his head down towards hers. She met his lips with hers and felt her breathing contract.

They each stopped moving. Lips pressed lightly together. Each of them breathing in the other. Lingering in the moment.

'Your lips feel amazing,' Luke said as he created a tiny bit of distance between them. 'But…'

'You need to go.' Jenna closed the distance a little. 'And I'm not stopping you.'

Luke laughed. 'God, I would like nothing more…'

She could feel his longing. And decided to be the grown-up. She put a hand on his chest and pushed. 'Go. You don't want to piss off your babysitter, cos then you won't come back.'

'I'm so lucky, really. Nathan's granny's been a star.'

'She'll be beyond pleased that you took Nathan on after her daughter died. I'm sure you won't have any—'

Jenna sat up, looking at the window. She hadn't fully closed the curtains when they'd entered the room – her mind being on other things. But although this was a ground-floor flat, her bedroom wasn't overlooked; you'd have to go to some effort to spy in.

'I thought I saw something there. Someone.' She pulled the quilt up over her breasts.

Movement just outside her window.
Shadows shifted.
The cold glitter of hard eyes and bare teeth.
Jenna screamed. 'There's someone outside.'

Chapter 21

Just when was the right time to tell your new girlfriend that you'd been in prison for causing someone's death?

That question had been rumbling through Luke's mind from the moment he realised he wanted Jenna in his life. Several times through the course of those first few dates the words had almost tumbled from his mouth, but something stopped him from speaking them.

Lying in her bed, about to dress and leave for the night, he'd opened his mouth in preparation to give a speech that could well ruin his first attempt at a relationship in years, when Jenna shouted an alarm and pointed at the window behind him.

Instantly, he was on high alert. He jumped into his jeans and rushed barefoot out of the flat and into the garden down the side, while Jenna screamed, 'Don't go.'

There was nothing to be seen outside, and all Luke got for his troubles was a chill on his bare flesh and a stubbed toe.

He limped back inside to find Jenna dressed and wrapped up in a quilt, sitting on the edge of the sofa.

'You okay?' she asked, looking down at his feet.

'Nobody there,' he said and limped over to sit beside her. 'To be fair it's so dark out they could have been a few feet from me and I would have missed them.' He cradled the big toe of his right foot.

'You okay?' Jenna repeated.

'Fine,' he replied, holding up a hand as he saw Jenna move closer. 'Stubbed toes always feel worse than they really are. Nothing's broken, and there's no blood, so your carpet's safe.' He instantly regretted his tone and his choice of words. 'I mean...'

'It's okay,' Jenna said. 'I've had a few sore toes in my time. It's never pleasant.' She looked over his shoulder, indicating the world beyond her four walls. 'There was nobody there?'

Luke shook his head. 'What did you see?'

Jenna shivered. 'It was too dark to make anything out, but there was somebody. I'm not going crazy.'

'I didn't say you—'

'I could make out a baseball cap. I think. And it was as if the light bounced back off their teeth.' Her bottom lip trembled. 'Jesus, that was scary. Who would do such a thing? God, I'll never feel safe here again.'

Luke got to his feet. He had been about to leave but there was no way he could abandon her like this. 'Right. Pack a bag, you're coming to mine, and then tomorrow I'll go round all your doors and windows, make sure you're safe. And maybe think about installing some lighting outside. Something that's triggered by movement, yeah?'

'You're sure?' Jenna's eyes were large with gratitude.

'I can't leave you like this. You're coming over to mine. No argument.'

'But what about Nathan? Isn't it a bit soon to be introducing him to me?'

'We'll think of something. Let me phone Gemma first and explain why I'm running late.'

*

Gemma met them at the door. She was wearing her coat, clearly ready to leave, but the line of her mouth was pursed tight with concern.

'Come away in, hen,' she said to Jenna, taking her by the arm and leading her inside. Luke followed, grateful for Gemma's no-nonsense approach.

In the living room she pointed to the sofa. Luke noted that it had been set up with pillows and a quilt.

'I wasn't sure what was what,' she said, as she coloured a little. 'But I thought you might appreciate a bed being ready for you.'

'Thank you,' Jenna said with a smile. 'That's very kind of you.'

'Nae bother, hen,' Gemma said. 'And Luke, the wean went down no bother.' Her face brightened, as it always did when she was talking about Nathan. 'He's a wee darlin'.'

'And so are you,' Luke said, and gave her a hug. Once they'd stepped apart he took her by the arm. 'C'mon and I'll walk you to your car.'

'Aye, maybe once I reach invalid status.' Gemma lifted her arm from his light grip and raised an eyebrow. 'I'll manage fine on my own.'

Luke laughed. 'Sorry, I didn't mean to suggest ... It's just we've had a fright tonight. There's some weirdos out there.'

'And if they try anything on me they'll feel the sharp edge of my tongue,' Gemma bristled. 'Anyway,' she added, 'I need my beauty sleep. I'll speak to you in the morning,' she said to Luke. Then she nodded in Jenna's direction. 'Hope you feel better, doll.'

Once Gemma had left, Luke sat beside Jenna on the sofa.

'She seems lovely,' Jenna said.

'She's amazing,' Luke replied. 'Don't know how I'd cope with the wee man without her.'

Jenna looked from the door to the sofa.

'I should sleep here, then,' she said patting the quilt.

Luke silently acknowledged the lead she was taking on this. His head was scrambled, and he wasn't sure what the right thing to do was.

'It will be less confusing for Nathan in the morning, I'm thinking.'

'Yeah, okay.' Luke nodded. 'Or I could sleep here, and you could have my bed?'

'Does Nathan climb in with you in the morning?'

'Ah, yes, he does,' Luke replied, feeling a smile spread on his face. He loved it when Nathan joined him each morning. His Fireman Sam pyjamas warmed through and soft with his body heat. And five minutes later the chatter would begin. Questions of the most random nature, mostly concerning his current favour-ite topic: dinosaurs.

'He'll get a bit of a fright if he sees me. I think Gemma had the right of it. I'll sleep here.'

'I could sleep on the armchair,' Luke offered. 'Keep you company?' He was unable to stifle a yawn that was so wide it almost dislocated his jaw.

Jenna crossed her arms, looking tiny. 'That would be nice. But only till I fall asleep, then you can go and stretch out on your bed.'

'Don't think either of us will get much sleep tonight. Fancy a drink of something?'

'Something herbal?'

'I was thinking of something harder, but that's the sensible idea. Camomile do you?'

Minutes later, Luke was back in the room bearing mugs. He handed one to Jenna and then sat in the armchair opposite her.

The subject of his past leaked into his mind, and from there to the tip of his tongue. He opened his mouth in preparation for speech.

'Thank you, Luke. For your kindness. I really appreciate it,' Jenna said.

'I couldn't leave you back there on your own. Not tonight,' Luke replied, feeling equal parts relief and frustration. Should he bring the conversation back onto the course he intended?

'I don't just mean that.' Jenna's smile was small, timid. A mouse peeking out from behind a wall. 'We never really got into why I was looking for therapy, and you've never pressed me since to find out why. I'm so thankful for that.'

'It's only my business when you make it my business,' he replied. 'But anytime you want to talk, I have a splendid pair of ears.' He cupped a hand behind each ear for emphasis and grinned.

Jenna's laughter was the music of his reward.

She cradled her cup and looked off into the near distance. 'I was such a fearful little girl. Dad had an accident at work when I was about five or six, and it terrified me. He recovered well, but that glimpse into the most important person in my life being so vulnerable...' She shook her head. 'It never really left me.' She sighed. 'Heart attack got him eventually, after I was a grown up, and I was fine. Handled that well, to be fair, but then Mum with this head injury brought it all back, you know?'

Luke nodded to show his understanding.

'But you distract yourself with busyness. You control what you can and accept what you can't ... and it lessens.' Her words were delivered with a half-certain smile.

Luke wondered if Jenna was still to convince herself of this but made a low noise of understanding. His impulse was to dig a little deeper, but he kept his mouth firmly closed. Now that they'd made the transition to lovers, he felt constrained by his first contact with her as a therapist. It felt like he could only use those skills from now on at her explicit request.

He looked into her eyes, saw her gratitude and read that it was being filtered through her barely acknowledged fear. Telling her about his past would be entirely the wrong thing to do now.

He would have to wait before revealing who the real Luke Forrest was.

Chapter 22

Jamie looked at the photo of the small boy on Luke's desk – the wide, trusting eyes and the flash of teeth – and felt a stir of guilt. Would what they were doing result in another child being left parentless? He considered his sister back home and quashed the thought. The only emotion they had room for was hate. Nothing else would see this done.

'Do you want me to repeat the question, Jamie?' Luke was asking.

Jamie shook his head. 'I was just thinking up an answer.'

'If you have to think up an answer, does that mean it might be less than genuine?'

'It's complicated,' Jamie answered. 'The more instant, obvious answer might be coming from the wrong place. It might be a knee-jerk reaction rather than careful thought.'

'Do you always prefer the rational?'

'What was the original question?' Jamie laughed. 'We've kinda gone round the houses here.'

'Your foster parents. Tell me about them.'

'It's this time of year,' Jamie started, 'full of not so happy memories. It was nearly Christmas when I was sent to them, you know. My first Christmas without Mum and Dad, and Amanda.' He crossed his arms. 'Not that Mum and Dad went overboard, like, but what they offered they did so without ... I'm trying to think of the right word. With the Millers it was always about consequences. Everything was a transaction. Do this – get that. Or don't.'

'Can you give me an example?'

Jamie was back in the Millers' kitchen. It was the first time he'd brought a friend over. And the last. Andy Calhoun. Andy lived two doors down. He was one of the best football players at school and as such was very popular. Jamie wanted to trade on that popularity to help him with the other kids at his new school.

Suppertime; the Millers always had tea and toast at 8pm. On the dot.

After playing with Top Trumps cards in his bedroom, Jamie led the way down to the kitchen at the appropriate time. Hoping there were biscuits, and ravenous after an early dinner from which his potatoes had been withdrawn because he had been late home from school. One of the newest of the rules that governed his every moment. Rules that appeared to come and go at a whim.

Sitting in the middle of the table was a plate consisting of several slabs of crusty bread, thickly buttered and bright with blackberry jam. On any other evening Jamie would have known the butter and jam was not for him. He got bread with a slimy spread of margarine, and cheap strawberry jelly. But, excited at the prospect of making a new friend – Andy appeared to enjoy playing with the cards – Jamie picked up the thickest piece of bread and took a massive bite.

'What do you think you're doing?' Mrs Miller shouted at him.

Jamie froze. The mass of bread in his mouth like a soured lump of guilt.

'Spit it out, boy. Spit it out.'

Jamie, aware that Andy was staring at him could do nothing but stand there and fight for breath, so big had the gobbet in his mouth become.

'Oh for goodness...' Mrs Miller grabbed him by the ear, dragged him over to the sink and bent him over it. There, she thrust her fingers in his mouth and sought the back of his throat.

Jamie gagged. Tears stung in his eyes. Blood rushed to his head, and his stomach heaved. Over and over again. Not only was the food in his mouth ejected, but his earlier meal too.

'Got to go. Bye,' Andy said, and Jamie was barely aware of him leaving.

It felt like his entire body was either stinging or pulsing.

'That didn't sound like a pleasant memory,' Luke said, his voice laden with concern and kindness.

'What?' Jamie shook himself. He forced a breath and almost felt Mrs Miller's sharp nails down the back of his throat. 'It's complicated,' Jamie managed to say, while his mind was full of the way Luke had spoken to him. He couldn't remember the last time anyone appeared so concerned about his well-being.

'Isn't that the hour up?' Jamie got to his feet, aware he was trying to distance himself from the emotions Luke was drawing out of him.

'We still have fifteen minutes left,' Luke replied.

'Yeah. Well.' Jamie reached for his coat and pushed one arm through a sleeve. 'Just remembered I have somewhere I need to be.'

*

Back home, and prostrate on his bed, there was a knock at his door.

'You're home early,' Amanda said as she opened the door just wide enough to be heard.

'Aye.'

'You did go, didn't you?'

'Leave me alone.'

He heard the door open a little more and Amanda step inside the room. Jamie turned on his side, showing her his back.

'Everything okay?'

What was that? Concern? Where was the usual snide, judgemental tone?

'You did go, yeah?'

'Yes. Now leave me alone.'

'Wait. You're upset. Is he doing, like, actual therapy shit on you?' She approached him, slow-footed but sure. A lean cat stalking a fat pigeon.

'Piss off.'

Silence.

'By the way, I found the boy's real father,' Amanda said in a sing-song. 'Shit's about to get real.'

'What do you mean?' Jamie asked.

'Luke Whatsisname doesn't get to be happy while our family are all in their graves,' she spat.

'What did you do?' Jamie asked.

'Life's about to get more difficult for a certain someone.'

'Amanda, what did you do?'

'What does Luke care about most in the world?' she asked him.

'I barely know the man,' Jamie replied, 'but I'm guessing his boy and his work.'

'He's about to lose them both,' Amanda said with a self-satisfied smile.

Chapter 23

A phone rang, percolating through Jenna's dreamscape. She sat up disorientated. Where was she? Luke's. Right. Weak street light pushing through a space in the curtains helped her pick out the detail of the room. Her phone stopped. It had sounded like it was coming from the floor. She nudged something solid with her foot. Her bag. Right. It felt like every thought was coming to her through a fog.

She leaned down, picked up her handbag, pulled out the phone and read the name of her mother's carer on the screen. Why would she be calling her?

It started to ring again. But this time her mother's ringtone sounded, and her name and number appeared on the screen.

'That stupid twat has only gone and resigned.' Her mother's voice sounded more slurred than normal. Anger and fatigue would do that, thought Jenna absently. She shook her head, willing clarity into her thoughts. Her mother was distressed. Wake up.

'Did you hear me? Resigned. Said she couldn't deal with my shit anymore.'

'I'm betting she didn't use those words,' Jenna replied. That would be so unlike Martie.

'You need to come over. I need a shower. My breakfast. What am I having for my fugging breakfast, Jenna?'

Fugging breakfast.

'What time is it?' Jenna asked.

'Breakfast time.'

It's her condition. It's not your mum. It's her condition talking.

After saying she'd be over as soon as she could, she cut the call and checked the time. 7:48. She took a deep breath, and willed energy into her body. This was not good. Her mother's latest carer was the third in six months, and was the only one to last more than two weeks. She worried her mother's reputation went before her, and the agency wouldn't be able to find someone else to work with her at such short notice. Besides, Christmas was approaching; staff had to have holidays. Would there be anyone spare? She'd have to phone the bookshop and take some time off.

Guilt and resentment fought for space in her mind. She couldn't not see to her mother, but she didn't want to lose her job. That and Luke were the only things keeping her sane right now.

With a start she realised that if she couldn't get a replacement carer, not only would she have to take leave from her work, she might also have to move in with her mother. And then her life would officially be over.

As she gathered her belongings together she focused her hearing in the direction of Luke's bedroom. Nothing. Good. It meant she didn't have to have any awkward conversations. He didn't sign up for a girlfriend with mother issues. Or one with an overactive imagination. Maybe the person looking in her window was all in her head.

Leave, Jenna. If she woke him up and told him why she was going, and perhaps why he was better off without her, he'd just do that nice guy thing he did and persuade her she was wrong.

No. He had enough on his plate with trying to build up his business, looking after Nathan, and then there was that freaky photo.

Time to leave.

She cast her eyes towards his bedroom, delaying her departure for just a moment, in the hope he would wake up and talk to her, and she would melt, going against all her instincts, which told her she should put relationships behind her.

Things had always been much more simple without men in her life.

Chapter 24

It was Friday night, and Anna had called to ask Luke to work. Over the last few weeks Friday nights had been spent with Jenna, but since she'd moved in with her mother, they had seen less and less of each other. Jenna explained that it was down to difficulties with her patient.

Luke believed her for the most part, but a nagging voice questioned just how difficult it would be to find a professional carer. Wouldn't the local authority provide something? And he had heard her mother in the background while he was talking to Jenna on the phone – conversations she always cut short – and she actually sounded okay. Demanding, but largely in possession of her faculties.

If Jenna was going cold on him he'd rather she was honest and end it.

He closed his eyes and acknowledged the churn in his stomach this thought produced. He had to admit he was falling in love with her.

'You alright, buddy?' Ken asked.

'Any better and I'd be surrounded by balloons.'

*

It didn't take long for the night to get busy, and things to turn south. Thirty minutes into their shift, a young guy, with a few of his Clearasil days still firmly ahead of him, ran out the door, bent over and puked all over Luke's feet. Presumably the toilets were out of reach when he felt the urge. And when Luke tried to calm down a young woman who was screaming black and blue murder at her boyfriend, both of them turned on him for 'dissing' her.

'When did we start to use words like that? "Dissing", for fuckssakes,' Luke asked Ken during a lull in the flow of punters.

'You need to get down with the kids, man,' Ken replied with a smile.

'No, I don't.' Luke clenched both fists while burying them in his pockets, feeling a burn of anger towards the couple, but annoyed at himself for letting them get to him. It was par for the course, people verbally abused him when he was on the door, so why was it bothering him so much tonight?

'You're not into this tonight, man,' said Ken, his face long with sympathy. 'You're more bothered about Jenna than you're letting on.'

'Bollocks,' Luke lied.

'I can see through you like you're made of glass, buddy.' Ken placed a meaty hand on his shoulder. 'I'll make your excuses. Say you suddenly felt sick and had to go home.'

'I'll be fine, big man,' Luke replied, hearing the doubt in his voice as he spoke.

'Honest, man. I can cope. Away and chill with a couple of beers.'

'Leave it, Ken. I'm fine.' Luke crossed his arms and turned away.

Just then an extended, pink limousine pulled up, emitting a booming, driving bassline almost with enough power to make the entire vehicle bounce. A grey-haired man, wearing a chauffeur hat and dark suit, climbed out of the driver's seat, and with all the energy of someone shuffling behind a coffin, walked towards the passenger door. Before he pulled it open, he made a face at Luke and Ken, and mouthed, 'Good luck.'

A burst of noise hit Luke's ears. A disco beat and energetic vocals. High-pitched singing. A squeal of laughter. Someone bossing someone else to finish their drinks. And then a surprising number of barely clad young women were teetering on high heels at their door.

'Ooo, I'll huv the big wan, Jo,' shouted someone. 'You can huv the short-arse.'

Luke heard a variation of this almost every night, and it never bothered him. But tonight, it bugged him.

'I don't mind the wee guy, Louise,' was the reply. 'Bet he's a pocket rocket.'

'Or he's got a rocket in his pocket,' another woman shouted. And then they were all laughing. Ear always tuned to the mood of a crowd, Luke could tell that the laughter was merely raucous and well-natured. But at a level that could burst an ear drum.

'Wonder if the big guy's got a rocket in his pocket.'

'Let's find out...'

In seconds Ken was surrounded by about a dozen drunk women, on his face a look of 'here we go again'. He tried to disguise it with a big smile, but Luke could tell the man was uncomfortable.

One woman stepped up to Ken and looked him up and down, pausing at his groin area for a moment. 'Is everything in proportion then?'

'If it was,' Ken replied, 'I'd be seven foot six.' It was an often-used line, and as Ken would have expected, his reward was a hoot of laughter. The women gathering even tighter around him.

Luke looked over to see if he needed to step in. His tall, blond, broad-shouldered friend was like a lighthouse sticking up in the middle of an island of halter tops, spray tan and shiny, straightened hair. Despite knowing that Ken was never quite comfortable with that sort of attention, he chuckled. Then he saw Ken flinch in a way that suggested someone had pinched his backside. Next, Ken's head and shoulders jerked forward and he shrunk in size a little, as if the attention had moved to his groin.

'Right, that's enough, ladies,' said Luke. He stepped towards the rabble, put his hand on one woman's shoulder and eased her to the side. The next woman was not for moving and was wearing a strange expression of ... what ... challenge?

'Sweetheart,' Luke shouted above the noise. 'Enough, eh? Can't you see the big guy's uncomfortable.'

The woman pulled at one side of her top and exposed a plump breast. 'How's about it, handsome?'

'Very nice,' said Luke. 'Now put it away. It's a bit too chilly for that tonight.' He tried to force jollity into his tone, but it sounded false even to him.

'This one thinks he's too good for us,' he heard a woman say. Now Luke was surrounded.

'Whoa. Back the hell off,' he said.

'Aww, come on, wee lad. It's only a wee bit of fun.'

Fingers grabbed at his backside, his chest, his arms. He felt a stab of panic. A rise in body temperature. He recognised the symptoms. The next step was always anger. He forced a smile onto his face and hoped that would send a different signal to his body. Relax. This was just a bit of fun. Why was he over-reacting here? He'd been in similar situations. Loads of times.

'Enough, ladies,' a deep voice sounded to his right. 'Why don't we get inside out of the cold?' he heard Ken say.

But the ladies were having too much fun. As if they sensed Luke's increasing discomfort, they all moved closer, the better to have a laugh at his expense. Hands were all over him. Touching his face, his shoulders, his backside. One hand brushed over, and then squeezed, his dick.

'Oi. Enough.' He pushed at someone. A squeal. Note of alarm. A handbag went flying back, and the woman were now crowding round one of their friends who was on the ground.

Ken sent Luke a look: *Really?*

'They ... they...'

'He groped me,' a woman shouted. 'Bloody touched me up.'

'Pervert.'

'Prick.'

'What's wrong wi' you. We were just havin' a laugh.'

A dozen faces tight with accusation stared. A woman prodded him in the chest. Somebody pushed him.

Women or not, thought Luke, if one more person laid their hands on him...

A couple of women at the front of the group read his

expression, their faces blanched and they stepped back. But one of them was not for leaving it.

'How bloody dare you...' She lashed out. Luke felt a flare of pain down the side of his face.

Then Ken was there and hoisted the woman out of Luke's reach.

Then, a female face that Luke recognised through the haze. His boss, Anna. 'Free cocktails inside, ladies. Free cocktails at the bar,' she shouted. Lured by the promise of free booze, the women dispersed. A few of them pausing to aim one last insult at Luke.

'My brother will have you, mate.'

'Prick.'

Anna squared up to Luke. The hands on her hips were a clue to her mental state, but her face was unreadable.

'My office,' she said. 'Now.'

Chapter 25

Before going to the office, Luke made for the gents to check on his injuries. Looking at himself in the mirror over the sinks, he could see the mess that had been made of his face. Two livid scratch marks ran from just under his right eye, down his cheek and stopped level with his top lip.

'Shit.' He winced as he splashed it with water. He soaked a hand towel and dabbed that on. When he lifted it away he saw blood on the grey of the towel and winced again. The sight of his blood made the injury somehow worse.

In Anna's office, which was really nothing more than a broom cupboard with a desk, two chairs and a CCTV monitor, Luke sat, arms crossed, and waited for her to arrive. His mind was a stew. He knew better. His job was to deflect situations not amplify them. He'd managed effectively hundreds of times, why was tonight so different?

Stupid question.

Admit it, you're rattled. Very rattled. He shouldn't be so hard on himself. Who wouldn't be rattled when faced with a struggling business, mounting debts and a failing relationship, then a photo that hinted at a threat against a child he deeply cared for.

He should have taken the night off. He should have listened to the big man and gone home. What was he thinking? He could lose his job here.

Maybe Anna would be sympathetic. The women were out of order, groping him and Ken like that. And surely the big guy would back him up.

He stewed some more.

On the CCTV monitor he could see a number of views. Ken, big and solid and centred, arms by his side, opening the door and smiling at people as they entered. Anna at the bar, surrounded by the women who'd effectively assaulted him and Ken. All of them now armed with tall glasses bedecked with paper umbrellas. A visible demonstration of the maxim that the customer was always right.

Minutes later Anna pushed open the door and stepped inside. She took a seat, chewed on the inside of her cheek.

'They're making serious allegations against you, Luke.'

'Aww, come on...'

'One of them said you grabbed her breast. Another that you cupped her...' Anna made quote marks in the air '..."front bottom".'

'That's ridiculous. No way did I do that. They just want some free drinks. And by the way, get a load of the damage to my face. Just who's come off worst here?'

Anna stepped closer to look at his face. She winced. Then turned to the CCTV monitor as if comparing the damage to her employee with the possible damage to her business.

'They're serious, Luke. Talking about going on Twitter etc and trashing us.' Anna's face was pale. Business wasn't exactly going down the pan, but a hounding on social media could have a disastrous impact on the place. 'One of them showed me a photo of you on her phone. And you were looking pretty scary. Pretty bloody scary.'

'What about this?' He pointed to his face. 'And them grabbing my dick? And groping Ken? Is that okay? Give them a free cocktail and everything's dandy.'

'All I saw on the CCTV was you surrounded by a bunch of drunk women. Then someone gets pushed to the ground.' Anna's face was tight. 'It's your job to keep a lid on things, Luke. That down there was the opposite of keeping a lid on things.'

'They were all over us, Anna. They were well out of order.'

'High spirits and lots of booze. Nothing more than you've dealt with hundreds of times.' She paused. 'Unless you can prove otherwise?'

Luke sat forward on his seat and looked over at the CCTV screen. 'Anything on there? You must have been able to see what they were doing?'

'Nope. There's only one camera aimed at that doorway. As I said, all I could see was a scrum of people round you. And then a girl being sent flying. And now I have women alleging sexual assault.'

'I'm not a piece of meat, boss. I'm not going to just stand there and let anyone manhandle me.'

'So you assault them right back?' Her face was long with disbelief. 'I'm going to have to get the police in, Luke; you realise that, don't you?' she demanded. She shook her head. 'Jesus. You've dealt with that kind of thing numerous times, Luke. What the hell?'

Doesn't make it right, he wanted to say, but didn't, because it would make him sound whiny and weak.

Luke looked down at his hands, clasped on his lap. He had no answer. She was right. He had lost it.

'Why don't you just go home? Have the rest of the night off, eh?'

'Boss...'

'I'll get in touch when I want you back in.' Her face was resolute. 'In the meantime, don't go anywhere, and expect a visit from the boys in blue.'

'Fuck.' He rubbed his scalp hard with the knuckles of his right hand. 'Boss...'

There was no arguing with her. She opened a drawer under the desk with her right hand, and pulled out a small, square tin. She unlocked it and pulled out a handful of notes. Folding them she pushed a small parcel of money towards him across the top of the desk.

'This should cover you for tonight. I'll get your wage slip to you in the post.' The conversation was over. And judging by the face on Anna, no way would he get another night's work with her. Ever.

*

In his car, he pushed back into the driver's seat, head against the headrest and stared up at the roof of the car. What the hell was he going to do now? He really needed the extra money that the door work brought in. Once word got out his name would be dirt.

Fuck.

How quickly had his life turned? Just getting back on track after Lisa. The wee man settling down, not scared to let him out of his sight, as he was for a long time after his mum died. And his own suffocating grief ... He squeezed his eyes shut and clamped down on his jaw muscles. *Don't go there, Luke.* There might be no way back this time.

Depression hit him hard after Lisa died, and if it wasn't for Nathan and Gemma he might have ended up as one more addition to the suicide statistics.

Right, breathe. What could be done about all of this? *There's always a way*, he heard Lisa say in his mind. That was her favourite saying. Nothing stifled her. If she wanted something, she went for it. If something proved more difficult than she first thought, there was always a way.

Perhaps he could go back and have a word with Ken. See if he could persuade Anna to change her mind.

Not going to happen, mate, he thought as he reminded himself of the look on her face. You don't come back from that kind of allegation. His time on the doors of this city were over.

But how had it turned so quickly?

He scanned the events of the evening, feeling his emotions being triggered yet again by the actions of the women surrounding him.

A moment snagged his attention. A dark-haired woman in a shiny silver top. Face rouged with drink. But there was something about her. A focus.

Nah, he was seeing things that weren't there. Trying to justify his loss of professionalism. But the moment snagged again. That look on her face. It was something approaching triumph when the other woman fell. What was that about? And she was the first one to shout that she'd been molested by him when anyone not doused with alcohol could tell she was too far away.

He dropped his gaze from the roof of the car, and spotted something white and square tucked under one of the windscreen wipers. Who'd be dropping flyers at this time of night?

No, it couldn't be...

In a flash he was out of the car and plucking the paper off the screen. He unfolded it and saw a similar image to the photo that had been on his doorstep. Him and Nathan at the park, this time kicking a ball back and forth. The little boy's face shining and wide with delight.

A noise sounded from his car. His mobile phone, which was tucked into his jacket pocket. Probably Ken checking up on him. Bugger it. He couldn't be bothered talking to anyone. He'd get the big guy in the morning and see if he could persuade Anna to change her mind. Maybe by then common sense would have prevailed, and she would have calmed down.

The phone stopped. And then immediately started ringing again.

'Take a telling, for Godssakes,' he shouted. Waited. It stopped ringing. And then started up almost immediately.

Crying out loud.

He stomped over to the door, sat inside and reached across to his jacket. Pulling out the phone, he read the notification. It was Gemma. Jesus, something must be up. She never phoned while he was working.

'Luke. It's Nathan,' Gemma said in a breathless panic when he picked up. 'That arsehole of a father. His dad. His other dad.' She started crying.

His other dad?

She must mean his biological father, Rab Cameron. Where had he appeared from?

With the heavy weight of anxiety in his stomach Luke an-

chored himself by making a fist with his free hand and forced calm
into his voice.

'I'll be home in twenty minutes. In the meantime, tell me
exactly what happened.'

'He turned up at the door, barged in and dragged the wee fella
from his bed. I couldn't stop him. He was too strong. And wee
Nathan ... the poor wee mite was screaming for you. Oh God,
Luke. What are we going to do?'

'Wait a minute. You saying Rab Cameron came over in the
middle of the night and took Nathan away?'

Gemma managed a sentence through her sobs. 'He said he was
Nathan's real dad, he was well within his rights, and we'd never
see him again.'

Chapter 26

Jamie had watched from around the corner as Rab Cameron half dragged, half carried the little boy to his car. A small red Ford. Once inside the car, on the backseat, Nathan launched himself at the window in attempt to get free, his little mouth making panicked shapes behind the glass. Calling for his gran.

She was at Cameron's back, then around at his face, pummelling him, but Cameron just shrugged her off as if her fists were butterfly wings.

'You're a waster, Cameron. What do you think you're doing with my grandson?' she screamed at him.

'Gie's peace, Gemma,' Cameron said, and Jamie gave him a little credit for being mostly gentle with the woman.

As if she judged that her efforts were wasted Gemma appeared to rein them in.

'Why? Why after all this time, Rab? Eh? The wean doesn't know you. He's terrified.'

'He'll be fine once I get him home.'

'This is his home, Rab. It's all he's ever known.'

'Aye, well. It's time I sorted that mistake.'

'There's proper channels for this, son. Speak to a lawyer. In the meantime we could arrange visits. Take it from there, eh? Nice and slow,' she wheedled.

'Aye, that's going to happen. You and white-knight guy hate my guts.' Cameron had a hand on the driver's door handle.

'Luke's a reasonable guy. He realises Nathan needs to know who his real father is.' She paused. 'The wee man asks about you all the time.' Even from where he was standing, Jamie could hear it was a lie.

'Whatever,' Rab said, pulled the door open and jumped inside. Jamie could hear Nathan's plaintive cry: 'Graaaaaan.'

It was shut off when Cameron slammed the door and drove off.

*

When he returned to the bungalow and parked outside, Jamie could see that the living-room lights were on. It was way past Amanda's usual bedtime, so she must be waiting up for him to report on what happened with the boy.

He felt a little sick at the thought of the boy's anguish, recognising the pain in his cries as the same as he felt when he was ripped from his own family.

Think about Forrest, he told himself. *His* pain was the point of all of this. The boy would be fine. Children adapt, didn't they? Hadn't he flourished?

The lie of that last statement lay like leaking blood on his tongue as he walked into the house. He made straight for the kitchen, and despite the time he made himself a coffee. When he opened the fridge door for the milk he spotted a six-pack of beer that Amanda had ordered in for him. Why, he had no idea. He hated the stuff and couldn't understand why people would turn to drink to take their mind off things. Everybody was so fucking weak.

When he closed the fridge door, Amanda was standing just behind it.

'Well?' she asked. She was on her tiptoes, as if every part of her was sparking with excitement.

'Went as planned. Cameron's got the boy.'

She cocked her head to the left and narrowed her eyes as she assessed him. 'You don't look so pleased about it.'

'I'm all for making Forrest pay, but we should leave the kid out of it.'

'Pfft, he'll be fine. Kids adapt. Look at you and me, we didn't do too badly, did we?' Amanda said, in an echo of his own thoughts.

Jamie turned away from her to locate the sugar and add some to his coffee. He gave it a stir and sipped.

'We didn't do too badly? You got married to a man forty years your senior, and you rarely leave the house. I'm on all kinds of drugs—'

'Jesus, you're such a negative ninny.'

'Who says negative ninny?' Jamie said, fighting back a grin.

As if sensing she'd breached Jamie's defences Amanda stepped closer and laid her head on his shoulder, then reached down, grabbed his wrist and tried to position his hand on her back.

Jamie stood there. Wooden. The heat from the coffee almost scalding his hand. He put it down on the counter-top. He couldn't remember the last time they'd expressed any emotion in this way.

She looked up at him. 'Hey, ninny. Gimme a hug for Chrissakes.'

'Oh,' he said, and relaxed a little more. This was nice, he had to admit. Affection. He hadn't experienced too much of it in his life.

Suspicion flared. 'Wait,' he said and reared back. Just a little. Part of him, the boy who had been lost and alone, needed this contact. This was good. Awkward, but good. But was she trying to manipulate him?

'We're family, Jamie. We need to start acting like it. Families hug, don't they?' Her eyes were large and a little wet, and her bottom lip carried a little tremble.

Jamie read genuine feeling in her face. He couldn't remember a time when Amanda appeared to be so emotionally open.

'Family,' Jamie repeated, while fighting to quiet the screams ringing along the corridors of his mind. Screams of a little boy being dragged into a car and away from the only home he'd ever known. Other, silenced screams, from another little boy, who remained unseen, unheard, and, he was certain, undeserving of love.

Chapter 27

Jenna's mother was napping in her favourite armchair, in front of the window. Winter sunshine was streaming in, casting her in a warm glow, sleep loosening the lines and folds of her face, reminding Jenna of the vibrant woman her mother had once been, and with a pang of loss she saw that relentless decline unravel along a threadbare carpet rolling out into their near future.

No. She couldn't afford to think that way. Her mother was still the woman who held her hand that first day of school, who moved into a smaller home to fund her university years, and who'd listened carefully to her tales of boyfriend woe, before she'd tilted her head and calmly, quietly, give her a dose of reality.

She was still the same woman within that weakening shroud of skin and bone, it was just that the signals in her brain were getting mixed up. She was still deserving of Jenna's love and attention, but, Jesus, did she have to be so difficult?

Jenna waved her hand in front of her mother's face. From experience she knew that the nap her mother seemed to need every day at this time would last around ninety minutes. Time to do some chores around the house. She ticked off a mental list: the washing, the ironing, clean the kitchen and the bathroom.

Her phone rang. With a start she looked at the screen, praying it was Luke, but *Mhairi Bookshop* was flashing there.

'Hey, doll,' Mhairi said when she answered. 'Just wanted to check in with you. See how you were doing.'

Was she seeing when she was coming back to work? Jenna wondered.

'Och, you know,' Jenna replied. 'She's hard work, but what can you do?'

'Hasn't the agency got someone new for you yet?'

'Not yet,' Jenna replied.

'I hate to do this to you, Jenna, but this is the busiest time of my year. I need the help. Any idea when you might be available again?'

'Sorry, Mhairi,' Jenna said, squirming a little. She knew what was coming.

'Okay.' In those two syllables Mhairi managed to convey sympathy and acceptance. 'I need to put an advert in the window for a new bookseller. But don't worry, I'll stress that it's temporary. I just thought I'd warn you. Don't want you to walk past the shop and see it, doll.'

'That's ... I understand,' Jenna said, trying to keep her voice light and cheery.

'God, I'm so sorry,' Mhairi said, clearly not convinced in the least by Jenna's attempt to brighten her speech. 'I've really no choice, Jenna.'

'I know,' Jenna said. 'It's not the fact that you're doing that.' Moving on, while she felt stuck. 'It's that you have to. I feel like I'm letting you down. Sorry.'

'Nonsense,' Mhairi replied. 'Family comes first. You don't really have a choice. But...' She paused. 'Make sure you look after yourself, eh?'

They said their goodbyes, and Jenna closed the connection.

She cringed.

Sorry. It felt like all she did these days was apologise. And feel guilty. And apologise for feeling guilty.

And then there was Luke. He'd tried to phone her several times over the last few days, and despite wanting to speak to him she'd ignored his calls. On one occasion he'd left a message:

'Hey, Jenna. Give me a call, will you?'

There was something in his voice, a tension that surprised Jenna. Luke was normally pretty relaxed. It was more than an unspoken query about her silence, she could tell, but she just didn't have the headspace for anyone else's problems right then. Give me a couple of weeks, she thought as she looked to her phone. Maybe then I'll have accepted things a little better. Besides, they'd only really known each other for a few weeks now, and she didn't feel she could put her burden on him just yet.

She walked to the window, feeling more than a little lost. She wasn't made for this care thing. She needed to be out and about, among other people. Working.

Across the street she could see that some of her neighbours had their Christmas trees up. Lights twinkling even in the daylight. Normally this was a sight that would give her a lift, but today all it did was remind her of something else to add her to-do list. She'd wait until her mother mentioned that it was time to put up the decorations. If it did even occur to her.

There was another important task she'd been putting off. A pile of papers lay on the table just to the side of where her mother rested. Among them was a power of attorney that needed both their signatures. Her mother was lucid enough to understand what it entailed and why it was necessary. But Jenna couldn't bring herself to complete and file the form with their lawyer. It just felt so irrevocable. An admission that her mother was on a downward trajectory. That she was never getting better.

Sally O'Neill strode through Jenna's childhood the very image of a modern woman: capable, energetic, intelligent, seemingly fearless, and occasionally a pain in the arse, and to see her brought so low was too painful to witness, and admit.

Oh, Mum. She made her way to her mother, sat on a chair beside her and held her hand. In response her mother shifted, as if Jenna's touch had intruded on her dreams. Sally murmured something and then settled again. In these quieter moments Jenna could remember and celebrate the woman her mother had been, and try to forget what the injury to her mind had made of her.

With a thumb, Jenna stroked the back of her mother's hand, tracing a blue vein that pushed past the hiccup of a pair of liver spots. Her skin felt dry and warm. She should put some moisturiser on them while she was still sleeping. Sally would never allow her to do it while she was awake.

'Stop fussing, Jenna,' she heard her say in her imagination.

She fetched some cocoa butter – her mother's favourite – from the bathroom and settled down to massage some into her mother's hands.

Her phone rang again.

Luke.

If she did answer it he would hear the helplessness in her voice and insist he come over and help. No. She would cope on her own.

A drop of moisturiser in the middle of the back of her mother's right hand, and Jenna got to work, finding a soothing in that moment. A reinforcement of her love for her mother. And a temporary easing of a daughter's guilt.

Her thumb stopped at a liver spot and she found herself slowly, absently running her thumb over it. Back and forth.

This role reversal made her almost itch with discomfort. The once-cared-for becomes the carer. The older person almost as helpless as the younger had once been.

'Hey,' her mother said, voice barely audible.

Jenna turned to her, saw that her eyes were open, and there, glinting in the amber of her iris, she recognised, just for that sparkling moment, the woman who walked through her childhood with certainty, humility and fabulous six-inch-high stilettos.

More often than not, in recent times, she'd look into her mother's eyes and see a stranger, as if the injury had meant someone else was inhabiting her mother's skin, muscle and bone. But there, in that gaze, in that moment, was the woman she'd loved and looked up to ever since she was a child.

Sally's eyes shone with love, then clouded over before she smiled uncertainly. 'This is lovely, dear, but who are you?'

Chapter 28

Luke was breathless with worry. Nathan would be beside himself with fear. Torn from everything he knew by a total stranger.

What on earth had happened that Rab Cameron felt the need to take back his son after all this time? He'd never attempted to see Nathan while Lisa was alive. Why take such steps now?

And what rights did Luke have to the boy? Legally, he wasn't sure he had a chance. Wouldn't the boy's biological father hold all the cards? It was his fault. Lisa had been saying for ages that he should formally adopt Nathan, in case something happened to her. She'd even had the papers drawn up, but he'd avoided signing them. Some soul-searching and a session with his counsellor, and he was able to admit the source of that hesitation was fear. Fear that he would let the boy down, that he wasn't up to the task.

And then the worst thing that could happen, happened, and formalities were driven from his mind by the day-to-day necessities of caring for this little boy.

With a child, you had to go into that kind of relationship with a full heart. And back then he didn't think he had it in him. He remembered holding Nathan, consoling him after a bad dream. Lisa was out with her friends. Somebody's birthday. Nathan curled up in his lap, head in the crook of his arm, relaxed back into sleep by Luke's attention. But Luke cleared a strand of hair from the boy's sweat-pearled forehead, while thinking, *Don't trust me, Nathan. I'll only let you down.* His past crimes cast their shadows, making him feel he was less than trustworthy. A lesser human being.

*

Luke walked down a familiar street. He hadn't been here since, well, since before his time at Her Majesty's pleasure.

This was an almost forgotten part of the city, directly under an elevated stretch of a three-lane motorway. People didn't even pass through anymore; they mostly drove over it. So most of the city's inhabitants could put the place out of their minds. They couldn't see it, so they didn't need to acknowledge the issues the people who lived here had.

Other than the arch of motorway overhead, the place hadn't changed. Rows and rows of tenement flats, many of the ground-floor windows boarded up, cracked pavements, every wall bristling with satellite dishes, and whatever greenery he could see was over-grown and was used as a dumping ground for all manner of detritus. Sitting in a clump in front of one house, like an art installation representing deprived inner-city life, he saw a brown, paisley-patterned sofa, a chocolate-coloured headboard and an old-fashioned box computer screen.

Luke's mother, who'd lived just a few streets over, used to leave things out on the pavement, knowing someone would come along, think it was better than whatever shit they had, and take it away. With a rueful laugh he decided that no one in their right mind would be interested in that sofa.

One thing that had changed was the kids. He'd barely seen any. In his day they would be out on the road, chasing a ball about. Screaming at each other. Seeing who could race the fastest, jump the highest, kick a ball the furthest.

Punch the hardest.

As if on cue, he heard a note of childish laughter. Nathan? His head shot round. In a doorway across the street, four small boys clustered round another boy, who was holding what looked like a computer tablet. He examined each of them, and with a sinking heart noted that they all had a good couple of years on Nathan.

'What you looking at, paedo?' One of the boys looked over at him. His mates joined in the group stare. The insult may have changed, but the attitude hadn't, thought Luke. Meet any stranger with a challenge. Let them know this wasn't their territory.

The decision to leave the car further away than necessary was an easy one. These boys might have done it some damage, just to prove they weren't to be messed with. And besides, he wanted to scout the lay of the land without alerting Rab Cameron to his presence.

He'd blanched when Gemma told him where Cameron was living.

'How did you know where he was?' he asked her, wondering if he had the courage to go back there.

'I know things,' she said simply. Her eyelids were pink, her mouth slumped in a sag of worry. 'Life's never easy, son. I knew Cameron would be back eventually.' So, she used her wide circle of friends and kept tabs, is what Luke read from that.

'Don't go in there mob-handed,' Gemma warned. 'That'll only make things worse.' Luke didn't have a mob, or anything approaching that. He'd turned his back on all the friends of his youth, and apart from Ken didn't really spend time with any other men. 'But bring my boy back, eh?' Gemma reached out and touched his forearm.

He felt that touch again now, a lingering ache, all of Gemma's fear and worry condensed into the heat from her hand.

'Well, if it isnae the Big Time Charlie,' Luke heard, and turned to see a man he'd first met a lifetime ago as a preschooler: Joseph Smith. They'd shared the last apple juice their first day of playgroup and built a bond that lasted almost three decades.

There had been three of them against the world at one point. Fraser and his twin brother, Josie. But Fraser had died when they were teenagers. Under mysterious circumstances. He'd been found dead on some local waste ground. The identity of whoever killed him remained a mystery to this day.

'The jungle drums still working then, Joe?' He'd always called him Josie, so by calling him Joe he was sending out a signal: we're no longer little boys. We've moved on.

His old school friend stood two paces away. Hands pushed

into the pockets of his grey sweatpants, though judging by the flab that pushed at the waist of the material the only sweating Joe had done recently was from reaching for the remote while the heating was turned on. He was a couple of inches taller than Luke. A fact he never let him forget when they were kids. Balding, narrow shouldered and wide-waisted. A white Le Croc polo shirt and black Adidas Samba shoes finished off his look. The temperature must have been close to freezing, yet Fraser was without a coat.

Luke remembered that this was typical of the man. A coat just got in the way, Joe used to say. Thought it made him look tough and resilient to go out in all weathers with just a short-sleeved shirt on.

Memory cast Luke back to Joe as a small boy, with spiked red hair that was never dry of a handful of gel, and a gap-toothed smile. He could recall, as if it was yesterday, the moment when he lost the tooth that gave him his trademark grin. They'd stolen a bike from outside a shop. Joe was on the seat peddling while Luke was side-saddle on the cross bar. The owner of the bike came charging out of the shop, roaring, 'Ya wee bastards.' The guy was six feet tall at least, a bit on the skinny side, but with enough attitude for six people, so the boys raced away.

Unfortunately, because his view was impeded, Joe didn't see a brick lying just off the kerb, and they'd both been pitched over the handle bars. Luke managed to roll over onto his feet with nothing but a bloody elbow. Joe was left with a mouthful of blood and one tooth less.

'Long time, no see,' Luke smiled, feeling the warmth of an old friendship. But the smile faltered as he recalled that he'd left Joe behind after he got out of prison. How many guys had he come across inside who were determined to go straight when they got out, but the second they got back to their old neighbourhoods, back in the company of old friends, slipped right back into bad habits? In double-quick time they were banged up again. But

Luke had been serious about rebuilding his life and knew his old friends could only be an impediment to that. Joe, and a few others, were casualties of that decision.

'Changed your name, I heard.' Joe paused. His eyes narrowed. 'Your da's name not good enough for you anymore?'

Luke had been born Duncan Luke Robertson, but when he got out of prison and tried to rebuild his life, it became clear that the old name came with too much baggage, so he adopted his mother's maiden name and dropped the Duncan. He'd never liked the name anyway. It always got shortened to Dunk, which, anytime they were near water, became a command the other boys were unable to ignore.

'How many kids you got now?' he asked, trying to dampen down any feelings of regret about his choices. It was never about thinking he was better than anyone else but about moving on. Moving away from the person he had once been.

'Three. That I know of.' Joe grinned, but haunting the cast of his eyes was the hurt of his oldest friend's rejection.

'Aye, right,' laughed Luke, and slipped into the insulting badinage he'd employed mercilessly as a youth. 'What self-respecting woman is going to want to shag you?'

Joe held up a middle finger and laughed. 'Roon ye.' Luke could see traces of the boy he'd known, grown up with and loved. Though any admissions of love would only ever have been made under the influence of a week-long drinking binge.

'Where you been, man?' Joe crossed his arms. The skin of his neck was mottled, as if with a rush of emotion. 'Since Danny—'

'Aye. Well,' Luke interrupted, feeling his face heat. Since Danny. He read the admonition. Heard a silent, *we needed you*. The reasons why he'd stayed away lined up in his mind, but he knew he couldn't list them without starting a conversation about why he'd left Joe behind.

They'd ruled this wee section of the city. Nothing illicit happened that they didn't get a slice of. With Danny and him out of the way, other ne'er-do-wells would have long since taken over, meaning Joe losing out on a substantial part of his income.

Too bad, thought Luke. That life was well and truly over. He'd done his time. Then he'd done the whole man-cave and hair-shirt thing. He'd not really returned anywhere near to himself until he met Lisa. Couldn't face up to the fact he'd been responsible for the death of one of his oldest friends.

He decided he'd had enough of the trip down memory lane.

'Do you know Rab Cameron?'

Joe screwed his face into an expression of confusion. 'Should I?'

'He lives just round the corner, man.'

'What's he done, like?'

Luke let out a long, frustrated sigh. 'How much time you got?'

'Let me go back in the house and get my wallet,' Joe said, with a note of eagerness that Luke thought was more to do with getting out of the house than spending time with him. 'We can go down The Black Bull and you can fill me in over a pint.'

The Black Bull. Luke felt his thighs weaken. He hadn't been back there since that night. Memory supplied him with an image of a bunch of bodies piling into his car after a marathon session of drink and whatever drugs were available. Only he and Danny were left at journey's end.

And then, only him.

'Sorry, man,' said Joe with a grimace. 'I wasn't thinking.'

'S'aright,' said Luke. Except it wasn't. Never would be.

'C'mon in the house and you can fill me in about this Cameron dude.'

'You sure?'

'Course, man,' said Joe, sounding anything but sure.

Luke debated whether he should take Joe up on his offer. It would be nice to spend a little bit of time with the man, despite the circumstances. And Joe might be able to find out more about Rab Cameron than he, now an outsider, could. There was, however, the issue of Joe's wife, Stephanie. Stef King was one of the coolest girls in the area when they were kids. Long black hair, large green eyes, a tight wee backside, and a clear-eyed way of looking at the world that cut through every boy's hard-fought bravado. She just 'knew' when you were talking crap and was happy to heap scorn on your head to prove it.

That Joe had ended up with her was considered a major coup by all the local lads, most of whom lusted after her. However, the last time Luke had been in her company she'd made it abundantly clear that if she ever saw him again she'd grab a knife and remove his balls.

Chapter 29

Walking along the streets of his childhood, his and Joe's footfall loud in his ears, Luke's thoughts were crowded with the names and faces of his old friends. And for the first time Luke realised what united them apart from their poverty: it was a lack of parents. Fathers in particular.

The Smith boys, Fraser and Joe, their father had disappeared when they were just babies, leaving their mother to cope on her own. As far as Luke knew the twins never heard from their father again.

When he and the Smith boys chatted, they always felt a little bit of envy towards Danny and his father. They thought that Danny was the lucky one. His old man was there. He had a good job. Provided well for the family. It was only one evening, years later, while they were neck deep in their third bottle of Buckfast that Danny told Luke what Gordon Morrison was really like.

'It was like abuse central round ours. Dad would scream and hit Mum. She would scream and hit him back, and if one of them wasn't around it was me that got it. Arseholes.' As Danny said this he was leaning forward in a low-slung chair, finger stabbing the air in front of him. Then he slumped back, drink and fatigue robbing him of energy, the memory of past pain in the half-light of his eyes. 'Thank the great god, Johnny Walker of Boozeville, they stopped at me. Our Amanda and Jamie were left alone. Or at least I think they were. Who knows what's happened since I walked out.'

Luke recalls listening to this, mouth open with surprise. Sure, he remembered times, particularly when they were younger, when Danny would show up for school with bruises or scratches on his face. When teachers asked what happened to him, he'd say, 'Ma ma (or ma da) were showing me how much they loved me, miss.' And he would say it with such a wide grin that nobody believed him. Besides, he had a bit of a reputation for being a troublemaker, so everyone thought it was just another one of those random acts of violence that young males experience in their lives.

But what about Luke's own father?

His absence from Luke's life was arguably a reason for his own poor behaviour as a youth. His father had been a shadowy figure in his early childhood. He had memories of hugs from someone with a scratchy face, strong arms pulling him out of a paddling pool, hearty chuckles and a rocking belly while they watched cartoons together.

Then nothing. His name was rarely mentioned in the house, and when it was, his mother used the past tense, making Luke think he was dead. But if he brought the subject up his mother would ignore him, shout at him, or worse, get tearful, so from a young age Luke learned not to ask about him.

'Me and you,' she'd say, and hug him tight to her. 'That's all we need. Just me and you.'

Until his fifteenth birthday.

A card dropped onto his door mat. He guessed it might be a birthday card, so ran to the door and reached it before his mother. Her face was white with shock when she saw what he held in his hand, and in a moment of insight, sudden as a curtain being ripped back, he saw that his mother did not want him to see what was in this envelope.

While she watched, all but wringing her hands, he opened it. The number 15 was a gold blaze on the front of the card. Accompanied by the word 'Son'.

Open mouthed, Luke opened the card, found a hand-written letter and some cash. He read the message inside the card:

Sorry I can't be with you again. But until the day we can properly meet, have a great time and spend the money well, son.

He looked over at his mother and read the last word: '...Dad.' He pulled out the cash – fifty pounds. 'But...'

His mother turned and walked along the hall to their small living room. He followed her, his mind a tumult of questions. As usual every surface shone, and everything was in its place. The furniture was proudly second-hand, but repurposed with a style that was the envy of his mother's friends. 'You should be on one of them TV shows,' they would say every time they entered the flat to see another nearly new piece being given the Bernadette Forrest treatment.

His mother reached for a cigarette packet – her once-a-day treat – and lit up. Luke could see her hand was shaking as she brought the cigarette to her mouth.

'My dad? I got money from my dad,' he said in stupefaction.

'Waster,' his mum said. 'We hear nothing from him for years, and he thinks fifty quid is going to patch it all up.'

Luke had a flash of memory. Several memories. Previous birthdays and Christmases. Envelopes being bundled into pockets, hidden before he could see what they were.

'You let me think he was dead,' Luke said to her, still struggling to compute what was in his hand. 'I thought my dad was dead, Mum. What the hell?'

'He was dead to me,' she said, chin tilted up as if ready to take on Luke's anger and disappointment. 'And you never asked.' She shouted now, as if thinking that attack might be the best form of defence. 'Not once did you ask, so I thought this wee life we built was enough for you. That I was enough for you...' She tailed off, eyes pleading.

'I learned a long time ago not to, Mum,' he replied. 'Anytime I did you'd go mental at me and then stay silent for days.' He paused. 'There's been other cards, hasn't there?' Luke took a step closer to her, brandishing the new one.

His mother turned away. 'He went off with that other woman, that bitch, without even a goodbye.' Then she turned back to Luke, brandishing her lit cigarette. 'I've been your mother and your father ever since. No one ever talks about that. About the sacrifices I made to keep you housed and fed.'

A storm of half-processed thought and unnameable emotion

swirled in Luke's mind and heart. He felt betrayed. Abandoned twice over. Once by his father, and now for a second time by the lies of his mother.

He ran to his room, slammed the door shut, curled up on his bed and held the card tight to his chest. He had a dad. And if he was sending him money he must care about him, right?

His mother was at his door. Gently knocking. 'Talk to me, son,' she pleaded.

He remained silent. Turned his back to the door and read the letter that came with the card and the cash. It was three pages long, handwritten and full of details of his father's new life with his second family; a wife called Carol and two kids, Sandra and Sarah. His father finished off by apologising for not trying harder to be in his life and said he was sad that Luke hadn't replied to his other letters but hoped he might reply to this one and they could begin to be a proper father and son again.

There were other letters too? His mother must have kept them from him. Who did that?

'How could you, Mum?' he shouted at the door, feeling a weight of disappointment in his mother.

There was a phone number in the letter. He didn't have a phone of his own, and feeling the need to speak to his father like an itch in his mind, he waited until he heard his mother go out for her shift at work before leaving his room and sitting at the house phone in the hall.

Mouth dry, heart pounding, he dialled. As he waited for the call to be answered he began to doubt himself. Could the card, letter and cash just be his dad going through the motions? He had all of this new family to worry about; did he really want him to get in touch? And his mother had clearly tried to keep him from his father. Why? Was there something wrong with him? He had all but convinced himself that he should hang up, when he heard a deep voice answer. And even after all this time he recognised his father in the two short syllables:

'Hello?'

'Dad?' he replied.

They arranged a meeting there and then for the following weekend. The night before, Luke stared at himself in the mirror, as if that might provide a curtain-raiser to the main event. His eyes everyone said were his mother's. But his nose, his jaw, that kink in the hair at the side of head whenever it grew too long – had they come to him from his father? Was that wariness in his half-smile a bequest from his absent dad?

To be fair, the answers his father gave as to why he had been absent were not critical of his mother. He seemed, to Luke at least, only to blame himself.

'Should have tried harder, son.' The gravel of his voice strained through with seams of shame and regret.

*

'We're here,' Joe said as he looked up at a window facing them. 'Just ca' canny with the missus. She's still pissed at you by the way.'

'Great,' Luke replied.

He and Stef had a history. He'd gone out with her before Joe, but cheated on her with her best friend. A best friend who was, at that time, going out with Danny. A best friend who died from an overdose. Stef was convinced her friend would still be alive if Danny and Luke hadn't been such bad influences.

Luke couldn't really argue with her reasoning.

'She'll be happy to see you, Dunk ... I mean, Luke.'

'Just keep her away from the knife rack, eh?'

'It was her that saw you out of the window. Told me to come and say hello.'

'Aye?' Maybe it was time to move on, thought Luke. If he and Stef could talk like grown-ups...

'She still hates your guts, like, but, hey, you can't have everything,' Joe grinned. Then he turned and indicated his doorway.

'What you doing with yourself now?' Luke asked as they walked up the path to the door.

'On the sick, mate,' answered Joe with an apologetic shrug. 'Been on the methadone now for a year. Turned it around, so I have. House husband an' that. Proper look after the weans while Stef goes to work.'

'Good for you,' said Luke. 'The modern man.' As he spoke he avoided meeting Joe's eyes. Didn't want him to read his disappointment that his old friend had fallen into addiction. Probably fed by his grief, trauma and unanswered questions over his brother's death all those years ago.

And who was he to judge anyway? They all had shit in their lives. It was just that Joe had been such a smart guy. He'd got into computers before anyone else but hidden his intelligence at school like they all did; then left as soon as he could and was one of the fortunates who got a trade. Plumber to the stars, mate, he used to joke with Luke when he got to install a new shower in a premier-league footballer's house.

Joe pushed open his door, and in silence they entered the close and walked up the communal stairs to the landing on the first floor. The door on the right was ajar, a boy's fire truck was abandoned in the middle of a doormat, the 'Welcome' sign faded. A voice that Luke recognised floated out into the hallway.

'Fraser Smith, if you don't come and finish your lunch you'll no' get to the swimming pool with your da this afternoon.'

'Aww, Mum...' came from just behind the door, and Luke felt a pang. How many times had he heard, or taken part in, that very same conversation with Nathan?

'You called your kid Fraser. That's a nice way to remember him,' Luke said.

'My only boy,' Joe said with unabashed pride. 'In you go,' he said placing a hand on his shoulder. 'The living room's straight ahead.'

Luke followed Joe's instructions, smiling at a small blond boy who stared up at him with undisguised curiosity, and walked into a well-lit room. Two pony-tailed girls sat either side of Stef on a corner sofa.

Stef looked up at him with an almost-smile. 'Duncan Robertson, as I live and breathe.' She said it as if she was going to use his new name only on her terms. And his old one from her mouth hit his ear with a discordant peel. He recoiled mentally and almost stumbled. A quizzical look appeared in her eyes. Stef missed nothing; she looked pleased that she'd made him feel uncomfortable. 'I nearly didn't recognise you. Been bulking up?' Luke read the tone and heard: *because there's nothing better to do in prison.* 'You're looking well on it.'

'So are you,' said Luke. She wasn't. She looked exhausted. The lustre had gone from her skin and her hair, and her too-lean frame was clothed in an overly large T-shirt and black leggings.

'You never were a good liar, Duncan,' Stef said as she smoothed back her hair.

One of the girls coughed. Stef looked from one to the other and back up to Luke, and as if she'd rather not, introduced him to her daughters. 'This is Emma...' She indicated the one on her right. Blonde hair, big eyes and wearing her dad's grin. 'The one with the cough...' she nudged the other girl '...is Chrissie.' Chrissie was her mother's double. 'Girls, this is ... Luke. An old friend of your dad's.' Stef placed a heavy emphasis on the word 'old'.

'Have a seat, man,' Joe said, indicating an armchair facing the forty-inch television. 'I'll get us a beer.'

Regretting that he'd allowed himself to be persuaded upstairs, Luke took a seat. Such was the lack of support in the chair that he felt himself sink almost to the floor.

'Girls, why don't you go into your room...' Stef reached behind her and pulled a laptop from underneath a cushion. It looked like it had been hidden there as some sort of punishment. 'And watch some stuff while your dad makes Luke and me *a nice cup of tea.*'

Joe made a face at Luke. 'Right enough. It's a bit early for booze. Cup of tea coming up.'

'Let your brother go with you, girls.'

'Aww, Mum...'

'Want me to take the laptop away, Emma?' Stef held a hand out as if to grab the computer.

Emma dodged out of her reach. 'If he doesn't sit at peace, I'll be chucking him out,' she said, as if that was the final word on the subject.

Then it was just Luke and Stef in the room.

She looked at him as if she was judge, jury and just possibly his executioner.

'Was it deliberate?' Stef asked.

'Sorry?'

'There was lots of chat when you went down for Danny's death. Some thought you got off lightly. Others thought you should have got a medal for taking that arsehole off the street.' An old hurt lingered in her eyes. Luke read that it was for Brenda, the girl who died.

'And what do you think, Stef?'

'You don't want to know what I think.' Her eyes narrowed as she spoke. 'Why are you here? You better not mess with his head.' She tilted her head in the direction of the kitchen.

Whatever scrapes they all got into as young men, Luke was usually one of the ring-leaders. And it was clear to him that what had happened to Joe in later life, Stef was certain it stemmed from Luke's bad example. He debated, just for a moment, standing up for himself. Perhaps it would do her good to hear that Joe was not an unwilling puppet in their games. But he decided against it. He didn't have the energy.

'Can we wait until Joe's back?' he asked. 'Don't want to go through all of this twice.'

Stef grunted, crossed her legs and arms, and leaned back in her seat. 'So where you been since you got out? You certainly stayed away from us. We too good for you now that you're a ... *therapist*?' There was amusement there. That one of *them* would try to pass in the wider world. Aim for betterment.

'You been checking into me?'

'The internet.' She uncrossed her arms. 'The new name got us foxed for, oh, about ten minutes.' She smiled. 'Nothing's secret anymore.'

'That's for sure.'

Joe walked back into the room, bearing a tray with three empty mugs, a jug of milk, a bowl of sugar and a plate of chocolate-covered digestive biscuits.

'Hey, what's going on? You giving my mate a hard time, Stef? It was your idea to invite him up,' said Joe.

'That was quick,' Luke jumped in to deflect the conversation. 'The kettle boiled already?'

'Nah,' said Joe. 'I thought I'd just crack open the biscuits first.'

'I was just about to tell Stef why I was round here this morning.'

'Oh aye?' Joe sat on the arm of the sofa next to Stef, and Luke couldn't help but read the body language; the way they each inclined to the other suggested that this couple were close.

Luke took a breath. Where to start? He couldn't talk about Nathan without talking about what had happened to him since he got out of prison, perhaps fuelling their resentment about his efforts to leave them all behind, so, he just opened his mouth and began to speak, hoping that his subconscious would push out the right words in the right order.

'Didn't think you had it in you,' Stef said when he stopped.

'Aye, good on you, mate. Taking on the poor lassie's wee boy,' Joe said while throwing an expression at Stef that was part *see, he's not that bad*, and part, *do you have to give him such hard time?*

'Who's this Rab Cameron character, then?' said Joe. 'Do you know him?' he asked Stef.

She shook her head. Thought about it some more. 'Changed times.' She shook her head again. 'You barely know your neighbours these days. Where did you say he was living?'

Luke gave the name of Rab's street, which was just around the corner.

'My mate Olive lives at number fifty-four...' She reached into the large handbag squatting at her feet and pulled out a mobile phone. 'And she's well tapped into the jungle drums. Give me a...' She thumbed her screen. Pressed something and held the phone to her ear. It was answered quickly.

'Hey, Olive.' They exchanged some pleasantries before Stef moved on to the reason for her call. 'I've got an old friend here, asking about Rab Cameron. Do you know him?' Then she made a few mmms and ahhhs. At each one it was all Luke could do not to reach across and pull the phone from Stef's hand. 'Thanks, honey. See you at the weekend, eh? Get your dancing shoes on, by the way.' Luke could hear the peals of laughter coming from the phone.

'Cameron's a waster, apparently,' Stef announced after she cut the connection. 'But you know that already. Got music on all hours. Doesn't work. A kid's appeared out of nowhere.' She nodded meaningfully at Luke. 'Cameron had a massive TV delivered yesterday. Oh and he picked up a new car this morning.' She paused. Smiled in admiration. 'Google would do well to give our Olive some work.'

A kid. Nathan.

'Olive's wondering where the money's coming from, seeing as he's been on the benefits for yonks.'

'Did Olive say anything about Nathan. The child?'

'Said he was quiet. Which is a blessing cos she lives through the wall and cannae be doing wi' anyone else's weans making a noise; hers make enough for Scotland.'

Luke jumped to his feet. Paced to the window. Then back to his seat.

'What are you going to do, Luke?' Stef asked, staring into his face with a worried expression. 'You've got that glazed-over thing going on. Don't be doing anything daft or you'll lose that kid forever.'

'I'm just going to go round. Make sure Nathan's in one piece.

Make sure Cameron has the wherewithal to look after him properly. Proper grown-up, adult chat.'

Stef looked down at his hands, which were both formed into fists. 'You sure? Looks like your body's saying otherwise.'

Luke stuffed his hands in his pockets as if he was hiding evidence.

Stef got to her feet. 'This needs a woman's touch. Watch the weans,' she said to Joe in a tone that brooked no dissent. 'Luke and me are going for a visit.'

Chapter 30

His heels were loud on the pavement as they walked round the corner to Rab Cameron's flat.

'Hey.' He felt Stef's hand on his arm. 'Nathan will be fine. Cameron's a lot of things, by all accounts, but I'm sure he's not a danger to the boy.'

'Aye,' Luke repeated, feeling Stef's support and good intentions bounce off the hard shell of his fear and concern. An image of Nathan appeared in his mind. An evening before he went off to work. Nathan was in his pyjamas, hair slicked back after his bath, and he had an armful of dinosaur figures that he was determined to detail to Luke before he left the house.

In a little bit of a rush, and worried he was going to be late, Luke had pretty much dismissed Nathan's attempt at conversation, patted him on the head and left. How he would love to have that time back, to have the opportunity to sit patiently and listen to every word that fell from that sweet little face.

If Cameron had touched a hair on Nathan's head...

Luke became aware that Stef had stopped walking.

'What?' He turned to her.

'You going to be okay?' Her breath fogged in the cold air as she burrowed into the depths of her padded coat. She looked worried. No, not worried; scared.

'Yeah ... I'm...' He studied her expression. She looked ready to run off in the opposite direction.

'You sure? Cos I don't need to be a witness to anything bad today. I've had it up to the back teeth with bad shit.'

'Wait.' Luke held a hand up. With a flash of insight he realised where she was coming from. When they were all young and stupid, and into all kinds of illegal stuff, he and Danny had been known to resort to violence. Danny was the ringleader for sure; it rarely kicked off when he wasn't there, but Luke often joined in.

Usually under the influence of some drug or another, but still, there was no real excuse. He was deeply ashamed of his behaviour back then. 'Sorry.' He felt his face heat. That old Luke was still the person Stef saw when she looked at him. 'I'm not that guy anymore,' he said.

'You sure?' Stef countered. 'Cos I've seen that face before.'

'Cross my heart, Stef. I'm a changed man.'

She narrowed her eyes. 'You better be. If anything happens in there' – she looked towards a door just a few yards from them – 'I'll be the polis' star witness at your trial.' She poked him in the chest. 'You hearing me?'

'Absolutely,' Luke replied, hand over his heart. 'I just want to make sure Nathan's okay, and maybe negotiate some time with him. Pick him up from school. Stuff like that.'

'Okay.' Stef appeared to be mollified. 'That wee boy, and bless him I've never met him, deserves the best care after losing his mother. That's the only reason I'm here, to help make sure that happens. If Cameron's got his act together and the wee fella appears happy, I'll be standing in your way if you try to kidnap him.'

'Aye, okay. Jesus,' Luke said, and read that Stef could still be a formidable woman when she put her mind to it. He held his hands up. 'No rough stuff. I get it.'

They arrived in front of the door.

'Did your pal say what number Cameron...'

'3B.'

Luke pressed the button. Waited.

Nothing.

He pressed again.

Nothing.

He rattled the door. "Sake, Cameron, where are you?'

'Calm down, eh? It's just gone one o'clock. Maybe they're having a wee nap. Or maybe Cameron's taken the wee fella across to the park.'

'There's a park?' Luke took a step back from the door and looked around. He shifted through some memories of the locale and couldn't think where a park might be. There certainly wasn't one when he was hanging about these streets.

'Remember the old church that became a bingo hall? It stood empty for yonks, became a bit of an eyesore.' She paused as if judging his reaction. 'Aye, even in these parts it was an eyesore. So they demolished it, landscaped the plot and put together this wee play area for the local weans.'

'Right. Let's go,' Luke said, walking in the direction of the old bingo hall.

Five minutes later, breath frosting in the air, they were standing before a line of black, iron railings. In front of them was a generous area of turf and safety matting studded with a group of brightly coloured play stations. On a bench at the far side huddled two men in padded jackets and baseball caps, shouting encouragement at a couple of kids on the climbing frame.

Luke studied the children. Both were about Nathan's age. But neither was him.

Stef studied his expression. Then appeared disappointed as she read it.

'I take it he's not here?'

Luke turned and started walking back in the direction they'd come from. There was an increased urgency to his movement now. Where on earth could Nathan be? If Cameron had caused any harm to that boy he would not be accountable for his actions.

Stef was breathless at his elbow. 'The wee fella will be just fine, Luke. You'll see.'

'Aye,' was all he could say in reply, his mind full of catastrophic images. He hoped the signal on his phone was good in this area, so he could phone the police and the local hospitals.

Minutes later they were back at the entrance to Cameron's block of flats. Luke pressed the button. Nothing. He pressed again. Then he rattled the door.

'I'll kick this in if I have to,' he said to no one in particular.

'Hold on,' Stef said, putting a hand on his arm. 'Olive lives one down. She's bound to know somebody who lives in the block. Let me try her. See if she can get one of her pals to get us past this door.'

Minutes later, after a phone call, the door lock buzzed, Luke pushed at the door, and it opened. He bounded up the stairs two at a time, Stef shouting at him to slow down and not do anything foolish. But Luke had moved past that. His mind was an unceasing run of terrifying images. He got to the door and knocked.

Nothing.

'Jesus,' said Stef when she breathlessly caught up with him. 'You'll knock the thing down.'

'That's not a bad idea,' Luke said as he took a step back and braced himself in preparation to put his shoulder through the wood.

Stef took a step towards the door, reached out for the handle and turned it. It opened.

'See you men, always got to be barging into stuff.'

'Aye,' said Luke, pushing the door open and taking a step inside. 'Nathan?' he shouted.

Nothing.

He was standing in a short, narrow corridor. Thin grey carpet, vanilla-coloured woodchip on the walls. A door was facing him, and there were two doors each side of the hallway.

'Nathan,' he shouted again as he pushed open the door immediately to his left. He saw a small window and in front of it a sink loaded with dirty dishes. Over to the left was a cooker, each ring bearing a pan encrusted with food. A cupboard was open, and Luke could see that it contained the brightly coloured packaging of children's cereal. Then he noticed a blue bowl on the countertop, half full of milk and dotted with the remnants of a cereal breakfast. A still-life tableau that until recently Luke saw every day. When he would chastise Nathan for not drinking all the milk.

He felt a shot of panic.

'Nathan,' he shouted.

A small voice sounded from his right. 'Dad?'

He barged past Stef, trying to locate where the sound was coming from.

'Dad.'

'Nathan,' he replied, 'I'm here, buddy.' It came out almost as a sob.

The door facing him at the end of the hallway. It must be the living room. He rushed over, opened it and scanned the room.

'Dad?'

Nathan was standing just beyond the door. He was wearing nothing but a pair of underpants and a white vest. He looked as if he had been at the point of reaching out to the man lying half on, half off a sofa. But as soon as he saw Luke he lifted his arms out wide and ran to him.

Luke gathered the little boy to his chest, feeling his small body wracked with sobs.

He took in the sofa. The man lying there, his head thrown back, Adam's apple prominent, mouth open, showing a curve of black fillings, eyes staring. He was wearing nothing but a pair of jeans. On the floor beside him Luke could see some tinfoil, a tablespoon and a piece of rubber tubing.

Then he saw what Nathan had been reaching for. A syringe was hanging from the crease of Cameron's arm, the long needle still inside a vein.

Chapter 31

Twenty-five years earlier

Fraser Smith, dead at his feet, was a moment Luke would never scrub from his mind. During his early years, violence or the threat of it was a worryingly predictable part of his life. Walk down the wrong street, be with the wrong friends, wear the wrong colour top, and a challenge could be issued. And if you backed down from that challenge your name was tarred and you could be the target of any spot-popping lad who wanted to make a name for themselves. It was an almost monthly, sometimes weekly, occurrence – a young man dead. Reason for his death?

Just because.

Feral young men, absent of parents, finding family and a sense of belonging with their peers. The older lads were the worst kind of example, but seeking their approval was like a gold medal to an athlete. They'd do anything to earn it.

Primarily, that meant violence.

But on this occasion, when the violence had been accidental – a mistimed throw of the hand, then a stumble and fall – the result was, at first, surreal, almost comical, until reality hit. Dead eyes. Open mouth. Blood seeping out in a dark spill. Another's pulse slowing to a dead stop.

He and Fraser were double-dating a pair of sisters, Lesley and Moira. Most nights they'd walk around the streets, trying to find quiet places they could hide away for a feel and a snog. Then, after the girls judged it was time to go home, the two boys would head across to a piece of waste ground that bordered their street. Fraser's house at one end, Luke's at the other.

The ground had at one time housed a row of shops, but they had been torn down in anticipation of a new shopping centre that the council never found the money for, so now it was a hodgepodge of uneven concrete beds, head-high railings, stunted bushes and piles of discarded goods that people hadn't the wherewithal to dispose of properly. These goods were a godsend to the local kids, and dotted around the place were various dens made of burst sofas, mattresses and bed frames.

On this particular night Luke had used some of his birthday money from his dad to take Linda to a movie. Van Damme in *Sudden Death*. Linda had protested. She wanted to see a comedy or a romance, but it was Luke's money so he got to pick. Besides, she'd made him watch *Bridges of Madison County* just a few weeks earlier so he thought she owed him, big time, for having to sit through that shite.

After the movie, and after he'd walked Linda home, he was on his way through the waste ground when he happened on Fraser walking home after his date.

'Slipped the hand tonight, mate,' Fraser said as he walked in step with Luke, holding his hands out before him at chest height and in a cup shape.

'Aye, so you did,' Luke said, and bumped his friend with his shoulder.

'Did,' Fraser asserted. 'Got a proper feel.'

Luke felt a pang of disappointment. He'd aimed for that during a quiet part of the movie, only for Linda to move his hand firmly away from his intended target.

'Was the film any good?' Fraser asked, envy clear in the cast of his face. 'That guy's some fighter, eh?'

'Aye,' Luke said, hopping into a Van Damme fighting stance, hands high while moving his head from side to side and making Bruce Lee noises.

Fraser snorted. 'You look constipated, mate.'

Luke shot out a leg, and his foot just missed Fraser's backside.

'Man, you're rubbish,' Fraser laughed. 'You do it like this.' He swung round, shot out a leg and caught Luke full force in the lower back area.

'Oww,' Luke yelled, and hobbled out of range. 'That was sore, man.'

'Sorry, buddy,' Fraser apologised, while trying to quell his laughter, clearly pleased that his effort had worked.

'Fuckssake,' Luke said as he bent over, riding out the pain. 'Did you need to do that, ya wanker?' He straightened up, hand at his back like an old man, and repeated his complaint. 'Fuckssake.'

'Sorry,' Fraser repeated. 'Ya big wean.' Then he laughed. 'Tell you what. If it makes you feel better you can take a Van Damme pot shot at me.' He stood facing Luke, feet wide apart.

'Don't be daft,' Luke replied, already better and feeling stupid at complaining so much.

'Naw, on ye go. Give it your best shot, mate,' Fraser grinned.

To shut him up, Luke swung at him half-heartedly.

'For Chrissakes,' Fraser laughed. 'What a poof. Is that your best shot?'

'You really want me to hit you?' Luke asked.

'Aye.'

'You really want me to hit you?' Luke repeated.

'On a count of three,' Fraser replied, closing his eyes. 'One, two...'

Grinning in anticipation at his friend's complaint that he didn't wait out the count properly, Luke swung, open-handed, judging a slap would cause less harm to his friend's face than a fist.

Fraser's head shot back. He lost his balance.

Almost as if it happened in slow motion, Luke watched as his friend fell to the side, and his head hit the kerb.

Fraser didn't move again.

'Right,' Luke said, 'You can get back up now.'

Nothing.

'Fraser?' Luke leaned forward in the near dark to assess his friend. 'You can stop kidding on now. It's not funny.'

Nothing.

'Fraser?' Luke peered down at the other boy. Saw a dark liquid pool at the side of his head. Read the utter stillness, and, heart surging with panic, he turned and ran.

Chapter 32

Jamie had his spare phone on the table in front of him while he was eating breakfast. Overnight oats with cream and blueberries. The phone vibrated against the table top and rang out. He gazed at the screen and recognised part of the number. Amanda looked up from her newspaper.

'Cameron?' she asked.

Jamie nodded.

'Well, answer it.'

'The boy's back with Forrest,' Jamie replied. 'We've no more use for him.'

'We knew Cameron would turn out to be useless, but that's fine. He's served his purpose.'

'Yes, but—'

'Answer the bloody phone, will you?' Amanda lifted the paper from her lap and gave it a snap in the air to show her irritation. 'See what he wants.'

'He's not getting any more money from us,' Jamie said. 'He'll just go and score some more drugs.' He looked away from Amanda and pressed the screen.

'Put it on loudspeaker,' Amanda whispered.

Jamie did so, and Cameron's nasal tones filled the room.

'Sorry about all that, folks,' he said straight away. 'That gear was fucking amazing. Near blew my head off.'

'How are you, Rab?' Amanda shouted from across the room. 'What happened?'

'Yes, Rab,' Jamie said. 'You messed up. We don't think we got our money's worth.'

'Aye, but—' Rab began.

'You were told to take the boy and keep him,' Amanda said. 'What did you do? You got out of your skull on the smack, and Forrest comes over and takes the boy back. And he probably took some photos as evidence that you are an unfit father and should never be allowed near your son again.'

'Aye,' Cameron wheedled. 'But it won't happen again.'

'Correct, Rab,' Amanda said. 'It won't happen again because we have no further need of your services.'

'Haw, ya snooty cow,' Cameron shouted back. 'I made a mistake, right? It happens.' He paused, and his tone when he began speaking again was more placatory. 'Lesson learned, eh? I'll get the boy back when Forrest's out the house, and I'll pure look after him proper this time.'

'You're a loose cannon, Mr Cameron,' Amanda said. 'No thanks. We'll do without you from now on.'

Cameron's attempt at composure didn't last long. 'I'll give you loose cannon, missus. I want another five grand or I'll be round Luke Forrest's house soon as I get off this phone. I've got an interesting story to tell him, ya pair of fuckin' weirdos. Who the hell pays somebody to nick a wean?'

'He's your own child, Rab,' Amanda said, her eyes taking on a calculating look. 'We're just righting a wrong.'

'My arse,' Cameron replied. 'I'm no' fuckin' stupid. You've got something on that guy, and you're using me to get back at him. I'm sure he'll pay handsomely to hear what the hell is going on.'

'Okay. Let's not do anything rash,' Amanda said, her tone measured. She paused as if thinking, but Jamie could see that she was already several steps ahead of Cameron. And him. 'My brother will be over later to negotiate a new deal with you.'

'He will?' Rab sounded pleased at this turn of events. 'But no funny business. I want the cash in tens and twenties. And in a nice wee Under Armour sports bag.'

When he ended the call Jamie turned on his sister. 'What the hell?' But he instantly calmed down when he read her expression. 'Okay, what are you thinking?' he asked.

'I'm thinking Rab Cameron needs to have an accident,' Amanda replied.

'What?' Jamie pushed himself away from the table and stood up.

'Shouldn't be too difficult for you to arrange. The man's a mess.'

Jamie held his hands up, then let them fall to slap at his thighs. 'I'm out. I didn't sign up for this.'

Amanda simply crossed her arms and studied him. 'Don't play coy with me, brother. We both know it wouldn't be the first time.'

Jamie felt his face and throat heat. That was then. He was a different person now. A better person. 'You don't know what you're talking about.'

'But I can make a good guess.' Amanda narrowed her eyes. 'Your foster parents died just a week or so after you moved out.'

'Shut up.'

'Carbon monoxide poisoning.'

'Shut up.' Jamie took a step towards his sister. Every part of him rigid.

'The newspaper report said the family were baffled, given that the gas boiler had not long been serviced.'

Jamie saw his sister's mouth move, but couldn't hear her properly because of the roar in his ears and the thunder raging in his mind. 'I'm not. I can't...'

Amanda got to her feet and approached her brother as a trainer might approach a near-wild stallion, all quivering muscle and repressed action. She put a hand on his shoulder, her expression now one of affection. He felt the heat from her hand, closed his eyes, and took note of the cool air at his nostrils as he took a long slow breath. Focusing on these helped him anchor himself in the present.

'Hey,' she shooshed him. 'Don't worry. One way or another Cameron's clock is going to be punched. You'll just be ... pushing him towards the inevitable.'

Jamie stepped back, shrugging off her touch. He knew what she was doing. She was trying to manipulate him. One minute scolding, the next pacifying him like a nurse about to inject a needle-phobic.

'Fuck off, sis,' he said, feeling every part of him bristle. 'I'm done being your bitch. Do your own dirty work.'

Chapter 33

Luke felt his pulse rise and his mouth dry as he walked up the long drive to Jenna's mother's door, worried about how Jenna might react to seeing him. He'd tried several times since Nathan came home to get back in touch with her, but each time his calls and messages had been ignored.

Now that the wee fella was safe, he felt it was time to sort out his relationship with Jenna once and for all. They'd been getting on so well prior to this silence, he couldn't fathom why she was shutting him out. If she felt he'd gone off the boil when he was worried about Nathan he would reassure her that wasn't the case. But he'd have to actually speak to her in person. Phone calls or text messages just didn't work. Not for the important stuff.

To his left a large patch of lawn, bordered with mature shrubs and trees, stretched up towards the impressive, two-storey, semi-detached sandstone building. The front door was under a portico off to the side and painted racing green.

Long ago he would have been impressed and perhaps even intimidated by the wealth this substantial house suggested, but having come across a handful of men in prison who elongated their vowels, as well as those, like him, who spat them out in a guttural rush, he now understood that financial status was a poor signifier of an individual's worth.

As a kid growing up in a neighbourhood that measured its wealth by the number of individuals in the house who could claim benefit, this area, which was only twenty minutes away in the car, might as well be on the other side of the moon. Such was the disparity in this city.

So here he was ringing Jenna's doorbell to get a final answer from her. If she felt there was something between them worth investigating, that would be wonderful. If she didn't, he'd disappear and she would never hear from him again.

As he was raising his hand to ring the bell, the door opened. On the other side was a distracted Jenna. She was wearing a coat and was wrapping a scarf around her neck while shouting over her shoulder at someone inside.

'Yes,' she said. 'I'll remember to pick up your prescription.' Then under her breath, 'Jesus, woman...' Then she became aware of Luke's presence, looked up into his eyes. 'Oh.' Her face pinked.

'If this is a bad time,' Luke said, and took a step back. Right hand up, palm facing her, he added, 'I'll come back...'

'No. No,' Jenna said. She smoothed the front of her coat. 'There's a row of shops two streets over. I need some stuff. You can walk with me.' As she spoke her eyes were everywhere but on his face. When she did eventually look at him, her mouth quivered into a smile.

'I wish you would come into the room when you're talking to me.' A voice sounded from along the hall. 'Who are you talking to?'

'It's nobody, Mum,' she shouted back, raising her eyebrows at Luke in apology.

Nobody. Luke didn't have that much of an ego that he would take this personally, but the thought registered for just a moment: this was how she now thought of him.

'I'll be back soon,' Jenna called to her mother. Then mouthed, 'Sorry.'

Whatever her mother said in response was shut off as Jenna stepped outside and closed the door behind her.

'Sorry. She's...' Jenna began.

'Hard work?' Luke offered with a smile.

'Och, I shouldn't complain. It's not her, it's her condition.'

Luke could see how weighed down she was by the effort of caring for her mother.

'None of my business, but you could try one of those respite places. I'm sure your doctor or someone would be able to help with that.'

'Thanks, yeah, I'll look into that,' Jenna replied, and Luke could see that she had no intention of doing so.

'Nice part of town,' he said, looking around.

'S'pose,' Jenna replied.

Twinkling lights in a window caught his attention, just as Jenna said, 'It's a bit early for that.'

'Aye, we're barely into December,' Luke agreed.

They fell into a clumsy quiet, Luke mentally cursing the loss of the easy way they previously had with each other. *Barely into December*. Jeez. How lame a conversation was that.

Jenna ducked her head. 'Cold, isn't it.'

'Aye. We've had a bit of a cold snap recently, eh?' He groaned inwardly. Was this the level they'd reached? Filling the silences with inane chat?

There were a few moments of silence while they negotiated the traffic as they crossed the road. Just ahead there was a row of shops, and Luke spotted the red awning of a café.

'Do you have time for a coffee, or do you have to rush back?'

Jenna paused, looked back over her shoulder in the direction of her mother's house. 'Oh, why not? Doing grown-up things would be nice for a wee while.'

A small heater above the door of the café gave them a welcome blast of heat as they stepped inside. Luke spotted an empty table at the back of the room. They sat down and each ordered coffee, and a slice of carrot cake to share.

'How's your mum?' Luke asked as soon as the waitress walked away.

'Och you know,' Jenna replied. 'One minute a saint, the next a demon.' As she spoke she offered a jaunty shake of the head, but Luke saw right through it.

'It's tough though, eh?' he asked. 'Can't be easy doing this whole role-reversal thing.'

Their coffees and cake arrived. The waitress made a show of placing the cake in the middle of the table as if this was the most romantic thing she'd seen all day.

'Yeah,' said Jenna, jumping back into their conversation. 'Mum gets frustrated that she's not the same woman.' She sighed, and, after a pause, as if debating whether or not to say it, she added, 'And last night she wet her bed.'

'Really? Did you get much sleep?'

'Oh God,' Jenna replied, leaning back into her seat and pulling at the skin under her eyes. 'I've got massive bags, haven't I?'

'Didn't notice,' Luke lied. 'I was thinking more about you having to change bedding in the middle of the night.'

'It's fine,' Jenna said as she lifted her chin up and crossed her arms. 'We're doing okay, all things considered.'

Luke saw that this assertion cost Jenna some energy, and he wanted to ask how she really was.

'Look at that poor cake,' Jenna said just as he decided it was time to start an honest conversation. 'Sitting there unloved.' She smiled, cut some off with her fork and popped it into her mouth, umming with delight. 'This is so good. You have to try some.' She swallowed and washed that down with some coffee. 'How's Nathan?'

He told her about his recent troubles; about how he'd lost his job at the club, and as he did so he didn't skimp on any detail that might make him look like an idiot. When he told her about Nathan being taken by his real father, her face lengthened with shock and sympathy.

'When I got there the wee man was reaching out towards Cameron. Looked like he was going for the syringe in his arm.'

'Oh my God,' she said, and reached across the table to grab his hand. 'That must have been awful for you both.' She shook her head. 'And here's me moaning about my mother. You must think I'm so self- centred.'

'Not at all,' Luke replied, enjoying the feel of her hand on his. 'I think it's fair to say that neither of us have had an easy time of it recently.' He looked across the table at her; the line of her shoulders suggested she was in a more relaxed state of mind now. 'Mind if I ask you something?'

'Uhuh...'

'I've been, well, I've been posted missing the last few weeks or so because I was out of my mind with worry about Nathan, and then I've been afraid to let him out of my sight. But...' He looked her in the eye. 'If you no longer want to see me, that's fine, but I need to know.' He bit his lip and steeled himself against an answer that he wouldn't like. 'You didn't return any of my calls. If it's too hard for you to look after your mum and have a relationship, I understand, but surely we could still carve out some time to be together? And I'm sure Nathan would grow to love you as much as I do...'

He stopped. He'd just made a huge admission. He gave himself a shake; this surely wasn't the way Jenna would want to discover the depth of his feeling for her.

Her eyes grew large and damp. 'Oh, Luke,' she said.

Guilt had him recoil slightly from her sympathy. She still didn't know the worst of him. He hadn't gotten round to telling her about that.

And now was the time. He couldn't delay any longer. Not if he wanted their relationship to be based in truth. And to work.

'Before we go any further...' he began.

She sat back in her chair, brow furrowed, arms crossed, as if in reaction to his change in tone.

'Cards on the table?' he added. 'There's something you need to know.'

'Luke, you're scaring me,' she said, eyes large.

He coughed. 'I've been in prison.'

Her hands were clasped in her lap. 'Oh.' Her eyes darted to the door, and he imagined she was calculating how quickly it would take her to get out of his company.

He held a hand up. 'It was an accident. Car accident. The morning after the night before. Well, a night that didn't really end, to be honest. I was left with driver duties. And...' He took a breath, his face hot with the admission he was about to make. 'And I fell asleep at the wheel, and somebody died.'

'God,' Jenna whispered. 'Oh my God.'

His phone rang.

'Shit,' he said, resenting the intrusion. He was finding it difficult to read her reaction; all he could see was shock. He needed more time with her to work out if one of the worst things that had ever happened to him would mean she would want him gone. The phone continued to ring. The number on the screen unrecognisable. 'Shit, I really should answer. This could be the school. Someone wanting to talk to me about Nathan.'

'Sure.' Jenna leaned away, staring at the table top as if she was struggling to make sense of what he had just said.

Luke picked up the phone. 'Hello?'

'What the hell have you done?' a female voice demanded. He recognised it immediately.

'Stef? How did you get my—?'

'What the hell have you done, Forrest? I've just had the cops round here. I said you were with me. I told you I would. Cos you might have been the last person to see him alive. Jesus, Dunc, I'm bricking it here. The polis were like murder this, murder that, and...' In her upset she didn't have the presence of mind to use his new name.

'Stef. What the hell are you talking about?'

'Cameron,' she replied. 'He's dead.'

Chapter 34

'Can I speak to the officers investigatin' the murder o' Rab Cameron.'

'Name, please?'

'I just want to talk to som'dy.'

'If you give me your name I can put you through to the correct person.'

'Smithy.'

'Smithy?'

'Aye, it's a common enough name, like. You got an issue with it?'

'Not at all, ma'am. Let me put you through.'

'Detective Sergeant Rossi. How can I help you?'

'That Rab Cameron – I'm his neighbour. Heard him fighting the other day. Just afore he died.'

'What's your address, Smithy?'

'That's nane o' yur business. Rab Cameron – are you investigating his murder?'

'Early indications are that his death was accidental. If you have any evidence to the contrary we would appreciate you coming down to the office and making a statement.'

'Aye. Right. I'm no' making no statement, hen. But I will say that Luke Forrest already done time for endin' som'dy. Managed to disguise that wan as an accident as well. Look no further, Detective Sergeant Rossi. He's yur man.'

'We appreciate the phone call, eh ... Smithy, but we can't base an investigation on hearsay and gossip. If you have any actual evidence we would love to see it. You don't even have to come into the office. Let me know where you are, and I'll send some officers round.'

'Aye will ye. Forget it, hen. But what I will say is that Luke Forrest's been acting the white knight, looking after Rab's wean since the mother died. Rab grabbed the boy back. Then Luke paid him a wee visit. Next thing, Cameron's toast. Join the dots, hen.'

'Thank you for your—'

'And if you think Forrest's no longer dealing then you're as stupid as you sound.'

Amanda ended the connection, opened up the back of her phone and removed the SIM card. Then she looked triumphantly over at Jamie, who had been sitting right beside her as she talked, the phone on loudspeaker.

'You put just the right amount of nasal into that,' Jamie said. 'Well done. But how do you know the police will do anything? The death has been ruled as accidental.'

'They have to follow up the tip, Jamie. Next part of the plan, you go for some therapy.' She pulled a little plastic bag out of her pocket and tossed it to him. 'You drop this in his shed somewhere. The police call in for a wee chat. Find it. Test it. Note that it's of similar vintage to the stuff that killed Cameron, and *voilà*.' Amanda nodded, clearly satisfied with her efforts. 'Let's see Forrest wriggle out of this.'

Chapter 35

As soon as he stepped inside The Therapy Shed, Jamie felt it was much warmer than the last time he'd visited. He looked around to locate the source, and saw, there in the corner, a little cast-iron wood burner.

'Good, eh?' Luke said from behind his desk, looking rather pleased for himself. 'The little electric radiator wasn't cutting it,' he added. 'And a friend offered me this when he was replacing his with a bigger version. I couldn't resist.' Luke got up from behind his desk, walked to the little stove and held his hands out to it. 'Such a simple pleasure. The heat coming off it is incredible.'

Jamie faked a smile, appearing to join in the other man's pleasure at such a simple thing.

'You can feel it as soon as you walk in the door,' Jamie said, and studied Luke. There was something different about him today. A brighter light to his eyes, a more relaxed cast to his shoulders. Had something happened, he wondered? Something good? Because if the police had been for a visit, it had clearly had no impact.

He reminded himself that Amanda had only called in a couple of days ago. Maybe it was too soon for them to act. Plus, it was only a few weeks till Christmas. Perhaps there were staff holidays to take into account before the end of the year. He had no idea how the police organised that among themselves, but they had to have holidays, surely?

Jamie took a seat, but before he sat down he stuffed a hand in his trouser pocket and located the small packet of lethal drugs he was about to drop.

For all he'd tried to resist his sister's goading about sorting Cameron out, when he heard her talking on the phone to some dodgy individual, about to give them directions to their house, he stepped in. He found a source for the heroin, then worked out how to adulterate it, before visiting Cameron and offering some to him as a 'peace offering'.

Cameron's eyes lit up when he saw the drugs, already anticipating the high and mentally spending the bribe money Jamie was holding out to him. Then all Jamie had to do was wait for Cameron to needle up, take back his cash, wipe down all the surfaces, and leave.

'What's on your mind today, Jamie?' Luke asked, throwing him from his thoughts.

Jamie shifted against the cushion of his chair and crossed his legs. He studied Luke, seeing nothing but genuine concern in his eyes. 'It's this time of year,' he said. 'We're all supposed to be cheery and kind, and I hate it. Christmases were nothing much round our house, and after Danny died they were miserable. Then, when I got fostered they became...' He paused and in his mind's eye saw a large pile of gaudily wrapped parcels under a massive tree in his foster parents' house, knowing he was about to discover they were mostly empty. Mostly for show; placed in front of the large bay window – a Christmas art installation for the neighbours' benefit. 'Aye. Not my favourite time of the year.'

Luke leaned forward in his chair. 'We haven't talked much about your foster parents...?' There was a rising inflection at the end of the statement, making it a question. 'Do you keep in touch with them?'

'They died years ago.'

'Sorry, I didn't know. Did they leave much of an impression on you?'

Jamie crossed his arms. 'Let's just say their Christianity didn't extend to any actual real kindness.'

'Uhuh...'

Jamie fingered the packet. Looked round and noted that the small table in the corner of the room, which usually bore some kind of refreshments, had no water.

'Could do with a glass of water, mate,' he said.

'I've no other clients this morning,' Luke replied. 'We can just chat – about anything. I could tell you more about what me and Danny got up to.' He moved his head from side to side as if making a judgement call. 'Well, some of it. Anyway, what I'm saying is we can take our time. And I could make you something warm? A coffee? Tea? Fancy something to eat?'

'Water's fine,' Jamie replied, feeling himself try, and fail, to resist Luke's good humour. 'Something's different about you today,' he said. 'You look like a man who won the lottery. Or...' He looked back towards the wood burner and dismissed financial gain as a reason for Luke's obvious uplift in mood. If he'd won the actual lottery he'd have bought a bigger house, bigger shed and a bigger stove. 'Been lucky in love?' he smiled.

'God, is it that obvious?' Luke grinned, then shrugged in a self-deprecatory fashion. 'We were having some issues, but we've sorted them out, thankfully.' He slapped a hand on the top of his desk. 'And there I go talking about me. The first sin of the therapist.'

'And here's me thinking we were more than therapist and client,' Jamie said, acknowledging openly for the first time Luke's attempts at friendship. He took his hand out of his pocket, allowing the packet to fall safely inside before he did so, where he imagined it burning a hole in his thigh. 'Coffee. Milk. One sugar, please.'

Minutes later, once they'd both been furnished with a hot cup of coffee, Luke sat back down, but this time on the same side of the table as Jamie.

'Christmases weren't very nice for you, then?' he asked.

'Putting it mildly.'

Luke nodded to himself as if making a decision. 'Then we need to do something about that.'

'Excuse me?'

'This therapy thing doesn't feel proper to me. Not with you. Too much going on.' He looked deep into Jamie's eyes, and Jamie read nothing but concern for him emanating from the man. 'We ... me and Jenna,' he ducked his head a little self-consciously, 'we're taking Nathan to the big Christmas funfair at the exhibition centre. Want to come?'

'I think I grew out of funfairs a long time ago.' Jamie heard himself laugh, feeling a little pleased at the prospect.

'Nonsense,' Luke replied. 'We're never too old to have fun.' He slapped at his thigh with his free hand. 'That's it settled. You, me, Jenna and Nathan on the dodgems, eating candy floss. It'll be a hoot.'

'It'll be a mess. Candy floss on the dodgems?'

Luke gazed over Jamie's shoulder at the door. There was a knock. Luke appeared to be mystified.

'Who on earth?' He got to his feet. 'Give me a second, Jamie,' he said.

Luke went to the door, and opened it.

'Mr Forrest? Mr Luke Forrest?' Jamie heard a female voice.

'Yes?'

'Detective Sergeant Rossi. Mind if we have a word?'

Chapter 36

Luke examined the woman standing on his garden path, just a few paces from his shed. She was tall and slim with dark, shoulder-length hair. Her dark wool coat was unbuttoned, and he could see a navy-blue suit and white shirt ensemble underneath. He recognised the look in her eyes. That questioning, assessing gaze that every police officer he'd ever dealt with used.

A man was standing just behind her. Similar kind of clothing and that same look.

'This is Detective Drain,' Rossi said.

Shit. He'd allowed himself to believe that the incident at the nightclub wasn't being investigated, but now it looked like it was coming home to roost after all.

Idiot. He was an ex-con. If a complaint was made, of course they were going to investigate.

'I'm sorry. I'm in the middle of something right now,' he said, feeling a weakness in his thighs and hoping that he didn't sound defensive.

He became aware of movement behind him and turned to see Jamie had his coat on and was clearly aiming to leave.

Luke held his hand up to stop him. 'You don't need to—'

'I'll get back to you ... about that thing,' Jamie said. 'Sounds good.' Then he stepped past Luke and was away along the path and out towards the front of the house.

Luke crossed his arms, deflecting his worry into irritation. 'You scared away my client,' he said. 'I was just beginning to get somewhere.'

'My apologies,' Rossi replied, and she sounded genuine. 'But we have some questions for you.'

'Yeah?'

Shit.

'Mind if we come inside?'

'Don't know that I have much choice,' Luke said, and stepped aside to let the pair in.

They sat around the desk, the visitors taking their coats off first.

Rossi gave her colleague a look, then she faced Luke. 'It's about your connection with Rab Cameron.'

'No problem,' Luke answered, feeling relief that it wasn't about the fracas at Neon, and making a mental note to call Ken and ask if he knew whether the boss actually did call in the cops or not.

Then the question slammed in: could they think he had something to do with Cameron's death? Shit. Wasn't it a drug death, after all? If it wasn't, and he was the last person in Cameron's house before he died, he could be in real bother. His mind raced through a number of scenarios as he struggled to show a calm face and answer the detective's question.

'He's the biological father of Nathan, the boy I look after,' Luke managed to say. Then he went on to explain about his deceased partner, and her wish that he adopt the boy. How after years of no contact between Cameron and Nathan, the man had turned up and basically kidnapped the child.

'And you visited Cameron to make sure Nathan was being looked after?' Rossi asked.

'Yes. I knew nothing about him other than he was fond of getting high, so I was worried. Rightly so, as it turns out.'

'What makes you say that?'

'I arrived to see Cameron out cold on the sofa, a needle in his arm, and Nathan reaching for the needle.' He felt himself bristle with concern all over again.

'What happened next?' Drain asked.

'I took Nathan home.'

'And Stef Cuthbert was with you all of the time?' This time Rossi was the questioner.

'Yes.'

'What's your legal standing with the child?'

'I ... eh ... His mother had all the forms organised for me to adopt Nathan ... just before she died.'

'And?'

'I was booked in with the lawyer to sort everything out. She died ... and I never got round to filing the paperwork.'

'You never got round to formally adopting Nathan?'

'Listen.' Luke sat upright in his chair. 'That boy has been with me almost every day of his life, if you think—'

Drain held a hand up. 'Just ascertaining the facts, Mr Forrest.'

Luke took a deep breath, and he was back in those days after Lisa died, head and heart heavy with her loss, trying to deal with his grief, and with Nathan's at the same time. 'It just felt like acknowledging that Lisa was really dead, you know? I couldn't quite bring myself to do it. But now?' He shook his head with regret at his own inaction. 'I'm worried the courts could take the boy off me.'

'Was Cameron still alive when you left him?' Rossi asked.

'Sorry?' Luke thought back to that moment. Pulling Nathan away from the man on the sofa.

'Was Cameron alive when you left him?'

Luke paused for a moment.

'You know, it's awful, but I didn't think to check.'

Chapter 37

They kissed in greeting, and there was heat there, and a little awkwardness – they still hadn't talked through her feelings about him being in prison.

She'd heard his words, saw the dimmed light in his eyes, and read the way his hands pulled and twisted at each other. This was something of huge significance in his life. Something that had haunted him every day since.

He was a genuinely kind guy; even with her poor track record with men she could see that. And he'd paid his debt to society. He seemed genuinely remorseful.

Was that all good enough for her?

The conversation with him had rumbled through her mind through the hours of darkness and into the light of a weak dawn, and it was only now, when she saw him in person, that she knew she could trust him.

She relaxed into the heat of him and tried to let him know with her eyes how she was feeling after his revelation, but she could tell that he was distracted.

'The police paid me a visit today,' he said. She stepped back from him and ushered him out of the cold and into the hall of her mother's house.

'Oh?' Jenna reached for his hand. Noted the chill of his skin. 'Why?'

'Apparently me and Stef were the last people to see Cameron alive.'

'So? Wasn't it an accidental overdose or something?'

'Jenna? Who is it?' her mother shouted from the living room.

'It's just Luke, Mum.'

In response, her mother muttered something unintelligible. Which, she thought, was just as well. She'd had enough of her mother's brand of honesty for the day.

'By the way,' Luke said. 'I've got Nathan in the car. Didn't want to leave him on his own.'

'Don't leave him out there. Bring him in,' Jenna said, looking over his shoulder towards the vehicle. As she did she felt her stomach shift, a slight wobble of nerves. Would they get on? She appreciated that for Luke this was a big step, so she offered him a little smile of thanks.

'You sure?' Luke asked.

'Of course,' she replied. 'The wee soul will be freezing out there.'

Luke stretched out his left hand and waved Nathan out of the car. As if he'd been released from a race trap, within seconds Nathan was out the door, down the path and standing looking adorably up at Luke.

'Hi,' he said to Jenna from behind Luke's thigh. Eyes big, teeth on show. 'Gran says you're Dad's girlfriend.'

'Well, hi,' Jenna replied, momentarily taken aback by the child's directness. 'You must be Nathan.'

He nodded his head vigorously.

'For fug sakes will you people come in the house and away from the fugging door,' Jenna's mother shouted along to them.

Jenna looked to the ceiling, gave Luke a silent apology and ushered them down the hallway and into the living room. Once there Luke and Nathan sat on the sofa facing her mother.

'Mum, this is Luke and Nathan. Luke and Nathan meet mother.'

'I've got a name,' her mother replied. 'It's Sally.'

'Hello, Sally,' Nathan replied brightly. Then as if he realised his voice was too loud in the space, he turned his face away and pressed his forehead into Luke's side.

'Hello, Nathan.' She then turned to Luke. 'I know you?' she asked as she searched his face. Then she turned to Jenna. 'Reminds me of that loser you used to date. Sammy. Or Larry. Whatever.' She waved a hand in the air, frustrated by her poor memory. 'The one that died. He's got the same shifty look about him.'

'Mum,' Jenna scolded. 'You can be rude all you like to me, but please don't be rude to my guests.'

'Well he has,' Sally huffed. 'And you, Nathan. What age are you?'

'I'm six,' he said proudly.

'Come here so I see you better?' Sally beckoned him closer. With a quick look at his dad, the boy walked over and stood by her side.

'Are you sick?' he asked. 'I sit cosy with a blanket when I'm sick.'

Jenna noticed Luke open his mouth as if to remonstrate with the boy, but he was cut off by Sally's chuckle.

Jenna and Luke shared a smile, and as she noted the lift in her mother's demeanour she felt an inward sigh of relief.

'Can you bring him round every day?' she said to Luke. 'I think they're going to get along famously.'

Leaving Nathan and Sally to chat, Jenna and Luke went into the kitchen, where Jenna put the kettle on.

'Coffee?' She turned to face him and leaned against the worktop.

He moved closer, lined his body with hers and kissed her. Long and slow.

'Mmmm,' he groaned, and she could feel the vibration through their lips. 'I've missed you.'

She laughed. 'I was just with you yesterday.'

'I know,' he grinned. 'That was ages ago.'

'Anything happened since.' She paused, and grimaced. 'Apart from a visit from the police?'

'Jamie was round for therapy.'

Jenna put a hand on Luke's shoulder and gently pushed him away, reaching for some mugs to pretend that was the reason for doing so. The truth was the young man made her feel uncomfortable.

'I feel so guilty, you know?' said Luke, unaware of her reservations. 'He has no one, really. No family, apart from a sister who has her own issues, as Jamie tells it...'

'You're being hard on yourself, honey.'

He smiled in acknowledgement and then continued. 'So, I asked him if he wanted to come with us to the Shows at the exhibition centre. He's not had a real Christmas for years, and it would be nice to show him what proper families do.'

'Oh,' Jenna replied. She found herself mentally recoiling from the suggestion that they all go together to the Shows, but the statement at the end – *what proper families do* – melted her heart a little. Luke saw them as a family?

'Daaaaad,' Nathan chanted from the living room, cutting off whatever she was going to say next.

'So you're okay with that?' Luke asked as he stepped away from her to check on the boy.

'Yeah. Yeah, that sounds fine,' replied Jenna to a now-empty room, thinking of Jamie and all those times he'd walked past the bookshop, trying to get a glimpse of her. Worryingly, remove the beard and he was like a slighter, younger version of an old boyfriend.

To be fair he had stopped the walk-pasts, and the couple of times they'd met since he'd been perfectly pleasant. But still, although she was delighted at the prospect of a nice Christmassy day out with Luke and Nathan, the shine was tarnished by the thought of Jamie being there as well. There was just something about the young man that made her uneasy.

Chapter 38

Twenty years earlier

Luke was in a café in Byres Road. It was only a short hop from his usual haunts in the city but might as well have been on the other side of the moon. That was one of the observations strangers to the city made: how poverty and wealth sat cheek by jowl.

He was with a new girlfriend, Felice Jenkins. Felice had gone to Hutchesons', a private school in the city, and with her long neck, designer clothes and hugely positive life expectations, she was like a different species from the women he normally dated. Why she was spending time with him was not too much of a mystery. He knew she fancied a wee bit of rough from time to time. Being proximal to some danger. And he did have a reputation: designer drugs and being handy with his fists.

The truth was that reputation was more to do with Danny. Luke himself tried to keep his distance from all of that stuff. Unless it got him an exciting and exotic girlfriend, in which case he was more than happy to ham it up.

Felice crossed her legs and kicked slightly, allowing her sandal to slap against her heel. It was such a mindless gesture, but it gave Luke a tingle in all the right places. Carefree and confident was such an attractive combination in women, he felt.

'My treat,' Felice said. 'What do you fancy?'

Luke examined the list of hot drinks chalked onto a board, some of which he didn't entirely recognise, and said, 'Why don't they just do black coffee, and coffee with milk rather than all this fake Italian nonsense?'

'Philistine,' Felice grinned, and reached for his hand. She gave it a squeeze, allowed the touch to linger, and then tucked the straight and gleaming strand of hair on the right side of her head behind a perfect little ear.

Her eyes looked deep into his, and he felt his breath quicken at the thought of what they were going to be doing back at her flat.

Of course he knew what all the coffees were. He enjoyed them, but he had a part to play.

'That pastry I had the last time I was here. That was good. I could fair go one of them.'

'What, a croissant?'

'Aye. It had some chocolate spread or something inside it. Thought I'd died and gone to taste heaven. It was magic.'

She looked at him as if thinking, *Poor thing, first time with a croissant?*

'I'll take you to Paris one day,' she said. 'Eat a croissant there, and you'll really know what taste heaven is.'

He leaned forward in his chair and whispered to her where exactly on her body he thought heaven might be.

She flushed, slowly licked at her lips and leaned back. 'White coffee it is then,' she laughed.

Luke became aware of movement behind her. A man was at the doorway. Danny. He took a puff from a cigarette, and then, with the thin stick poking from between his knuckles, he beckoned Luke towards him.

Luke felt himself bristle. He sent a silent 'piss off' to his friend. Danny cocked an eyebrow, stepped inside the door, leaned against the glass wall and stared at Felice. Giving her the once-over. He raised his eyebrows approvingly. Mouthed the word 'nice' and then made a grotesque licking motion.

Luke made sure Felice's eyes were elsewhere before he sent Danny a warning glare. But Danny was nonplussed. His relaxed stance told Luke he was going nowhere.

'What is it?' Felice asked.

'Oh, nothing,' Luke replied. Then thought it might be fairer to give her a warning. 'One of my arsehole pals is about to crash our date.'

Sure enough, looking as if he owned the place, Danny swaggered over to their table and stood over them. He was wearing his usual uniform of black jeans, black leather jacket and black T-shirt. He hadn't shaved for a few days, and his chin-length hair was slicked back. There was an energy and force about him that few could deny being affected by. And Luke could see that Felice was instantly uncomfortable with his presence, could sense the threat from him. Without a word, he stood there, stared down at Felice's cleavage and then examined Luke with a smile. A smile that asked, *Is this the hill you want to die on?*

'A word?' Danny said. Without waiting for a response, he turned and walked out of the café.

Standing up, Luke wondered how the hell Danny had found him. 'Sorry, Felice. This will just take a second.'

'Who is that arsehole?' she demanded, crossing her arms, and Luke realised that not only had he lost any chance of a sweaty afternoon in her bed, but he'd also lost her respect.

Outside on the street Luke faced up to Danny.

'What the fuck, man?'

Luke stepped in close so that they were almost chin to chin. Danny's raised eyebrow was an eloquent dismissal of any and all of Luke's concerns. It let him know that, wherever he was, Danny would find him, and pull him back down to his level.

'Remember the Delaney twins?'

'Of course I fucking remember the Delaney twins.' Luke didn't think he would ever forget those girls. They were the year below them at school. The hot girls that everybody fancied. Danny bet the guys he would not only shag them both but he'd get them hooked on heroin. They all thought he was full of shit. They hadn't yet learned how dangerous he could be.

Luke shivered involuntarily.

Danny caught it. 'Aye. You know what I'm capable of.' His eyes searched Luke's. 'And *I* know what *you're* capable of.'

'What's that supposed to mean?' Instantly, Luke went to that moment he was standing over a dead Fraser Smith.

'I see you, *buddy*,' Danny said, his eyes full of knowledge and threat.

Chapter 39

Jamie looked at the blip on the screen of his phone and recognised the spot where Jenna had parked her car.

Amanda had insisted he plant the tiny devices on both Jenna and Luke's cars, saying you never knew when they might come in handy. He'd resisted initially, but as usual his sister persisted until he caved in.

'You know we'll get there in the end,' she'd said, hands on hips. 'So why not just give in at the start and save us both some time.'

'What? Like you're the first female pope? Infallible. Has to be obeyed?'

Her answering smirk infuriated him, setting off a full-blown row in which they both said things that were difficult to retreat from. Standing toe to toe in the hallway of their house, screaming at each other, flecks of her spit landing on his face.

She slapped him.

He slapped her back, with just as much force.

She held her hand to her face, eyes wide with disbelief. 'You hit me,' she said.

'This isn't a movie, sis. A slap in this world earns one right back. Next time I might not be so lenient.'

Her eyes sparked, and he could see a battle going on there. She wanted to hit him again, but trusted his threat. She turned and ran to her bedroom, slamming the door behind her. He followed. When he opened the door she was lying on her side, away from him. Anger spent, he edged over the threshold.

'Okay?'

She mumbled something. Then sat up, facing him, her expression one of resolution.

'I hate always being the bad one here, Jamie. It's on both of us to set this right, but I feel I'm losing you to this ... this arsehole.'

'Nonsense. You're not losing me to anyone.'

'Aren't I?' She leaned forward, demanding. 'I'm not an idiot, Jamie, I can see you're not into this with the same enthusiasm. You didn't even plant the drugs as we agreed. Have you forgotten what he did?'

'No,' he replied instantly.

'Sure?'

'Yes. It's just...'

'What?'

'I think he's changed.'

'Black and white, Jamie. He messed up our lives. If it wasn't for him I wouldn't have had to whore myself out to that old man. And you wouldn't have had to go through what you did with that couple. We're in this together, Jamie. I can't do this on my own.' She shook her head wildly. 'I can't stand this.' She moved her hands up and down in front of herself. 'What he made of me.' Her face was a looking glass of expression. Never had he seen her so raw, so vulnerable. 'I loathe what I've become.' Her eyes shone. 'It was someone's fault, and they have to pay.'

Jamie didn't know where to look. He couldn't deal with the intensity, the honesty, of her pain.

'C'mere,' she said, her voice soft. She patted the bed at her side. 'C'mon, have a seat.'

He approached and sat on the edge of her bed. She inched forward so that the front of her body lined the back of his. She pulled him closer, leaned her head against his shoulder and rested there for a moment. Then she turned to face him. 'Show me you're a man, Jamie. That you're the man of this family.'

He couldn't say anything, but he felt that strong link between them. Blood calling to blood. A connection so deep that it felt to him like it reached back through a thick, swirling fog to the beginning of time. And the little boy inside him, so starved of affection, relished the touch.

And now, here he was, fingers and toes numb with the cold, standing behind a leafless tree only a few feet from two people, listening attentively while they discovered a dark secret.

Chapter 40

Next day, her mind full of Nathan's chatter and her mother's delight, Jenna found herself going on a detour on the way home from the supermarket.

There was a tarmac'd semi-circular parking area before a knee-high sandstone wall topped with head-high iron railings. An opening just wide enough for a hearse to pass through led to a two-storey Victorian gatehouse, and beyond that rows and rows of graves.

It had been such a long time since she'd visited this place. What had brought her here? she wondered. Her mother's oblique mention of an old boyfriend who Luke reminded her of, and her ham-fisted attempts at remembering his name?

Perhaps.

And perhaps now that she'd found happiness with someone she could trust, someone who saw her for who she was, she was finally able to move on and let go of the guilt that crowded her mind whenever thoughts of him arrived.

Or was it the time of year? It had been just before Christmas when she found out he'd died. And feeling that she couldn't not, she had visited his grave. Despite everything, despite the way he had been with her, cossetting, closeting, demanding her whole attention, they'd had a deep connection, and she regretted that she hadn't been able to make it work.

Or was she kidding herself? Adding a patina of glamour to a relationship that had a bright start, but ultimately never really went anywhere, and to a man who was deeply flawed.

Out of the car, leaning into the chill, she walked through the gates. Chin deep in her scarf, she felt the air spark against her exposed skin and heard her shoes crunching on the frost-furred pebbles. Her hands were fisted so tight inside her gloves she felt the strain all the way into the cords of her neck.

Memory led her faultlessly to his stone. A modest, black, upright slab of marble. The gilded name had lost none of its lustre, but the stone itself was dulled by time and Glasgow's weather, reminding her that she probably was romanticising the man, while the truth was much less bright.

She stood on the path in front of it, reluctant to move closer, noting that most of the other gravestones around were wreathed in flowers, while this one was bare. The small granite bowl at the side looked like it hadn't held a bloom since his body was interred. And this, more than anything else, set off the tears. A silent slide of emotion down her cheek that she wiped at with the side of her glove.

Stamping her feet, willing heat into her thighs, she looked around, again questioning why she'd made the journey. There was nothing here for her. Never had been, really.

Behind her, she noticed, was an older section of the graveyard. Here, the stones were much grander – the loss of life observed in a very public, large-scale way. Here, see how big our grief is. Be impressed by how much we spent on lifeless remains.

To her right was a roofless structure, wide enough to fit three coffins. Marble walls rose to head height, on top of which sat a series of pillars, all pushing the memorial into the tree canopy. Above a metal gate stretched a lintel of marble, on which had been carved a winged creature, reminiscent of another culture.

Directly behind her an angel stood serenely on a plinth. Head bowed, sightless eyes downcast, wings tall and proud, and one hand slightly raised, as if pausing while offering a blessing.

Jenna stood there for a long moment, captured by the statue's grace, feeling a momentary stillness that had evaded her most of her life settle in her mind. Another tear sparked in the corner of her eye. She tilted her neck to examine the sky, saw that it was a uniform, earnest grey. Then she realised, no, it was not a tear, but a first fall of snow.

Face turned upward, she closed her eyes and felt the benediction of the skies spark wet and cold on her forehead, her right cheek, her left eyelid. The wind lifted, sighed in her ear, and she fancied it spoke to her, told her that old life was long gone. That it was time to enjoy and embrace the new.

Silly woman; she laughed at the notion, but savoured the sentiment.

A shift in the air, scuff of shoe underfoot, and she became aware of another's presence. She turned when she heard a familiar voice.

'Jenna? What are you doing here?'

She stepped back in surprise. Momentarily unable to speak, she pointed to the small, black stone. And there, with the snow falling around them like ash, reducing the world to a hush and a single, loud heartbeat, she heard Luke ask...

No, demand...

'How the hell did you know Danny Morrison?'

Chapter 41

There was something about this time of year – past mistakes a weight on the mind before the promise of a new year offered the shine of a clean slate – that always made Luke think of an old associate. That thought, and its attendant guilt, would lead to an almost automatic trudge to a certain graveside.

So here he was.

And so was Jenna – and what a shock to his heart it was to see her.

Luke stared at her, struggling to deal with the clamour in his head and heart. Jenna had been Danny's lover? Even in death the man was able to ruin his life.

Jenna had been Danny's girlfriend?

How anyone could willingly enter into a relationship with that man was beyond him. And what did this say about the woman he was in love with? He turned slightly, enough to see that her arms were crossed and she was now staring at her feet, as if unable to comprehend what *she* had just learned.

'What the hell? Danny was the guy you went to prison for killing in the car?' she asked as she took a step away from him. 'You were friends? But how did we never meet? He never mentioned you, not once in all the time…' A light came on in her eyes. 'I was a junior reporter at the time. When the case went to…' She stared at him. 'The guy changed his plea to guilty so the case didn't go to trial, but I'm certain his name wasn't Luke Forrest. It was Duncan something.' She stared off into space as if rifling through some mental files.

'Robertson,' Luke replied.

Her mouth fell open in shock. 'Oh my God,' she said. 'Who changes their name?'

'Somebody who wants to rebuild—'

'He never mentioned you,' she repeated, talking over him.

'When I got the details from the court official that day the name of the...' her voice came out in a whisper '...accused, was a complete unknown to me, and the gossip that day was that they ... you ... were the best of friends.' Her eyes were an essay in confusion. 'How can someone you love not know who your oldest friends are?' she asked Luke as she shook her head slowly.

Someone you love. The words hit Luke with the power of a sledgehammer.

He took a breath, felt the chill air fill his lungs and stamped his feet against the cold.

Luke needed to know, desperately, how Jenna came to be with Danny and if she was holding on to any feelings for him, but he could tell from the clamp of her jaw that she wasn't going to speak anytime soon. It was down to him to get the conversation going. And he didn't know if he wanted to. Now that he knew she'd been with Danny.

It was long minutes later that they spoke, and they did it at the same time.

'How—?'

'What—?'

'You go first,' Jenna said quietly, all but shrinking into her coat, as if she really didn't want to hear what was about to come from Luke's mouth. As if she couldn't wait to get away from him. As if she was judging him for his part in Danny's death.

'It all began as a laugh, a way of getting extra money.' Luke spoke looking straight ahead. 'We were young and daft. Or so I thought. When I think back to what Danny was like ... There was always a calculation in what he did. Anyway. It was a chance to buy some good clothes, buy lots of drink and impress the girls, aye? Dealing a wee bit of hash here, some contraband fags there. The odd bit of stolen goods.' Luke saw Danny in his mind's eye, the glow in his expression as another deal went down and he made another load of cash. 'I'm not proud of who I was back then. Despite everything with my mum, the lies she told about Dad, I had a good upbringing. I was the only one of my friends where there was no drink or drugs in the house, and Mum had proper work. A decent job for the council, so we were comparatively well off.'

'Why did you go off the rails, then?

Luke gazed into the distance. 'I was so fucking angry with Mum, lying about Dad. If you grow up thinking one of your parents has no interest in you it's like a wrecking ball to your growing psyche. Those circumstances provided fertile ground for the influence of a friend like Danny.' As Luke spoke he recognised that the training in psychology and counselling he had undertaken in prison was bleeding into his speech, making the explanation of his life sound like an oral essay. He needed to use more everyday language here.

'That just doesn't sound like the man I knew,' Jenna said.

'You know, I'm fed up thinking about him. Fed up having him in my head.' Luke popped the heel of his right hand against his forehead. 'He's had way too much time in here.' He caught himself and dropped his hand. Then said, making an effort at a more conciliatory tone, 'I think we knew very different men. I got the worst of him, and it sounds like you got the best.'

Jenna didn't reply for a moment. She simply looked into his eyes as if assessing him and his words. 'I don't understand how our paths didn't cross. He didn't mention you while we were together. Not once. Then the week after we split up he's in a car with you, his oldest friend, apparently, and dies in a crash.' She shrugged and held both hands out in a *what the hell* gesture.

Again, Luke considered carefully what he should say. Which truth he needed to detail.

'I decided to leave Glasgow. Stayed away for a couple of years. Without a word to anyone, I went up to Aberdeen to stay with my dad. Got a job on the rigs, changed my phone, completely cut myself off from my old life. Even my mum didn't have my contact details.'

'What? That's a bit extreme.'

'I knew Danny would go and see her. Turn on the charm. And next thing he'd be knocking on my door, demanding I come back to Glasgow. I stayed in touch with Mum, of course I did. I phoned every time I could, and I sent her cash to come up and visit me. It was a bit of a risk, knowing that Danny could easily follow her. But, you know, I couldn't cut off contact with her altogether.' Luke felt a brief smile form on his face as he thought about those times. 'I was earning plenty, to be fair, so I put Mum up in a different posh hotel each visit. She loved Skibo Castle.' He paused. 'It was so nice to be able to spoil her. In spite of what happened when I was a boy, I knew she did her very best for me.'

'But why stay away from Danny?' Jenna asked.

'He was toxic,' Luke replied instantly. 'He may have been able to hide it with you, but I knew if I stayed, one of us would end up dead.'

'Which is what happened as soon as you came back,' Jenna said. She looked as if she was making a mental calculation. 'Less than a week after I left him, you guys were in that crash.' She paused. 'Why did you come back?'

'Mum's funeral,' Luke replied. 'Even that was a worry,' he re-called. 'Cos I knew Danny would seek me out, but what kind of son would I have been if I stayed away for that?'

'Did you know he was seeing someone while you were away?'

'Joe might have mentioned it on one of the few times we spoke, but I didn't pay much attention. Danny was dead to me. I had no interest in him whatsoever.'

'Whenever he was drunk he would talk about you. Kinda. Without naming you,' she said, as if the memory had just popped into her head.

'What did he say?'

'Just about the people who'd abandoned him. Good friends who'd walked out, after all the time and effort he'd invested in their friendship.'

Luke fell to silence; he'd run out of words for the moment. He was unsure how to convince Jenna who the real Danny was, and watched as she burrowed her chin into the collar of her coat.

'I'm struggling,' she admitted. 'The man you've just described in no way matches the one in my head.' She crossed her arms, tucking her hands under them. 'He could be so kind. Vulnerable.'

'Was he really?' he challenged. 'Or did you see what you wanted to see?'

'I'm not an idiot, Luke,' she snapped.

'I didn't say you were. When we fall in love with someone we're blind to who they really are. Because, if we've fallen in love with a bad human being, what does that say about us?'

'You mean, what does that say about me?' Her eyes were laden with regret – and anger.

'Listen, I'm not one to criticise when it comes to Danny. I let that man control me for years.'

'Why? It's not like you were in love with him or anything. Or were you?'

Luke snorted a dismissal of her question.

'So, what, then? If he was such a horrible human being why did you hang around? What hold did he have over you?'

One punch.

All it took was one punch and one of his friends died.

Luke studied Jenna's expression. She looked like she couldn't wait to get away from him. She knew that he was responsible for her ex's death. And now the future of their relationship was at stake. Could she take the knowledge that he was responsible for another?

Chapter 42

Jenna was at a loss as to what to do next. The man she was falling in love with had good as killed the only other man she'd really loved.

He'd changed his name. Had he changed as a person?

She heard her mother in her ear:

Wasters. You were only ever interested in wasters.

Maybe Luke used to be that guy, but he wasn't now. Unless he was putting on an Oscar-worthy performance.

With a start, she remembered her notes. She'd started to do a little digging into the events of the night Danny died, but it had been too painful. Then her father died, throwing all such thoughts from her head. She'd moved back into her parents' house by then. Might her notebook still be here?

Don't go there, she told herself. How could she possibly benefit from unearthing it all? Luke, or Duncan, or whatever his name was, had done his time. Danny was dead and wasn't coming back.

What was she to do next? Luke had quickly become an essential part of her life, but now she couldn't bear the thought of being with him. And he'd appeared just as confused. He looked like he couldn't wait to get away from her at the cemetery.

But why? He was the one in the wrong, surely? All she did was fall in love with the wrong man.

Twice.

'Put the heating on,' her mother shouted from her bedroom.

'It's on,' she shouted back.

'Put the fugging heating on,' Sally shouted again.

'It's on, Mother,' Jenna shot back, and then felt guilty about getting angry.

Her phone pinged an alert.

Hazel, looking to chat. She hadn't heard from her for a while. Maybe talking to Hazel was just what she needed – an unbiased ear.

First, she'd sort out the heating. She propped herself up on her bed and looked at her phone. It was 7:50am. The heating wasn't due to come on until 8:00.

'That's it on, Mum,' she shouted through the wall. A white lie. What harm could it do?

'Did I not tell you never to lie,' her mother shouted back.

'Takes a while to heat up, for God's sake.'

'I'm freezing.'

Jenna shot up out of bed, picked her dressing gown off the chair at the side of her bed and quickly put it on against the chill. Her mother wasn't wrong, it was freezing. In her furry slippers she stamped through to her mother's room, allowing her irritation to get the better of her.

'Jesus, Mum. The heating'll be on soon...' But as she entered her mother's room, she saw that the quilt had mostly fallen off her, and, unable to claw it back up, she was lying there only in her thin nightdress.

'Oh, Mum. Why didn't you say?' she scolded.

'I did,' her mother replied, shooting her looks of fury. 'Hundreds times. Weren't listening. Always on that phone. Never bothered about your mother. I worked my fingers to the bone for you, girl. And what thanks do I get?'

Jenna let the words wash over her, guilt that she hadn't responded more quickly to her mother's request for help dampening down any response she might have had.

'Yes, Mum. Yes, Mum,' was all she said as she fixed the sheets and the quilt, being sure to tuck them in so that they wouldn't fall off again before the heat came on. 'When do you want your breakfast?'

'Nine o'clock,' Sally replied in her *are you an idiot?* voice. 'Like I have it every day, and don't make my porridge all milky like that last time. Oats, water and salt, that's all it takes. Your granny will be birling in her grave looking at that nonsense you gave me the other day.'

That nonsense was a porridge Jenna made for her weeks ago. Every day since, she'd received the same warning.

It was with relief at the thought of speaking to another grown-up that she answered the message from Hazel.

Chapter 43

Amanda gave a little cheer when Jenna answered her message. She'd built this online persona years ago, waiting for just the right time to bring her into action. It hadn't been too difficult to research Jenna's past, and when she'd found out she'd been at university and which course she'd been on, it had been easy to set up a fake profile. How many people remember everybody they met at university?

And so Hazel was born.

—*Lovely to hear from you, Hazel. How's you and the family?*

—*Och you know. Just getting on with things like everybody else.*

Amanda paused to look at her notes, she'd scripted a full biography for Hazel so she could be better at the kind of chat she might come up with. She'd designed the woman to be completely unthreatening; Hazel was all about emojis, loving and pampering yourself – and kittens. Amanda had also furnished her page with the pictures of a fake husband and children, picked up from websites with stock images.

—*Anna's a wee madam. But she's 13. You know what we were like at that age.*

Amanda rolled her eyes as she typed. Jesus, she would hate this woman in real life.

—*But the kids are great, parents are still alive and kicking, and that husband of mine is still giving me grief. You know how men are.*

Amanda tacked that last sentence on, hoping that Jenna might respond and open up on that aspect of her life.

—*Can't remember what I told you last time we spoke*, Jenna responded. *Can't be bothered scrolling back up the chat. But I've moved back in with Mum. Had this great carer, but she dumped us. She was the sixth one we'd had in as many months. None of them could cope with Mum. A couple only lasted a matter of days, meaning each time I had to run out of work to see to her. And I can't take the hassle of trying to find another one and having to leave work time and time again. Maybe I'll try again after Xmas. There was a pause. God, soz. I just splurged all of that out on you.*

—*What I'm here for, lovely,* Amanda replied. *I know we don't chat too often, but I love it when we do. You're one of the few people I can be honest with.*

—*Everything okay, hun?*

—*Just man trouble.*

Before she continued, Amanda had a quick check of her notes to remind herself what Hazel's husband was called. Geoff. Time to sow some marital discord.

—*Geoff was away in Amsterdam with the boys on a stag weekend. He was best man to Craig Dunlop. Remember him? Went bald really young. Bandy legs. Was always out running? Anyway, at the actual wedding I was in the ladies and overheard two women saying Geoff and Dave paid for a blowjob in a strip club. I'm devastated. Haven't confronted him yet. Don't know what to do. And typical, mindless Geoff has no clue that I'm pissed off at him.*

—*Shit. That's awful. Want to do this old-fashioned, and actually talk in person?*

Amanda waited a few moments before replying, even going so far as acting out a pantomime that she was crying and wiping away some tears.

—*Thanks, hun, but I'm a mess right now. This is SO much easier. I can cry and you don't have to see the snot and runny mascara.*

—*Well, anytime you need to meet up, just give me, like, three weeks' notice – to find a carer and I'll be there.*

A sense of humour, thought Amanda. You're going to need that. Then she carried on.

—*Please tell me something nice to cheer me up. Tell me about your new hunky man. That he's lovely and kind and honest and trust-worthy. And a good shag. All that interesting stuff.*

There was a long minute before Jenna replied.

—*Oh God. Things were going so well, but I've just found out something awful, and like you I don't know what to do next. I mean, I like him. Really like him, but he went to prison for a REALLY bad thing. I thought I was done with the bad boys.*

Amanda knew the bad-boy tag was about Danny and wondered if she could divert the conversation a little and get Jenna to talk about her time with her older brother again. She knew every time she did this she was at risk of exposing herself. But she couldn't help it. Jenna was one of the only people she knew who'd known her big brother, and she loved hearing about him.

—*OMG. What did he do?*

—*Killed someone. It was an accident really. Driving while he was off his head on something. Killed his passenger. Only just found out the passenger was an ex of mine. A guy called Danny.*

—*OMG.* As Amanda typed those three letters her heart gave a little flip. Poor Danny. *Maybe talking about Danny will help you put your feelings about Luke into perspective?*

There was a long silence before Jenna replied. And as Amanda waited she realised her mistake. She's used Luke's name and Jenna hadn't mentioned it yet.

Damn. How could she cover that up?

—*Did I tell you his name?* Jenna replied. *Do you know him?*

Shit. Think, Amanda. Think.

—*Caught. Oops. You know how us girls are. Gossips are us, eh? I actually popped into the bookshop to order the latest Margaret Atwood. You weren't in, and that woman who owns the place was happy to fill me in on your latest. All about this hunky guy you'd met in the actual shop, like something out of a movie. How cute is that??!!*

Jenna didn't reply straight away, so Amanda rambled on.

—*AND, feeling sorry for myself about that hubby of mine, I was desperate to hear some good news, and thought I'd get in touch. Sounds like my timing is way off. SO sorry.*

Jenna then opened up, telling Amanda things that she knew already, but she posted sad-face emojiis in all the right places.

—*Thing is,* Jenna continued. *I don't know how I feel about him*

*now. He's responsible for the death of a man I loved. Who I still –
and it surprises me – have feelings for. Even though he's long dead.
How messed up is that?*

*—Tell me more about … Danny, wasn't it? He sounds like such a
cool guy.*

*—We've talked about him loads, eh? He was so sad, you know?
Broken. Had this vulnerability that all those so-called bad boys try to
hide, but with him it was obvious. He could be tender and kind. He
was so nice, I couldn't, wouldn't, believe all the bad stuff people told me
about him. I was sure they were all lying. Jealous of what we had.*

—What do you know about how he died?

*—Car accident. God, I don't even like typing this. Luke was
driving. They were both out of their skulls on a bunch of different
chemicals. Anyway, the car went off the road, killing Danny. Luke
was charged, found guilty and did seven, or might have been eight
years.*

—Not much for killing someone, is it? Amanda typed.

*—No. It's not. And to complicate matters I was a junior reporter
on the local newspaper, and I was in court the day he was due to go
on trial.*

—OMG. That must have been tough for you.

*—He changed his plea to guilty so I avoided the whole trial thing.
Not sure I could have coped with that. Then, when the sentencing
happened, I was off work helping Mum sort stuff out after Dad died.
And this was all around the time I lost the baby.*

*—Wow. What a tough time for you. It's a wonder you're still
standing. And how are you feeling about this new guy now that you
know this?*

*—Changes everything. I think. God, I don't know where my head
is. Before Dad died I was going to go full Lois Lane. I've got a notebook somewhere full of stuff, but then with Dad, you know? And
Mum was a mess.*

*—What do you mean about going Lois Lane. Did you do a little
bit of digging?* Amanda pressed.

—Started to. But it was too painful. Then, with Dad dying, that knocked the stuffing out of me. I'm sure I still have that notebook somewhere in the house.

Amanda felt her face tingle. There was something important here. Something she could use. She knew it. Having Jenna and Luke at loggerheads over this would be just wonderful.

—You should check it out.

This was so frustrating. Amanda wanted nothing more than to scream at the woman to go find the notes now and tell her exactly what was in them. But she had to do this the right way. She'd waited so long to put all of this into play, there was no sense in rushing it now.

—It's all so patchy in my mind, Jenna replied. *Like the memories are someone else's, you know? I'd almost forgotten how upset I was when I heard Danny was dead. How can you forget something like that?*

—The brain does strange things to us, eh? Amanda typed, thinking, yeah you're a weirdo. How could you forget? It's stayed with me every day of my life.

There was a pause of a few minutes before the little message box in her screen filled with letters.

—There was something about the case I thought was strange. A witness. Can't remember the details, but I remember thinking if the court heard this guy the sentence might have been longer. Shit. Wish I could remember.

Go get the notes now, Amanda wanted to say. She wanted to reach into the screen, pull Jenna through and give her a good slap. God, this woman was so wet. How could she not remember this stuff?

—But I'm so conflicted. Luke's done his time. And what good would it do Danny now to rake through all of this? But still. He deserves better, you know? I was crazy about the guy and it still hurts to think of him going like that.

Another pause.

—God, I can barely see the screen to type for tears. I thought this grief was long in the past.

Amanda softened a little. Gratified to read of Jenna's upset.

No. She steeled herself. She couldn't afford to think like that. This woman dumped him. And worse. And everyone knows what happened next. Her poor brother, broken and bloody at the side of a country road, and her family ripped apart.

And for that, somebody had to pay.

Chapter 44

As agreed, Luke picked Jamie up outside the Oxfam on Byres Road.

'Ready to have some fun?' he asked Jamie as he climbed into the car, with a glance over to the back seat and Nathan.

As if he twigged that this comment was really for the little boy's benefit, Jamie replied, 'I can't wait to go on the dodgems and the slides, and I'm going to eat every toffee apple in the place.'

'Yes, Daddy, can I have a toffee apple,' Nathan piped up.

'I think the magic word is please.'

'Pleeeeeeeese,' Nathan replied, and Luke could see in the mirror that he'd accompanied the word with the widest, toothiest smile he could muster.

'I'm sure we can manage that,' Luke replied as he shot a 'well-played' smile at Jamie. They only had a short drive to the exhibition centre, where the funfair was sited, but as usual this part of the city was heavy with traffic. After a stop-start twenty-five minutes they eventually turned into the car park, clambered out, and an overly-excited child pulled Luke by the hand to the main door.

Inside, they stopped as if hitting a wall, assailed by the lights and the happy commotion. Mechanical tunes, Christmas songs, and children's screams of excitement blended into an ill-tuned or-chestra of fun. Lights blared, giant, rose-cheeked Santas grinned from every surface that wasn't given up to angels, elves and tinsel. Luke hadn't been here for years and had forgotten just how frantic this place could be. People milled around – families, couples – and every child looked like their head was about to explode with the endless possibilities. Chief of which was Permission Granted: make as much noise as you can.

It was a massive space, you could fit dozens of football pitches under the giant roof, and every inch of it was crammed with something that would delight a child and dizzy their parent. It would be so easy to lose a kid in here, Luke thought, as he gripped Nathan's hand a bit tighter. He shook that notion from his head and looked down at a little boy, who was jumping up and down on the spot.

'Where do you want to go first?' Luke asked.

'Dodgems,' shouted Nathan.

'I'm not sure where they are, wee man,' Luke replied, moving his head down closer to the boy's. 'Let's start walking, and if you see anything you fancy before we get there, let me know, eh?' He turned to Jamie, who had the same startled look on his face as Nathan. 'Any requests, Jamie?' he asked, half shouting above the noise.

Jamie tore his eyes away from the tumult around him. 'Just … wherever, mate. Not bothered.' He grinned. 'It's up to Nathan. It's his day.'

*

Holding Nathan's other hand, it felt to Jamie like the little boy's excitement had travelled up his short arm to his own, and was now sparking off in his brain. He'd never experienced anything like this. No one, not even his much vaunted big brother, had thought to bring him here.

How could this be an annual event in his home city, and he get to this age and never experience it?

Nathan pulled him to a toffee apple stand, looked from him to Luke, and then back to Jamie, as if he was recruiting him as an ally.

'Jamie wants a toffee apple,' he said.

'Cute,' replied Luke with a massive smile. Then in a whisper to Jamie, 'This boy's going to grow up to be a politician.'

Jamie read Luke's pride and ached for the child he had once been. The small boy who rarely, if ever, received such attention.

Then he heard Amanda's voice in his mind. Saw her at the door to their house as she waved him away. 'This is your chance, Jamie. Fuck him up. Fuck him up bad.'

He shook her voice out of his head. Not today, Amanda. Let the boy have today. It was more than he ever had.

'What?' Nathan looked up at him, his cheeks sticky with toffee, and the trust in his eyes was almost enough to break Jamie's convictions.

'Let's go and get you on something fun, eh?' Jamie replied, wondering if he'd actually said something aloud.

'You alright, buddy?' Luke asked him.

'Sure. Sure.' He forced a grin. 'All of this...' He looked around. 'Kinda takes you aback, aye?'

'Sure does,' Luke replied. Then he looked away. 'There,' he pointed. 'Want to go on the slide, Nathan?'

The slide was shaped like a lighthouse, and from where Jamie was standing he could see children entering the door in the middle. They climbed up inside, and then slid down a ramp that followed the curve of the wall, all the way down from the light at the top to the floor, where one child had just spilled out on to a thick carpet, giggling and brushing off his mother's concern.

'Yay,' Nathan cheered, pulled his hand from Jamie and ran to the entrance. There, a man in a light-blue baseball cap put a hand in front of Nathan to stop his progress, looking up to see if there was an adult with him.

Jamie caught his eye and nodded. And the man let Nathan past.

'The wee fella's having a blast,' he said to Luke.

'Sure is,' Luke replied, his face shining as if it was he himself who was about to go on the ride.

Once the boy was bored with that slide, they found another, and another. Then they took a break from sliding and jumping around, and found somewhere they could throw things. Darts on a certain card would win something. The choices looked like cheap rubbish, but rubbish that kids adored.

Three darts on the same card, and Jamie won a prize. He chose a giant teddy bear and handed it to Nathan, who looked fit to burst when he took it from him.

'Daddy, this is the best day ever,' he said.

'Yeah,' Luke said. 'Absolutely.' Then he smiled his thanks to Jamie. 'How about we take it down a notch? There's a café over there. Fancy a coffee, Jamie? My treat, seeing as you're winning all the prizes for us?'

Jamie laughed. 'I could fair go a hot drink. Is the wee man allowed a cola?'

Luke rolled his eyes in a mock fashion. 'Aye, okay. It's not as if he's not already climbing the walls.'

Jamie was beginning to feel dizzy and strangely on edge, too aware of the pulse point in his temples, so he welcomed the break in the action. A chance for some relative quiet. His ambivalence about the task Amanda had set him almost had his head bursting. Nathan was having such a good time, he was all but levitating with joy. How could you not respond to that? And the little boy's life had been pretty difficult so far; he was only a couple of years younger than Jamie was when tragedy struck his family, so he knew how it felt. He'd been stuck in a kind of numb limbo for a long time. To witness the fortitude of this kid was like a life lesson. He wondered how much of that was down to having a stable, loving home –Luke clearly adored the ground he walked on. The boy wasn't even his son, and he'd set about fathering the child as if his life depended on it.

Maybe it did?

With a flash of insight Jamie realised this was Luke's way to make amends – to reconcile himself with his sins.

But did he care? Should he? Amanda didn't. Old Testament-style retribution was her focus. She couldn't see past Luke's history and simply wanted him to suffer.

That was how Jamie felt too. Or it had been. His resolve had been weakened a little by this time he was spending with Luke and the boy. Their affection for each other was like a drill working through the defences he'd set up all those years ago. Bit by bit, the brick and the lye was being chipped away. But only slowly.

Pain strobed just above his left eye. Jamie pressed a thumb into the spot as if the pressure might alleviate the stabbing sensation, and wondered how he could comply with his sister's wishes before the din, the lights, the heart-stopping clamour, and the two warring sides of his nature fractured his mind into a million tiny pieces.

*

They grabbed a table and chairs in a little area off the beaten track, in front of a catering caravan. A woman with the broadest smile and a dizzying burst of hair, pulled back from her forehead with a tie-dyed piece of cloth, brought them their drinks and a hot dog for Nathan.

'Having a nice time, guys?' she asked as she handed Nathan his cola.

'The best,' he beamed.

'Merry Christmas when it comes, wee darling,' she said, patted him on the head and then went back to her station inside the van.

'You'd think all this Christmas cheer would get to her eventually,' Jamie said, nodding in the woman's direction.

'You'd think,' Luke agreed. A song he recognised started playing from the van's speakers. A song that everyone would know. 'But maybe she's one of those who wishes it was Christmas every day.' He sang the last few words in tune with the song.

Jamie groaned. 'Got any corn to go with that?'

Luke laughed.

'Hey,' Jamie said, leaning closer. 'I thought Jenna was going to be with us today.'

Luke shifted in his seat a little, wondering how to respond.

Jamie held a hand up. 'Sorry I asked. Life's complicated, eh?'

'S'okay,' Luke replied, and allowed a little of the sadness of missing Jenna cloud his eyes. 'I'm hoping we get through this, you know?'

'Help to talk about it?'

Luke reached across and patted Jamie's shoulder. 'Thanks, mate. Appreciate it. I just need to process it myself first, you know?' He sat back in his chair. Attention fully on Jamie, aware that his smile was strained and his eyes appeared to be too large. 'You've never been to anything quite like this, have you?'

Jamie shook his head. 'Truth? No. But there's a wee boy in here' – he pointed at his head – 'who's glad it happened at last.'

Studying the gleam in Jamie's eyes, Luke could see that the man was working at being open and honest, trying to keep his defences down. Then, as if aware of how deep Luke's scrutiny had been, the shutters slammed back up.

Luke watched as Jamie slowly stroked the sides of his legs. He worried he didn't have the tools to give Jamie the help he really needed. Something told him there was way more to the psychological workings of this young man than he first realised.

*

Jamie could tell that Nathan was more than ready to get going again. His feet were drumming his need to move into the carpet beneath them. The sweet drink and the hot dog had clearly replenished his energy. His little head was on a swivel as he looked around them as if working out where to go next.

'There,' he pointed.

Jamie and Luke followed the direction of his finger.

'Dodgems,' they all exclaimed at the same time.

After a short wait in the queue, Luke and Nathan jumped in one car, and Jamie in another. They chased each other around the circle, occasionally hitting other cars and bumping into each other. The look of excitement and delight on Nathan's face didn't ease up the entire time they were on the ride. When their time came to an end, Jamie could hear him chanting, even above the noise of the music:

'Again. Again. Again.'

Jamie joined them as Luke was explaining to the boy that they would have to go back to the end of the queue and wait for another turn.

'Okay,' Nathan said. 'Let's go.' And started pulling Luke with him.

This time their wait was longer. Luke caught Jamie's eye, just as Jamie felt his phone vibrate an alert in his pocket.

'That coffee's gone right through me,' Luke said. 'You mind looking after the wee fella while I go find a loo?'

'Sure,' Jamie said, taking Nathan's hand. 'We're going to have so much fun,' he said to the boy. 'Bet we can go around three times before your dad gets back.'

'Yay,' Nathan sang in reply.

Luke walked away, smiling, and Jamie checked his phone. A text had arrived from his sister.

Well?

Jamie felt the little boy's hand grip his, shook his head as if trying to clear it and released himself from Nathan. 'Just need to answer my phone, mate,' he said to the boy.

Both hands free now, he tamped down his reservations and thumbed out a reply.

Don't worry, sis. Mr Forrest's day is about to go horribly wrong.

Chapter 45

Jenna's knees were sore, her neck was aching with the crouch she'd forced herself into, and her nostrils and throat were sanded with irritation from the dust in her mother's attic. In order to give herself a little breather she'd moved into the centre of the steep A-shaped space and straightened herself out.

She'd climbed up the creaking loft ladder ostensibly to find her mother's Christmas decorations – a notion her mother had sneered at: *Fuggin' Christmas – waste of time – never liked it –* which was a patent lie when you considered the sheer number of decorations that had been boxed and labelled. Although perhaps it was her father's writing on the boxes, and he was the one who loved this time of year.

Whatever the truth of that was, it also gave her an opportunity to look for her old papers and the moleskin notebook she'd begun to use when she'd heard that Danny had died in a car accident. The case was to be tried in the sheriff court that had been part of her beat as a junior reporter.

Now, with the perspective of time, she was able to view her actions as those of someone struggling to grieve; someone feeling that in some way she didn't deserve to. She'd abandoned the guy knowing he was fragile, guessing that he would find a destructive way to deal with her departure.

She'd felt every bit as guilty as the guy who was driving the car.

How she hadn't twigged until recently that the car had been driven by Luke was difficult to understand. She'd seen his photo. Or had she? Memory was playing tricks on her. When she went there she came up empty. But then again, perhaps this was not so unbelievable. She was a mess at the time, and her dad had fallen ill and subsequently died. That had pulled the feet from under her. Any interest in the cause of Danny's death had paled in comparison with the loss of her father.

Her phone sounded an alert. She picked it up, and her heart gave a little twist. It was a reminder that they were due to take Nathan to the Christmas funfair today.

Luke had called the previous two evenings, no doubt to see if she was going with them, but she simply stared at the phone as it rang, mind swinging back and forth on a confused pendulum. Yes. No. Yes. No. In the end she settled for not answering the phone at all. Which, of course, was an answer in itself.

She looked around. In the weak glow of the naked lightbulb she saw nothing but dust-covered boxes and dark corners. Working slowly and methodically, she placed the boxes labelled *Xmas Decs* in a neat pile by the entrance to the attic.

The next box she opened in her search contained a surprise. It was her parents' wedding album. A white, cushioned cover with gold lettering opened to a page of crisp tissue. She pulled that back and lost herself in a swoon of feeling. Her dad was in his army uniform, her mother in a white fish-tail gown. Clear-eyed and smiling, they both looked into the lens of the camera as if certain of life's future joys.

Theirs was a good marriage, as far as their only daughter could tell. She rarely heard a cross word, and both appeared consistently committed to each other and to her. She must have been a disappointment to them both. An expensive education, an honours degree, and now two damaged lovers into a wasted adulthood.

Oh, Dad. She traced her index finger over his face. Not once did he express any of that disappointment. The best lessons, he'd said on one occasion she'd come home in tears, are the ones you learn for yourself. So, go, learn your lessons and know that when you need to lick your wounds – he'd put one great paw lightly on her shoulder – there will always be a place here for you. As he spoke her mother was sitting by his side, nodding in agreement.

It was such a shame that it took these photographs to remind her of those sentiments.

Realising she was growing maudlin, she carefully closed the

album and placed it back in the box, to revisit some time when she was able to view it from a place of contentment.

She moved that box to the side and scanned the space. Where might her stuff be?

There.

A black plastic bag had something underneath it. A gift bag, its once-bright primary colours now dim with age and dust.

Inside there were some photos, some cards, and a notebook.

Chapter 46

Mere seconds after Luke had disappeared into the throng to find a toilet, Nathan became agitated, holding his hands over his crotch.

'Need a pee too,' he said, eyes beseeching.

'Could you not have said when Luke mentioned he was going?' The small boy shrugged.

'Okay, wee man,' Jamie said. 'Let's find you a loo, and maybe we'll be there and back before your dad?'

Nathan nodded his head with the intent only a small child could, eyes bright at the notion of turning it into a game.

Jamie started off in the same direction as Luke, Nathan's hot little hand in his. To his surprise he found he enjoyed the responsibility. But he heard his sister's voice: *Eyes on the prize*. They were among her last words to him when he'd left to meet Luke.

It's okay for you, he thought. Hiding behind your laptop, at a safe distance from the complications that actual human contact can elicit.

'I'm bursting,' Nathan said as he tugged at Jamie's hand.

'Sorry, wee pal,' Jamie replied. 'Give us a minute and you'll be right as rain.' He looked around for any signs telling them where to find the toilets.

There. A sign for the gents. Leading in a different direction to the one Luke had sped off in. He pointed up at it and smiled down at the boy.

Minutes later he was standing outside a cubicle while Nathan did his business inside. When he came out, ready to go back to the fun, Nathan made straight for the exit.

'Eh, did your dad not teach you to wash your hands?' Jamie asked.

Nathan gave a little shrug that read *caught* and walked over to the row of sinks, where he rinsed his hands in the minimum amount of water possible, waved his hands at a dryer and then ran to Jamie at the exit.

As they walked back to the little caravan where they'd had their break, Jamie spotted an empty stand. It was six paces from one end to the other and about the same as deep, and it was lined with waist-high elves and, in a central position, sat a large, high-backed chair on a purple-carpeted plinth. It had been set up for Santa's grotto, Jamie realised. Except Santa had taken the day off.

Jamie reached in and pulled a hat off one of the elves and put it on Nathan's head.

'New game,' he said. 'But you mustn't tell your dad, okay?'

Nathan nodded eagerly. 'Okay.'

'Promise not to tell your dad?'

Nathan nodded again. 'Promise.'

'Want to play hide and seek?'

Chapter 47

A man brushed past Luke as he left the toilet; and he looked so like Danny it rocked him. And he was back in that time, fifteen years earlier, having just buried his mother.

When Luke walked out through the doors of the hotel where they'd held the funeral tea, there was Danny, in his usual uniform of dark jeans, white T and black leather jacket. He was leaning against a black BMW, arms crossed, but he was unshaven and his hair unkempt, as if he'd just got out of bed. Even from twenty paces, his eyes managed to convey a brittleness that even Luke, who had been used to the man's moods, found unsettling.

Luke examined the car. Read the registration plate. There was no way this belonged to Danny. He was sure he'd either borrowed it or hired it for the day to reinforce his 'message'.

'Get in,' Danny said before climbing into the car. His manner showed there was no question in Danny's head that he owned Luke, even after his absence.

Mind, body and soul.

Anger flooded Luke's mind. Pent-up frustration that after one of the worst days of his life, Danny thought he could just pick up where they'd left off, as if the last two years had never happened.

Danny opened the window. 'Get fucking in.'

Luke exhaled, softened his shoulders, vowed that he would bide his time and got into the car.

'Sorry for your loss,' Danny said, without feeling. 'I'm guessing you could do with a wee hit...' He put his left hand into the pocket of his jacket and pulled out a little white packet. Then he reached across Luke to the glove compartment, pulled out a baking tray, and on its aluminium surface lined up a hit.

'Here?' Luke shot a glance back at the hotel and his fellow mourners. 'You're fucking kidding me.'

'I'm no' asking,' Danny said.

Luke met his old friend's unwavering gaze with one of his own. This was part of the act that Danny used to demonstrate he was the alpha. He was in control and you better not forget it.

Luke considered his next step. A rant was coming, for sure. Luke could probably script it. What kind of pal was he that he'd just up and leave and never get in touch. Think you're done with me? I'll say when we're done…

Problem was, if he knew Danny, Danny knew him just as well. Too well. If he appeared cowed, Danny would know he had plans to leave again. Put up too much resistance, and Danny would reel him back in the most painful way he could think of.

But his anger surged past his thoughts. 'Fuck you,' Luke said. He climbed out of the car and walked away, down the hill to a row of houses.

He'd left the hotel, needing to clear his head after hours of accepting the condolences of family, friends and old neighbours. He'd enjoyed talking about his mother and seeing how fondly people remembered her, but he was starting to feel hemmed in. As her only son it seemed that everyone wanted to speak to him.

And then he came out only to meet Danny Fucking Morrison.

As he walked, Luke ignored his impulse to check back to see what Danny was doing, and savoured the early-spring sunshine on his head and neck. He tried to seem carefree, sending Danny a message – hands in his pocket, shoulders back, chin up. This was a new guy and he wouldn't be so easily controlled.

A car pulled him beside him.

Luke kept on walking.

The car edged forward and the window opened.

'Aye, awright. The coke was a wrong move.'

'You don't say,' Luke replied.

'Good. We're mates again,' Danny laughed and stopped the car. 'Now get fucking in.'

Luke had made his point, so he got inside.

'How long you in town for?' Danny asked.

Luke studied his old friend and noted how tired he looked. Saw a fresh hurt behind his eyes.

'That it?' he asked. 'No rant about what an arsehole friend I am. You're not going to give me a hard time about vanishing for two years?'

Danny shrugged. 'Bygones, eh?' Then he smiled, and a bit of the old Danny, the fun Danny, appeared. 'What do you say we get the boys together for one mammoth session. Send your wee maw off in style? When you going back up to Aberdeen?'

'I was going to drive back tomorrow.'

'No time like the present, then,' Danny said, and patted Luke's knee. 'The boys'll meet us in The Black Bull. You up for it?'

*

Luke walked away from the toilet, thighs trembling. He shot a glance back at the man, just to make sure he wasn't Danny.

Of course he wasn't Danny. He'd seen him die. Waited on the emergency services, the light in his eyes gone forever, his mouth agape, the dying pink of his tongue just visible behind his teeth. An image he saw every night as he tried to sleep.

He needed to slough off that part of his past. Forever. He'd been punished. And was now making his way back into life. With the help of the sweetest little boy you could ever meet.

And with Jenna too. He couldn't ignore how he felt about her. Whenever he was with her he felt lighter; switched on to life and its quiet affirmations. Her hand in his – warm, soft – was enough to send sparks of pleasure flowing through his body.

But now, the spectre of Danny hung over them. Toxins flowing from his ever-strong memory, poisons that leached into Luke's every vein, every muscle; tainting every thought, perception and action.

Jenna's face that day: 'You,' she said. No single syllable was ever weighed down so heavily. She judged him in that moment, and he doubted if he would ever recover his place in her heart.

Still, he had Nathan, and while that boy was in his life, he had enough purpose for ten people. Thoughts of Nathan, and that beguiling, trusting smile of his added a boost to Luke's step as he found his way back to the snack caravan.

As he approached, he felt a tug on his arm. He turned and saw the panicked expression on Jamie's face, and even before Jamie spoke, knew his world was about to turn upside down.

'Where's Nathan?'

Jamie all but wrung his hands. 'Isn't he with you?'

Chapter 48

Jenna held the notebook up to her nose. She caught the scent of beer and cigarettes, some of which would have been from her old habits, and some of it from her mentor when she was working on the local newspaper, the *Glasgow Post*. Doug Logan was so slim he used to stand side on to you and ask, with a half-smile, can you see me? He always had a pencil behind one ear, and he subsisted on Mars bars and diet drinks. The smoking ban was a calumny of the worst kind, according to Logan, and he always had to have a cigarette to hand, unlit or not.

'We're like the fourth emergency service, hen,' he said to her the first day on the job, after a stream of people appeared at the reception desk, each of them looking to highlight an important issue that the local council were unable or unwilling to clear up for them.

Mere weeks into the job and she made it to the local sheriff court, and the stories she gathered there often made up the bulk of the paper, aside from the adverts. But she quickly grew bored. When she broke up with Danny, she'd thrown herself into the job to distract herself from thinking so much about the irrevocable step she had taken. The guilt and shame almost crushed her. Doing that to herself. To her own baby. So she worked all hours, pulling extra shifts. The busier she was, the easier it was to cope with life without him.

And without her.

She never knew the sex of the baby, but she was convinced she was a girl. It was a little girl who whispered to her in all those dark moments since. In the quiet hours while the rest of the world slept, she'd wake, and hear her. Berating. Haranguing.

Shaming.

Then the news hit that he was dead. That drugs and alcohol played a part came as no surprise. She thought of him as being like an ill-fated popstar, without the back catalogue.

When she opened the notebook a couple of yellowed pages spilled out. They were printouts from the BBC Scotland news website. Both articles were painfully brief. Male aged twenty-nine dead at scene. A notorious bend in the road. The car had rolled over and over, down a hill, and would have been out of the sight of any passing motorists. The driver survived with miraculously minor injuries, but the ambulance crew were too late to save the passenger. Drink and drugs were expected to be a factor in the man's death. In the other article: male appears for sentencing. And his name: Duncan Luke Robertson.

There was a small photo of a man, in handcuffs, being escorted from the back of the court into a big van. She studied that image for what felt like hours, staring at it so hard the photo became a blur. He had a goatee beard and his hair was chin length, and he was scowling at the photographer. Caught forever in an expression that was alien to the man she'd come to know. Indeed there was nothing in that photograph that she could relate to Luke. It was like he was an entirely different person.

The pages of her notebook were only half filled, most of it a barely legible scribble. She flicked through her notes once more, and came upon an entry at the very end that was clearer than the rest. It held a telephone number, then a name and a phrase that was underlined, followed with four question marks, as if she was sending a message to her future self. See this. Take note. But for the life of her she couldn't remember what she was to take note of.

Uncle Sandy.
Check the time!!!!

Chapter 49

It felt like Luke's stomach had dropped down to his toes.

'What do you mean, is Nathan with me? I left him with you.' He prodded Jamie in the chest with two daggered fingers.

'He followed you. Came straight after you.'

'What?' A roar of anguish went off inside Luke's head. He felt his skin tighten, his mouth go dry and his palms start to sweat. 'I told you to wait with him.'

'But he was right behind you. I could see him walk up to you.' Jamie's face was pale, and he took a step back.

'We'll find him. He'll be around here somewhere,' Luke said, hoping that saying the words out loud would wind them into truth. 'Kids go missing all the time here, I'm sure.'

Luke spotted a steward. A young man barely out of his teens dressed in black apart from a neon tabard with his designation printed across it. His name badge said 'Bobby'.

'We've lost a wee boy,' Luke said breathlessly, feeling panic rise in him. 'Nathan. About yay high.' He held a hand out at about hip height. 'He's got blond hair and he's wearing a navy-blue puffer jacket.'

'Aye?' the young steward answered, as if this was about the twentieth child that had dodged their parents that day.

'Do you have a lost-children section or something?' Luke asked.

Bobby held a hand up. 'I'll put out a call, mate. I'm sure he'll be here somewhere. Digging into a giant puff of candyfloss and getting a pure sugar rush or something, aye?'

Luke wanted to slap the nonchalance out of him, but held himself in check as he swivelled round on the spot, looking for a small blond head atop a blue padded jacket.

'He's called Nathan.' Bobby was talking into a hand-held short-wave radio. 'Blond hair. Blue puffer jaikit.'

A male voice replied and Bobby nodded. Then he cut the connection and addressed Luke. 'Right, the word is out, mate. We'll have him with you any minute. We haven't lost one yet.'

Luke knew this was intended to reassure, but the word 'lost' bounced around his skull like a pea in a just-blown whistle.

'Take me back to where you last saw him,' Bobby said. Luke nodded and turned back to the caravan where they had their drinks.

The table and chairs they'd been sitting on were now occupied by a young family, both parents looking exhausted and relieved to have found a seat and some relative quiet. A small boy and a smaller girl sat on a chair each, sipping from a straw and kicking their feet in the air as if anxious to get going again.

Luke approached them. 'You haven't seen a wee boy; blond hair, blue jacket, about yay high?'

Both parents shook their heads, while wearing matching expressions of concern at the thought of losing one of theirs.

'Right,' Bobby began. 'Why don't we move in a wee circle round this area and then increase the circle each time we go around, aye?'

From just behind Luke, Jamie said, 'Good idea.'

As Luke walked, he desperately scanned the crowd. He saw several blond boys. None of them was Nathan. Then he saw one just ahead. The right height. Wearing the right colour of coat.

'Nathan,' he shouted, running over and putting a hand on the boy's shoulder.

'Hoy,' a man with a lined face and trim grey beard faced up to him. 'What do you think you're doing?'

It wasn't Nathan. Looked nothing like him. Luke had been seeing what he wanted to see.

Bobby reached them and stood between the two men. 'Sorry, sir,' he said. 'This fella's lost his wee yin, and we're getting a bit worried. He's about the same height as your wee man here. Called Nathan. Keep an eye out, aye?'

Bobby pulled Luke away and under his breath said, 'Sir, you need to try and stay calm.'

Luke opened his mouth to answer him, but nothing came out. His mind was filling with catastrophic visions. He was at the morgue. Standing in front of a small body under a sheet. *Get a grip. He'll be fine.*

'If anything happens...' he gulped, fighting for breath. 'He's all I've...'

Then.

'Daddy.'

Jamie striding towards him, holding a little boy by the hand. In the other he was holding the large bear he'd won for Nathan earlier.

'Daddy,' Nathan repeated, and he was running, jumping, in his arms. His face was bright with excitement, and he was wearing a little red elf hat. 'Hide and seek,' he said. 'I was playing hide and seek.'

Luke buried his face into Nathan's little padded chest, and breathed in the actuality of him. *Jesus,* he thought, *I'm never letting you out of my sight again.*

'See,' Jamie was saying. 'Told you we'd find him.'

'You shouldn't have lost him in the first place,' Luke snapped. Then seeing the hurt that flashed into Jamie's eyes he held his hand up. 'Sorry. It's just that if anything...' But Jamie turned away, rendering his efforts at an apology useless.

'Jamie,' Luke tried, but he had moved away, so Luke turned his attention back to his boy. He held Nathan out so he could see his face as he spoke. 'Don't ever do that to me again. Whenever we're in a busy place like this you stay with a grown-up. Got that?'

Nathan stared at Jamie's retreating form as if looking for some sort of back-up.

'But—' Nathan began to protest.

'Enough excitement for the day, son.' Luke interrupted. 'We're going home.'

Chapter 50

Jenna held the notebook open and read the entry over and over again. It would be so easy to take it downstairs, dial that number and ask to speak to Uncle Sandy.

A face filled her mind. So complete that Jenna could have been looking at a photograph. Where had this memory been hiding, she wondered? The face was deeply lined and the skin sagged as if he had lost a huge amount of weight. He had watery-blue eyes, and his hair was cut short – dark but patched with grey. One side of his moustache and the outer edge of an eyebrow were tinged in yellow, as if he had been smoking sixty unfiltered cigarettes a day from the moment he learned to walk.

He had turned up to the trial expecting to be called as a witness, Jenna recalled, but was let go when Robertson changed his plea. Jenna had come across him as she left the court house: an old man hunched over a banister as he eased a bad hip down onto the next step. Looking to ease his journey a little, she'd walked over to him.

'There's a lift, sir,' she said as she approached.

'There is, aye?' The man cackled. 'Is that the wan that's broke?'

'It's broken again?' she asked. 'Goodness. That's awful.' She pointed at the wheelchair lift nearby. 'How about that? Would that help?'

The old man muttered something about being the eejit who went on a wheelchair lift without an actual chair with a set of wheels. Then he turned to her.

'Here, you're our Danny's girl, aye? I'm his Uncle Sandy. Well, no' his uncle, uncle. I used to be their neighbour. Knew all the family.' He scratched his face. 'I saw you up the town with Danny one day. Arm in arm, like love's young dream.' He winked. Then under his breath added, more soberly, 'You're better off without him, doll, he was one bad bastard, but.'

His honesty took her aback.

'Ah say it as ah see it, hen. He was a trial to his poor mum and dad from the day he was born that boy.'

At that moment a couple walked past. The man must have heard Sandy's words because he stared at him and growled, 'For God's sake, Sandy, can it, will ye?' The man then looked Jenna up and down, his face a sneer. He shook his head and said something to the woman by his side. She shot Jenna a look full of hatred, mouthed the word 'whore' and walked on. Both then clipped down the stone stairs as if desperate to get out of the building.

Jenna felt scored through with hurt by their brief examination. But then recognising the cast of the man's features, she stepped back, hand over her heart in shock.

'That's...?'

'His dad. And his mum, hen.' Sandy shook his head. 'Took it awfy bad.'

They must know, she thought. Danny must have told them about the baby.

Sandy shook his big head slowly, unmindful of the state she was now in, eyes shining as if they held the wisdom of Solomon. 'They came here expecting answers. And when that bastard changed his plea, that got hit on the head.' His eyes now offered an apology on their behalf. 'And now, troubled as they were by their son's ongoings...' he made a face at that word, an expression that hinted at deeply unsocial behaviour '...they're hitting out at anyone. Everyone. When a child dies you need an explanation, or a target, eh?'

Jenna wanted to say, *But I loved him.*

Then a quiet voice added, *at first.*

'Word is he was fair besotted wi' you, hen.'

'Yeah.' She felt a surge of emotion, and wiped away a tear.

'As I said, you're well shot. If you hadn't chucked him there's a fair chance he would have taken you down wi' him.'

Jenna felt a hit of anger. 'If you aren't so proud of Danny why are you here?'

'I'm a witness, doll. I saw Danny just afore the crash. Him and that Robertson boy. They were out Drymen way, driving towards the loch. I live just outside the town there, and was making my way into Milngavie when I passed them. Must have been just a matter of moments afore the accident.'

Danny's father's voice roared up the stairwell.

'Sandy, are you coming or what?'

'My old neighbour. We used to be like brothers.' Sandy rolled his eyes to the ceiling. 'Allowances are being made.' He looked down at her hands. At her notebook. 'You work for the local rag, aye?'

'Yes,' Jenna answered.

'Something I'd like to talk to you about, hen. Might be worth a wee write-up.' He chanted out his telephone number and asked her to call him. He said something else, explaining what he wanted her to know, but Danny's father came charging back up the stairs, heckling Sandy to 'get his arse downstairs if you want a lift.'

Jenna desperately wanted to tell him she was sorry for his loss, that she really didn't have a choice, but this time he didn't even give her a second glance, so she knew any approach would be rebuffed. In her distraction she missed most of what Sandy saying, except something about an hour and that something didn't add up.

Danny's father turned away and before he followed him, Sandy pulled her close. 'Well rid, hen. Well rid,' Sandy said. 'I knew him since he was a bairn, and, God rest his soul, but when he and that Robertson fella get thigither they're pure poison.'

That Robertson fella.

Pure poison.

He had been talking about Luke.

Chapter 51

As soon as Jamie got home, Amanda was in his face.

'Well?'

'For Chrissakes, can I get in the door?' Jamie complained.

'You're a bit touchy. What happened?'

'Everything went to plan, sis,' he said, and he told her about 'losing' Nathan, and Luke's panic, and then delivering the boy to him like a hero.

'And?' Amanda was disappointed. 'I was hoping you'd do something more than that. He's got the boy back. How is that in any way part of our plan?'

'Nothing happens to that boy, understand?' Jamie leaned in close to Amanda, pointing.

'Yeah, but—'

'Yeah but nothing. My plan was to lose the boy and then worm my way into an even better position of trust when I saved him. But it didn't work out the way I thought.'

'Oh?'

'Oh, he was polite enough. Too polite. I know he was furious at me. Practically told me he never wanted to see me again.'

'Is that what he said?'

'Not quite, but it was obvious. He wasn't happy.'

Amanda's eyes shone. 'That's you seeing the real Duncan Luke Robertson, or whatever his name is now. That whole therapist thing...' she waved her hands in the air '...is all an act. He's an arrogant, nasty arsehole and we've got him just where we want him.'

'We do?' Jamie asked.

'I've just been messaging his girlfriend...'

Chapter 52

Jenna recognised the signs. She was prevaricating. Even her mother gave her a side-eyed look when she fixed the sheets at the corners of her bed for the fourth time that morning.

'What the fug?' Sally asked. Then she shoo'ed her away like one would a mewling cat looking for a second breakfast. 'Can you not go back to that shop and give me some peace?'

'I can't go back to the shop, Mum. I need to stay here and look after you,' Jenna snapped. But her fuse mended as quickly as it broke, and she felt a hot rush of regret. 'Sorry, Mum. That was uncalled for.'

'But true,' her mother replied, her face slumped with self-loathing. 'I hate being a burden on you, Jenna.'

'You're not a burden, Mum,' Jenna said, and stroked Sally's hand. 'It's this other stuff.'

'That man, is it?' Her mother's eyes were keen, and in this moment her mind was entirely lucid. 'You can tell me, dear. Might help to talk about it?' It was clear she desperately wanted to help, to add a touch of reciprocation to what had become an entirely one-sided relationship. But Jenna knew if she told her mother what was going on it would boomerang back on her when her mother's mind was less sharp and her frustrations got the better of her.

'It'll all work out in the end, Mum. For better or worse.'

'You're trotting out some of your father's sayings now?' Sally smiled.

Jenna laughed. 'My favourite was: time to piss or get off the potty.'

Sally laughed. A throaty, head-back chuckle. It had been so long since Jenna heard her mother properly laugh that a tear spilled onto her cheek. She wiped it off before her mother noticed.

'That was a last-resort statement. He used to get annoyed at me talking an issue to death. His way of telling me move on or do something.'

'I miss him so much,' Jenna said.

'Me too, honey.'

Jenna looked into her mother's eyes and gave her hand a little squeeze. These moments of sharing and genuine communication were becoming rarer, and she vowed to treasure them when they arrived.

'Fancy a cuppa?' Jenna titled her chin up and added brightness to her tone. Time to stop feeling sorry for herself.

Her phone sounded an alert.

'Always on that fuggin' phone,' Sally shouted. Her mental bridge to aggression snapping into place.

'And we're back,' Jenna mumbled to herself as she left the room.

At the kitchen table she fired up her laptop. Hazel was asking how she was today.

—*Just had a nice wee moment wi Mum*, she replied. *I'll take that as a win.*

—*Lovely. Take them where you find them, eh?* Hazel wrote. *Ever find that notebook?*

—*Couldn't remember half of that stuff. I think with Danny dying, then my dad...* She almost added something about her baby but stopped herself. Hazel didn't need to know that. *With all of that going on I think my memories of that time are in a mess. But I'd written down Luke's proper name and everything. No idea how I didn't connect him with the guy who killed Danny. I'm such an idiot.*

—*Being harsh there, lovely. Different name, and a different context. I saw a guy in a café the other day. He waved hello, and I'm, like, who the hell are you, mate? Then it twigged. He used to be on the tills in Aldi and we'd chat every week, but because I saw him away from that till I had no clue who he was. So not knowing who Luke is/was makes perfect sense to me.*

—*You're too nice,* Jenna replied.

—*Find anything interesting in those notes? Apart from realising you've a memory of a goldfish.*

—*I met this old guy at the court. He had been a neighbour of Danny's parents and was still in contact with them. He was a witness apparently. He'd passed Danny and Luke in the car when they were heading out towards Drymen. I noted something about the time not adding up. Can't remember what I was getting at.*

—*This old guy passed them just before the crash?*

—*Yeah. Didn't get to describe what he saw cos the case didn't go to trial. And he didn't get to tell me cos Danny's dad wanted to leave and they'd given Sandy a lift in his car.*

—*You met his dad at the trial? What was he like?*

—*Angry.*

—*Did you speak to him?*

—*Not really. He just gave me a dirty look and swore at this old guy, Sandy, to get downstairs and into the car or he would leave him there to get a taxi.*

—*What about his mum? Did you meet Danny's mum?*

Jenna paused her fingers above the keyboard, wondering why Hazel was so keen to know about Danny's parents. With a shrug, she answered:

—*She just looked incredibly sad. Heartbroken.*

There was a long pause before Hazel replied.

—*Poor woman. As a mother myself I can't begin to imagine what pain she was in. What about this old guy? What else did he say?*

Jenna stopped again. Hazel was really showing an interest in this.

—*He was pretty rude about Danny tbh. Said he was a – I'm paraphrasing here cos I can't remember exactly – he said Danny was a trial to his parents from the moment he was born. A bad lad who brought shame to the family, essentially.*

—*This Sandy sounds like a wee arsehole.*

—*What? Do you know this family, Haze? You're sounding, I don't know, almost angry about this.*

Jenna waited several minutes for Hazel's reply to this. As she waited, she scrolled up the conversation. Sandy was indeed a little man, but she didn't actually describe him as such to Hazel.

A reply appeared.

—*Soz, hun. Had to answer the door there. Hubby and his online purchases. I swear he's going to bankrupt us. No. Not angry, and I don't know this family. It's just I feel so sad for the mum and dad. They lost their boy. They don't get their day in court, and this former neighbour is being a wee bit disrespectful. It just, I don't know, hit a chord there. Soz. Didn't mean to sound crabbit.*

—*That's okay, lovely. I understand,* Jenna replied. She didn't really, but as an explanation it felt honest.

—*What now, super sleuth? You going to follow up with Sandy?*

—*I hadn't thought that far, tbh,*

—*Can I offer you some advice? I'm giving it to you whether you want it or not. Sounds like this has got under your skin, and it's going to eat at you until you get to the truth of the matter. Don't you think you owe it to Danny to find out what really happened?*

Chapter 53

As Amanda read and typed, Jamie was watching over her shoulder.

'Careful,' he said. 'She might be distracted with all the stuff that's happening now, but she's not stupid. You're showing a little bit too much interest in Danny's ... our ... parents there.'

Amanda's face pinched into a scowl. 'Shut up. She's fine. Just needs a nudge in the right direction. And she's not as clever as you think she is. And that old arsehole saying all that stuff about Danny. If he was here...' She made a fist.

'Do you remember Sandy?' Jamie asked her.

'Aye. He was a creep. Always putting a hand on my shoulder or arm when he talked to me. He was one of those types who had to say what he thought.' Amanda looked off the side, her mind mired in memory. 'He acted like it was a virtue to be brutally honest. Mum couldn't stand him, but Dad and him had a laugh. And they both liked a drink.'

'I'm struggling to picture him, to be honest.'

'And what was he like, saying that stuff about Danny. What a prick. Danny was not a bad lad who brought shame to the family. Mum and Dad loved him like crazy.'

'Did they, aye?' Jamie said, raising his eyebrows.

Jamie slumped back in his chair, and it looked to Amanda that it was his turn to be lost in the past.

'What?' she asked him.

'I met Jenna once back then. I never told you.' He looked into her eyes. 'I never told anyone.'

'Why? What happened? How on earth did you meet that...?' She paused, made a calculation. 'Danny brought her round to ours when he knew we'd all be out?'

Jamie shook his head. 'Every now and again he would meet me at the school and walk me part of the way home.' Studying Jamie's expression, it felt to Amanda that he had collected memories like a magpie would gather jewels. 'Every time, he would say, "You and me, Jamie. It's you and me against the world." And I loved that attention, you know? You said Mum and Dad loved him? They were constantly furious at him. He knew it. Couldn't handle the arguments, so he stayed away.' Jamie shook his head. 'He told me that one day he'd lose it with the old man and do something he'd regret. Something that would get him locked up for a long time. So I think you need to revise your memories, sis; our Danny wasn't some plaster saint.'

'I'm not stupid, Jamie. I know that.' Amanda crossed her arms. Danny may have been somebody who didn't follow the rules but he was her big brother and she adored him. 'Anyway,' she added. 'You were talking about Jenna.'

'This one time, we went on a kind of detour, through a little park. And Jenna was sitting on a bench there. At the time I thought it was a surprise encounter, but now I can see that Danny had arranged it. He wanted me to meet her.'

'What was she like?' Amanda asked, almost despite herself. She didn't want Jamie's resolve to be softened by honey-coated memory.

'The same as she is now. She has a few more lines, but to be fair she's aged well.'

Amanda tutted. 'I meant as a person. What was she like as a person?'

Jamie rolled his eyes. 'Nice enough, I think. Didn't really say much. You remember what Danny was like. He kind of dominated.'

There was more to this than what Jamie was saying, Amanda could see. There was an assessment going on behind his eyes, as if he was debating telling her something. She guessed that whatever it was it wouldn't show Danny in a good light.

'Go on, just tell me. Feels like you're holding back.'

'What?'

'I can read you like a book, Jamie. Whatever it is, I can handle it.'

'Okay,' he said, and pursed his lips as if working out the best way to tell the story. 'We were walking through the park. No one else around us. And Jenna disagreed with something Danny said. Can't remember what it was, but Danny didn't like it.' Jamie examined one of his nails. 'And he started on her. "What do I see in you?" All that kind of shit. "Best thing about you is your boobs. Cracking set of tits, Jamie," he said. "Want to see them?"'

'I don't believe you.'

Jamie pressed on. 'He went on about how I was just a boy but I would need something to start off the wank bank when I was old enough. And shouted at Jenna over and over to show me her tits.'

'Oh, come on,' Amanda said, shaking her head. This was nonsense. No way would Danny behave like that to a woman. He was always respectful around her whenever anything sexual arose in the conversation. Warning her off boys, threatening to castrate anyone who even looked at her in a certain way.

'Then he grabbed Jenna and pulled at her top.'

'You're making this up,' Amanda shouted. 'I don't believe a word of this.'

'I remember her running away, crying, and Danny just laughing.'

'Jamie, please. I know you want me to have a ... more realistic view of what Danny was like, but do you expect me to believe that pile of crap?'

Jamie's answering shrug infuriated Amanda. She wanted to slap him. She wanted to storm out of the room as she called him every bad name she could think of.

'You believe whatever you want to, sis. I was there. I pretended to laugh along with Danny. He was my big brother, and I doted on him, but he could be proper scary.'

'Was not. He was just ... assertive.'

Jamie snorted. 'What are you on, Amanda? Sure, once Danny died our lives turned to shit, and by all means look to make these people suffer, but admit what Danny was really like. He had a bad side to him. There was some sort of personality disorder going on there.'

'Crap.'

'Did you know Dad and Mum used to beat him?'

'What?' Amanda shook her head fiercely. 'Now you really are losing it.'

'I was just a tot, to be fair. Tiny. So they probably just forgot about me. Dad was drunk. All I can remember is Dad shouting at him, until Danny shouted back, and then Dad started hitting him, with everything he could get his hands on. Shoes, a belt, the poker. And Danny just smiled. Every time Dad hit him he just gave him that smile, as if he was asking, is that your best shot?'

'Jesus, this is like one of those shit movies you watch.' Amanda shot to her feet. 'I've had enough of listening to this.'

'That badness had to come from somewhere, Amanda.'

'Pff.'

She turned and walked away as Jamie raised his voice to make sure she heard him: 'We've all got it, sis. That badness. If I was a superstitious person, I'd say this family was cursed.'

Chapter 54

Amanda couldn't let it rest. Jamie was sorely mistaken if he thought that episode with Jenna at the park, even if it was true, was any indication of what Danny was really like. Probably some sort of wish fulfilment going on there, Jamie remembering something like that.

No way would Danny treat a girlfriend that way.

She searched her memory for how Danny was with her for clues that might prove Jamie wrong. Amanda would have been around eleven at the time, and there were a couple of girls who came to the house in tears, looking for Danny. Both times it was her job to get rid of them. To pretend he wasn't in the house, and she didn't know where he was or when he'd be back.

One of them looked her up and down. 'Lying wee bitch,' she said, before turning and walking away with as much dignity as she could muster.

The other just wept, and Amanda almost felt sorry enough for her to bring her into the house, but that would have meant losing out on the tenner Danny promised to give her when the young woman had gone.

'I'm trying to let them down gently, poppet,' Danny explained to her when they were on their own. 'But you girls need a different tactic when you're ending it with a boy. Remember that time you cut your knee, and I pulled the plaster off in the one go?'

Amanda remembered it well. The pain was sharp but short-lived.

'That's how you should finish it with your boyfriends. The ones that get past me that is, eh?' he winked, and she laughed, heart full of love for this handsome, funny young man who was giving her his full attention. 'Some fellas don't want to hear it and stick around way past their welcome. So be blunt. Be fucking brutal, don't leave any room for doubt and they won't pester you anymore.' They'd both laughed, and he'd asked her what she was going to spend her money on. Unlike anyone else in the family, he sat and listened to what she had to say.

Now, she lay in her bed, head hot against her pillow, restless as a six-month-old pup. She tried sleeping on one side, then on the other, but her mind wouldn't let her rest. It continuously threw out images of Danny. Him smiling, being attentive, giving her stuff, especially at Christmas and birthdays. His presents were always the ones she looked out for. Sure, he had his bad side. Who didn't? But Jamie was remembering a different man if that was the stuff he was coming out with.

Finally she gave up, climbed out of bed and located her laptop. Once it was fired up she checked to see if Jenna was online, and bingo. She made straight for her chat box with Jenna.

—*You can't sleep either?*

Thirty seconds, no more and a reply came in.

—*Too much on my mind. You too?*

A pause and then Jenna typed some more.

—*And sorry. The chat these days has all been about me. I forget to ask about you. I'm a bad friend.*

—*Rubbish. You're lovely. And you've got a lot on your plate. Besides, my stuff is boring. A brother who's doing my head in. A child who is on his computer WAY too late, and a sleazeball husband. But let's not dwell.*

—*You didn't say you had a brother.*

—*Want to take him off my hands?* Amanda considered how she might bring the conversation round to Danny and his death. *It's just an old uncle has been sent to a nursing home. He dotes on my brother, but he won't bother his arse to go and see him.* Amanda grimaced at the thought that the next thing she typed might be a bit too obvious, but she hoped that Jenna was tired at this hour and less able to think straight. *Talking of old uncles. Clang. Have you thought more about that old uncle, or was he a neighbour? The man who wanted to be a witness? Thought about getting in touch?*

There was a long silence. Too long, and it made Amanda think she'd overplayed her hand. The three little dots appeared, suggesting that Jenna was typing. Then they disappeared. They appeared again. Went off. Appeared again.

Shit. She'd messed it up.

Then the box filled.

That's what's keeping me awake, tbh. Should I do anything about this? Sleeping dogs and all that. I was only with Danny for a year or so. But he made such an impression on me. Standing by his grave recently was an emotional moment, and I can't believe how hurt I was when I discovered Luke's involvement. That was a real lightning bolt. Felt like my heart was being pulled apart.

—Did he have family? Amanda regretted typing this question the moment she pressed send. What if she didn't like the answer?

—He rarely talked about them when we were together. I was with him pretty much every waking moment – which was too much, I guess – and he never visited them. He missed his wee brother. Talked about him, but his parents, according to him, were horrible. Violent towards him, so I can see why he wanted nothing to do with them.

Amanda's breath was coming in short blasts. She felt light-headed and at the same time wanted to scream her disappointment into the night sky. He missed Jamie? No mention of a sister?

She tried to force relaxation into her shoulders and tried the calming technique she'd picked up online. Chanted five things she could see. Four things she could physically feel. Three things she could hear. Two things she could smell. And one thing she could taste. Then repeated that until her mind was a little more calm.

Jenna was clearly misremembering. There was no way Danny didn't mention a little sister.

—That was his only sibling? A young brother? Do you think he's still about? Worth contacting him?

—I vaguely remember the brother. Couldn't pick him out in a

photo, to be honest but I do remember he was a handsome wee thing. Danny took me to meet him after school one day. Didn't go well. We had a falling out. One of the few times Danny was nasty to me. Like he was a different person, just for that moment, you know?

Amanda waited to see if there would be more. If there wasn't, that meant two things: one, Jenna hadn't twigged that the Jamie she met in the shop, and with Luke, was the little boy she met all those years ago. And two, the falling out in the park didn't involve Danny pulling at her top. The crap that Jamie talked about, demanding Jenna show him her boobs, was just that: crap.

Trying to set aside her crushing disappointment that Danny hadn't talked about her to someone he was supposedly in love with, Amanda carried on.

—*If I was you, I'd be in touch with this old guy. This is clearly affecting you more than you realise. Peace of mind? Worth it for that?*

Silence.

Then.

—*You're right.* Then Jenna added, *After Christmas though. It's too close to the holidays. Nobody wants to speak to anyone other than families and shop assistants over the next wee while. Aye. After Christmas.*

For fuckssakes, Amanda thought. It's just one day. Why does the world have to stop for two weeks for the sake of one day?

Chapter 55

It was only just noon on Christmas Day, and Luke was fit for nothing but bedtime. Nathan had woken him up at 5am, bouncing on the spot at the foot of his bed, his eyes shining so bright he could almost see them in the half-light.

'Santa's been. Santa's been,' the boy chanted.

'He has, eh?'

Luke judged if he brought the boy under the covers it might give him another thirty minutes of rest. So he lifted up the corner of the quilt.

'C'mon in, buddy. The older person in the house needs a little more sleep this morning.'

Nathan lay still for about a minute, as Luke's thoughts drifted to Jenna and how her Christmas Day might turn out. Depending on the mood of her mother, it might not have much festive cheer about it.

But his rest didn't last long. The boy shifted beside him as if he had ants under his pyjamas.

'Sure Santa's real, Dad?' he asked. 'Donna Brady says he isn't – that it's your mum and dad that buy you presents. And I don't have a mum anymore so it must be you.' Then he added, as if hedging his bets, 'But I don't believe her.'

'Santa's real, son,' Luke replied. Then he propped himself up on his elbows and looked Nathan in the eye, the better to deliver this statement. 'He's real.'

'I knew it.' His face gleamed.

'I'm not going to get back to sleep, am I?' Luke asked him.

Nathan was at his side, squatting on his heels. He pushed out his bottom lip while tucking in his chin, which was as close as he came to being openly defiant.

'Okay, let's make a deal,' Luke said.

Nathan nodded his head furiously.

'We open two big presents now, and we wait until Granny comes over before we open the rest. How does that sound?'

'Yay,' Nathan shouted, and then rolled back off the bed, feet over his head, and landed perfectly on the carpet.

*

Granny Gemma arrived at 11:30 laden with more parcels. After she greeted Nathan she handed Luke an envelope.

'Found this on your mat,' she said. 'A late Christmas card?' she suggested.

He opened it, and his stomach gave a hard twist. It was an image of Nathan. He was in their local park, head tilted back as if talking to someone much taller: an adult. Luke could make out a figure just behind him, sitting on a bench. Himself, and he was caught in a moment when he was looking off to the side. Jesus, he thought, could these people not leave him alone?

'What is it?' Gemma asked.

'Nothing,' he replied, pushing a smile onto his face as he folded the page and shoved it into his back pocket. When he found out who was doing this...

'Presents,' Nathan chanted, momentarily throwing him from his dark imaginings.

'Okay, wee pal, let's do it.' Luke got down onto his knees and watched as an excited little boy began to open his gifts.

The result was a mess of gaudy paper, boxes, toys, books and sweets spread across the living-room floor. Nathan sat in the middle with a stunned look on his face, as if he was choosing which was going to provide his next moment of joy.

'He's a happy wee boy,' Gemma beamed from her armchair. She looked just as tired as Luke felt. Then her eyes moistened. 'It's a shame Lisa isn't here to see how her wee boy's thriving.'

'Aye,' Luke replied. 'He's a credit to her.'

'And you, Luke,' Gemma said, looking over her glasses. She

wasn't one for paying compliments. A gruff little humph in acknowledgement of a job well done was her usual, but the Christmas spirit must have got to her. 'You've done a rare job, so you have. Lots of men would have vanished when left with a child who wasn't their own.'

'I've been with him most of his life,' Luke replied. 'I might not have been present at the conception, but he's my son.' In truth, whenever anyone said something like this, Luke couldn't take it as a compliment. There was no choice in the matter. He was just doing the right thing. What else would he have done?

'Just sayin',' Gemma replied. 'If you hadn't stepped up like that, I don't know what kind of mess we would be in.' She wiped at a tear.

Luke felt his throat tighten. 'Wheesht, woman,' he replied, because he knew she hated being addressed in this way. 'You'll have me crying as well.'

They settled into a moment's silence.

'What are you having for dinner?' Gemma asked.

Luke shot a glance at Nathan, remembering a conversation they'd had just a week ago. Not being one for a traditional meal, he asked Nathan what his very favourite food was and promised that would be their Christmas meal.

'Sausages. And chocolate cake,' Nathan replied almost instantly.

'Sausages and chocolate cake on the one plate? That's going to be messy.'

'No, silly.' Nathan rolled his eyes dramatically. 'Sausages, with mash. And beans. Then after that, chocolate cake and chocolate ice cream. With chocolate sauce.' The last part added with hooded eyes, as if he knew he was chancing his luck.

'That enough chocolate for you?' Luke grinned. Nathan's studied expression suggested he believed there could never be enough chocolate.

'And to think I'm going out for Christmas lunch with our Betty. What am I missing out on?'

'You're welcome to stay,' Luke said.

'Ha. Betty's taken up thon Facebook. If I didn't show she'd be telling the world she had the world's worst sister. Besides, I'm a sucker for the whole Christmas dinner thing.' She laughed. 'I never look at turkey for the rest of the year, but you have to have it at Christmas, don't you?'

He laughed, then looked over at Nathan. 'Fancy a movie?' The little boy nodded eager assent, and Luke set it up.

With Nathan cradled in his arm and the theme tune playing, his thoughts turned again to Jenna. He'd sent her a text message wishing her a happy Christmas and asking her if she wanted to chat. She'd replied with a simple *Happy Christmas*, ignoring the possibility of a talk.

Fair enough. Who could understand that more than him?

Nonetheless, although finding out about Danny and her had muddled his thinking, he had to acknowledge that he still had feelings for her. He was almost constantly drifting off into thoughts about her. What was she doing? Thinking? He'd even seen something online that he thought he should share with her, but stopped himself in time.

What a mess.

Jamie was next to enter his head. He hadn't spoken to the young man since the funfair. Sure, he'd been annoyed with him at the time; after all, he'd trusted him to look after Nathan, and although ultimate responsibility would always rest with him, Jamie had let him down. But he'd managed to push that to the side and act pleasant. Hadn't he? So why had Jamie gone silent on him as well?

How was he to make it right with people if they didn't give him the chance?

Chapter 56

Jenna looked at her phone, read a message from Luke and wondered if she should just call him. His message seemed so sad, and with a pang, she realised she was missing him as well.

At this thought she shook her head. The man had done terrible things; how could she be so confused as to still have feelings for him? What was wrong with her that she always fell for these damaged men?

She heard laughter from the television in the living room. She'd left her mother in there watching reruns of Morecambe & Wise Christmas specials. Occasionally she even heard her hooting along with the studio audience.

She looked at the turkey crown in its tray on the table, then covered it in foil and with a sigh put it back in the fridge.

'Looking forward to your Christmas dinner?' she'd asked her mother that morning after they'd opened their paltry collection of parcels.

'Pfft,' her mother answered. 'It's just another day. I hate turkey, and what the fug are trimmings. That's a bloody stupid word for stuffing, gravy and sprouts.' She'd paused then to throw a disdainful look in the direction of the kitchen. 'Brussels sprouts are evil, by the way. Nothing but little green bombs of disgust.'

Her mother had never before voiced such an opinion about any of these foods, but Jenna mentally deleted the turkey, sprouts and stuffing from the menu she'd prepared. She'd feed her mother them on Boxing Day when she'd have forgotten her complaints. In the meantime, mentally surveying the contents of the freezer, it was a microwave meal for them both.

Food decisions made, she sat at the kitchen table and scrolled through her social media, looking at all the festive messages from the people she knew. Many of them looked like they were having a fabulous time, but she doubted the truth of their assertions.

She'd be willing to bet that many of them were just as miserable as she was.

A familiar theme tune sounded from down the hall. It was for *The Golden Girls*, and before long her mother was chuckling along.

Jesus, was this what her life had become? Old TV comedies. Being envious of other peoples' lives on social media. Life without Luke. Life without men. That's it, she'd just go without, become a committed spinster. It would be much simpler on her own. And in the New Year she'd think about what Hazel had said and go check out old Sandy.

Thoughts of Hazel brought her back to what they'd been talking about before Christmas. Maybe she should have another read through her notebook and see what it prompted?

On her bed, pillows plumped up and ready, she reached to pull her notebook out of her bedside cabinet. But she'd misjudged the distance and nearly toppled over. In the moment it took to correct herself she dropped the notebook onto the floor. When she moved to the edge of the bed and leaned down to retrieve it, she noticed something had fallen out. A little, clouded black-and-white image.

Her twelve-week scan.

Oh my God. A sob bubbled up from her throat. When must she have put it in there? She had no recollection of doing so. And why hadn't she noticed it before now? To be fair, she had only written in the first third of the book, this must have been tucked into the back.

With her heart thumping she picked it up from the floor, righted herself on the bed, and held the image of her once-foetus in the cradle of her cupped hands. And started to cry.

My poor baby, she thought. What did I do to you?

Another memory rose in her mind: Danny screaming at her the week before she found out she was pregnant. She was trying to tell him it was over. She knew he would always be special to her, she'd told him. He was her first, but the relationship was no longer working for her. He was becoming too clingy. Too dependant on her.

To say he didn't take it well was an understatement. At first he shouted at her. Calling her all the offensive names he could think of. But when she ran to the bathroom and started packing her toiletries, he changed tactic. Actually got down on his knees. Apologised. Begged her to stay. He was only being horrible because he was scared of losing her.

He kept on for hours. And eventually persuaded her to stay. 'I'm going through a tricky patch,' he said. 'But once I get through this, it's all gaunna be sunshine and flowers, babe, you'll see. I'll be the Danny you fell in love with.' He gripped both her hands and stared into her eyes.

'I'm...' she began, unsure once again. His temper had been scary. But he was a good guy, wasn't he? He could make her happy.

'God, I love you, babe,' he said, and planted rapid kisses all over her face until she melted and they were both giggling.

The unease left her. But only for a few days. She turned away from the bathroom mirror one morning to find him in the doorway, staring at her. His face was impassive. He was about to state fact. 'You leave me,' he said. 'And I'll kill myself.'

'Jesus,' she replied, shivering. He turned away and walked out of the door. 'Danny,' she shouted after him. But he was down the stairs, out of the door and gone.

It wasn't long before she realised she must be pregnant. She'd missed a couple of periods, knowing deep within herself what it meant but unable to face the truth, until her mother noticed something was different.

'Are you pregnant?' she asked at the end of one Sunday dinner, while they washed the dishes together.

Jenna stared dumbly down at the dish in her hand.

Sally placed a hand on her back. 'Have you had a test yet?'

Jenna coughed. Offered a weak smile. 'I couldn't.'

Turned out she was eleven weeks gone. A scan was booked, and the little piece of paper she now held in her hand was produced as evidence.

Danny was beside himself. 'I'm going to be a dad,' he sang. 'I'm going to be a great fucking dad.'

And the look he gave her tore at her heart and weighed her down with an expectation she knew she couldn't ever deliver. It wasn't a look of love and togetherness. It was a look of ownership. A look that said: got you. You're going nowhere now.

The next Sunday dinner her mother once again caught her as they washed dishes. Danny didn't ever come to lunch with her. He said her parents didn't like him and he wasn't about to put himself through their scrutiny week in, week out.

'Where's the glow?' Sally asked, staring into Jenna's eyes.

'I'm just tired, Mum,' she replied. 'Honestly. Wiped out.'

'Mmm,' her mum said, and put an arm over her shoulder. 'Talk to me, honey. I've known you all your life. I've watched you nearly every moment, and I know when my baby is troubled.'

Jenna started crying. 'I'm too young for this. I've got my job and...' She was sobbing, gulping for breath.

'And?' Sally prompted.

'I tried to break it off before I found out I was pregnant, and he threatened to kill himself if I ever leave him.' The words left her in a torrent of sound. She barely paused for breath as she detailed their almost fall-out, his tactics of persuasion, his look of ownership. And then she told her about the afternoon he'd taken her to meet his little brother.

'He did what?' her mother asked in disbelief.

'But there's a kindness there. A vulnerable side.'

'Who are you trying to persuade, dear?'

Jenna cried some more.

'Do you want out?' Sally asked, feet braced as if she was ready to take on the world to save her daughter.

Jenna nodded.

'Do you want to keep the baby?'

Jenna paused, then slowly shook her head from side to side.

She stayed at her parents that night. Left a lie on Danny's phone to say that her mum was ill and she was staying over to keep a watch on her, and then she threw her phone into the sink along with the dishes so he couldn't reply. The very next morning her mother started the process for a termination.

Jenna held a hand over the image, then lightly applied the pad of her index finger to the tiny spot where her baby lay. Sorrow, she recognised, was a stain that would never leave her soul.

That was the most difficult period of her life. The termination. Danny being killed. Then her dad's heart attack. It was a wonder her head and heart didn't both give way.

She'd managed to keep all of that mostly tamped down, until now. Until she met Luke. And then her awakening feelings for him had stirred everything up.

In the mess that was her brain was her love for, and fear of, Danny. Her guilt that she'd killed their baby, and suspicion she'd driven him to his death.

She knew then, with the suddenness of a door being slammed open by a cold, hard wind, that she had to face up to all of that or she would never know peace. Plus, if she and Luke were going to stay part of each other's lives she had to know exactly what happened that day with Danny, or it would play on her mind and ruin any chance of happiness that they had. She clearly didn't have the best instincts when it came to judging men, but as sure as Christmas came with excess, Luke was hiding something.

Having made that decision, she felt lighter than she had for weeks. Yes. This was absolutely the right thing to do, and it started with following up what she had begun all those years ago.

As soon as the holidays were over she was going on a trip to meet one of the last people to see Danny alive.

Chapter 57

Jamie and Amanda sat down to a Christmas meal right out of a television advert. Roast potatoes, a giant turkey crown and all the usual vegetables. Followed by Christmas pudding with brandy sauce. And then a glass of port each.

Looking across the table it seemed to Jamie that Amanda had set to eating with grim determination. She was *absolutely* going to enjoy this. Wasn't this what Christmas was all about – a set menu and overeating? For the entirety of the meal they didn't say a word to each other. The only sound in the room was of them masticating and swallowing.

After dinner, they even watched the Queen's speech.

Jamie opened his mouth to ask why they were watching it, but Amanda shushed him. Then they watched Christmas episodes of all of the soaps. And then a Christmas movie. Throughout it all, Jamie was bored out of his mind, but he felt a strange fascination, watching his sister. It was as if she felt this was her last Christmas on Earth and she was going to be damned sure she would follow the ideal and enjoy it.

'Well, wasn't that jolly?' Jamie said at the end of the film.

Amanda exploded. 'You've had a sour puss on you all day. You could have at least tried to enjoy yourself.'

'For fuckssake, Amanda. This is supposed to be a holiday where you do what pleases you, not "what is written". He formed air quotes as he spoke. 'This is like sitting through a Christmas commandment. You *will* eat this and you *will* watch that. Fucking pathetic. Don't be such a sheep.' He left the room and went to his bed.

Lying there, staring upward. As cars drove by outside, shadows waxed and waned against the ceiling. Watching the indistinct shapes move above him he realised he felt just as lacking in substance. Like he was a slice of darkness growing and shrinking, dependant on the light from someone else. That was what his entire life was like. And it was time for change.

Everyone who had ever been part of his life had let him down, including the sainted Danny, even if it wasn't his fault. And what about his mum and dad? Sure, he was fed and watered, but the more he tried to look back, the more he couldn't remember a kind word or a soft hand. Ever. They were too busy fighting each other and drinking.

Then there were the foster parents. Pure evil. What kind of way was that to treat a little boy desperate for a family; desperate for any small act of love and affection?

The shapes on the ceiling continued to move, to shift, to reach down and pull him in. A memory. Nothing but a boy, his voice hadn't even broken yet, and he was in a bath. She was on her knees by his side, reaching in, losing the soap, finding it again.

'We need to wash the sin out of you,' she said as she held the soap to his groin and began to rub. Hard. 'The sins of the child, and the sins of the man to come.'

While she worked the soap into a lather her husband stood at her back. His hand stroking her hair, a secret smile working its way into the corners of his mouth.

He recoiled from a memory that visited him from time to time in his dreams. He was certain there was more, otherwise why would there be so much fear and anticipation attached to that memory? But his mind protected him from the detail. Memory held fast a black, iron door and wouldn't let him through.

He was glad they were dead. And how easy was that to organise. A little adaptation to their boiler while they slept, and fatal gases filled the house instead of flowing out into the night air.

Finally in the roll-call of those who had let him down: Luke. He'd begun to let him in, to trust him. It had been almost soothing to watch him and Nathan. To see how people who cared about each other actually behaved. But he allowed his yearnings for a proper family to cloud his judgement. Luke was no better than the rest of them. And that was made worse by the man behaving like he was some kind of saint.

His acts of caring were clearly just that: acts.

He'd never forget the barely suppressed anger in his eyes at the funfair. Oh, he'd tried to hide it. Tried to pretend that everything was fine, that he wasn't furious that Jamie had lost his precious wee boy. For the rest of that day he barely spoke to him, concentrating entirely on Nathan. He felt ignored and dismissed, as if he was nothing and nobody.

After all he'd 'found' the boy, and shouldn't that have been the main consideration in Luke's mind?

Luke had led Jamie to believe he was better than that. But like everyone else he was a liar. A fraud.

As far as he was concerned the man deserved everything that was coming to him.

Chapter 58

Nathan stood in the middle of the living room, hands on his hips, and surveyed the space around him. Concerned that the boy was upset about something, Luke asked what was wrong.

'What's owld clays? And I don't like porridge. It's yuck.'

It took Luke a moment to work out what he was talking about. Gemma had been round the day before and helped them take down all of the Christmas decorations and stow away the tree.

She must have said something to Nathan when he was out of the room. The Scottish phrase that got trotted out after every celebration: 'It's back to auld claes and porridge.' Time to put the glad rags away and go back to boring food.

'Old clothes, she means. Put your nice stuff away till the next party. And stop eating all that sweet and fancy food. Cos it will give you a big belly.' With that he advanced on the boy, grabbed him and started tickling said belly.

After a few minutes of laughter he sat the boy down on the sofa.

'Want to watch a movie while I do some work?'

'Yes, please,' Nathan said. '*Lion King*?'

'We got you lots of new ones from Santa. Don't you want to...'

Nathan shook his head.

'*Lion King* it is.'

With the boy happily watching his favourite movie and singing along to the songs, Luke booted up his laptop. He really needed to drum up some business for the New Year.

Following the incident when he was on the nightclub door, he'd had to accept that his days doing that kind of work were over. Which was no real loss. It was a handy way to get some quick earnings to help out when things were tight, but it was uncomfortably close to the old version of him and he needed to move on. And what about the potential complaint? He'd still heard nothing from the police.

Thoughts of the law had him reaching for his phone. They hadn't been back to talk to him after that initial chat about Cameron either. Did that mean they were happy with his version of events?

Ken answered within a couple of rings. 'Merry Christmas, wee man,' he said.

'Aye...' Luke answered absently. 'I meant to ask you: did Anna ever bring in the cops after that night at the club?'

'Did she not get back and tell you?' Ken asked.

'Tell me what?' Luke felt a spark of irritation. If there had been any developments he should have been kept informed.

'The ladies, and I'm using that word loosely for this gang, were fed free cocktails for the rest of the night and went away drunk and happy.'

'So...?'

'So Anna decided if they weren't still complaining at the end of the night, and there was no social media fallout, there was no point in her bringing in the cops. The matter was dealt with. Cost her a bit of cash, like; those women were thirsty, but as far as she was concerned it was over.'

'She might have told me,' Luke said.

'Probably wanted you to stew in it for a wee while.'

'Aye,' Luke replied, thinking with everything else going on the worry about it had only been a small distraction.

The men said their farewells, promised to meet up soon, and cut the connection.

At least that was sorted, Luke thought. But he still needed to boost his income and that meant a fresh concentration on building up his therapy business. Determined that he would make it work, he looked up other similar kinds of businesses online to see what he could learn from them. If he found an approach from someone else that seemed to work, he wasn't above copying it and tailoring it to his needs.

While he was online, it occurred to him he should look in on his social media accounts in case there were any requests for appointments or even some positive reviews that he could use in ongoing promotions.

There were no contacts that needed following up, he noted with a sigh, but he had been tagged in a few posts.

Oh. Excellent.

With a hitch of excitement in his chest he clicked through to see what was being said. Hopefully it would be good enough to stick in an ad, or something. His happiness was short-lived when he read what they'd said about him.

Absolute charlatan. Don't waste your money, said one.

Mansplainer and borderline inappropriate, said another. *Always sitting with his legs so wide. Yuck.*

What the hell does that even mean, he thought? And who are these people? He read the names. None of them had been to him for therapy. This must be a case of mistaken identity.

The last one he read almost had steam coming out of his ears.

If I thought this idiot belonged to a professional body I'd be straight on them to have him disbarred, or whatever you do to stop these people. But he probably got his 'qualification' from a £20 online course. Don't use this guy, he's a joke.

He angrily typed out a reply, but before he pressed send, he read the comment again. It was by a woman called Hazel Williams. Who was she? He'd never heard of her in his life. How could someone be so malicious as to try and ruin him professionally, because that was exactly what she was trying to do.

Clicking through to her account he saw that she'd studied journalism, had a husband and a couple of kids. But there was something odd about the people in the photos – they seemed too shiny, with matching expressions, and their clothes all looked like they'd just come out of a box. The photos looked staged, not like these were real people at all. And the images of the woman were all selfies – she was in none of the photos with the husband or children.

Internal sirens blaring, he looked on. This Hazel woman had had her account for some years, but there were very few entries. Two kids, but only one birthday party mentioned. Why would you celebrate one kid online and not the other?

There was something off about this. Way off.

This was a troll. Had to be. But why would someone troll his business? Was there a competitor out there trying to kill off the competition? If there was, they were wasting their time; his business wasn't exactly thriving.

Next, he clicked on this woman's friend list, and there were only about a dozen.

With a jolt he recognised the face on one of the thumbnail pictures.

Jenna.

Chapter 59

The sun was wintering low in the sky, the glare forcing Jenna to wear her sunglasses. She took the approaching bend slowly, wondering as she did so if this was the place where Luke and Danny went off the road.

'That's what I like,' Hazel said beside her. 'A careful driver.'

Jenna took her eyes off the road just long enough to send her passenger a quick smile.

'Thanks for coming along with me today. I'm not sure I would have actually done this if you weren't with me.'

'No problem,' Hazel said. 'It struck me that you needed to. And what kind of friend would I be if I didn't come and keep you company? You never know, this old guy could be some kind of pervert. If there's two of us you're bound to be safer.'

As the holidays had dragged on, Jenna's mind had gone more and more to the events of the past – Danny, Luke, the old man she met at the court. And to Danny's parents. And she knew she wouldn't be able to think straight until she'd sorted it all out in her head.

She said as much to Hazel when they chatted online, and Hazel offered her company and support when she'd said the time had come to talk to Uncle Sandy.

Taken aback by how keen she was to help, Jenna agreed. It would be nice to meet Hazel in person, after all her support over the previous weeks.

When she saw her waving as she pulled into the car park, Jenna was surprised. They must be in the same age bracket, but time had been kind to her. She looked like she'd just left university a matter of months ago. When she'd looked at Hazel's photos on social media she'd thought her youthful looks were down to the use of a filter, but it was clear the lucky woman didn't need any.

'Hey,' Jenna said. 'Nice to see you in the flesh after all this time.'

As she spoke she fought for memories of her during their time at university. But came up blank. Which wasn't so odd, really. There were so many people who'd come and gone in her small circle of friends over the years she spent there. It was very plausible that they had met and Hazel hadn't made an impression. They were all still finding out who they were at that age. Some used that to blend into the background, others tried everything to stand out. Hazel must have been one of the former.

'Oh, man, it is so good to get out of the house. Feels like I've been indoors for years.' Hazel gave her a quick up-and-down of assessment. 'You look well.'

There was a grudging admission in her voice that surprised Jenna.

As if she recognised she'd allowed too much honesty to leak into her speech, Hazel added a qualification. 'For someone who's looking after an invalid mother, you actually look amazing.'

'You're being too kind,' Jenna replied, then paused. 'Thank you for doing this, Hazel.' She exhaled. 'I'm feeling a little nervous.'

'Why?' Hazel asked.

'What if I find out something that I really don't want to know?'

Chapter 60

The living room of Sandy's house was like a tribute to the 1990s. Dark-green, sponge-painted walls, dado rails, a sofa and chairs with floral print, and round occasional tables with skirted covers. And on top of every surface a display of Wedgewood figurines.

Amanda looked around for clues as to what kind of man he was and how he spent his time. There were a couple of photos of Sandy as a young man with his arm round a young woman.

'You brought a friend?' Sandy said to Jenna, his face bright with smiles. Apart from being more than a few pounds lighter, he hadn't changed much in the years since Amanda last saw him. Then, seeing the movement of Amanda's eyes, Sandy nodded towards the photos. 'That's our Jean. She's out for a coffee and a natter with her pal. No' sure when she'll be back, you know what you women are like once you get started.' He paused. 'To be fair, I'm every bit as bad,' he added with a self-mocking grin. 'You might meet her afore ye leave.'

Hope not, thought Amanda. One more person who might recognise her.

'What if Sandy recognises you?' Jamie had asked when she told him she was going on a trip with Jenna to see their old neighbour.

'God, it's been at least fifteen years since he saw me, and I was barely into my teens then. I'm thinking it's worth the risk. You'd be a problem.' She looked at her brother. 'You look like Dad, and there's a bit of Danny in you, across the eyes. I take more from our mum's side.'

Now, Jenna was speaking to the old man: 'Yes, this is my friend, Hazel. I hope you don't mind her tagging along?' Jenna spoke brightly, as if trying to keep the mood up.

'Why would I mind having two beautiful young women in my house?' Sandy laughed. He rubbed his hands as if warming himself up. 'Sit down, ladies.' He pointed to the sofa, and once they were seated he lowered himself by increments into his arm-chair. Knee or hip problems, wondered Amanda.

'Do I know you, hen?' he asked Amanda, his eyes steady on hers.

'If I remind you of someone I hope they were very lovely,' Amanda replied with a chuckle. 'But no, we've never met. I'm sure I would remember a charmer like yourself.'

'Jings,' Sandy said. 'Can you come back next week? Two minutes in my house and I feel ten years younger already.'

The two women exchanged looks and chuckled dutifully. Amanda felt relief that she'd passed the first test. Hopefully that would push from his mind any notions that their paths had crossed.

They talked about the holidays just past, the excesses of Christmas, the cold start to the year, any wishes they had that they were in for a nice summer. Then Sandy climbed out of his chair, saying something about a kettle, and appeared a couple of minutes later with a tray bearing mugs, milk, tea, coffee and biscuits. The biscuits were Rich Tea and digestives, and Amanda felt a charge of recognition. This was what her mother always gave to visitors. Indeed, it looked exactly like a plate she might have arranged.

Once they'd had their drinks and biscuits, Jenna brought the conversation round to the reason why she was visiting.

'And gosh,' she said, 'you've barely changed in all those years since I saw you at the court. And you've lost some weight.'

Sandy preened a little. Patted his belly. 'Eventually got the hip op, but it's my knees that are giving me jip now. It might not look like it, but I'm definitely more mobile than I was.'

'Do you remember much about that time? When Danny died.'

Ouch, thought Amanda. That was a bit clumsy.

But Sandy laughed good-naturedly. 'Listen, I might not remember what I had for dinner last night, but my long-term memory is spot on.'

'Sorry,' Jenna said. Then she reached into her handbag and

pulled out her old notebook. She waved it at Sandy. 'Your memory might be good, but mine's shocking. I have to write everything down.'

'It was such a difficult time, but,' Sandy said. 'What with Danny dying. He might have been a bad bastard, like, and you'll forgive me for speaking ill of the dead, but there was something deeply wrong with that fella. Anyhoo, the trial, then his mum and dad dying in a car crash themselves – what a weird twist of fate that was. So much pain, so much death in such a short time.' His sigh after he spoke seemed to come up from his feet. 'And then there was they two kiddies. Jamie and Amanda.' He shook his head slowly.

Amanda clenched both fists and clamped her lips shut.

'What happened to them?' Jenna asked.

'Don't know, hen,' Sandy said. 'Word was that they were fostered, and to different families, which was horrible. Imagine losing your brother and your parents in car accidents, and then the authorities parcel you out separately? Poor kids. Wouldn't happen now, I don't think. I often wonder what happened to them. A damned shame. It's them I feel worse for. James was just eight or nine, I think. Amanda was about eleven or twelve.'

The sadness in his voice was so evident that Amanda could feel herself respond. Slightly turning to the side, she tried to wipe away a tear before anyone saw her.

'Awright, hen?' Sandy asked. Of course he missed nothing.

'Dust allergy,' she replied. 'I'm very sensitive.'

'Oh.' Sandy looked around himself. 'I have a woman who comes in on Thursdays,' he winked, clearly talking about his wife. 'I'll have a word. Can't have my guests sneezing at everything.'

Amanda waved away his concern. 'I'm fine. Honest, I'm fine.'

He was peering at her now. 'You sure we've never met? You ... just, you remind me of someone.'

'I've got one of those faces,' Amanda replied. 'Anyway, Jenna was just about to...' She shot a look at Jenna.

'Yes,' Jenna said. 'Poor Amanda and Jamie. So much pain in their young lives.' She shook her head. 'How would you cope with that?'

'Aye. That's a lot of tragedy for a young mind to cope with,' Sandy agreed.

'So...' Jenna opened her notebook. 'You were disappointed not to give evidence, as I recall.'

'Yeah. You build yourself up for it, you know? It's quite a daunting place, a court room.'

'What would your evidence have been?' Amanda asked.

Chapter 61

Fifteen years earlier

It was a road Sandy had driven many times over the years since he moved out of the city. He loved small-town life, the closeness to the countryside, being away from the blare of the urban sprawl. But for his wife, the shopping just wasn't as good, so every now and again they'd jump in the car and drive to Marks and Spencer in Milngavie.

Jean had gone to the supermarket, and she liked to take her time, so he'd wondered over to the local bookshop, chosen a book to read while drinking a coffee, then, as arranged, he'd met Jean back in the car park and helped her load the shopping into the car. He was a man of habit and he had to get home by noon to have his porridge.

On the road, and Sandy was looking forward to his oatmeal, when a car and its passengers caught his attention. It was only for a few seconds, but he could see the young men in the car were arguing. There was an intensity to their focus on each other, and a sharpness in the way in which their mouths were moving.

Then they were passed him.

And he realised who the passenger was.

'That was Danny,' he said to Jean. 'Gordon and Fiona's boy.'

'What would he be doing out this way?' Jean asked. 'Who was he with? Time that young man got himself a good woman. Might help him settle down.'

Sandy laughed. 'God, you're so predictable. Always looking to pair people up. And no, he was with a man.'

'Whatever takes your fancy,' Jean replied.

'Don't get the impression that's what Danny's into,' Sandy said. 'And anyway if he is, I just witnessed a lover's tiff. They were shouting blue murder at each other.'

*

Sandy looked at his two guests.

'And that was that. Or so I thought. Then it was on the news just a few days later that Danny had died in a car crash. And that drink or drugs were involved.' Sandy stuck out his chin as if daring anyone to defy his version of events. 'I might be naïve when it comes to drugs and all that. But if they guys were under the influence, my name's Johnny Walker.'

'You sure about that?' Jenna asked. 'You said you only saw them for a moment.'

'You can pick up a lot about people in a second or two,' Sandy asserted. 'It was plenty of time to see that they were arguing and that they were both pretty sober.'

Amanda really wanted to believe his version of events.

'Just playing devil's advocate,' she said, 'but can you really tell that in the seconds it takes for a car to drive past you?'

'I could be wrong, aye,' Sandy replied. 'But I don't think so. I've seen plenty of drunks in my time, darling. Scotland can't be too proud of its record in that regard.' He shook his head. 'They were sober.'

'The post-mortem said that Danny had enough booze and drugs in his system to render him unconscious, even without the massive damage he suffered in the crash. How does that tally with what you saw?' Jenna asked.

'I have a theory,' Sandy said. His eyes narrowed, and he spoke slowly and clearly as if he'd repeated this speech every day since his appearance in court was cancelled. 'Danny was legendary for his ability to handle the booze. I daresay it would have been the same for whatever drugs he was taking. Robertson did admit, apparently, that they had been on a bender that week. Maybe they were coming out the other side of that, and there was enough stuff in their bodies to register in any drugs tests, but mentally they were, or they *thought* they were, on the ball...' There was a moment's pause while they all considered this. 'I know hee-haw about blood alcohol levels and all that stuff,' Sandy continued, 'but I have had the odd boozing session in my life, and I know I've felt more than capable of driving when my body was still full of whisky.'

Jenna looked up from her notebook. 'When you talked to me back then, you said that the timings didn't add up? Something about them being off?'

'Yeah,' he said, while shaking his head. 'It was a long time ago.' He shifted in his seat. 'The more I think about that, the more I feel it was me who got the wrong end of the stick.'

'Maybe over time you've allowed the news reports to throw doubt on what you remember?' Jenna asked.

'Maybe,' Sandy said.

'Let's forget about the timings given by the police over the accident. What do you recall happening?' asked Jenna.

'The guys passed us just before noon. That time sticks in my head cos when we go into town I like to be home around about noon for some scran.'

'You're a creature of habit then,' she said. 'You need to be back home for your lunch.' She paused. 'And that's why you remember when you passed them in the car.'

'Aye.' Sandy scratched the side of his head. 'I read in the paper – or maybe I heard it on the radio – that the call came in to the emergency services just before 2pm. But I passed them as they approached the spot where the accident happened just before noon. So they must have crashed just after we saw them – not around two o'clock.'

'Really?' asked Jenna. 'Could they not have driven somewhere else and came back, and the accident happened then, just before the call came in to the paramedics?'

'I drove past the spot later, hen. Saw the bright-yellow accident tape across the gap in the hedging. There were skid marks on the road, and the direction they pointed in was as if the car had been coming from Milngavie, not from Glasgow.' He held his hands out. 'To my mind that suggests the car went off the road just after they passed us.'

Amanda shivered. The old man was one of the last people to have seen Danny alive.

As if he read her thoughts, Sandy continued. 'I've asked myself every day since: What if I waved them down? Could I have done anything to stop the accident?'

'You're being hard on yourself, don't you think?' Jenna asked.

'Sure, that's what your logical brain tells you, but the conscience is a right nag. What if...?' Sandy crossed his arms, and his legs. His gaze was on the floor, but his mind was locked in memory. 'The paramedics were quoted in the local paper...' He looked to Jenna in query.

'Wasn't me who interviewed them,' she replied. 'My dad had just died, and I was on compassionate leave by then.'

'They were quoted as saying that if they had gotten there just a little while earlier, they could have saved the deceased man. What if we'd been a little later to hit the road? What if I'd waited a wee while longer in the bookshop? Read a few more pages? We might have seen it happen. We could have phoned it in then, and maybe Danny would still be alive today.' His eyes were dull with what-ifs and lost possibilities, his conscience a weight on his memory.

'To be fair, the lad was in self-destruct mode, so maybe I'm feeling guilty over nothing. If he hadn't died that day I'm sure he would have been killed long before now.'

Amanda was more than a little annoyed about Sandy criticising Danny again, and she was also anxious, now, that his wife might come in and possibly recognise her. So she looked at her watch, exaggerating the movement.

Sandy took the hint. 'I suppose you ladies need to be leaving soon,' he said, and pushed himself to his feet with a groan. They said their goodbyes as they made their way to the door.

But as they approached it, Amanda couldn't resist – she needed to hear one last thing about her family from someone who knew them.

'I'm just fascinated by this whole story,' she said. 'I'm a bit of a wannabe writer. And this would all make a great novel, don't you think?' she trilled, ignoring Jenna's look of surprise. 'You knew the family. This Danny guy's parents. What were they like?'

'I was a bit of a drinker back then, so I got on okay with the dad. His mum was a poor wee soul. Always looked like she needed a good night's sleep and a proper feed. Again...' Sandy exhaled long and slow and made a face of apology '...I don't like to speak badly of the dead, but there was something wrong with that family. The screaming I used to hear coming through the wall. And she gave as good as she got, by the way. Nah, that wasn't the way to speak to your weans or your partner. Proper nasty it was at times.' He shuddered, as if at other memories too dark to articulate. 'I was glad to move away, if I'm being honest.'

'But Danny's parents gave you a lift to the court that day,' Jenna said. 'I got the impression you were all friends.'

Sandy sucked on his bottom lip as if considering how much to say. 'You got away, you know? But they had a way of reeling you back in.'

The door opened before Sandy could say anything more, and a small, female version of him stood in front of them, wearing matching red hat and gloves, and a gold-coloured padded jacket.

Sandy made the introductions, and Jean shook both their hands. Her eyes lingered on Amanda for longer than she was comfortable with.

'Gosh,' Jean said. 'You're so like—'

'Hi, I'm Hazel.' Amanda repeated her name. 'I've got one of those faces. A day doesn't go by without someone saying I remind them of someone else. But I'm just me, I'm afraid. Nothing exciting.'

But as she walked out of the door, *they had a way of reeling you back in* rang in her ears. How disrespectful. She was sick of people lying about her family.

Chapter 62

The two women were mostly silent on the way back into Milngavie. On each bend of the road, Jenna again wondered if this might be the one where the accident happened. She had planned, long ago, to drive along here and work it all out, where exactly the tragedy had unfolded, but a tragedy of her own had intervened, meaning she hadn't truly put to rest one of the worst periods of her life.

'You okay?' she asked Hazel. 'You're really quiet.'

Amanda looked out of her window, then back to Jenna. 'It's just so sad,' she said. 'What a waste of a life. Every one that was touched by ... this guy's death has never really recovered. Sandy's wracked with guilt, the mum and dad died in a car crash, of all things, this Luke fella sounds like he's still affected by it, and you. All these years later and you're still trying to make sense of it all.'

'True,' Jenna replied.

'And what happened to the siblings? Where did they go?'

'Poor kids.' Jenna looked at Hazel. 'It's the ones left behind that suffer most, eh?'

'You don't want to look them up? Find out what they remember?'

'They were just weans,' Jenna replied. 'I'm not sure they'll be worth talking to.' Something in Hazel's expression made her add a qualification. 'About the accident, I mean.' She focused back on the road, wondering if she'd imagined the look that passed over Hazel's face. It was as if she was taking this all too personally.

She glanced back, and the woman looked very relaxed, her eyes ahead and her hands on her lap. She gave herself a mental ticking off. She was seeing problems where there were none.

Her mobile rang. She looked at the screen and saw that it was Luke.

'I'll just ignore it,' she said to Hazel. But as she spoke, she had to negotiate a bend in the road on a rise that was so steep, she couldn't see if anything was coming towards them. As they reached the top, she found she'd taken it too fast, and the car pulled towards the centre of the road. With a sigh of relief she noted that the way ahead was clear. Perhaps this was where the accident had happened.

'I don't mind,' Hazel said. 'If you don't have hands-free, pull over if you want to talk to him. Whatever you think.'

In truth, Jenna wasn't doing much thinking at this point. Her heart and mind were a tangle of half-formed thought and soured emotion. And the day had been going so well until he phoned.

Sandy had been very helpful, willing to tell his version of events – a version that begged the question, why was there a two-hour discrepancy between the time when he saw the men in the car to the time when the emergency services were called?

She felt a chill at this, and she wished she'd never bumped into Luke Forrest. Going to him for therapy was a waste of time and money, and why did he come into her shop? Her life had been swimming along just fine before he showed up. And now she felt she was lost at sea, in a whirlpool, being buffeted by waves, ears and eyes full of water, entirely unable to work out in which direction to kick, and where to find the surface.

Chapter 63

Luke could feel his frustrations building and building. He'd already snapped at Nathan twice that morning, earning a hurt look of rebuke from the boy. He apologised each time and each time his words were met with a quiet, 'S'ok, Dad.' Which made him feel even worse.

He needed to go for a run, punch a bag, lift some weights or sit down with some pan pipes in the background.

In the kitchen he turned on the coffee machine.

Then he got down on the floor and did forty press-ups. After that his chest was aching and his breathing was slightly awry, but he didn't feel any better.

He needed to get out of the house.

He called Gemma. She didn't answer.

Next, he tried Jenna, and neither did she. He gave Jamie a try, with the same result.

Ken. He should call Ken. It would be good to speak to someone completely unconnected with all the shit going on in his life. The big man answered within two rings.

'My favourite arsehole,' Ken said. 'How you doing?'

'Fancy a coffee?'

'Aye. Where?'

'Mine.'

'When?'

'Now?'

'That's what I like about chatting with you, wee man. The brevity. It's good for the soul. See you in twenty.'

Good as his word, Ken arrived at Luke's door on time. After a round of throwing Nathan in the air and chatting about their individual Christmases, Ken and Luke made for the kitchen, where Ken brought the subject round to Luke's need for a chat.

'My life's turning to shit, man,' Luke answered as he flicked on the kettle.

'Bit dramatic, but I'm listening,' Ken said with a smile, then, when he realised Luke was being serious, his smile faltered.

'First, that photo arrives on my doormat, then the wee fella's taken by his fuckwit father. Said fuckwit dies. The police visit me cos I was the last person to see him alive, apparently.'

'Jeez,' said Ken as he leaned against the kitchen worktop.

'I find a woman. Fall in love. Lose my job at the club. Then Jenna finds out I killed her ex in an accident, and now she won't return my calls.'

'Holy fuck, mate.'

'And now some fucker is trying to ruin my business.'

'Man, that's a lot of shit to deal with,' Ken said.

'And I'm totally skint. If this business doesn't work, I don't know how I can support the wee man.' Luke went to the door and looked down to the living room, where he could see that Nathan was sitting cross-legged in front of the TV. Then he turned back to Ken. 'There was a little bit of life insurance when Lisa died, and her mum will help out, but I can't rely on that. I want to leave the life insurance for when Nathan's going to uni, or something.' Having said all of that out loud made Luke feel momentarily worse. 'Sorry, mate.' He looked at Ken. He laughed. 'And how are you?'

Ken joined in the laughter. 'I thought my life was shit, but now I'm enjoying the comparison.'

'Fuck off.' Luke surprised himself by managing a grin.

'Seriously, though. Is this one of those conversations where you just want someone to listen, or are you looking for advice?'

'I don't know what the hell I want.'

'Anything come of the police thing with Cameron?' Ken asked.

'Haven't heard back,' Luke replied. 'Not sure if I'm a person of interest or not anymore.'

'Don't you want to find out?'

'What, and draw attention to myself again? Best to let sleeping dogs lie and all that. They must have decided that there was nothing in it, that Cameron's death was simply down to an over-dose. There was certainly nothing to suggest he'd been held down and forced to take the drugs when I saw him. So...' Luke shrugged. Matter closed.

'What about work? Want me to get the word out to the other pubs and clubs? See if anyone needs anyone on the door?'

'Beggars can't be choosers,' Luke replied. 'I need the cash. But that kind of work...' He sent Ken a look of apology, but the big man just shrugged. He understood where Luke was coming from. He was one of the few people Luke had trusted with his past – he'd not gone into detail, but he'd provided the bones of the story. Not that he didn't trust Ken with all the ins and outs, but he didn't want to see that look of judgement in his eyes when he realised who the real Luke Forrest was.

They'd been talking so long the kettle needed to be switched on again. Luke set about sorting out the drinks. 'And then there's Jamie. I really want to make it right with the guy, but he won't return my calls. And neither will Jenna.'

Ken pursed his lips and exhaled. 'You've been through it, mate.'

'You're not joking. Feels like the world is conspiring against me.' He brought out his phone and opened his social-media apps, then showed Ken the profile of the woman who was trashing his business.

'That feels a bit personal,' Ken said. 'An ex-girlfriend, maybe?'

'I can't think of any who might hate me that much.'

'What, even back in the day when you and Danny were cock of the walk? Any girls you treated like shit who could be out for blood?'

'I wasn't that bad,' Luke bristled. 'I wasn't exactly a saint, but the worst I got was to two-time somebody. It was Danny that did the real damage.'

He thought back to the evening before Christmas when he was working on the door with Ken, and the hen party kicked up a fuss. There was a woman in the crowd. He could see her face yet. A perfect mix of spite and pleasure. He described her to Ken.

'Remember her?'

'I was too busy trying to fend them off, mate.'

'There's a pattern here,' Luke said absently. Then stopped in the motion of pouring water into a mug. He put the kettle down, shaking a little now, his mind suddenly scrabbling as pieces seemed to fall into place. 'And when I think about it, it all began the moment I met Jenna.'

Ken snorted his disbelief. 'What you saying, man?'

'You should have seen her that day she met me at Danny's grave.' Luke's heart gave a lurch. 'Maybe she knew who I was all along? Maybe she's the one behind all of this? Oh my God. What if it's Jenna,' he said. 'What if she's the one who's out for revenge.'

Chapter 64

Jenna dropped Hazel off at the car park she'd picked her up from a few hours earlier. With effusive thanks and promises to keep in touch, she drove away.

With her eyes on the road and her mind on the recent past, she reviewed her conversation with Sandy. He was every bit as hard on Danny as he had been the last time they spoke. And he did it with a great deal more knowledge than she had. He'd spent years living around the man – when he was younger to be fair, but wouldn't it still give him a good knowledge of what he was really like?

She assessed her own reactions to Danny, again. Was she idealising their relationship? For sure he was her first, big heart connection, and perhaps they'd had unfinished business, but was she putting him up a pedestal? Was her guilt about the baby clouding how she felt about him at the end?

A memory slammed into her mind, with claws so sharp she had to pull over.

Meeting his little brother after school in that little park. How many times had that happened? A handful? She'd talked to Hazel about some of those occasions. But this one time it was different; they started arguing. She couldn't remember what it was about. But he changed, became this other man, and started to humiliate her. She remembered his face, the dead eyes as he grabbed at her top. What was he doing that for? Then: 'Show the wee man your tits.'

Oh God. She flushed with the shame of it. But why did she feel shame? He was the arsehole.

He'd changed back to the man she knew so quickly it was as if it never happened. And he carried on, chatting and laughing with his little brother. The little boy was as mortified as she was, but they kept on walking through the park and onto the kid's street, where they said goodbye before Danny's parents saw him.

How on earth had she forgotten that?

And what prompted the memory now?

As she made her way back home she wondered what else had gone on that she'd consigned to a dark place in her mind? Had she misremembered their entire time together?

No. She refused to believe that. They did have fun together. It was lovely at first, knowing that this man was so in love with her that he'd put the rest of his life behind him to concentrate on her. What young girl wouldn't be flattered by that kind of attention? But it did become too much. And he was more than a little clingy.

Actually, no: suffocating.

She thought about the way he made her feel at the end. She felt weighed down by him. Smothered. He wouldn't let her out of his sight. The more it went on the more she realised it wasn't healthy. *They* weren't healthy.

Her mind pulled at a thread, and a question formed. No, not a question, an idea. If that was the way Danny was with her, what would he have been like with an old friend, like Luke?

Danny's death was recorded as an accident. If Sandy was right and there was some missing time before the emergency services arrived, was there something else at play here? Had Luke killed Danny and passed it off as a crash?

She gave herself a mental shake. That kind of stuff happened in the movies. Who behaved like that in real life?

No. Despite everything, and pushing aside her poor judgement of Danny, she could see that there was a lot of good in Luke. From the brief time she'd spent with him as a client, she could see that he knew what he was talking about, and that he cared. That was something you couldn't fake.

Just who was the real Danny Morrison?

And who was the real Luke Forrest?

She pulled up outside her mother's house. Climbing out of the car, she locked it and then made her way to her front door. Eyes on the pavement, mind elsewhere, she became aware of a presence, and heard a voice.

'Can we talk?'

If he'd been wearing a cap it would have been in his hand. It was Luke.

Chapter 65

The post-holiday traffic suggested life was getting back to normal. All the way across town, Luke negotiated rowdy schoolkids, one red light after another, bad drivers, cyclists, bus drivers changing lanes without signalling, and even at one point a motorised wheelchair, all while building himself up to confront Jenna.

'What if you're wrong?' Ken had asked. 'What if you've taken two and two, and turned it into twenty-three dozen?'

'What kind of stupid analogy is that?' Luke had replied.

'I'm just trying to slow you down and make you think. You could be making a huge mistake here.'

'Nope.' Luke felt a cold certainty. There had been a consistent campaign against him, and Jenna was the common denominator. But quite how she managed to get Rab Cameron to abduct Nathan was beyond him. That suggested a very devious person.

'Mind staying here with the wee fella for a bit?' he'd asked Ken.

'Sure, but—'

'See ya.' Luke reached for his car keys. 'Don't let Nathan eat too much sugar.'

But now, at her mum's place, as she walked towards him, looking innocent and a little bit lost herself, much of his earlier certainty died. Was he, as Ken suggested, turning a lot of nothing into a whole lot of something momentous?

'Can we talk?' he asked her.

She stopped as if she'd walked into a brick wall. Crossed her arms. Not a good sign. 'Okay.'

He opened his mouth. Closed it again.

'How's Nathan?' she asked. 'Did he have a nice Christmas?' He wondered whether she would have liked to have been there to see him open his presents.

'He did, thanks. He was spoiled. Got way too much.'

'That's what it's all about, eh? Spoiling the kids.'

'Yeah,' he replied. How did this conversation become small talk about Christmas when he'd come over here to read her the riot act?

'And did you have a nice time?' she asked him.

'Other than watching Nathan, it was pretty bloody...' He shook his head. 'What are we doing, Jenna?'

'Not sure what you mean. You came over to see me.'

He wanted to hold her hands. Or hug her. Stroke the sleek darkness of her hair. Take her home and make love to her. Go for a slow walk in a beauty spot. Smooth that worried look from her face. He wanted to hold her and never let go.

Instead, he let his arms drop to his side, and he asked her, 'Who's Hazel?'

'Sorry?' she asked.

'The social-media account for my business is full of trash talk. As if someone is trying to ruin my business. And one of the worst is from a woman called Hazel. She's a friend of yours on social media.'

'I...' Jenna shook her head. And squared off to him. 'I've got a question of my own, Luke. Did you mean to kill Danny?'

'What?'

'I've been with a guy today called Sandy. He was one of the witnesses due to give evidence at your trial. He saw you and Danny the day he died. Just before the crash. And he said you were both sober.'

'I've been to prison for that. I pled guilty. I don't know what more you need,' he said, stomach churning. All his thoughts of love for her shrivelled. She was so suspicious of him she had gone out of her way to look into his old case, and here he was, mooning over her like some love-sick fool. 'You've got it in for me, haven't you?' he said, previous certainties slamming back up in his mind. 'Ever since we met, all of these things have been going wrong.'

'What on earth are you talking about?' she asked, taking a step back from him.

He edged forward. 'The threatening photos, losing my job at the club, the bad reviews, it's all been you.' He stabbed the air in front of him with his finger. 'Oh, you were clever, so bloody clever.'

'Luke, what on earth are you talking about?'

'It's been a great act. Oscar-worthy. Trying to get close to me. Make me love you, and then turn my life to shit. That was the plan, eh? But how you got Cameron to abduct Nathan is beyond me. Very clever, Jenna. Very clever indeed.' He stalked back to his car, anger sparking in every cell of his body.

She followed him. 'I don't know what you think you know, Luke, but you're off. Way off.'

'Save it,' he said. 'You got your wish. My life is crap. I have no job. No business. Happy?'

'Luke...'

'Goodbye, Jenna. Danny's been avenged. You win.'

Chapter 66

Jenna stayed standing by her front door long after Luke drove away. Shivering with the cold, nonetheless she remained where she was, trying to make sense of his words.

She heard her mother shout her name. Over and over. Eventually she went inside.

'What were you doing out there?' her mother asked. 'And what was all the fugging shouting about? The neighbours will be on to the police.'

Jenna walked into the living room, shucking her coat and bag as she went, carelessly dropping them onto the carpet, as if the simple act of putting them somewhere tidy was beyond her.

What on earth was going on in Luke's head?

Sally was in her usual seat armchair, a pink crocheted blanket on her lap, her face sagging into an expression of worry. 'You okay, love?' she asked. 'What's going on?'

'I'm fine, Mum,' Jenna said. 'Needing anything? A hot drink? Need the loo? Hungry?'

Sally waved away her daughter's concerns. 'I'm fine. Are you going to tell me what is going on?'

'Luke...' Jenna began, pulling her hair back from her face. 'He's not happy with me for some reason.' She thought through his accusations. Sure, she'd sought out old Sandy, and that didn't necessarily look good, but the other stuff? Rab Cameron, and Hazel? How on earth Luke thought she could have influenced either of those, she didn't know. And getting him to lose his job? And what photos? And what on earth was Hazel doing trashing his business?

'Jenna, tell me...'

'You don't need anything, Mum, no? In that case I'm off to my room. There's things I need to try and sort out.'

Ignoring further protests from her mother, Jenna retrieved her laptop from the kitchen and carried it through to her bedroom. Once there she studied Luke's social-media pages. Scanning them, hoping they made some sense of his accusations.

But...

Nothing.

No negative reviews. No good ones either. And certainly nothing from Hazel. He was certainly upset about something. Luke didn't strike her as a person to make stuff up, but what on earth was he on about? There was nothing here.

Chapter 67

Amanda felt a little frisson of pleasure at her own cleverness when Jenna phoned to tell her how Luke had been behaving. Immediately after he responded to her online review, she deleted it. And how typically arrogant of him was his reply:

I don't know who you are. You've never received treatment from me. Delete this immediately.

How high and mighty was he? Demanding that she delete her comments. No 'please'. No attempt to mollify. Just 'get rid'.

Okay, done, mate. See how you like it now.

The man was unravelling. She rubbed her hands at the thought.

'Luke's just been here,' Jenna said when Amanda answered Hazel's phone. She judged that it was time to progress to more actual phone calls rather than messaging, now that they'd met in person. It was more intimate, and, besides, typed conversations could take ages.

'And? Did you kiss and make up?' Amanda asked.

'Not bloody likely,' Jenna replied. 'He was going mental. Saying all this nonsense about me trying to ruin his life. He got some photos, apparently. Threatening ones. What does that even mean?'

Amanda pressed her hand over her mouth to stifle the sound of her laughter. That was the first time she'd heard Jenna swear. She must be rattled. Once she recovered her equilibrium she said, 'That sounds crazy. Poor you. What else did he say?'

'Something about Rab Cameron abducting Nathan, and how on earth did I manage to arrange that? The man's lost it. And Cameron was the boy's biological father, so I'm not sure abduction is the right word.'

'Wow,' Amanda said.

There was silence from the other end of the phone. Then the sound of crying.

'Poor you,' Amanda said. 'He's really got to you, eh?'

'Yeah, he thinks I've co-ordinated this attempt to ruin his life,' Jenna managed through her sobs. 'How mental is that? My life isn't exactly a picnic, mate.'

'Oh, honey, I wish I was there to give you a hug.'

The sound of Jenna sniffing came down the phone line.

'God. Snot and tears,' she said with a half-laugh. 'It's not pretty.'

'I hope you told the prick to piss off,' Amanda said.

'Didn't get the chance,' Jenna said, her emotions sounding as if they were more in check. 'He kinda flounced off to his car.'

'Flounced,' Amanda repeated. 'Love it.'

Both women laughed, their laughter feeding each other and before long they were in fits of giggles.

'Oh, lordy,' said Jenna. 'That was just what the doctor ordered. You can't beat a good laugh.'

'True. And what now?' Amanda pressed.

'To be honest, I'm not happy the way we left it. Him getting the last word.' Jenna paused. 'He did mention you by name. Or someone else called Hazel who had written some awful reviews for his business, and that was part of my plan to ruin his life. Idiot. But when I went online and looked there was nothing there. And if there was nothing there, how does he know your name? How does he even know you exist? Has he been looking through all of my friends? And if so, why pick on you?'

At this Amanda gave herself a double pat on the back. Jenna's thinking was all over the place. One stone thrown in to the water and the ripple effect was just starting.

'Do you think he's got that stalker thing in him?' she asked.

'Who knows? He's killed someone, so what's a little bit of stalking to someone like that? Should I be worried?'

Amanda thought carefully about how she should respond to this. What would be the best result for her and Jamie? Jenna was getting close to the truth, she could feel it in her gut, and when she did, wouldn't the impact on them be greater if Luke and Jenna were together?

But would Jenna stop digging if they made up?

There would be a way round that, Amanda thought. There was always a way.

'An accidental killing, and stalking? Strikes me there's two different kind of personalities going on there. Has Luke shown any previous behaviour to suggest he could be that kind of creep?'

'No,' Jenna replied instantly. 'He was always respectful. Always giving me space. But he's rattled. Threats to Nathan and to his livelihood, if that's how he sees it, have to be unsettling. And when people feel threatened they tend not to act rationally.'

'What do you do now?' Amanda asked. 'Do you want to have the last word.'

'Not sure I *need* the last word,' Jenna bristled. 'But I want the chance to argue my side of the story.'

Chapter 68

Good riddance, thought Luke, all the way home. They'd had some nice times together since they met, but everything else had turned to shit. Was he wrong to go over there and try to have it out with her? She did look completely amazed at his accusations, but then she would, wouldn't she? If she was a good enough actress to hook him and reel him in, then she would be good enough to deny everything.

But what if he was wrong? What if it was all just a coincidence, and he'd just ruined the best thing that had happened to him for years?

Back home he thanked Ken for his babysitting skills and offered to make him his dinner.

'No, thanks, mate. I've got work tomorrow,' Ken replied with a grimace that suggested he thought Luke's cooking wasn't up to much.

'Piss off, *mate*,' Luke replied, allowing himself to be affected by his friend's humour. 'My cooking's not that bad.'

Ken left, and Luke made dinner for him and Nathan. The boy attacked his meal as if he hadn't eaten for days, while Luke picked at his, eventually throwing most of it into the bin.

Then it was some TV time and an early bed, with a mind full of contradictory thoughts and emotions. He lay on his side, on his back, then on his other side, the sweat of forbidden and foreboding thoughts dampening the cotton underneath him. Then a bent and broken body rose in his mind, reminding him of his own lack, his own failings, his own immutable shame.

*

Next day, head still in a swirl, he got Nathan up, fed and off to his first day back at school. Then at home, he set up his calming space in the shed and worked at getting himself back into some sort of peace before he could start a fresh round of marketing for his business.

'New Year: New You' was the approach by every freelance therapist, personal trainer and alternative health practitioner he followed online. Why reinvent the wheel? So after a session of yoga nidra that he knew would help reset his frame of mind, he got out a pad and pen, and started to scribble down some copy that might grab the attention of prospective clients.

One hour and three coffees later all he had written down was *New Year: New You* and some doodles that, if he tilted his head and screwed his eyes near to shutting, looked like a three-horned devil.

He threw his pen across the room, frustrated with himself and his situation, and thought about just getting his running shoes on and going for a jog. That might help clear his head.

The light outside shifted. Movement. He got to his feet and went to the door.

'Hi,' he heard a small voice. 'It's me.'

'Jenna?' Luke opened the door. She looked so confused and small that the first words out of his mouth were, 'You okay?'

Her head moved slowly from side to side, then up and down.

'Can I come in?' she asked. 'It's bloody freezing.'

Luke stepped to the side to let her inside, then walked past her and over to his side of the desk.

She gave a small self-conscious laugh. 'I haven't been in here since my doomed attempt at seeking therapy.'

Luke sat down, and crossed his arms and his legs. Forcing himself to relax he loosened his limbs and let his hands fall onto his lap. Jenna sat down on the other side of the desk.

'Can I get you something to drink?' Luke asked. This was his place of work, his place to help people, the offer of hospitality was automatic, but he wondered if it was prudent.

Looking at her expression, the downward cast of her eyes, the shadows under them, her normally plump lips pulled tight, he could see she was as confused as he was. He heard her take a deep breath in preparation of speech. But she paused. Held her arms out, pink, delicate palms facing up. She was laid bare. There was no artifice he could detect here, but instead, a reminder of his own bad judgement, of his own shame at how he had mistreated her. He'd vowed to be a better person; a better man. What happened to that treaty he'd made with himself? The things he'd done under cover of darkness, obscured by cloud and an unseeing moon – who was he to judge anyone? He should hear her out. Let her words, tone, the movement of her limbs, the play of the tiny muscles under the skin of her face – the orchestra of her – communicate with him; let all of that wash over his brain and gut, and then perhaps he could honestly and accurately make some kind of sense of what was going on.

'The postcard,' she began. 'The reviews, all of that stuff you mentioned yesterday. None of it was me. I've never even met Rab Cameron, so God knows how I could have persuaded him to do anything.'

'I'm—'

'Please,' Jenna said. 'Let me finish. There's all of this ... stuff going on my head that I can't make sense of. I was ... I am in love with you, Luke. But I was also in love with Danny. It was only a short time, but I was young, inexperienced. This was fifteen years ago. I was just turning twenty-one – finding myself really – and he was none of the things other people warned me about.' Her gaze was fixed on his desktop. A memory clouded her eyes. 'Except this one time that...'

'That what?' Luke knew exactly what Danny could be like and worried what this one time was all about.

'It's not important. Like every relationship, there was good and bad, but the good did outweigh the bad. So it was a shock – I can't tell you how much of a shock – to find out you were the guy who killed him.'

'Accidentally.'

'Nonetheless, he'd still be alive...' She shook her head as if freeing herself from that avenue of thought, as if it made little sense to travel down there. 'Anyway. Loving you after loving him, can't you see how that would trouble me?'

'Yes, but...'

'But I have no interest in trying to carry out some sort of revenge on you. None of the things you accused me of are down to me. To be honest it all sounds a bit fanciful. As if you're striking out at everyone around you rather than looking to yourself for blame; as if delaying that moment when you have to knuckle down and take responsibility for your own actions.'

Luke was stung by this accusation. 'That's not fair, Jenna. The last seven years, since I got out of prison, have been about taking responsibility for my actions. You don't cause someone's death and go, "oh well, never mind". That shit haunts you forever.'

'Okay, I apologise for saying that, but know this: all of that stuff? None of it was me.'

'Who's this Hazel woman?'

'There's nothing on your account from Hazel. And why would she do that? You're nothing to her.'

'But you are. Something to her.'

'You're saying she made some misguided attempt to trash her friend's ex's business?' Jenna snorted. 'We're sort of friends. We chat now and again, but I seriously doubt she feels we have such a strong connection that she needs to defend me. Or set out to ruin you.'

'It might all be deleted now, but I didn't imagine it, Jenna. The comments were there. And they came from that woman you call a friend. What else am I to think?' Luke felt his irritation rise, could hear it in the pitch of his voice. He coughed as if that might clear it. Took a breath. 'Sorry, I want to hear you out. I want to believe you. I just need to understand what's going on.'

'You and me both,' Jenna said. 'That offer of a drink still available?'

'Something hot?' Luke asked.

'Too early for gin,' Jenna laughed. 'Even for me.'

As Luke prepared their drinks, he sneaked a look at Jenna. He could see she was trying to be honest. There was no reason for her to come over. The fact she had showed a willingness to keep their dialogue going, to keep it open and meaningful. If he wanted to repair their relationship perhaps it was time to set aside his own priorities and see what would work for Jenna.

'What do you need, Jenna?' he said. 'What's going to make sense of all of this for you?' He was serious. He would tell her everything.

Almost everything.

Straight away she answered. No pause. No hesitation: 'I need to know exactly what happened that day. And I need to hear it directly from you.'

Chapter 69

Fifteen years earlier

The morning after his mother's funeral, Luke and Danny were in the car after a night of boozing and pill-popping. Luke was exhausted, but Danny, whose capacity for drink was legendary, looked like he was ready to go again. After a lock-in at The Black Bull, the boys all piled into the car, and by dint of the fact that Luke had fallen asleep at one point, and no one else could be arsed to do it, he was the designated driver.

Truth be told, Luke hadn't missed the lifestyle while he'd lived up north, and nothing that happened since he returned would alter that. He couldn't wait to go back to his life and work up in Aberdeen and leave this city behind him. Now that his mother was dead there was absolutely nothing left for him here. Besides, he had just met someone. Her name was Angie. Pretty, with a wise head and a great sense of humour. And he planned on spending more time with her and forgetting all about his life in Glasgow.

As the night had progressed he had done what he could to avoid keeping pace with the rest of them, but Danny missed nothing.

'C'mon you,' he said, time and time again. 'Have a drink. You've gone all soft on us, living up there wi all those sheep-shaggers.'

'Piss off,' Luke replied each time he was called out, and pretended to drink. Slowing right back down when the attention moved on from him.

'Ah need ma bed,' Chris said from the backseat. 'Take me hame, there's a good fellow.' He patted Luke on the back of the head.

'Aye, me an all,' Dickie Hirst said. 'Think I'm gonna huv a hert attack if I don't lie doon for like a week.'

'Jesus, what a bunch of lightweights,' Danny said as he fiddled about with the car's sound system. He found a station that was playing some nineties dance tracks. 'Take them home, Luke. Then you and me can go for a wee run.'

'Eh?' Luke said. 'I'm done, mate.'

Danny leaned towards Luke and spoke quietly, in a voice designed only for Luke's ears. 'You're done when I say you're done.'

'Whit was that?' Joe asked.

'Go to sleep, wanker,' Danny said. 'The big boys is talking.'

Here it comes, thought Luke. Danny had been nothing but pleasant since he picked him up after the funeral, and all night he'd waited for the real Danny to show up. He always had a way of letting Luke know what he wanted from him, and did it with just a look and the angle of his head. In the smirk around the mouth and the contempt and mockery in his eyes.

'You're mine,' Danny said under his breath, so the other guys couldn't hear him over the music. 'And don't you ever forget it.'

'Fuck off, Danny,' Luke replied.

'What's up wi you two?' Dickie said from the back.

'Nothing,' Luke and Danny replied at exactly the same time.

'Not happenin', mate,' Luke replied to Danny. 'I moved to get away from you, and I'm never coming back.'

'Izzat right?' Danny asked, cool as a man with nothing to bother his conscience. 'Mind of wee Fraser Smith?' he shouted over his shoulder to the guys in the back seat.

'Who?' Dickie asked.

'Shut it, Danny,' Luke warned.

Danny said nothing in reply. He simply smiled. The man with all the cards.

Resentment at Danny rose in Luke like a wave. He thought this part of his life was over. This part of his life *was* over. But here Danny was trying to pull him back down. The man was like a piece of glass under his heel, grit in his eye, a toxic coil wound round his heart. If he didn't get out from under him now he would spend his life in thrall to a man who just knew how to get what he wanted while making him feel as bad as he possibly could.

*

Dickie lived in a bedsit in Clydebank and was the last to be dropped off. With a tired wave aimed at the two of them in the car, Dickie pushed open the door to his building. As Luke watched him disappear inside he felt a pang of envy. Shook his head. Today would be the very last day that Danny got what he wanted.

He rejoined the traffic, and for a few minutes they drove, listening to the heavy drumbeat of the sound system.

'I've a wee notion for a picnic at the top of a hill. Hey.' Danny nudged Luke so hard the car swerved. 'Mind that time we had the magic mushrooms? Let's get some shrooms,' he shouted over the music.

'Jesus,' Luke said as he corrected the car. Then, 'Aye, shrooms. I've no idea where you're going to get them at this time of day.' Playing at agreement was always easiest with Danny. Often a different idea would soon take root, and he'd insist that was the one they'd go for. Until something else popped in to his head. Luke decided to bide his time. He'd wait until Danny was asleep, and then he'd abandon the guy again. And if he followed him up to Aberdeen, that was his backyard now and he'd do whatever was necessary to make sure Danny got the message.

'Or Buckfast?' Danny grinned. 'Haven't had Buckie for ages.' He looked around. 'Where are we going, by the way?'

'Fucked if I know. I'm just driving.'

'Find me a hill,' Danny said, leaning forward towards the windscreen as if willing the car faster.

'Better put your seatbelt on,' Luke said.

'Sorry, mother,' Danny said, making no move to do so.

Luke carried on driving. He saw a tourist sign, brown with a thistle at the top and the legend, *Loch Lomond*. Danny must have also noticed it because he started singing.

'You tak the high road and I'll tak the low road and I'll be in Scotland afore ye.'

Then Danny stopped, turned the volume of the music down and twisted in his seat so he was facing Luke.

'What's it like to kill some'dy?'

Luke shifted his view from the road to glance at Danny in disbelief. The other man's eyes were gleaming, his mouth open as if he was breathing heavily. What on earth was going on in his head?

'You're sick,' Luke replied.

'Tell me, man. You're the only person I know who's done it. What does it feel like?'

'It's shite. It hangs over every thought that forms in your head. Every decision. Every moment it's there, fucking you up. I wake up with that boy every morning...' Luke tailed off, lacking the energy to carry on. Fraser Smith was there, just out of sight beyond the edge of his vision. He hadn't aged a day since that moment all those years ago, and Luke could feel his eyes bore into him in silent accusation. *You carry on living while I don't have that luxury*, he said. *I'll never have a wife, or kids, or drink beer at sunset in a back garden, or watch football, or laugh at a shit joke, or listen to music, or, or, or...* The list was endless, and Luke regularly thought of going to the police and Fraser's family, but then he'd have to face Joe's grief.

But then the torment would be over.

That was something he didn't deserve. It was only right that he suffered with this every day for the rest of his life.

Luke noticed the houses thin out, replaced with hedges and trees, and that the roads were smaller and winding. He closed his eyes at one point, struggling to keep them open.

The car lurched to the right. With his pulse thundering in his ears, Luke managed to correct it.

'Fuckssake, nearly went off the road,' Danny accused.

'Would that be such a bad thing?' Luke replied.

'Aye. Cos I've been thinking,' Danny said.

Luke groaned. He knew what Danny's thinking meant: half-baked ideas and a full load of problems.

'It's time you left that Aberdeen shit-hole and came back to Glasgow. Time you earned some proper cash.'

'You're deluded, mate,' Luke replied. Quietly. Working up some defiance. 'My life's up there now.'

'What was that?'

Luke reached across and turned off the music. 'So you can hear me, Danny. You're on your own. Wherever this wee road trip ends up, after that I never want to see you again. You're toxic, man, you're always going to be toxic, and I've had it up to here.'

Danny was silent for a moment. Luke stewed, only half his mind on the road, the other half full of determination. Whatever Danny threatened, he would deal with. This time it was for real. He and Danny were done.

Danny started clapping. Slow, and so loud in the shell of the car, it sounded like gunshot.

'Nice speech, mate. Nice speech. Shame it's never going to happen, cos I own you. Heart and soul.'

'You think? Kick a dog and it's only so long before it bites back, arsehole. I'm done. We're over. I never want to see you again.'

'Oh aye? Want to set up a nice wee life, do ye? What's her name again? Angie?'

How the hell did he find out about her? Luke shot a look at Danny. His eyes were gleaming. Triumphant.

'Did ye think I wouldn't find out?'

'Danny, you touch her. You as much as breathe in her direction...'

'She likes a wee bit of blow, I hear. Wouldn't take long to get her worked up to something way more addict—'

Luke back-handed him. Without another thought, without a care for the ramifications, he took his left hand off the wheel and with as much force as he could generate in that small space he whipped his hand back and hit Danny in the face.

'You fucking wanker,' Danny said, and punched him back. Full on the chin, just as he breached the top of a small rise on a bend.

A hedge rushed towards them. With a crunch the car hit it, and kept moving at speed. The car flipped. The windscreen shattered. Luke's ears were full of the roaring of the engine. And screaming – his and Danny's. The car rolled. Both men buffeted from side to side. Seconds were like hours. Luke was aware of Danny still screaming. And a final shuddering crash as the vehicle was forced to a stop, by a wall or a tree or ... whatever it was, Luke was grateful the torture was over.

Then, silence.

Chapter 70

As Jenna listened to Luke's version of events, she watched him, assessing his body movements for congruence with his words. His description tallied with the one she'd built up back when she'd started to investigate the case – and with Sandy's version too.

'Next thing I know,' Luke added. 'A man in green's standing over me. I was covered in blood.' He put a hand to his forehead and his nose as if reliving old hurts. 'He spoke so gently to me. So reassuringly, I felt myself being calmed.' He shook his head slowly. 'The effect was remarkable. After all that noise...' He tailed off. 'Then I heard a woman, the other paramedic, shout him over. That there was a body. Not another person. A body.'

'Goodness,' Jenna said. 'Must have been terrifying.' Then a thought. 'If Danny punched you just before you lost control, why didn't you cite that in your defence? Surely you weren't to blame, in that case? I can't imagine anyone could keep their car on that road after having taken one to the chin?'

'The lawyers got to me. That's why I changed my plea at the last minute. They said the court would go easier on me with a guilty plea. My blood scores were enough to convict me, they said. I should never have been driving with that level of booze in my blood. I didn't stand a chance at trial. So...' He shrugged, his eyes briefly displaying the bewilderment the accused young man must have felt when faced with the might of the legal system.

Jenna looked at him, saying nothing, waiting to see if he would bridge the silence.

Luke simply looked back at her, but there was a wealth of information going on behind those pale-blue eyes. If only she could read them accurately. She could sense, when he spoke about his plea, that he felt he deserved what he got, but also that he felt little if any guilt over Danny's death. She said as much.

Luke made a face of apology. 'I know it's not what you want to hear, Jenna, but I would never have been able to change my life if Danny was still alive. Was I glad he was dead? No, I could never celebrate someone dying, but was I pleased he wasn't around? Absolutely.'

'But...' Jenna paused, unsure how to ask what had been bothering her as she listened to Luke's account.

'But what?' Luke nudged. He was leaning forward, his arms out, palms up. 'You can ask me anything.'

'What I don't understand is what Danny had over you. Why couldn't you break away from him?'

'You heard what he threatened to do. He was going to turn Angie into an addict.'

Jenna narrowed her eyes. 'Really? Surely you could have protected her from him?' She still struggled to marry her own experience of Danny with the man Luke said he knew, but there was certainty on Luke's face. He truly believed Danny would have done what he threatened to do.

'You're lucky,' Luke said as if reading her thoughts. 'It seems he had you fooled.'

She reacted with a sharp intake of breath.

'Either that,' he added hastily, 'or you got the best of him. But believe me, the people who did are few and far between. Even his parents treated him with caution.'

They sat in silence. Each of them trapped in the weave of their own thought and emotion, unsure or unable to push through and find a way back to each other.

The wind picked up. The shed groaned as it shifted. Rain fell on the roof, a light but urgent pattern, like soft fingers lightly drumming their insistence that the truth be revealed.

Luke regarded Jenna, hoping that what he'd said to her would be enough, but he could see as she sat back, crossing her legs and arms, that something caused her doubt. He felt a tremble at the thought that only the absolute truth would satisfy her.

Jenna's phone sounded from her handbag. She looked at it, then looked away as if dismissing the need to answer.

'On you go,' Luke said.

'Sure?'

He nodded.

She pulled the phone from her bag and read the screen. 'It's Sandy,' she said.

'Hi, Sandy,' Jenna said. 'Can I call you back?'

Sandy carried on regardless. Luke could hear the man on the line speak clearly in the quiet of the space: 'It's just, hen, that our Jean's been pushing me to call you.'

'Yeah?' Jenna asked, making a face of apology towards Luke.

'That girl you were with the other day? Hazel? Our Jean's been nagging me. She said the girl's face was familiar. Very familiar, and she's since been looking out old photos to try and convince me. Cos I don't know why anyone would pretend to be someone else. I think she's havering, but she insisted.'

Luke sat up straight, and as if she picked up on his alertness, Jenna did too. 'What did you just say there? Pretending to be who?'

'This Hazel lassie. Jean's sure she's not who she says she is.'

There was a pause, and Luke could make out some conversation in the background, then a woman saying, 'Give me that phone.'

'Hi, Jenna is it? This is Jean, Sandy's wife. For my sins.'

'Hello, Jean. Yes, we met briefly the other day,' Jenna replied, widening her eyes at Luke in confusion. 'What were you saying?'

'That Hazel girl. I knew her as soon as I saw her. I just didn't trust myself, you know? She's Amanda Morrison, Danny's wee sister. The spit of her mother, God rest her soul. I'd watch out if I was you. That family were all a wee bit strange. And if that lassie's pretending to be someone else, she's up to no good. No good at all.'

Chapter 71

Amanda was ten. Dancing with perfect form in her pink tights, leotard and ballet shoes. The ribbons of her shoes kept coming loose. Every now and again she'd trip over them. Then she'd have to stop in the middle of the show, lean forward and wind the ribbon around her calf.

But no matter how tightly she tied them, they'd work their way loose. Every time they came loose, she stopped to retie them. And every time she did that the music stopped. And everyone stared. Some people even laughed. And pointed. Her parents were in the front row, and they were so drunk they didn't even notice she'd messed up. They were just sitting there, vacant-eyed, stooped with alcohol. Amanda was worried about what would come next. First came the sleepiness. Then, they'd snooze, and wake up minutes later in a fury. And start shouting at each other.

But the anticipated fight didn't come. Instead, her mother pointed. At her. Laughed. At her.

Her da, hard-faced: who do you think you are? Ballet my arse. For poofs and ponces.

Her ma: it's a life on a supermarket checkout, hen, don't get ideas above your station. She does look pretty, right enough. I used to could dance, she added wistfully.

Her da: bollocks, you had two left feet. Nothing but a big heifer.

Stung, her mother swung her handbag at him. Then they were toe to toe, chin to chin, shouting at each other. As Amanda's face burned, men in suits escorted them from the theatre.

The music started up.

Stopped.

Amanda looked down. Her ballet shoes were loose again.

Her parents were in the front row, vacant eyes, sodden with alcohol.

*

Breathless, Amanda knocked on Jamie's bedroom door.

'Go away. I'm sleeping,' he replied.

'Hardly,' she replied, turned the door handle and walked in. 'Unless you sleep with your bedside lamp on?' She looked around at the pristine space. Every surface was bare, and if any dust dared to rest there she was sure Jamie would flick it off with his duster the moment it landed. 'Jesus,' she added. 'Can't you act like other lads your age and be a bit of a sloth? This neat-freak thing is not becoming.'

'Piss off,' he replied as he moved up onto his elbows. His eyes were blinking as if indeed he had been on the verge of sleep. 'What do you want? It's two o'clock in the morning.'

'Can I come in beside you? I'm scared.' She lifted up the corner of his quilt. He put a hand over hers and slammed it back down.

'No, you can't, weirdo. We're not weans, and I've got nothing on.'

'Pfft,' she replied. 'It's just a penis. I've seen one of them before. I was married, you know.'

'That's ... disturbing,' he replied. 'Now please, fuck off.'

'I had that dream again, you arsehole.'

Jamie groaned, and edged across the bed. While he did so he plucked one of the pillows from under his head and placed it between them. 'There,' he said. 'If you're sleeping here, stay on your side of that and on top of the quilt. And zip it. I'm knackered.'

'My,' Amanda said, hand over her heart as she allowed herself to fall on top of the bed. 'My virtue protected by a rectangle of foam.'

Jamie groaned. 'For someone who's scared, you're pretty bloody chipper.'

'Aye, well,' she replied, and for a moment she allowed the terror she felt in her dream to leak into her mind. 'The humour is me just trying to play it down.'

'Do you get night terrors as well?' Jamie asked.

'Aye, now and again,' Amanda admitted.

'Why did you never say before?'

'Why did *you* never say before?' she countered.

They lapsed into silence as they each considered the other's experience.

'Right,' Jamie replied. Subject closed. And he turned onto his side, away from her, reached across and switched off his lamp.

'You can go under the covers if you want,' Jamie said in a voice that suggested this was a huge concession on his part. The room was chilly, despite the housecoat over her light fleece pyjamas, so Amanda burrowed under the quilt.

'Now can we get some sleep?'

Amanda felt the mattress give slightly as Jamie moved, and she heard what she imagined was him drawing his knees up into the foetal position.

'We're getting close, little brother. Things are coming to a head. I can feel it.'

'Right,' Jamie mumbled.

'Jenna O'Neill and Luke Forrest Robertson, or whatever his name is, have no idea what's coming. I have plans, little brother. Big plans. We're going to make them wish they'd never been born.'

'Uhuh,' Jamie responded.

'We're going to cut the feet from them. Watch them bleed.'

Amanda lay beside her brother, matching his breathing, whispering words of misery and mayhem. And as his body twitched in early sleep she filled the air between them with susurrating sounds, knowing her suggestions would find their way over the stretch of bleached linen between them and filter in through his slumbering conscious mind to find fertile soil in the bleak imaginings of his little-boy mind.

He was her Old Testament.

The Jekyll to her Hyde.

The sharp end of her knife.

Chapter 72

Luke watched as realisation dawned on Jenna. Her eyes grew large, her mouth fell open, and she shivered as she realised who this Hazel woman was, and what she might be up to.

'I've been done up like a kipper as well,' he said.

'How do you mean?'

'Jamie.'

'Shit.' Jenna's hand shot to her mouth.

'He's been following me everywhere, hasn't he?' Luke thought through his interactions with the young man. 'They must be in cahoots. Just think of everything that happened since he came into my life.' He thought about that first meeting outside the bookshop, the photos of Nathan, the shadowy figure at Jenna's bedroom window. 'Oh my God. The Christmas fairground at the exhibition centre.'

Jenna gasped. Paused. 'Nathan was lost and then Jamie found him? What could he gain by that little pantomime?'

'My trust? First push me over the edge with worry, then act as the saviour when he finds him and brings him back to me.'

'Do you think he might have had something worse in mind and then chickened out?' Jenna asked, her face pale at the thought.

Luke shook his head. 'He didn't reveal that much about himself during our brief sessions. I learned enough to think that he wouldn't actually cause physical harm to anyone, least of all a child. Or I thought I did.'

'But why now? Why do this – whatever this is? Why do it now, after all these years?'

'They've grown up?' Luke suggested. 'They were both kids when Danny died – and this is all about him, I'm assuming. And I was inside. It takes time to set up a deception like this. How long has Hazel been your friend on social media?'

'I could check my computer to see when we became online

friends. I'll do that when I get home. Don't have it on my phone,' she explained. 'But it must be a few years now.' She sat back in her chair as if the callousness of the siblings' actions had just been revealed to her. 'Hazel – Amanda, I mean – she's been on this for years. Jesus. Who does that?'

'Amanda watches over us for years. We meet. Get it together...' Luke continued. 'Perhaps seeing me happy...' He softened his voice. 'Seeing I was falling for you.' He coughed. 'That set them off?'

'But all I did was fall in love with him...' Jenna said. Her eyes clouded, just for a moment, as if she'd gone somewhere uncomfortable in her mind. Could she be hiding something as well?

Whatever had happened between Jenna and Danny was her business. If she wanted to tell him she would, but in her own good time. Rather than press on that, Luke decided to carry on with the topic at hand.

'And when you dumped him Danny got back to his old tricks with his mates. Namely, me. And you know what happened next...'

'So I'm to blame for Danny getting killed? That's ridiculous.'

'Maybe they're thinking if you had stayed with him he might still be alive.'

Jenna stared off into the distance, as if allowing that idea to settle. Then she added quietly, 'He might well be. But what kind of state would I be in if I'd stayed with him?'

They were silent for a moment, then Luke reminded her about losing his job at the club. 'Could she have set that up as well? Dear God, what would those two not do to us?'

Jenna shrunk in her chair as a thought hit her. 'Rab Cameron,' she said. 'Do you think...?'

'What – that Jamie and Amanda killed him, or had him killed?' He shook his head. 'No, surely not.' He remembered what Stef and Joe's neighbour had said, that Cameron suddenly came into money just before a kid appeared in his house. He detailed this out to Jenna. 'They could have paid him to take Nathan away from me. Anyone with a pair of eyes knows I dote on the kid. If I lost him I don't know how I would ever handle it.'

'What do we do?' Jenna asked. 'Now that we know this, what do we do with it?'

'Depends on how far they take it,' Luke replied.

'Do we go to the police?' Jenna asked.

'And say what? There's no tangible proof of anything, and have they committed any actual crime?'

'What about Cameron? A bit of a coincidence, isn't it, that once you have Nathan back, he dies? Maybe they were afraid he'd come to you and tell you everything, and they fed him a doctored batch of whatever junk he was on?'

'The police came to see me, remember? Not sure I want to draw their attention again. I'm an ex-con. And again, we've no proof.'

Luke quickly ran through his interactions with Jamie. Was there anything in there to suggest he was capable of the ultimate crime? Were they in physical danger? He thought they'd become friends. He'd actually become fond of the young man. Was all of that a lie?

'They've toyed with us like a cat might with a mouse,' he thought out loud. 'What else do they have planned? Just how far are they going to take this?'

Chapter 73

Jenna returned to her mother's, mind full of Hazel's deception, scared about what else was to come and worried that someone was so full of hate for her that she would become their target. How was she to trust anyone ever again?

When she got home she saw to it that her mother was comfortable: she'd been to the toilet, she was warm, and didn't need food or drink. Now Jenna could focus. She approached her laptop on the kitchen table as if it was mined.

Bracing herself, she opened her social-media accounts and looked to see how long she'd been friends with Hazel. Four years. Dear God. That was how long this woman had been planning her revenge. Or perhaps even longer.

She ran through their encounter a few days earlier. All the way in the car out to Sandy's, was there anything in Amanda's demeanour that suggested the hate that must surely fuel such an enterprise? She couldn't see it. Like Luke with Jamie, she'd been completely taken in. At least Jamie hadn't lied about who he was. Did that make Luke even more stupid than she was, or was it the other way around?

Hindsight provided her with twenty-twenty vision: when she looked at Hazel's profile page it was clear, or it felt clear, that this wasn't a real account. There was little in there that was personal. No depth. No humour even. Just a bland piece of occasional reportage designed to pull her in. God, she'd been an idiot.

Or was she? Had there been a real Hazel among her university alumni?

She looked through her contacts for anyone she knew was definitely at university with her. There. Catherine Diamond. Cathy was a real character. Liked a drink. Loved the men, and rumour had it, the occasional girl. Cathy played hard, and then buckled down just before exam season and worked round the clock to get a pass. If she owned any candles they had burned-out wicks at either end. Jenna sent her a message.

*

A reply pinged through the next morning.

—*Great to hear from you, Jenna. Did you get to put that hard-won degree to good use, lol? A few years at a national in London for me. Then I fell pregnant. Got two smashers now. Wouldn't change any of it. What's been happening? Anything juicy? Re: this Hazel person I've never heard of her, and I knew, like, EVERYBODY.*

As soon as she read the reply, Jenna called Luke.

'Can I come round?' she asked. 'We need to decide what to do. Ignore this and hope it goes away? Or...'

'There's no sign that they're going to stop, is there?

'In that case we need to confront them. And that needs to be done face to face.'

'Sure,' Luke replied. 'The wee man's off sick. A tummy bug, but he's sleeping so he won't disturb us.'

Part of her mind filed away the small charge of positivity she heard in his voice when he answered; and the small thrill in her heart when she recognised this. Enough, she told herself. Her feelings for Luke had to be placed on hold until she knew exactly what was going on. He was still hiding something, she was sure.

But then, so was she.

When would be the right time to tell him about the abortion? Would he understand? Would he judge her and find her seriously wanting?

Did he even have the right to know? That was her business – a very private pain. And private it would stay. No one needed to know. Only two other people did; her mum and Danny. Her mother wasn't going to tell anyone, and she hoped that it was a secret Danny took to his grave.

When she arrived at his place, he guided her into the living room. 'Should I stick my head in and say hi to Nathan?' she asked, wanting nothing more than to be warmed by the little boy's smile.

'Maybe later,' Luke replied. 'He's still asleep.'

Disappointed, she followed Luke into the living room. Sitting on the sofa, while Luke took the armchair opposite her, she could see that he was tired. Shadows hung under his eyes, and the line of his mouth was tight and cold.

She relayed to him what she'd just learned. What she'd begun to suspect.

'What do we do now?' she asked him.

'To be honest,' Luke replied, 'I just don't trust my judgement right now. I want to go round to hers, wherever that is, and confront her. But I don't know if that would make it worse.'

Jenna quickly twigged what Luke was hinting at. 'Yeah, you're an ex-convict. She calls the police, and regardless of how strong you think your story is, you're the one that gets huckled into the back of a police car.'

'But still' – Luke sounded like he was charged with a cold fury – 'they can't get away with this.'

'Say we did confront them? Not saying we should,' Jenna added quickly. 'How do we even find them? Do you know where Jamie lives? I picked Hazel – sorry, Amanda – up in Milngavie in a car park.' She shook her head at this. With the benefit of hindsight, and adding all the pieces together, this was a strong clue that Amanda was hiding something.

'God, yeah,' Luke replied. 'I only ever saw Jamie at mine, or on the one occasion I did pick up him, it was on a busy, public street, not at home.' He paused. 'That was in the West End of the city, if that helps?'

'Oh.' Jenna received a flash of memory. 'Jamie ordered a book from the shop. Would it be too easy if he gave his actual address when he made the order?'

'Worth a phone call?'

Jenna nodded. Pulled her phone from her bag and called the shop.

'Sorry I can't chat,' she replied to the bright and cheery response from Mhairi. 'There was a book order a couple of months ago. Jamie Morrison. Did he leave an address?'

'Hang on a mo,' Mhairi replied. There was a pause in the chat, and Jenna could hear the clicks from a computer keyboard. 'Yes,' she said. 'It's...'

'Would you mind texting it to me, please, Mhairi?' Jenna asked.

'I'm not sure that's appropriate,' Mhairi replied.

'I know, and I'm sorry. But it is important. Do you trust me?'

'Course I do.'

'I'll explain next time I see you, I promise, but in the meantime...' Jenna left her request unrepeated, and waited.

With a sigh, Mhairi gave Jenna the address. 'If anything comes back to me on this, I won't be a happy bunny, Jenna.'

'Understood.'

'How's your mum?' Mhairi asked.

'She's doing okay, all things considered.'

'Great,' Mhairi replied. 'I'll send this text through to you. Oh, and keep me posted? You're a good worker, Jenna, and there's not too many of you to the pound these days.'

The women said cheerio, with promises to meet soon, and Jenna hung up. Moments later a text came through with Jamie's address. She showed Luke the screen.

Luke read the street name. 'It's not too far from where I picked Jamie up.' He looked into Jenna's eyes. Held her gaze. 'There's only one way to find out.'

Chapter 74

They climbed into Luke's car and headed across town to the address on the text. But not before Luke had once again called on the babysitting prowess of his friend, Ken.

Happily, he was free and delighted to be called in to look after Nathan. In no time at all he was bounding into the house, arms full of comics and DVDs.

'Where did you get that lot?' Luke asked, delighted that his friend was clearly so enthusiastic about looking after the boy – probably because it gave him a chance to act like a kid for a few hours.

'Where's your charger, mate? Phone's dead.' Ken held his phone in the air while dismissing Luke's question. Of course he was going to have stuff on hand for when he was next asked to babysit.

Nathan woke up as soon as he heard Ken's booming voice, and he ran downstairs in his pyjamas, hair looking like he'd just come out of a wind tunnel.

Just as they were leaving, and before Luke gave him a quick hug and kiss, he squatted down and looked at Nathan carefully.

'Do you remember the day we went to the place with all the Santas and you were on the slide, and the dodgems...'

'And I got the toffee apple and the ... the big, pink, fluffy sweet?'

'Candy floss,' prompted Luke. 'Yeah, that's right. And do you remember Jamie was there, and just before we left he brought you over to me?'

'Were you angry with him?' Nathan asked, furrowed his brow, and then clamped his lips tight as if he'd just remembered something.

'This isn't going to get you into trouble, buddy. Or Jamie,' Luke replied, surprised that the little boy had read his mood on the day so accurately; he was sure at the time that he'd managed to hide how he was feeling.

'Is Jamie still your friend? I haven't seen him for lots,' Nathan said.

'I thought he'd lost you that day, buddy. That's why I was angry.' Luke made light of this statement by throwing his hands up in the air in a 'silly me' gesture.

'You were silly, Daddy, cos I wasn't lost. Jamie told me to hide in with the elves cos we were playing hide and seek. And you didn't find me cos I had a hat on,' Nathan crowed.

'Right,' Luke said as he plastered a smile on his face, while thinking once again of how he'd been duped by Jamie Morrison. He'd trusted that young man with his family, and that was the biggest betrayal of them all. 'Anyway.' He turned to Ken. 'He's been up sick most of the night, and he's off school. So that means no games.'

'Aww, Dad,' the boy protested.

'Aww, Dad,' Ken grinned.

'Maybe one. A quick one,' Luke relented.

*

In the car, while negotiating the traffic, his mind ran through the various ways he'd been fooled by Jamie. He tried to figure out if the young man had ever given away, or even offered as much as a hint as to what his true intentions were. But he came up blank.

He looked across to the passenger seat at Jenna and guessed that from her distant expression she was going through the same mental journey.

'They had us fooled, eh?' he asked.

'Yes,' Jenna replied, briefly shooting him a look.

'You okay?' he asked, reaching across and putting his hand on hers. 'They've been very clever. I think anyone would have been caught out by them.'

Jenna pulled her hand away from his and tucked it under her arm. 'I know. But I just feel so stupid. Once you put it all together all of these little nothings become something major.' Her eyes grew wide as a thought occurred. 'What do you think their endgame is here? Do you think they want us ... well, dead?' She paled.

Luke exhaled sharply. 'They're displaying the behaviour of highly disturbed people, but there's nothing here that points to them committing actual bodily harm.'

'Can you stop the car, please?' Jenna asked.

'Excuse me?'

'Please. Just stop the car a moment, will you?'

'But we're almost...'

'Stop. Please?'

Luke spotted a space at the side of the road, between two cars. He parked, then turned in his seat to face Jenna.

'Sorry,' she began. 'I just need to know. Is there something you're not telling me?'

'Oh, Jenna.' His stomach twisted.

'Please,' she said. 'If I go in there and confront this woman, and she lobs a bomb at my feet, I don't know that I'll recover from it. We need to talk to her from a position of strength. Show her that we're together. And if she throws something at us that I already know, then it will defuse the whole situation, won't it? Put the onus back on her to explain what the hell is going on.'

'But—'

'But, nothing, Luke. I've been with you long enough to know when you're holding on to something. There's something I don't know, and I'm worried it will give her and Jamie the advantage. So, if you're going to tell me the truth, Luke, it needs to be now.'

'Okay.' He steeled himself, wondering exactly how much to tell her, and if it would be obvious that he was holding something back. 'There was this lad...'

Chapter 75

Twenty four years earlier

Memory slammed him straight back to that moment when he was standing on the waste ground just yards from his mother's house, with Fraser prostate at his feet.

'Stop pissing about,' he remembered shouting down at Fraser, struggling to ignore the fact that his friend wasn't pretending anything.

This was as serious as it got.

He leaned over the boy, read his preternatural stillness, and in the darkness was able to make out what he thought was blood spooling out from Fraser's head.

Panicked, Luke turned and ran.

And ran.

Eventually, he found himself pounding on Danny's front door, and thankfully it was him who answered and not one of his parents. Breathlessly, Luke told Danny what happened.

'Right,' Danny said as he dragged him into his bedroom. 'You've been with me all night. We've been in this house playing *Grand Theft Auto* since we got home from school.'

'But I've killed him, Danny. Killed him.'

Danny slapped the panic out of him, grabbed him by the collar and pulled his face close. He spoke carefully and slowly, enunciating every word. 'You've been here all night playing *Grand Theft Auto*. What have you been doing?'

Luke had enough presence of mind to repeat Danny's words. Then he spent the rest of the night in a welter of worry, thinking every noise in the house was notice that the police were on their way to arrest him.

'What are you going to do?' Danny asked him. 'Do you know he's dead for sure?'

Luke was certain he would never forget the sight of his friend, pale at his feet, deathly still with blood blooming around his head. 'Aye. He's dead.'

'Stay here,' Danny said, throwing the handset for the game at him. 'Play with that. I'm going out to check.'

'What? Check what, for Chrissake?'

'That he is actually dead. Stay.' Danny put a hand on his chest. 'I'll be ten minutes.'

Danny disappeared for what was the longest fifteen minutes of Luke's young life.

When he returned it was with a ghostly face of confirmation. 'You need to get out of town,' Danny said. Then he put the ceiling light on and examined Luke's clothing. 'You've no blood on you.'

'Jesus,' Luke said, as he jiggled on the spot. 'How can you be so calm about this?'

'Got any cash?'

'I could go to my dad's. He's up in Aberdeen.'

'He is?' Danny asked. He looked miffed that Luke had kept this from him. Truth was that Luke kept it from all of his friends. He wasn't sure why, other than that he didn't want his family situation to be a topic for gossip.

'Long story. Aye, and he's in Aberdeen.'

'Perfect.' Danny rooted under his bed, came out with a small tin – a lunchbox with superheroes on the cover. He opened it and pulled out a wad of cash. He handed the money to Luke.

'Where did you get all that...?'

'Stay here tonight. We'll pack you a bag, then in the morning you can get the first bus to Aberdeen.'

It was at that point that the realisation of what happened properly hit Luke. 'Oh my God.' His legs went from under him and he fell to the floor. Head in his hands, he mumbled, 'I should go to the police. I should hand myself in. God, what have I done?'

There was a loud banging on the wall. 'What's going on in

there?' Danny's mother shouted. 'You got a girl in there, Danny Morrison?'

'Naw, Mum. Gie it a rest, eh? Duncan's here. I told ye already,' Danny shouted back. Then he turned to Luke. 'Shut it. Forget the polis. Go to your dad's. Lie low for a few weeks, then when you come back down it will all be over. Fraser will just be another statistic.'

Luke did just that. All but shrinking into himself with guilt he jumped onto the bus to Aberdeen, and a taxi got him from there to a surprised but delighted father. His mother called to speak to him the next day, in a panic, worried that their falling-out over the missing letters had sent him into the arms of the man she hated most in the world.

As much as his father and his new wife continued to try to make him feel welcome, Luke felt he was imposing on the family, and once Danny got in touch to say that the funeral had happened and that the police had filed Fraser's death as an unresolved crime, he got on the first bus back down to Glasgow.

Chapter 76

Jenna watched Luke speak, shrinking back from him as he did, wishing there was more room in the car. He'd killed someone else? Sure, neither death had been planned, and could be deemed accidental, but still.

She didn't know how she felt about this. But she recognised the guilt and shame that coated every word out of Luke's mouth, like rust on metal, and that was the reason she stayed where she was.

'If you never want to speak to me again, that's fine,' Luke said. 'I'll understand.'

'You saw Fraser's brother and his wife just before Christmas, yeah? Do they know any of this?'

Luke shook his head. 'I couldn't bear it if Joe knew what had happened to Fraser.'

'Oh my God, Luke, his death will still be down as unresolved. His family have a right to know what happened to their boy.'

'You're right. They do. But I can't bring myself to tell them.' Luke's face was pale, his eyes shifting back and forward, as if everything they saw was a reminder of his sins.

'When you were with them, it didn't feel awkward?'

'Course it did. Joe thinks I've kept away from them because I feel I'm better than them. That I've been trying to improve my life and they just hold me back.' He hung his head. 'When it's just down to good old-fashioned guilt. I can't look at Joe without seeing Fraser.'

'Bloody hell.' Jenna shook her head. 'What a mess you've made of your life.'

Luke reared back as if stung, then slumped as if accepting this summary as fair. 'So, yeah. Whatever I touch turns to poison. You're better off not speaking to me again.'

'But first,' Jenna shifted in her seat and looked ahead, praying that her own secret wasn't about to come to light, 'we've got some comeuppance to deliver.'

Chapter 77

Jamie felt like there were two people living under his skin. The little boy who craved love and attention. And the one who wanted to set fire to the world.

On the way to the local shop that morning for some bread and milk, he walked past an older man, broad in the shoulder and with an open, benevolent cast to his face. He found himself stopping the man and asking for the time. The man pulled out his phone, a question in his eyes: *Don't you have one of these?* And then told Jamie the time.

'Thanks,' Jamie mumbled.

'You okay, son?' the man asked, looking deep into his eyes, his concern for a stranger so potent Jamie almost held his hand up to shield himself. There was a solidity about him, feet planted wide, braced to support all of those around him; his eyes clear, as if certain about who he was. Jamie wanted to ask him if he had half an hour to sit and talk somewhere. To counsel him. Perhaps even to wrap those brawny arms of his around Jamie, to provide a cocoon of muscle and heart. But of course, that would be crazy, so he dragged up a smile, and replied:

'I've had better days,' he said. 'But thanks.'

'Aye. Hope it gets better for you soon, son.' And with a wave the man turned and went on his way.

Ten minutes later, on the way home from the shops, and his hard-won peace shattered. Two teenage boys, blazers and ties, leery with testosterone and attitude, and obviously avoiding school, jostled past him, arguing about some game or another.

'Hey,' Jamie challenged when he got knocked out of his stride.

The boys turned to him. 'Want to make something of it?' One was taller than Jamie, the other was short and wide. Too much gaming and pizza. Both wore matching gelled and spiked hair cuts, and snarls.

Jamie imagined a throat punch to one followed by stamping on the knees of the other. He felt a surge of anger and adrenaline, then managed to ease off a little. But he couldn't stop it from smouldering, just under his skin, like a lava field needing just one more degree of heat before exploding.

He turned and walked away, ignoring the jeers that got louder the further he walked. He shook his head at himself, recognising the see-saw swing of his nature these days.

He thought he was gaining some equilibrium after meeting Luke and Nathan. He'd never known peace like that, just in the few hours he'd spent in their company. And missed it greatly since that last day at the funfair.

Luke's face. The disappointment in his eyes. And barely suppressed anger. He was no different than those boys back there. All knuckles and barely tamped down aggression. He'd been pretending to like Jamie, all the while just assuaging his guilt at what happened to Danny.

Amanda's voice sounded in his head, demanding biblical retribution. She'd recognised that his willingness to be part of her scheme had been softening. And in turn he recognised that being so intent on their plan was not good for his state of mind.

'Why don't we just satisfy ourselves with the damage we've caused so far?' he asked her.

She exploded from her seat and stabbed the air in front of her with her index finger. 'Never. They need to suffer like we suffered. One of them killed him. The other all but drove him into the killer's arms. They deserve everything they get, so, no, I won't be satisfied until they're on their knees.'

But he'd had a glimpse now of what a normal life could be.

But he didn't deserve it, did he?

But.

But.

But the chatter never ceased. One way then the other. Strike out. Sit in peace. What he would give to have a moment, just a moment, in someone else's head. When the monkey mind was stilled.

When he reached the corner of his street, some instinct made him pause. He sniffed the air the way a predator might, but recognised nothing but a linger of cigarette smoke and diesel fumes.

He saw low hedges, tall trees and clipped lawns. A row of red-roofed bungalows on either side of the road. A woman and two small children, all of them wrapped in coats, hats and scarves, the children's light, happy chatter flitting into the air like birdsong. And there, two houses down from where he and Amanda lived, a car he recognised.

Two people sat inside, and even from this angle, when all he could see was the shoulder of one and the side of the head of the other, he knew who they were.

He stepped back around the corner, pulled out his phone and called Amanda.

'Luke and Jenna are outside in his car,' he said before she could speak.

He heard her intake of breath. Then: 'How the hell did they find us?'

'No idea,' Jamie replied.

A moment's silence.

'Get yourself in here, and we hear what they have to say. Or...'

'Or what?' he asked.

'Let's take it up a notch. Will the kid be at home?'

'Nathan should be in school,' Jamie answered, thinking about the two boys in uniform he'd just encountered.

'How long will it take you to get to his place?'

'Depends on traffic, but probably about twenty, thirty minutes. Why?'

'Just thinking. If you managed to drop a lit match while passing his door, it wouldn't be the worst thing in the world.'

Chapter 78

Jenna cast a glance to Luke, who was standing at her shoulder, before knocking at the door. It was solid red, with a brass knocker in the middle at head height. She'd examined the house and garden as she walked up the path, wondering how someone so young could have afforded a house like this.

Sandstone bay windows on either side of the entrance, and a loft conversion; a herringbone-patterned red-brick drive, and plenty of space in front of the house and down either side, planted with mature shrubs and trees.

She'd given a low whistle as she walked up the drive to the house. 'Jeez, if this is in good nick you're talking half a million.'

The door opened.

The woman Jenna knew as Hazel stood there, a half-smile working its way across her mouth, but her eyes were hard, challenging. Her hair was blonde, shoulder length and straightened to a gleam. She was wearing grey yoga pants and a navy hoodie, and Jenna wondered how she could ever have thought this woman was the same age as her.

'Amanda Morrison?' Jenna said. All the way over she'd been thinking about what to say when she saw 'Hazel' and settled for using the woman's real name. She felt a massive sense of satisfaction as she did so. She wanted to pull off her mask like you might rip off a plaster.

A sharp light of recognition appeared in Amanda's eyes, but she quickly recovered her equilibrium, as if she'd had advanced warning of their arrival. She stepped back, out of their way. 'You'd better come in.'

Jenna paused to allow Luke to enter first, as if on some silent signal that he would be the better to meet any physical threat. But all that greeted them was a hallway with a plush, grey carpet that from the tramlines looked like it had recently been hoovered. To the side, an occasional table holding a small red bowl, edged in gilt, and a tall mirror, and she wondered about malice given a veneer of respectability. How many people, on how many streets just like this across the country, were hiding the poisoned apple of their heart with a throw blanket, a nice rug and some scatter cushions?

'I've just put the kettle on,' Amanda said. 'Anyone fancy a brew?'

'Really?' Jenna replied, almost admiring the nonchalance of the young woman while wanting to slap the cheek out of her. 'That's where we are? Tea and coffee?'

'Might as well be civilised about it,' Amanda replied. 'Let's go through to the conservatory. You catch the winter sun there just lovely.'

'Where's Jamie?' Luke asked.

Amanda ignored him and kept walking.

They entered a conservatory that had brick walls to waist height, patio doors facing them, and leaves resting on the glass roof. A three-piece bamboo suite and coffee table sat in the middle.

'Haven't got round to updating yet,' Amanda said. 'Been kinda busy.'

'Give it a rest,' Jenna said, feeling Luke stiffen at her side.

Amanda sat on an armchair, indicating the sofa to Jenna and Luke. He sat, but Jenna stayed standing. She could see he was studying Amanda's face.

'We did meet back then,' Amanda said, also reading Luke's expression. 'Well, *met* is an exaggeration. Danny brought you round a few times, and you completely ignored me.'

Luke opened his mouth to reply, then closed it again as if deciding it wasn't worth the effort.

'I can't believe you had me fooled about being in the same class at uni,' Jenna said. 'What are you, twenty-five, twenty six?'

'Does it matter what age I am?' Amanda sat back and crossed

her legs. 'What gave it away? Sandy and Jean?' She saw Jenna's re-action. 'Damn. If only we'd left there five minutes earlier.'

'*If only* you hadn't turned into some vengeful monster,' Jenna countered. 'What did I ever do to you? I loved your brother.' Jenna heard emotion in her voice, hated herself for it and cleared it from her throat with a cough.

'You loved him until you didn't.'

'He was not an easy man to love.'

'What, do you want sympathy?'

'I can understand why you targeted me,' Luke interrupted. 'Well, I can't, cos this is shit that crazy people do. But why go after Jenna? She had nothing to do with Danny's death.'

Amanda didn't react. It was as if Luke wasn't there, hadn't spoken. Her gaze was stuck on Jenna.

'Look at you,' she said, her eyes full of knowledge. 'Little Miss Butter-Wouldn't-Melt.'

Jenna's stomach lurched. There was no doubt in her mind. Amanda knew, and the only person who could have told her was Danny. And seeing the shine in her eyes, Jenna was sure she was about to wield that fact like a sword. Better that she take that moment of surprise away from her.

'Danny told you about the abortion?' she asked, quickly glanc-ing at Luke, ducking her head in apology.

'What?' Luke asked quietly. 'A what? Why didn't you tell me?' His eyes were soft, his expression one of empathy.

'I'm—' she began,

'She's a whore,' Amanda interrupted. 'At least that's how Danny described her when he told me.'

'You were only a kid,' Jenna said, trying to hide the sting she felt at Amanda's words. 'Why would he tell you something like that?'

'Did it without even telling him first, eh? What kind of coward does that? Ran away with mummy to the hospital. God knows what sob story you told them.'

'It ... it was complicated,' Jenna replied, struggling to find the right words.

'God, how awful for you,' Luke said, reaching for her hand.

Jenna tried gently to shrug it off. Now was not the time for sympathy. She had to harden herself and deal with this young woman. She and Luke could talk about the termination another time.

'Complicated?' Amanda asked. 'That's it? That's your explanation for killing my brother's child?'

'I did what I had to do,' Jenna replied, sitting up straight. 'You weren't there. You couldn't possibly understand.'

'My brother was ruined – ruined after that. Yeah, I was just a kid, but I was old enough to see that what happened messed him up.' She narrowed her eyes. 'I remember just before. He was in the kitchen with Mum on one of his rare visits. Dad was out,' she added by way of explanation. 'And he was telling Mum you were going to be the saving of him. That he'd changed his ways and all it took was the love of a good woman.' Amanda sat forward in her chair as if to get closer to Jenna. 'Can you imagine the betrayal he felt? The woman he thought was going to be his saviour goes and does that to him? How you can even stand under the weight of all of that is beyond me,' Amanda sneered. 'You are a vile human being—'

'Enough,' Luke interrupted. 'Jenna did what she had to do, and that's good enough for me. Your big brother was dangerous, Amanda. There was something in him that could be pretty bloody scary. And it sounds like Jenna woke up to that just in time. Perhaps we leave Jenna out of this. It's me you really want.'

'I couldn't believe it when you two got together,' Amanda said, completely ignoring Luke. 'I mean, what are the chances?'

'Regardless,' Luke said. 'Jenna was young, and in an impossible situation – realising that the man she was in love with, and who'd just made her pregnant, had a screw loose.' He looked across at Jenna, and she read that he was keen to show her his understanding. 'So, let's leave her out of it, shall we?' he repeated.

'Nope,' Amanda said, shaking her head.

Luke jumped to his feet. 'You are nothing but a silly little girl, and Jamie's a silly little boy. There's nothing more here than a case of arrested development. You were both badly treated by your parents, they died, and you went on to even worse treatment by the people who were chosen to look after you. Trauma on trauma. Blah, blah.' Jenna knew Luke well enough to know that he took the effects of trauma on the developing mind very seriously indeed. He was trying to rile her. 'Well, time to grow up, little girl. Lots of people have a difficult start, and they go on to lead productive lives. You need to start taking responsibility. You got dealt a shitty hand. Move on.'

'A shitty hand? You know nothing, Duncan Robertson.' Amanda's nostrils flared, and she leaned forward and smiled, but the light in her eyes didn't change, didn't hint at the thoughts behind the smile. Her right hand, though, tucked under her left, was clenched. Even as she tried to display a controlled façade her body was betraying her. Luke's comments had got to her.

'Everything was fine until *she* came along,' Amanda said. 'Danny was a great brother. The best. Then nothing. He stopped coming round. Never even phoned. And Mum laughed. My mother *laughed* at me. She laughed at my disappointment. What kind of mother does that? Then, when you dumped him and killed his baby, he was changed. Had no time for women, regardless of who they were. As far as he was concerned you had ruined that for him. At least he knew where he was with the guys, he said. Women were a different species, and he wouldn't trust any of them ever again.' Her lips were a tight, white line of barely supressed anger. 'You ruined my brother, you witch. Happy?'

'Oh, for God's sake,' Jenna said.

'And you drove him back to the company of this arsehole. And we all know what happened next, don't we?'

'Danny was a grown man,' Jenna said. 'He made his own choices.'

'And we all know what happened next, Duncan,' Amanda repeated. 'Or do we?' Her focus was lasered on Luke.

'What's that supposed to mean?' Jenna asked.

'You were there, or have you forgotten, you daft bint? When Sandy told us about the time he passed Danny and Dunc.' She continued to bore into Luke's face. 'On that road. Hours before the paramedics reported they were called. What happened, Duncan? What *really* happened?'

'You know what happened. It's a matter of public record.'

'Public record, my backside. Even when I was a wee girl I knew the whole thing stank. You saw a chance to get control over Danny's business empire and you tried to take it. It's just a pity,' she spat, 'your ploy didn't work out for you, and you landed in jail.' Amanda looked over at Jenna. 'Even she knows we never got to the truth.'

'Business empire,' Luke snorted. 'Danny was a petty criminal with delusions.'

'And what does that say about you?' Amanda replied.

'I'm not proud of who I was back then, and I've spent years trying to make amends.'

'Thing is,' Amanda said, 'we're not buying this new nice-guy version. I can still see your spots, Mr Leopard.'

'When your view of the world is as distorted as yours, Amanda, it's no wonder you can't understand – can't see when someone's made a change to their life.'

'Shall I get some Brasso out and give your halo a wee polish?' Amanda sneered. 'Bollocks. It's all bollocks.'

'Where's Jamie?' Luke asked, looking back into the house. 'I assume he lives here with you?'

'Tell you what,' Amanda said, completely ignoring the question. 'At this point in time you have nothing. You can't go to the police, cos there's nothing actionable. Computers and the internet are my business. There's nothing there for the police to work with, believe me. So why don't we make a deal? You tell me what really happened, and I back off.'

'You know what happened,' Luke replied.

'Stop it,' Amanda shouted. She was on her feet, face red. The change in her behaviour was so abrupt that Jenna dropped into a seat as if that might create some distance. 'You killed him. It was never an accident.' Her mouth was twisted in hate. 'You got him tanked up, stayed sober yourself and then drove into that field. Probably after you unfastened his seatbelt. And then you waited just long enough to phone the ambulance so that people would think it was an accident. Tell me I'm right, and then you two can go back to your dreary little existence.'

Jenna could see Luke was studying Amanda's face for subterfuge.

'That's a promise?' Luke asked as he sat back down.

Jenna stared at Luke, mouth open in shock.

That suggested there *was* more to the events of the day Danny died. Did she want to know? Fascinated and repelled, she resisted the urge to press her hands over her ears and listened as Luke told his story.

Chapter 79

Fifteen years earlier

Luke was sick. Sick of the life he was leading, of feeling adrift. Of hiding up there in Aberdeen just so he could avoid Danny. Feeling that if he were to die no one would mourn him. He hated everyone he knew, especially the man screaming in the chair beside him. And so, when he misjudged the bend, the speed, the bright sun sharp in his eyes, he forced himself to relax and prayed as the car shot through the hedging and he rocked back and forward, and up and down in his seat, aware of Danny's yells, the roar of the engine, and the sound of metal buckling. As his senses slowed down and picked everything up, he prayed that he would die and that the end would be quick.

Instead.

One final bang. A stop so sudden he felt as if his head was about to be torn from his shoulders.

And a silence so profound he thought his ears had stopped working.

Then darkness.

*

When he came too, it could have been minutes, or hours later, he had no way of knowing. He took a breath, and felt pain. In his face, neck and chest. Smarting, stabbing, sharp pain worse than any he'd received during the fights he'd experienced in his life.

Moving his head to the side, carefully, slowly, he struggled to make sense of what he saw. The passenger seat was empty. The airbag had deployed, cracking the windscreen. The door was wide open.

'Danny?' he shouted. Then again. 'Danny?'

Nothing.

Creating as little movement as possible, Luke reached down and unfastened his seatbelt, and recalled that Danny had refused to wear one.

He passed out again.

Next thing he remembered was being outside the car on his hands and knees, crawling around the back. The front was almost embedded in a tree.

And there, off to the side, a tangled bundle of arms and legs. They were still.

Perfectly still.

'Danny?' he shouted.

This time his question was rewarded with a groan. Luke crawled over.

For a moment, the sharpest of moments, his disappointment was acute. Danny was alive. Just.

'Fuck,' Danny mumbled. His face was unrecognisable. Blood and bone. His lips moved, and Luke could see a mouth of broken teeth, smeared red. 'Phone. Ambulance.'

Luke reached out to touch Danny's shoulder, to reassure, but he found he couldn't do either. Touch the man, or offer any re-assurance.

'Phone. Need help,' Danny said, his voice noticeably weaker.

Luke felt panic rise in his chest. What do you do? How do you help? He looked back up the hill and saw the passage the car had taken in the torn turf and burst hedging.

Danny wheezed. A bubble of blood appeared on his lips. 'Bastard,' he whispered. 'I hope you're worse than me.' There was no edge of humour in his voice. He meant what he was saying. Even in his worst moment, this man, who he'd known for most of his life, had nothing in him but spite and bile.

'Ambulance,' Danny repeated. 'Phone?'

His phone was in his jeans. Should he do the right thing? He patted his pocket, and let his hand fall away.

'Don't have it, Danny. Can't find it. Must have been thrown out of the car during the...' He looked back up towards the road, imagining his phone flying through the air.

'Mine,' Danny said. 'Try mine.'

Luke scanned down Danny's body and saw the flat rectangle shape at the side of his jeans. Managing his pain as best he could, Luke crawled closer, slowly reached into Danny's pocket and pulled out his phone.

The screen was cracked, but there was enough power to light the screen. Enough power to see three little bars suggesting there was a good signal.

He thought about the years Danny had held him under his thumb, the women he'd got hooked on heroin. The havoc this man created in the lives of everyone around him.

'No signal, mate,' he said and felt the weight of his decision. He had no real choice, did he? Or his 'mate' here would continue to rain havoc down on him. They weren't friends. Hadn't been for a very long time. Their relationship was all about Danny and what Luke could do for him.

Through the blood and hair and torn skin he could make out Danny's one good eye. It was large. Staring. Accusing. In the weakening light of that small orb Luke could read that Danny knew exactly what was happening. To avoid his glare, Luke allowed himself to fall to the turf, and felt the soft, wet surface on the side of his face. A cooling, solid embrace.

He could hear a car passing on the road, and wondered if the driver could see down this far. Then another. But there was no sound of brakes. No shouts of assistance. Then he heard birdsong, as if nature was reclaiming the air around them.

Other sounds. Danny trying to speak. A rattle in his throat.

'Any last words, Danny? Want to try and make amends before you die? Apologise to all of the people whose lives you messed up?' Luke fought to prop himself up on an elbow to assess what was happening with Danny.

He saw Danny's mouth open and close. Open and close, as if it was taking the last amount of energy he owned.

'Cunt,' he said. And then he fought for a breath as if that exclamation had emptied his lungs. He didn't say another word after that. And Luke made himself watch as Danny struggled, fought for one breath after another.

And then slowly, interminably, stopped breathing altogether.

Chapter 80

Luke had watched Danny die? He'd waited until he was sure he was dead before he called for help? Who does that?'

Rather than shooting across town for an act of arson, an act that, when Amanda first mentioned it, he'd instantly rejected, Jamie had waited until Luke and Jenna entered the house, then shot up the drive, round the side, and hunkered down below the low wall of the conservatory, just under a slightly open window, knowing that was where Amanda would lead them.

He listened in mounting horror as the man he'd come to respect gave Amanda the missing piece she'd been looking for all of these years. Some instinct had told her that there was more to Danny's death. Jamie had thought it was the product of a twisted mind, but she was right all along.

Maybe that was not all she was right about.

The see-saw swing of his recent moods were exhausting, and he thought it was because the better part of his nature needed to be observed. Now, having heard the truth, he was thinking the opposite. The wolf had to be unleashed.

On his hands and knees, and full of a kind of resolve he hadn't felt for a long time, Jamie crawled back the way he came, and then ran to his car for the journey across town. Via a petrol station.

Outside Luke's house, he paused, felt the certainty of his actions, and checked up and down the street that he wasn't being observed. It was empty. The windows on every house blinked back at him blindly. This street was inhabited mostly by workers he guessed. All these drones would be scattered around the city, working to raise the cash to pay the bills for the items they didn't need but judged essential because of the status they conferred.

Sheep. The lot of them. He despised them all.

He drove back around the block slowly, checking for movement, pausing at the end of the street, where a row of garages were situated. A man with a young child got into a car. He waited until they were gone then he went to the back of his car, filled a bottle with petrol and pushed a rag into the neck to act as a wick.

Then he drove along to Luke's, checked again for movement, and, satisfied there was none, climbed out of the car again. He judged the distance from where he was standing to the front door, and, feeling confident he could make the throw, lit the rag.

He cocked his arm back and threw, and mentally cheered when he heard the smash and roar as the bottle landed at the door, and the flames took hold.

Something caught his eye.

Movement.

A boy at an upstairs window. He obviously had no understanding about what he had just witnessed. Yet.

Because the little boy was waving in recognition.

And smiling.

Chapter 81

Luke felt an easing. Just for a moment. A secret he'd harboured for so long was no longer secret. Guilt from it had dripped into his mind over the years, like rancid water from a rust-ridden tap. But then he looked at Jenna, at the horror on her face, and was charged with regret.

The truth was out, but at the cost of any future with her. Jenna looked as if any more time spent in his company would be too much. As if she'd just discovered he was harbouring some dread disease, and she had been contaminated with it.

Amanda, on the other hand, looked vindicated. An Olympic winner on the rostrum. A woman who'd just brought her life's work to fruition.

'You made a promise,' Luke said, feeling empty. 'And I'm trusting you to keep it.'

She smiled. For the first time since he'd been in her presence he felt her smile was genuine.

'It's not me you need to worry about,' she said.

'What the hell's that supposed to mean?' Luke demanded. Then realisation struck. 'Jamie. Where is he?'

Amanda raised her right eyebrow. 'Just follow the sound of the fire engines.'

Chapter 82

Fear was a storm under his skin, an unceasing list of catastrophic what-ifs in his mind. Luke wanted to force Jamie's intentions out of Amanda. He stood up and approached her, his hands blunted into fists.

'Fire engines?' he demanded.

A frightened look from Jenna worked its way past his fury and stopped him in his tracks.

'Is Jamie headed over to my house?'

Amanda simply smiled.

'Fuck. Nathan's off school today. Anything happens to him and I'll—'

'He's not at school?' Amanda asked. Then her face fell as Luke's increased state of agitation provided her with an answer. 'We didn't...'

'Didn't what?'

Amanda's arms were wide in supplication. Her face long, and eyes contrite.

'God.' Amanda jumped to her feet. 'The boy's at school, no?'

'What's happening, Amanda?' Luke demanded. 'What's Jamie up to?'

'I'll phone him,' she said, looking around. 'Shit. Where's my phone?'

'Fire engines,' Luke said. 'You mentioned fire engines. Why?'

'Shit,' Amanda said as she pushed past Luke and moved into the kitchen. 'How long have you been here?' she asked as she plucked her phone from the work surface.

'About thirty minutes or so,' Jenna said as she followed Amanda and Luke. 'What's going on?'

'Is that long enough to get from here to yours?' Amanda asked Luke, her face white with concern.

With a lead weight in his gut and shortening breath Luke

worked out what Amanda was getting at. He pushed his hands under his arms and held them tight as she dialled Jamie and waited.

Then. The unmistakeable sound of a phone ringing somewhere in the house. It was faint, but it had clearly started when Amanda dialled the number. She followed the sound, Luke and Jenna behind her. It sounded stronger in the conservatory. It was coming from just outside the window.

'Shit,' Amanda said.

'What?' Luke demanded. 'What?'

Without answering, Amanda exited the conservatory, took a left, and there under the window was Jamie's phone.

'He must have doubled back,' Amanda said.

'What do you mean?' Luke asked.

Jenna wore a look of sharp comprehension. 'He must have been squatting behind that wall, listening to everything we said.' She looked up at the open window.

Amanda's open mouth was all Luke needed for his anxiety to soar. 'You have to stop him,' she said.

Luke ran from the house, followed by a wordless Jenna and they jumped in the car. Even before she had her seatbelt fastened Luke pulled away from the kerb. Ignoring the screech of brakes and blasts of a horn as a car nearly crashed into the back of them, Luke pushed his foot down on the accelerator. The light at the end of the street was about to change. He drove straight through.

'Luke,' Jenna admonished a little breathlessly. 'If we crash we're not going to be of help to anyone.'

'There,' he said gesturing towards his phone that was sitting in a compartment above the gear stick. 'Phone Ken for me.'

He was now behind a black estate car. It was being driven exactly at the speed limit.

'For Chrissakes,' Luke shouted. Beeped his horn. Drove as close to the car as he could. 'Move,' he shouted. The road ahead was suddenly clear. No oncoming traffic. Luke overtook, the owner flashing his lights in annoyance. Two hundred yards ahead, another set of lights were changing.

Amber.

He sped up.

Red.

He had to jump on his brakes, and with them screaming in protest and his forehead inches away from the windscreen, he managed to stop at the crossing, where an old woman paused in her journey across to shoot him the finger, while mouthing, 'Arsehole.'

'Luke,' Jenna shouted. Her voice broke through the panic of his thoughts. 'We can't help Nathan if we crash the car.'

'Jesus.' Luke drummed on the steering wheel as he waited for the lights to change. A little of Jenna's good sense leaked through to him. He took a breath. The light changed. He took off. Turned right, but was forced to slow down by the sheer volume of traffic he was now in the middle of.

He looked at the clock on the dashboard: 11:45. Just before lunch break. Workers and the city's schoolkids would be at their stations. That might mean the motorway would be relatively quiet.

'Phone Ken for me will you?' he repeated, and told her his passcode.

She keyed it in, found Ken's name under contacts and dialled.

It rang out unanswered, then switched to his answering service.

'Ken's a nightmare with his mobile,' Luke said. 'Try again.'

She did. With the same result.

'Shit.'

'Try the motorway?' Jenna asked. 'Might be better at this time of day?'

'Just what I was thinking.' Luke studied the road ahead. If he turned at the next lights, just a hundred yards beyond that was a ramp down onto the M8, the main arterial route that sliced across the city.

Just minutes later they were on the motorway, and Luke felt his hopes lift as he put his foot down and felt the car respond. They were now only about fifteen minutes away from his house and coasting at fifty miles an hour. The exit he had been aiming for appeared ahead. Soon he was off the motorway and moving closer to home.

Another ten minutes, his forehead almost pressed against the windscreen in his willingness to get home, and with his heart about to burst out of his chest with worry, he turned the corner into the top of his street.

His worst fears were all but confirmed. There was a wall of flashing lights. A fire engine, a pair of ambulances and a couple of police cars all added to the visual din. A police car was parked across the street to stop passage through the area where the emergency services vehicles were working.

Luke jumped on his brakes and flew out of the car.

'Move your car.' A policeman approached him. Stern. Pointing. 'You're causing an obstruction.'

'That's my...' Luke said, fighting to be heard above the clamour, fear stealing any volume from his voice. 'My house.'

'I won't tell you again, sir. Emergency vehicles need access. You have to move.' The officer moved closer to Luke.

'You're not hearing me, man,' Luke attempted again, as he tried to move past the policeman.

'Luke.' Jenna was in his ear. 'Give me your keys. I'll move the car.'

A fresh blare of noise, and an ambulance with its lights churning left the throng and moved towards them. The driver pressed down hard on his horn, his mouth moving fast, his intent and frustration clear.

'Luke. Your keys,' Jenna insisted.

'Who's in that ambulance? Officer – who's in that ambulance?'

'If you don't move your car and let this ambulance out this second I'm going to have to arrest you.'

'Luke,' Jenna shouted, then reached for his hand. Dumb-founded, Luke glanced down. His car keys. The weight of them. How did they…?

Jenna plucked them out of his grip, ran to the car and reversed it out of the way.

The ambulance scorched past them.

Luke's anxiety made him unable to sequence events. All he could think about was the ambulance leaving quickly; it could only mean whoever was inside was in a bad way.

'Nathan,' he shouted into the distance.

Faces surrounded him. Mouths moving.

Maybe it wasn't Nathan inside that ambulance. He turned back to the throng of vehicles around his house and made to move towards it. Hope stirred in him that his son was fine. He's being attended to right now by some friendly ambulance technician, charming the last pound coin out of him. Surely?

Anything else was unthinkable.

'I need to…' he said to the officer.

Jenna reached them. 'It's his house,' she shouted. 'His son.'

The officer's demeanour changed instantly. 'Right,' he said. 'Why didn't you say so? Come with me.'

In his urgency Luke didn't hear what the man said, he simply read the change in body language and ran past him towards the house, his pulse thundering in his ears, his breath ragged, and his eyes searching for any sight of his little boy.

A pair of firemen were holding a hose and aiming it at his roof. Another pair were aiming their hose at his front door. He saw more smoke than flames, and part of his mind filed that away as a good sign. But where was Nathan? The house could burn to the ground for all he cared, as long as his boy was alive and well.

The policeman caught up with him. 'Sir,' he said, and the seri-ousness of his expression almost whipped the strength from Luke's thighs. 'Your boy's safe. If you just come with me.'

Luke opened his mouth, but nothing came out other than a

squeak of worry. He coughed. Once. Twice. 'He's safe?' he asked, struggling to breathe.

Jenna had caught up with him. She reached out and gripped his arm. 'He's trying to tell you, Luke. Nathan's safe.'

The cop nodded at Jenna and then turned to Luke. 'The ambulance just here...'

'He's in an ambulance?'

'And he's absolutely fine. A wee bit shaken, but he's a right wee trooper. If you just...'

Luke moved towards the ambulance.

'Nathan,' Luke shouted as he ran.

'Daddy?' came the high-pitched query.

'Nathan?'

The front door of the ambulance opened, and a little body jumped out and into Luke's arms.

'Oh my God,' Luke said, faint with relief. 'You're okay?' He held Nathan out from his body, searching for any sign of damage, and apart from a dirty face, there was none. He pulled the boy back into a hug.

'I'm never letting you out of my sight ever again.'

After a moment, Nathan kicked his legs a little in protest. 'Daddy, I can't breathe.'

'Sorry, buddy.' Luke relaxed his grip, and pressed his lips against the warm square of the boy's forehead.

'Daddy, Jamie saved us. He kicked the door down and saved us. And he saved Tritops.'

Tritops was Nathan's favourite dinosaur.

'Jamie saved Tritops as well?'

'Yes, he was very brave.' Nathan nodded his head slowly to emphasise just how brave he thought Jamie was.

Luke didn't have the heart to voice his certainty that Jamie had set the fire in the first place. But what made him spring into action and try to save everybody afterwards? Did he think the house was empty, and then see some movement?

A paramedic came over to them. 'He's a wee star,' the man in green said. 'I've just been showing him how the lights flash.'

'Oh aye?' Luke looked around himself, remembering an ambulance had just sped off. 'Ken. My friend Ken was with him. Is he...?'

'He's in the back of this one,' the medic said. 'We're just patching him up. Then we'll take him to the hospital for further tests, but he should be fine. C'mon and I'll take you to him. But you should know your other friend is in a bad way. Smoke inhalation.'

'Other friend?' Jenna asked.

'He got the boy out, then he ran back into the building to help Ken here, but he collapsed.' His expression was grave. 'He's in the ambulance that took off earlier.'

The paramedic led them to the back of the ambulance and opened the door. Inside he saw Ken sitting up on a gurney, bandages over his hands. His face was smeared with smoke and ash, the skin around his eyes was red with inflammation, and the eyes themselves were dull with pain.

'Hey man.' Luke put a hand on his shoulder. 'How you feeling?'

'Been worse,' Ken replied in a croak.

'What the hell happened?'

'Not sure,' Ken said. He paused, slightly breathless. 'We were upstairs in the wee man's room, having a nap. Something woke me up. There was a crash at the door, and I smelt burning. I went out into the hall and saw all these flames. It was fucking scary, man. So I got a bath towel, soaked it, and covered Nathan. And that was enough time for the fire to grow even stronger. The smoke.' Ken shook his head. 'Never seen so much smoke. I couldn't see a bloody thing. Got completely disorientated.' He swallowed, and judging by his expression it was painful. 'But your man, Jamie, burst through, ran up the stairs and helped us both outside. Nathan was going on about his dinosaurs melting so Jamie went back in.'

'He did?' Jenna asked in disbelief.

'I know. Nutter, but he said if Nathan wanted his dinosaurs

then he'd get them for him. From what I saw he barely made it back out alive.'

'Aye, the medic just told me he's in a bad way.'

Something in Luke's voice made Ken study his friend's eyes. 'Are you thinking what I'm thinking?'

'It's a bit of a coincidence that he's there when my house goes up in flames, eh?'

'Nathan told me he saw your friend Jamie from the window while I was sleeping,' Ken replied.

'Do you think...' Jenna began '...he started it, thinking the house was empty. Then when he saw you two were inside he realised what a mistake he'd made and jumped in to save you.'

'He set the house on fire, and then he saved our lives,' Ken said. 'How do you make sense of that?'

A middle-aged woman approached them, dark suit, black hair pulled back from her face. Her eyes were trained on Luke, and he sensed straight away that she was a cop. He'd seen enough of them in his time to recognise one at twenty paces.

'Mr Forrest?' She studied Luke. 'You're the owner of the house?'

'I am,' he replied.

'Mind if I have a word in private?'

'Of course,' he replied.

Luke asked Nathan to stay with Jenna and Ken for a moment, and the woman guided him a few feet away from the ambulance.

'You okay?' she asked, her human face showing briefly.

'A bit shocked,' Luke answered. 'But Nathan's alive and well, and that's all that really matters.'

'Absolutely,' she agreed, then, as if an internal switch had been applied she was back in police mode. 'The chief fire officer says that early indications show the fire was started deliberately. Do you have any idea who would want to set your house on fire?'

Luke nodded grimly, crossed his arms, set his eyes in the direction the other ambulance had sped off in, thought about Jamie trying to atone for his mistake, causing himself serious damage in the process, and he prayed, despite everything, that the young man would survive.

Chapter 83

After he finished speaking to the policewoman, the paramedic told Luke he was taking Ken to the hospital.

'He's fine. We just need to observe him in case there are any complications coming from breathing in all that smoke.'

'That's a thing? That happens?'

'Absolutely,' the medic answered. 'The wee fella's absolutely fine, but we should probably admit him for the night as well. We can take you all across to the Queen Elizabeth in this ambulance...'

'Okay,' Luke replied, and held a hand out for Jenna. 'Let's go.'

*

Once over at the hospital, Luke and Jenna saw to it that Ken and Nathan were comfortable before seeking out Jamie. They were directed to his room by a nurse, and with a mind roiling with uncertainty Luke entered. The young man stretched out on that bed, propped up by a small hill of pillows, had set his house on fire, but had then rescued Nathan and Ken. How was he supposed to assimilate all that?

Jamie stirred when he saw Luke, tried to push himself up, but the activity set off a paroxysm of coughing.

When it stopped, sweat was beading on his forehead, and the pulse reading on the small screen by the bed shot up.

'Hey,' Luke said as he moved closer. 'You need to relax.'

'Nathan okay?' Jamie managed to ask. His voice little more than a squeak, his eyes stark with worry.

'He's absolutely fine. Saying you're his hero.'

'He is?' Much of the worry seeped from Jamie's expression, and he fell back onto the pillows. He closed his eyes. Tears leaked out. 'Sorry. So sorry,' he said. 'I could never forgive ... if...' He started coughing again. When it stopped he held a hand out to Luke, his eyes beseeching, begging Luke's forgiveness.

Luke accepted the hand, held it tight. Felt the weakness there.

'So sorry,' Jamie replied. 'For everything.' This set off another fit of coughing. Luke was alarmed at how much pain the young man appeared to be in.

'Hey,' he said. 'Don't worry about it.' He gave his hand a squeeze. 'Let's get you better, eh?'

Jamie turned his head away. 'I don't deserve...'

'Hey,' Luke said. 'Don't say that.'

His mind crowded with all the things he wanted to say. This young man never had a chance. Any promise he had as an individual had been distorted by all the adults in his life. Everyone in a position to help him had done the opposite. It's not too late, he wanted to say. We'll get you better. Sort you out.

'All I want,' Jamie said. 'A friend.' He coughed. 'You ... the closest ... and what do I do?' The light in his eyes had dimmed with self-loathing, his face was cloaked in cobwebs of self-recrimination.

His head sagged to the side, his mouth dropped open, the machine at his side emitted a loud warning. Then Jamie's legs started to shake violently.

'Nurse,' Luke shouted. 'Nurse.'

A group of them charged into the room, pushing a cart. One of them pulled Luke to the side and guided him out of the room.

'Let the team work,' the nurse said.

'But...' Luke stretched, trying to see past all the bodies working around and on Jamie. 'Will he be okay?' he asked.

'He's in the best possible hands,' the nurse said. 'If you just wait out here?'

They closed the door behind them.

Luke paced in the corridor. Several times he held his head to the door, trying to hear what was going on beyond, but he could make out nothing from the muffled sounds that leaked out.

Finally, one of the team opened the door and stepped outside. As she pulled off her face mask, her eyes were dropping with apology. She was speaking. Syllables floated towards Luke and past his head.

'But he was fine,' Luke said, finding it impossible to believe what she was saying. 'He was coughing, aye, but he was sitting up in bed. He was fine.'

'I'm so sorry, sir,' she said, her disappointment palpable. 'It's frighteningly common with smoke inhalation. It puts the lungs, and then the heart, under a huge amount of stress.' She paused. 'We couldn't save your friend. I'm so sorry.'

Chapter 84

One month later

Stef and Joe were sitting either side of him on armchairs, while Luke sat on the sofa. The children, including Nathan, had all been sent to a bedroom to play some games on someone's device.

'How are you liking staying at the in-laws?' Stef asked.

'Ach, Gemma's a sweetheart. She loves having Nathan around, so we're no bother to her. And I've got an invite to go up and stay with my dad whenever I want.'

'That's cool,' Joe said. 'You've patched things up again with your old man?'

'Aye,' Luke replied.

'When's your own place going to be ready?' Stef asked.

'These things take ages,' Luke replied, thinking of the smoke damage in the house and his attempts to get answers from his insurance company.

'And Jamie died, aye?' Joe asked.

Luke nodded, and thought about Jamie's last moments. The young man's plea for forgiveness, and Luke's hope that Jamie understood he was trying to do just that before his heart gave out. Luke could feel the emotion tighten his throat, coughed, and switched his thoughts to the real reason he was here.

Jenna was still struggling with Luke's revelations and was unsure if they had a future, but appeared willing to try, for now at least, to work through her feelings. Their contact was spread out, but regular enough to keep Luke optimistic that there might eventually be a way to bring them back together. One of Jenna's stipulations, in order for that to happen, was for Luke to talk with Joe and tell him the truth about that night with his brother, Fraser.

'Yeah,' Luke replied to Joe, now. 'Smoke inhalation, when he saved Nathan, Ken and the dinosaurs; led to his throat becoming inflamed and that, combined with oxygen deprivation, led to a fatal heart attack.'

'Jesus.' Joe shook his head. 'And he was the one you think actually set the fire?'

Luke nodded. 'Had to be.'

'And what about the sister?' Steph asked. 'Is she still in the picture?'

Amanda had arrived at the hospital that day, just as he was leaving. He saw her rushing in the main doors, her eyes wide with panic.

Luke pulled her to the side and as gently as he could he told her Jamie was dead. She'd studied him, looking for any sense of satisfaction in his statement of a terrible truth. She saw none, and in that gaze Luke read her deep regret and everlasting sorrow at her complicity in Jamie's actions. Her grievous loss at Jamie's death was apparent in the hang of her eyes, the angle of her head, and the drag of her feet as she wordlessly turned and walked away.

'I don't think I need to worry about Amanda Morrison.'

'Danny Morrison, eh? The gift that keeps giving,' Joe said. Luke had told them earlier that Jamie and Amanda were Danny's lost siblings.

'There's something else though, eh?' Stef asked. She was studying Luke, reading him, and Luke smiled ruefully. There wasn't much that got past Stef.

'Well, yes.' Luke glanced down at his hands, then clasped them as if in prayer. 'There's something you need to know.' He looked over to Joe. 'A couple of things.'

'Aye?' Joe and Stef said at the same time.

'The crash that killed Danny?' Luke took a deep breath. 'I waited until I was sure he was dead before I called 999.'

There was a moment of silence, then Joe exhaled loudly. 'Fuck me, that's callous.'

'Aye,' Luke replied. What else could he say.

Stef studied him as if she'd suspected something all along. 'I'm sure you had your reasons.'

'Aye,' Joe agreed with his wife. 'Good enough for him. He was one bad bastard.'

'What was the other thing?' Stef asked.

Luke forced a breath. Braced himself. 'The real reason I've not been about, the real reason I've been avoiding you guys since I got out of jail … and for a long time before that, to be honest…'

'Aye?' Joe leaned forward in his seat.

'Guilt,' Luke said. 'I was there the night Fraser died.' He realised he was prevaricating, and forced himself to offer a proper explanation. 'Mind that piece of waste ground we used to congregate on, aye? We met there one night after I'd been to see a Van Damme movie.'

'Right…' Joe said, his expression one of confusion as if wondering where Luke was going with all of this.

'Fraser challenged me to hit him like Van Damme would. I did this stupid punch thing, not really wanting to hurt him. But Fraser fell back, tripped and hit his head,' Luke held his hands out in supplication. 'I'm so, so sorry. If I could take it back…'

'Just what are you saying, mate?' Joe asked, sitting up straight.

'One punch and he fell back and hit his head.' Luke closed his eyes against the image of Fraser at his feet in the near-dark, a small pool of blood just visible at his head. 'I didn't need to check. I knew. Just knew he was dead, and I panicked. I ran for it. Went up to Aberdeen to my dad's. I couldn't handle what I'd done.'

'I don't…' Joe shook his head. 'What the hell are you talking about?'

'The night Fraser died. It was me. I killed him. But it was just one punch … a kind of pathetic slap really. And he fell back…' Luke repeated. 'I'm so sorry. If I could take it back…'

'Hold on. Hold on.' Joe was on his feet. 'You're saying you killed Fraser?'

'Aye,' Luke replied unable to meet Joe's eyes.

'With one punch?'

Luke forced himself to look over at his old friend, and could see that both of his hands were gathered into fists. He stood up. Braced himself. Whatever Joe demanded from him, whatever the price, he was willing to pay.

'You were with him that night?' Joe asked.

Luke ran through events of that long-ago evening once more. Then told them that Danny had given him money for the bus to Aberdeen, and recalled that he'd hidden out at his father's for over a month, until he felt it was safe to come back to Glasgow.

Joe surprised him with what he said next, with the sympathy and care in his eyes:

'You've been holding on to that all these years?'

'Jesus. What more can I say? I killed your brother, and it's haunted me every bloody day since.'

'Danny fuckin' Morrison,' Joe said in a voice that suggested he'd just been given the final piece of a jigsaw, and that he was brimming with fury, but not at Luke. 'Honey, can you get the box with all of that official stuff?'

'What?' Luke asked. This reaction was not what he expected.

Joe motioned for him to give them a second. He'd explain.

Stef rarely did Joe's bidding, but on this occasion she did, returning moments later holding a red biscuit box with the legend *Victoria Selection* on the lid. Wordlessly, but with an expression of understanding, she put it on the coffee table in front of them.

Joe took the lid off and rumbled through the papers inside.

'Ah. Gotcha,' he said and handed Luke a piece of paper. It was an official document, typed, laid out in a format Luke recognised.

'This is...?' he began.

'Fraser's death certificate. Here.' He held the paper out. 'Read the cause of death.'

Luke searched the document. Found the wording and with a mind that reeled from what he read he spoke the words out loud. 'Suffocation.' He looked over at Joe. 'He died from suffocation?'

'Aye,' Joe replied. 'And last I heard bouncing your head off the kerb isn't going to cause that.'

Possibilities he was unable to articulate rumbled through Luke's mind.

'Exactly what happened when you went over to Danny's?' Stef asked.

Luke shook his head, still trying to make sense of what he'd just read, as if the black and white of officialdom couldn't quite shred the certainty of a long-held belief. 'I told him what had happened. He gave me the money and told me to go up to Aberdeen. He'd sort it.'

'Aye, did he,' Joe said. 'But before he gave you the money?'

'He went over to the waste ground to check that Fraser...' he looked over at Joe as the pieces fell into place '...was actually dead.'

Luke and Joe's eyes met. The picture they'd just assembled now clear to them both.

'Danny fuckin' Morrison,' Joe repeated. 'He went over there, saw our Fraser was still alive, and fuckin' strangled him.'

'Jesus,' Stef said. 'He was that cold? Why would he do that?'

Luke remembered that last day, in the car not long before the crash, Danny asking him what it was like to kill someone. He replayed the look on Danny's face. It hadn't struck him as true at the time. It didn't sit with the words that had just come out of his mouth, and now Luke knew why. He was toying with him. He knew exactly what it was like to kill someone, because he was Fraser's killer. And he did it because he could, and because he knew he would get away with it. And he knew just how to cash in on it.

'Holy shit,' Luke said. 'You think you know just how wrong somebody was, but they continue to surprise you.'

'All they years ago,' Joe's eyes narrowed, 'something told me you wanted to go straight. Danny as much as told me himself.' He shook his head as he read back into that moment. 'So that was him fuckin' with me. He knew you couldn't go straight cos he was holding Fraser's murder over you.'

Luke's answering smile was a grim one. He could clearly see now how he'd been part of his own downfall – but not for the reason he'd always thought. 'And if I'd come to you years ago and confessed, you could have put me right.' He considered everything that came from the state of mind Danny had allowed him to remain in and shook his head. 'What a bloody waste.'

Joe took the death certificate from Luke, placed it back in the tin and gently closed the lid. Luke could see that every part of him was trembling. Joe looked from Stef to Luke.

'You did us all a favour that day, mate. The world is a far better place without Danny Morrison,' Joe said. 'I fuckin' wish I could dig the bastard up, so I could kill him again myself.'

*

That evening in the bedroom he shared with Nathan – the bedroom that used to be Lisa's as a girl – as he tucked Nathan into the king-sized bed they would share until his own house was repaired, Nathan asked:

'Sure Jamie's in heaven?'

'He saved your life, so, yeah, could well be,' Luke replied.

'And he'll meet Mummy up there?'

'That's ... possible.'

Satisfied with the answer, Nathan turned onto his side, pulled his knees up towards his chest and closed his eyes. Viewing his long lashes, button nose and plump lower lip, Luke wondered if there could ever be another child so beautiful. Unable to resist, he leaned forward and pressed his lips for a moment against the warm, plump softness of his cheek.

'Night, night, buddy,' he said.

'Night, night, Daddy,' Nathan, already close to sleep, mumbled in reply.

Sitting back in his armchair by the window, Luke picked up a book he'd been meaning to read, *The Body Keeps the Score* – he'd had to buy another copy after the first was lost in the fire – and reviewed his answer to Nathan. It was such a simplistic view of the after-effects of Jamie's actions, but was there a better one? The young man had come from a troubled background; no one was coming out of that family unscathed. And he'd gone to foster parents who compounded that trauma with more. Jamie's last actions exemplified his state of mind: set the fire, put the fire out. With Amanda wittering in his ear, was it any wonder he'd come to such an end?

Could Luke have done more to help him? He sighed, breathing out – breathing away the impulse to blame himself. He'd had more than enough of guilt and its effects. And, boy, did he feel so much lighter knowing it wasn't him who killed Fraser.

And there, curled up on the bed, was the biggest reason of all to make sure he did just that. Was it okay that a part of him was seeking some form of rehabilitation by being a father to this little boy?

Was there any need to even ask the question? He was a better man because he'd accepted that role, and Nathan would also benefit greatly. Wasn't that all that mattered?

He got out of the chair, put out the light, and with the book in his hand he looked out of the window, at the darkening grey of the sky, at the roofs that paved his view for miles around, and at the warm bluster of the streetlights and the shadows beyond. If he chose to, all he would see was shadow, but he focused on the peaks of the roofs, the hard lines of the houses, the rows and rows of windows, like eyes stolidly returning his gaze. And he thought of the people around him, of their care and support and love, how fortunate he was, after everything, to have them. And stroking the cover of the book in his hand he considered that they were where the healing lay.

Acknowledgements

Writing is a solitary task ... until the edits begin. Good editors are worth their weight in gold, and I count myself lucky to be working with the best in the business. A massive thank you to Karen Sullivan and West Camel. This book is a much better read because of your diligence, hard work and attention to detail. Stars, the pair of you!

Writing is a solitary task ... but it brings you in touch with a wonderful community. Massive thanks to all the booksellers, bloggers, reviewers, writers, and readers for their companionship, willing ears, ribald jokes, and continuing support – it is hugely appreciated.

Book people really are the best people.